NEW YORK
NOCTURNAL

Officer Herring spotted the figure slumped among the ashcans near the entrance to 853. A woman was trying to pull a fat spaniel away. Reid parked the police car at the curb. Herring got out, flashlight in hand.

He played the light over the figure, resting it on the man's back. There was a small tear in the coat, and around the tear a wet stain had spread. "Son of a bitch," he said softly, then shone the light on the victim's face. A good face, like a minister's, he thought, a good man. The hair was gray at the temples. There was a dirty lump at the back of the man's ear. "Son of a bitch," he said again . . . "Call it in. It looks like a knife job."

Other Avon Books by
Dorothy Salisbury Davis

Tales for a Stormy Night
Where the Dark Streets Go

THE PALE BETRAYER

DOROTHY SALISBURY DAVIS

AVON
PUBLISHERS OF BARD, CAMELOT, DISCUS AND FLARE BOOKS

AVON BOOKS
A division of
The Hearst Corporation
1790 Broadway
New York, New York 10019

First Avon Printing: February 1987

AVON TRADEMARK REG. U.S. PAT. OFF. AND IN OTHER COUNTRIES, MARCA
REGISTRADA, HECHO EN U.S.A.

Printed in the U.S.A.

K-R 10 9 8 7 6 5 4 3 2 1

for Judy and Steve

THE PALE BETRAYER

Prologue

Altogether they had met only three times and that night, the twenty-fourth of May, they would gather without meeting, and for the last time. Eric Mather would stand in full view beneath the street lamp and give the sign by which the others would know that all was as he had said it would be; they would wait in the shadows and move after he had gone. A man's briefcase would be stolen. It was not likely that he would even go to the police, for he was a busy man and the briefcase, to his knowledge, would contain nothing irreplaceable. In the morning the briefcase would, as it were, advertise its owner: it would be discovered in a postal deposit box, its contents—again to the owner's best knowledge—intact. The joke would seem to have been on the thief who had stolen a few strips of highly publicized and widely disseminated film and the jottings of a noted physicist, his impressions of the international conference from which he had just returned.

Three times they met, Mather and his co-conspirators, whose names he knew only as Jerry and Tom. Nor did he want to know more of them. He had not even wanted to know what they specifically knew of him. After that night it would no longer matter.

The first meeting had occurred in New York's Washington Square. Mather, having finished his last lecture of the day at Central University, was standing in the February sun looking vainly for signs of spring. He was watching a group of students, two or three of his own among them, distributing ban-the-bomb literature, one of their leaflets in his hand.

"What good do you think that will do?" a man said. Mather had not noticed him until he spoke. Short, pudgy-faced, he seemed vaguely familiar. Afterwards Mather knew to whom "Jerry" bore a resemblance. At the time he supposed he knew him from the university corridors.

"As a friend of mine would say, it can't harm," Mather said. He started to walk away.

The stranger caught up with him, not saying anything for the moment and needing to take three steps to Mather's two in order to keep pace. Mather did not like it. He did not like Washington Square and wished he had walked out of the park instead of into it. He stopped abruptly. "Should I know you?"

"Let me put it this way, Eric: you will. My name is Jerry."

"Very likely," Mather tried to cut him. Vainly.

Jerry pointed a stubby finger at the handbill Mather was still carrying. "I am engaged in such business myself. I have been looking for a partner." There was a trace of foreignness in the way he said "partner." Otherwise his accent was what Mather would have called New York non-descript. "You have been recommended."

"By whom?" Mather's voice very nearly cracked, the tightening of fear catching his throat.

"It is not so much by whom, Eric, as by *what.*" He added, almost regretfully, "I know quite a lot about you. Can't we walk while we are talking?"

"There is nothing..." Mather stopped. Jerry was shaking his head, a look of mournful reproof in his small dark eyes.

"But we do not need to speak of that at all—not ever.

What I have in mind...Please, let us walk, like friends who happened to meet. Okay?"

This time Jerry set the pace. Mather noticed the people around them, several men idly watching from the benches. There was no way of knowing friend from foe among them. Most of them, the thought flickered through his mind, were, like himself, their own worst enemies.

"I am really an idealist, Eric, as you are. An idealist although you might not think it to look at me." Jerry glanced up at him. "What would you say I do for a living?"

"You sell fruit," Mather said bitingly.

Jerry snorted, a noise that passed with him for amusement. "That is very good. I sell fruit. You don't need to know anything more about me." He paused in his walking to gaze down at a chessboard on a bench, the game temporarily abandoned by its players.

"Don't touch that!" A man buying a bag of chestnuts from the corner vendor shook his fist at them.

Jerry held up his hands to indicate he had no intention of disturbing the board. To Mather he said: "I don't understand this game, not like you. It takes a particular brain—a scholar, not a fruit seller." He moved on, Mather following, inwardly cursing his cowardice, his vulnerability. "Eric, your friend, Peter Bradley—he will be going to Athens this spring, won't he—to the International Conference of Particle Physicists?"

"I have no idea," Mather said.

"But you do. I have just told you." He clicked his tongue in disgust at the litter along the path, stooped and picked up an empty cigarette packet which he dropped into the litterbasket. "People have so little pride. Eric, is he truly your friend? What I mean to say is, a man with such a deep involvement in science: what are friends to him? What is family? He has such an attractive wife. It is a shame you are..." Jerry shrugged, letting the gesture carry through his meaning.

Mather clasped his fists within his pockets. He was deprived of anger by his fear. His very skin was crawling with fear, fear and loathing, much of it of himself who could not lift his hand to smash this wily, syrup-tongued bastard in the mouth. And if he were psychologically able, what would come of it, a quarrel between two men in Washington Square?

"Wh-what do you want of me?" He sickened further, stuttering on the word.

"I want Dr. Bradley to bring something from Athens on his return."

"Go to him yourself then."

Jerry shook his head. "It is a delicate matter, and since you are very good in matters of delicacy, it is my hope that you will undertake the entire arrangement. I am a simple man, a man of action, not planning, and I would put myself under your direction." They were passing the chestnut vendor, the sweet fumes of the roasted nuts rising from the charcoal fire. "Do you like chestnuts?"

"I loathe them," Mather said.

"They are not very American," Jerry said, walking on. "Are you?"

"I pass," Jerry said amiably. "Shall I tell you now the problem I am hoping you will solve for me—for humanity you might say? You will agree I am sure that the kind of international exchange that goes on among scientists engaged in what they call basic research—loosely speaking, the peaceful potentials of nature's energy—you will agree, it is a good thing to exchange such information?"

"Does it matter whether or not I agree?"

Jerry shrugged. "It is more pleasant to work with people whose ideals you share."

"Ideals is a word like peace. It means what you want it to mean at the moment, so cut the crap."

"I am happy to do so. Well. At every such conference as will be held this May in Athens, a thriving side-business goes on in espionage. Information—often useless, sometimes critical—is passed there, much of it for money, some for, you will excuse the expression, ideals. Motive, as you would be the first to point out, is irrelevant to the betrayed government. Very simply, I am asking you to help me find a traitor."

"To whom?"

"To the Soviet Union," Jerry said unhesitatingly.

It might be supposed that Eric Mather, thirty-six years old, an assistant professor of English literature at Central University, born in the Midwest of New England ancestry, and with no more knowledge of international politics much less espionage than he gathered from the newspaper head-lines, would have considered the whole encounter a hoax, a campus madness, the after-term prank of a disgruntled student. The thought did cross his mind, but over it almost simultaneously swept the feeling that he had been waiting, expecting something of this kind to happen. There was even a familiar nuance to the sly persuasiveness of "Jerry," the intimation of an old affinity now to be renewed.

"You are not betraying your own country in this, Eric. What you are doing is striking a blow for international disarmament."

"A very fine distinction," Mather said.

"Perhaps, but I said it out of respect for your New England conscience." Jerry peeled the paper from a stick of gum and dropped it neatly into the next waste container. The incongruousness of someone on his mission chewing gum made Mather smile. Jerry was overplaying his role. Mather began to feel a needling sense of superiority.

"You seem to have a great deal of confidence in me," he said.

"My dear Eric," Jerry said, laying his hand on the teacher's arm, "you have given us every reason."

Mather shied at the man's touch, a reaction that made Jerry smile, but this was as close as he came to mentioning the source of his confidence in Mather's cooperation.

"Tell me what you want me to know," Mather said.

"We wish to intercept the highly secret military infor-mation intended for an American agent, and we want to have it brought to us here for evaluation. Such evaluation will tell us the source of the leak."

"You want it brought here—to the United States?"

"I know it is hard for you to believe, but take my word, we are safer here than anywhere in the world."

"I don't understand."

"Forgive me, Eric, but you do not need to. I will explain anyway: here we know our enemies and, perhaps fortunately for us, we have very few friends."

Mather liked the turn of phrase in spite of himself. It distracted him momentarily.

"Neither you nor we should like to interrupt the good work of such international exchanges, so it becomes essential that our carrier—in this case Dr. Bradley— be kept in entire ignorance of his role. That is why we are calling on you."

Mather felt he had missed something. "Why Peter Bradley?"

"Ah, of course. At the Athens conference our scientists will be making an extraordinary gesture. Grysenko will give film prints of a recent Soviet nuclear experiment to certain scientists of other countries who my government feels have contributed to world progress in that particular area of research. It is a magnificent gesture. And Peter Bradley of course is foremost among those scientists."

"I see."

"It is our problem to see that Dr. Bradley also brings home what in another kind of film is called 'a trailer.'"

It was a moment or two before Mather spoke. They had walked the distance of the park. As they approached the gate he said, but with no great hope of its meaning anything: "I wish you luck, but you don't need me."

"Ah, but we do and now we must have you. I have confided so much." Jerry turned back into the park and Mather, turning after him, felt himself to be treading a counter-moving path. "You see," Jerry went on, "in Athens itself we must establish Bradley as *the* man—there will be perhaps a half-dozen other American physicists there. It is too dangerous to use his name. You must find for him a mission—a particular, obscure work of antiquity—a monument perhaps?—something it will be imperative for him to visit because you, his friend, insist upon it. And on the day he returns he must be separated from his 'trailer,' but at the same time keep his innocence untouched."

"It is untouchable," Mather said with fervor.

Jerry had the effrontery then to laugh, and the instant Mather realized the source of his amusement his fury rose and exploded. "You son of a bitch!"

"I'm so sorry," Jerry said. "I forgot myself and that you are now my superior. It will not happen again." As he spoke he removed his hat and ran his hand through the black, lank hair, at the same time half-turning.

Another man who, Mather realized, seeing him, had passed them as they turned back from the gate, now joined them. He was Mather's height but twice his build. Blond and ruggedly handsome of feature, he looked like an aging ball player.

"This is Tom," Jerry said, "your other colleague."

Tom, standing very straight, his hands at his sides, said: "How do you do, sir."

Mather glowered at him and the other looked down at his own shoes. Mather knew his type from the classroom, the man who needed the grade and would do anything the teacher demanded in order to get it. A small tingle of satisfaction came with the realization.

Jerry, missing nothing, said: "You are going to find it surprisingly good sport, Eric. Think about Athens for a few days. We shall be available when you want us."

They met twice again in the intervening months, once in the same park when Mather was ready to talk to them—he had seen one or the other of them there several times, but when he made no sign they had not approached him—and once in his apartment. Then on the morning of May 24 Mather posted a notice on the third-floor bulletin board in the General Studies Building: PUPPIES FOR SALE—CALL EL 7-2390 AFTER 9:00 P.M. After posting it he set about organizing a small party to celebrate the return of Peter Bradley from Athens that night.

1

There came that moment of stillness which sometimes falls upon a crowded room. Several conversations were suspended at once and the only sound was the metallic clicking of the mantel clock. Even the street traffic beneath the open windows briefly ceased. Dr. Peter Bradley, host to a small party of students and faculty, had paused to search his memory for the name of a Greek physicist he had met at a conference in Athens from which he had returned that day. Robert Steinberg, an associate professor of physics under Bradley at Central University, had just told a joke to which no one got the point. His audience looked at one another questioningly.

Eric Mather, his back to the mantel, felt his heartbeat quicken to strike pace with the clock's loud tick. A moment out of time, it seemed, was being given him in which to weigh the last possibility of turning back. He could excuse himself to Janet Bradley who was showing him the dummied pages of her latest book, cross the room to her husband and say to him: "Peter, old man, I got you into something you didn't know about..." But suppose it turned out that nothing had happened in Athens, that contact had not been made at all? He had been given a moment in which only to relish the last sweet dregs of a cup he had once thought would be bitter tea. Watching Peter tap his head, the sycophants hanging breathlessly for the wisdom he was expected to shake loose, Mather had no regrets. After all, his own greatest moments had always come from turning chagrin into triumph.

Janet turned the last page of *Child of the City,* a photographic study of the East Twenties, where she and Peter lived, to the Bowery's edge. Mather noticed her fingers tremble. It gave him an unexpected, an almost shocking thrill, to discover that Janet cared so deeply that he liked the book and, by extension, that he liked her. He remembered then Jerry's intimation—the misfortune of Mather's inadequacy to such opportunity—and the memory crippled the brief, exquisite emotion. It would not spring again, wish as he might to conjure it. He pitied Janet almost as much as he did himself. He reached out his hand to her in the need to have and give sympathy. But Janet, interpreting the gesture by her own heart's dictate, clutched the book in both hands and looked toward her husband. Her lips met, about to say his name.

At that instant Bradley snapped his fingers. "Skaphidas," he cried. "That's the name, Nikos Skaphidas."

Steinberg, to those around him, said: "Oh, God. No wonder you didn't get the point. I forgot to say the man in the story..."

His wife, Louise, cut in: "Bob, you always *do* that!"

Spontaneously the murmur of conversation resumed all through the room. Mather watched Janet, trying to catch her eyes, to seek the best of himself reflected there, his lost salvation.

"Janet..." He caught her hand and kissed it. Anyone in the room, observing, would say it characteristic of him: Eric was a great kisser of hands.

But Janet said: "Thank you, Eric."

"It's a beautiful book, you know. One would expect it to be, coming from you."

She inclined her head in acknowledgment of his praise.

To escape the intimacy with which she could not cope, she said: "There's more coffee. Shall I warm it?"

He shook his head and forced her to endure a few seconds of his scrutiny. She suffered it with great poise, only the faint telltale pulse moving at her throat. Still she would not meet his eyes, keeping Peter within her gaze.

"Do you love him, Janet?" he asked quietly.

"Yes!" She tilted her chin and the word had come too quickly. A cry in the wilderness. Mather felt it at his own heart's core. The clock behind him rasped, about to strike the hour of nine. How bitterly ironic to reach two climaxes at once in a life so barren of such moments. The others in the room had begun to move, the eagerness of the young scientists to see the film irrepressible now that the time had come. Mather heard Peter say: "Mind, there may not be anything we don't know..." But even as he said the words his eyes were shining. He wanted to see it as much as they did.

Mather allowed himself one last thought of Janet: he wondered how he would feel about her after this night had passed. "I'd better go too," he said. "I've promised to look in on the Imagists."

"What are the Imagists?" Janet asked.

"Well, they're neither beats nor Beatles, certainly. They're latter-day worshippers of Eliot and Hume, and they're so square, they're cubed." He smiled down at her and brushed her cheek with the back of his hand. "Thank you, my dear, for everything."

As he moved across the room the clock struck nine. Louise Steinberg said to no one in particular, simply a despairing statement of fact: "Wouldn't you know they'd go to the laboratory, even tonight?"

Yes, Mather thought, one would.

"Damn you, Peter," Louise added, but without malice. Louise was getting plump. She liked comfort and was both proud and possessive of her husband who was finally making a comfortable living as well as a reputation in physics under Bradley.

"It won't take long," Bradley said. "I haven't seen Janet in a week.

"Eric, come look at some pictures with us. They're Russian."

It was Anne Russo who said it. Her purpose, Mather thought, was to forestall his interrupting her moment with Peter. Possibly she was single-minded enough to think the pictures might actually mean something to him. Anne, studying for her doctorate with Bradley, adored him. Most of the women in his classes did. Not that he had many— Anne was the only one in graduate work—and he did his best to discourage those he had. To make it in science a woman had to be able to take discouragement. The little beasts loved Peter for giving it to them. Anne did not look like a female scientist: more the social register sort. Quite tall, she had a good body, Mather supposed, but he doubted that any of this crew was aware of it.

"I haven't seen a Russian picture in years. They're much too hammy," he said, playing the scientists' clown. He sometimes thought it why they tolerated him, for they were snobs to the last man of them.

He put his hand on Bradley's shoulder. Peter was getting gray at the temples—at thirty-five—the burden of premature success. "How much of Athens did you see?"

"The Acropolis and the Plakka, like any week-end tourist."

"And the Byron monument?"

"We had a hell of a time finding it . . ."

We, Mather thought. He had supposed that Bradley walking in Athens even as at home would insist upon his solitude. He did not like to think Bradley might again break that pattern in the next few minutes.

But Bradley was true to habit. He picked up a magazine from the side-table waiting for the others to leave before him. Janet said he did much of his reading in such odd moments, able to absorb a page at a glance. And he had the remarkable faculty of doing it without giving offense, a sort of social sixth sense. As Mather reached the door and glanced back, Peter waved and called out, "We'll talk, Eric!"

Mather waited for a car to pass before crossing the street. There was the sound of water to the wheels' whine over the pavement. But it was heat only. It had been too hot a day for May. He tried to think about the heat, the children playing—if you could call it play, their deadly stalking of one another among parked cars and the shattering bray of their make-believe guns. Darkness had come, the murky darkness of ill-lighted streets over which the city brightness hung, a neon-tinted nebula of smoke and fume sealing in the night below. Mather took up his self-arranged vigil beneath a street lamp and looked up at the Bradley second-floor windows. As he gave the sign to his co-conspirators who were watching—from where he did not know; he could not even be sure they were watching—the kissing of his fingertips toward the house he had left, he saw Janet in the window facing him. How extraordinary that she should be there! It brought full circle the wheel within the wheel. She abruptly turned her back so that he supposed she had seen him and taken the gesture to her own heart. Good! So much the better if something should go wrong. It was the first time he had permitted himself even fleetingly that fear. Anne Russo was with her now, shaking back her dark long hair as she spoke to Janet. Had she seen him too? He could not be sure.

In the street directly below the windows, the three male students—Mather could not keep their names straight—were hallooing up to Anne. Steinberg joined them and the party started to move up the street. A few seconds later Anne loped after them. Louise Steinberg came out and paused on the stoop. Mather had almost forgotten her. She stood a moment breathing deeply of the fume-infested air: Louise was the sort who'd embrace an oyster; she loved the world. Sometimes she audited his classes. He remembered her best there for her description of Shelley as a proletarian poet!

A light went on in Bradley's study, a small room just off

the livingroom. Peter came to his desk near the window and opened his attaché case. He took a small box from it along with some papers which he put into the less important-looking lettercase. A few seconds later, switching off the light, he left the room. Janet was drawing the livingroom shades, talking over her shoulder to her husband.

Mather's job was done. All that remained was for him to walk away, which to the other watchers meant that Peter Bradley would now come. Mather moved quickly, for he wanted no part in what was to follow, however simple the snatching of the lettercase. Almost instantly he resented that Peter should be their dupe now that his own involvement was finished.

Mather angled his way through the half-commercial, half-residential streets that lay between the Bradleys' and Greenwich Village. He chose his route at random fancy, striding out, swinging his body like a country boy legging joyously over the fields. That image shot briefly through his mind, his favorite memory of himself: at the age of twelve running free, scattering ducks and chickens in his grandmother's yard, starting a partridge and her young as he dashed through a field, and then reaching the vast and silent woods unobserved, utterly free.

He was again free, exhilaratingly so, having successfully loaned his talents to a conspiracy which, he had convinced himself, would go far to destroy conspiracy. That he had been recruited less for his talents than for his availability, and that he had acted out of vulnerability more than conviction were circumstances he no longer believed himself. He had snatched honor from dishonor as perhaps did more men than he knew. Despite his continual playing on it, his knowledge of human nature was suspect to him underneath. But his problem now would be to keep his exultation secret. He knew his own weakness for the dramatic. One of the things he was going to have to avoid after the incident was over was the temptation to tell Peter Bradley the truth, that unbeknownst to himself, Bradley had been used by Soviet counterespionage.

Mather laughed dryly at his own expense: the temptation should be easily overcome. Bradley simply would not believe him; he would call it a splendid tale, worthy of Mather's imagination, fiction patterned to coincidence. Free? He was locked within his own contrivance.

His pace slowed with the diminished sense of triumph. The fact that Bradley would not believe him if he could tell the story rankled fiercely. Bradley did not know him that well. Nobody did. It sometimes troubled him that he suspected no one wanted to. Yet, he was welcomed in all company, even that of scientists. He could choose at that moment among a half-dozen groups of young intellectuals meeting by chance or habit at some Village shop or bar and find a welcome. He could retrace his steps to the house he had just left. Would Janet welcome him? She would want to. Or had a moment alone again with Peter cast the tempter from her mind?

When he reached the Red Lantern, the Imagists were in full flower: the word struck him as particularly apt. These were a group of young men distinguished by their carefulness of speech, their elegance of clothes and manner. Mather was amused by the affectation: to pursue elegance for its own sake on today's campus, among the consciously sloppy and unwashed, took its own kind of courage. The dark-paneled, hazily lighted tavern was crowded, tourist trade at most of the tables and regulars squaring their backs to it at the bar. He ambled toward his young friends. The only girl among them, wearing a scalloped paisley shawl and with her hair loosely nested on the top of her head—or was it a wig?—stuck out her tongue as a wolf-whistler paid her tribute on his way to the washroom. Sweeney among the nightingales.

The young people edged together to make as much room as Mather wanted, which was a whole bench to himself. Most of them called him Eric, off-campus. He often sat among them, sideways, a knee drawn up to his chin, his eyes closed as he listened to their talk. He bought his welcome possibly with his ability to quote from memory whole passages of poetry to either bolster or defeat the point in the making. Tonight it *was* "Sweeney" again. He would not stay long. He had always found Sweeney a bore as well as a boor.

Suddenly he opened his eyes and began reciting, the conversation falling off beneath his onslaught. He was as startled himself by his choice of lines as were his listeners. They had come from deep within his own subconscious and were as remote from Sweeney as London from the Dardanelles. In fact, until he found himself reciting them he had not been aware of knowing them at all:

> "Snatch from the ashes of your sires
> The embers of their former fires;
> And he who in the strife expires
> Will add to theirs a name of fear
> That tyranny all quake to hear..."

Having started, he found the impulse to carry on too strong to resist. He poured out stanza after stanza, plummeting the strange and hidden recesses of his own memory for them. And as he tumbled out the words, his delivery far more eloquent than the poem, he loosened his tie and then removed it, unbuttoned his shirt and spread the collar.

The young people watched him, fascinated, their eyes a mixture of amused puzzlement. Eliot? Surely not. Some of them could scarcely suppress laughter, and others let it go thinking it would prove them knowledgeable of the jingo he was counterpoising to Eliot's sardonicism.

He stopped abruptly. His listeners waited silently. He said: "Who?"

More silence. Then the girl giggled. "I know," she said with a grating drawl. "It's Byron."

"How could you tell?" he mocked.

Grinning vacuously, she gestured with her limp hand at her own neck, indicating his open collar, that bit of manly flair for which the romantic poet had been remembered when his lines were long forgotten.

"The testimony of fair woman," Mather again mocked. "The poet is soonest recognized who bares his throat to her fangs."

He gathered his long legs under him and slid out of the booth. "Forgive the interruption, gentlemen. Live, Sweeney! Agamemnon died tonight."

He moved quickly out of the tavern, pushing his way through the incoming crowd, ignoring the bartender's friendly salute. He was possessed of a wild restlessness, the need to do something flamboyant, to lose himself by calling attention to himself. Agamemnon died tonight! Well, hadn't he with honor's death? He began then a round of the taverns and coffee shops, conjuring a welcome from one group, then another with his fierce exuberance.

2

Janet was in the darkroom, which had probably served a previous tenant as a maid's room, when the phone rang. She was a few seconds getting used to the light as she stepped into the kitchen. The thought ran through her mind that Peter had become involved: something had turned up in the film which he and his group had not observed before. To Janet photography meant a study of persons, objects. Sometimes she experimented with non-objective effects—she had an exhibit of such studies showing now —but to Peter, a high-energy physicist, in his work film was the record of possible mathematical significants achieved in nuclear experiment.

It was Bob Steinberg on the phone. "Janet? Where the hell is Peter? We've been waiting here for over an hour and I've got an eight o'clock class in the morning."

"He left just after you did," Janet said. "I expected him home soon." The University was a brisk twenty minutes' walk.

"Did he say he was stopping any place?"

"No. And he was tired, Bob. He wanted to get home."

"Huh." Then as though to allay her concern by citing the seeming illogic which was sometimes characteristic of her husband, Steinberg added: "When he's tired, that's when he goes walking. Don't worry about him, Janet. He picked up a lot to think about in the last few days."

"If he doesn't come soon . . ."

"I'll call you," Steinberg interrupted. "We'll break up soon if he doesn't come and I'll call you."

"Thank you, Bob." Janet looked at her watch as she hung up the phone. It was twenty minutes to eleven. The latest it could have been when Peter had left the house was nine fifteen. He was not a man to hold to a timetable, but he was considerate of other people's time. He might have stopped for a few minutes at St. John's Church if it were open. He often did. Not that he was religious. It was just a place he liked to stop. She wondered if he might have fallen asleep, sitting there. They might even have locked him in! She gave a little laugh aloud at the thought. But even to herself the sound was edged with hysteria.

She returned to the darkroom and put away the materials with which she had been working when the phone rang. There was nothing she could do but wait. Peter would be annoyed if she started phoning. And where? The vicarage of St. John's? Peter would definitely be annoyed. There was no phone at the laboratory. Bob Steinberg would have had to go out to a corner box. She had ought to have become accustomed in eight years. She began to think of the circumstances under which Peter had instructed her she was not to worry: his staying an hour and a half in the bathtub; his failure to show up at mealtime or at bedtime. Onto something, he had on occasion stayed until dawn at the laboratory—and then walked to the tip of Manhattan where he bought fresh fish and brought it home for breakfast.

Worry about Peter, Janet thought as she sat down to it in earnest, had one sure if somewhat miserable advantage: it took her mind off Eric Mather—and off herself in her disgust at thinking so much about him.

* * *

Steinberg, leaving the public phone booth, stopped briefly at the corner newsstand. The vendor was folding copies of *The Times*. He had the only stand in the city, he liked to boast, that sold more *"Timeses* than *Newses."*

"Have you seen Dr. Bradley tonight, Hank?"

"Yeah," Hank said. Then he scratched his head. "No, I guess not. It was Miss Russo I seen — a little while ago."

It was a damned funny confusion, Steinberg thought. He remembered then that Anne had stopped home to get her glasses, arriving at the laboratory some time after the rest of them. He had never liked the idea of Anne's walking alone the two blocks from the newsstand to the laboratory. He didn't like to do it himself. Soon they would have a new building, but just now the laboratory was in a warehouse on the edge of one of the worst slums in the city. It was the rare landlord who wanted to have a cyclotron in his building, even a baby cyclotron.

3

Patrol car thirty-seven, operating out of the Houston Street precinct, cruised into East Tenth Street, Officer Tom Reid at the wheel. His partner, Wally Herring, was a Negro. They had long since ceased to be conscious of one another's color, but they were both very much aware of the mixtures in color and language of most of their territory. This part of Tenth Street represented its upper class, a conglomeration of old family houses long since converted to apartments, ten-year-old apartment buildings which from the day of construction had lacked charm, much less dignity, and were already half-slums, and a string of shops which Herring kept his eyes on, watching for signs of forced entry—antique shops, a shoemaker, taxidermist, Spanish delicatessen, art galleries... The two men were due to go off duty at midnight. So far it had been one of their quieter nights: good weather seemed to make good neighbors.

Herring spotted the figure slumped among the ashcans at the mouth of an arcade near the entrance to 853. A woman was trying to pull a fat spaniel away. Reid parked at the curb. Herring got out, flashlight in hand. The woman began at once to berate the policeman, blocking his way.

"Where do they get it? That's what I want to know. *Where* do they get it?"

The dog whimpered, straining at the leash.

Herring could not get past them. "Ma'am, you might try the corner tavern. Let me by, please."

"Oh, the arrogance of some people these days," the woman said, and to the dog: *"Will* you come, Dandy? Come!"

Reid, watching from the car, saw her put a sharp toe to the dog's most vulnerable parts. It yipped and swung around, fawning on her. Whereupon she made a great mothering fuss over it. If she had a husband, Reid thought, God pity him and his vulnerable parts.

Herring played the light over the figure, resting it then on the man's back. There was a small tear in the coat and around the tear a wet stain had spread. The policeman touched his finger to it although that was scarcely necessary. "Son of a bitch," he said softly, and shone the light on the victim's face. It had settled into repose like the face of a child about to cry. A good face, like a minister's he thought, a good man. The hair was gray at the temples. There was a dirty lump at the back of his ear. "Son of a bitch," he said again and then added all the vile epithets with which his own street upbringing had equipped him, a curious source of strength at such a moment. He returned to the car door.

"Get them rolling," he said to Reid. "It looks like a knife job." He looked at his watch: twenty minutes to eleven, and got out his report book. Then he remembered the woman. There was not another person within two blocks. He hurried after her as she turned into the corner building and called out: "Madam, one minute, please."

Before he reached her she started protesting: "I saw nothing. Nothing. A person ought to be able to walk their dog without the police chasing after them."

"Madam, the man is dead," Herring said.

"I'm not surprised," she said, as cold herself as the steel of a knife.

"When you were bringing the dog out . . ."

She interrupted. "I told you, Officer, I saw nothing."

Herring stiffened in authority. "May I have your name and address, please?"

"Mrs. Rose Finney, apartment 4A."

"The address of the building, please." He did not look up although the number was plainly visible.

"Eight-seven-one."

"Thank you, Ma'am." With alacrity he opened the door and held it for her.

She looked up at him, puzzled, suspicious, and then sailed in, yanking the dog after her. Herring showed her a beautiful set of teeth over which, when she had passed, his lips closed like the sudden drop of a curtain over footlights.

Inspector Joseph Fitzgerald and Lieutenant Dave Marks answered the call for Homicide. They were on the scene within fifteen minutes. The medical examiner arrived shortly afterwards along with the technical squad. By then people were hanging out of windows up and down the block; fire escapes were sagging with them. The precinct men had already roped off the area.

Fitzgerald, a veteran of twenty-four years on the detective force, ran his hand gingerly over the victim's hip and side pockets, and then eased it beneath the man to feel his breast pockets. He glanced up at Reid who had stayed with the body. "No identification?"

"No, sir." He reported on the finding of the victim, the failure of the one possible witness to contribute any information.

Fitzgerald grunted and looked up at the gallery of faces, like bobbing balloons in the eerie light of the kliegs. "All yours," he said to the medical examiner.

At the door of 853 Lieutenant Marks talked with the uniformed officer, Walter Herring, while the latter held his torch to the vestibule light fixture. The bulb had been smashed and the building superintendent from across the street was on a stepladder replacing it. This sort of vandalism was not uncommon in the neighborhood, especially where the super did not live on the premises.

The building was clean but old, a converted brownstone. The vestibule had been freshly painted. Marks threw his own flashlight on the mailboxes. There were four of them; one, the first floor, was without a nameplate, an invitation to mischief. Marks winced at the gritty sound of broken glass beneath his feet.

"Are any of these people home?"

"I don't know, sir," Herring said. "Nobody's gone in or out since we found him."

Marks studied the names, wondering the economic strata of the tenants. On the top floor was a Dr. A. J. Webb; then two names, neatly written in ink: Brannon, Russo—women he supposed since the first names were omitted; the next was Adam Britt and Joyce Liebling Britt, names vaguely familiar so that he speculated they might be theater people.

The overhead light came on and Herring helped the super out the door with his ladder. Marks studied the walls and floor. The glass from the broken bulb was ground to fragments where more than one pair of feet had scuffled through it. He could see no blood anywhere and the new yellow paint would have shown it easily. He moved out of the vestibule and the photographers and print men moved in. Marks at the first opportunity examined the shoes of the victim: tiny bits of glass glistened in the light. The same would hold for the shoes of his attackers if they could be got to soon enough. He crossed the street and looked up at the building. There was light in the top apartment, but the blinds were drawn and the windows closed. Otherwise the house was in darkness. Nor was there a window open in the whole building.

Marks was in the habit, where he could, of separating himself from the herd of detectives that converged on the scene of homicide. It was easier that night because Inspector Fitzgerald, his chief, had decided to ride with him when "the squeal" came in. Fitzgerald and the top precinct officer, Captain Redmond, whatever the ostensible business of their earnest conversation right now, were establishing lines of authority. Fitzgerald had the advantage of rank; Marks answering for Homicide would not have had it. Nor would it have troubled him—and that would have very much troubled Fitzgerald. Marks was one of the Commissioner's "bright young men," trained in the law. Despite the fact that he had his lieutenancy before reaching the age of thirty, he was by no means sure that he intended to make the detective force a lifetime career. It was somewhat ironic that, chiefly interested in the prevention of crime, he should have been assigned to homicide where what was past, fortunately for society, was rarely prologue.

He was recrossing the street, intent on finding out who was home on the fourth floor, when he noticed two uniformed men trying to restrain a young woman from entering the closed area.

". . . I tell you, Officer, that's where I live."

Marks quickly joined them and identified himself to Anne Russo. She gave him her name, and on his asking, told him where she had spent the evening.

Marks walked her slowly toward the building. "A man was killed here tonight. I wonder if there's a chance that you might be able to identify him."

The girl, almost his height and attractive in a non-made-up sort of way, flashed him a look of shock. For a second then, her teeth pressing her lower lip, she showed what he suspected to be a personal concern. He saw her throw it off.

"There is someone . . . ?" he suggested.

Anne shook her head.

Marks said quietly: "He's a good-looking man in his late thirties, I'd say. He'd be the sort that you might know."

The girl moistened her lips. "Dr. Bradley. . ." She hesitated, then went on: "A group of us were to meet Dr. Bradley at the laboratory. We waited till a little while ago but he didn't come."

"Dr. Bradley is a physicist?" Anne had told him the nature of her work, identifying herself.

"Yes. He's head of our group. He just got back today from a conference in Greece and he was going to show us some film..." Anne, having started to talk about Bradley and now full of fear for him, did not know where to stop.

Marks was careful not to interrupt her. Standing as they were in a concentration of light, he noticed that the Negro officer had taken his report book from his pocket. At a nod from Marks, he began unobtrusively to take down Anne's testimony. This was how young cops got on, Marks thought fleetingly. He was himself intent on what the girl had to tell. Anne told of the supper party, the wait at the laboratory, Bob Steinberg's call to Bradley's home...

Marks, getting both addresses, observed that both the laboratory and Bradley's home were within walking distance of where Anne lived.

"Yes, but..." Anne smiled nervously. "It's silly of me to be telling you all this."

Marks said: "If it turns out that way we can be grateful, can't we?"

Anne nodded doubtfully.

"Do you think you're up to taking a look at the victim, Miss Russo? If your Dr. Bradley has not shown up yet, we'd have to ask his wife to view...this unfortunate. You can save her that."

Anne nodded a determined willingness but she had gone deadly pale. Marks gave her his hand which she clutched without knowing it as he guided her through the jungle of men and equipment.

Anne was able to identify the murdered man.

A few minutes later in Anne's apartment, Marks filled Fitzgerald in on the girl's story. Anne opened the windows and then sat down, trying to grasp the reality of the situation hearing her own words restated.

Fitzgerald was impatient. He wanted a witness's story direct, not from the soft mouth of a sympathetic policeman, especially in the witness's presence. Himself a cop of the old school, he considered every witness hostile until proven otherwise by his testimony in court.

"You'll have to get in touch with his wife," he cut in. "Take a good man with you—a precinct man. I'll go over the young lady's story with her."

Anne thought then of Janet, still waiting. "Couldn't I be the one to tell her, Inspector?"

Fitzgerald had a daughter Anne's age himself. "All right," he said, "but first I want to hear about this movie you say the doctor was going to show you tonight. Was he carrying it with him?"

"Yes, but it wasn't a movie. It was film taken during recent experiment with..." Anne hesitated. Instinctively she knew better than tell a man like Fitzgerald that it was something he would not understand. She glanced at Marks. He nodded just a little, encouraging her. "With nuclear particles. The Soviet scientist, Grysenko provided prints of it for certain members of the conference."

"Did he?" Fitzgerald said. "A Russian?"

"A scientist," Anne said.

Marks felt that she might be a match for the old man—which would not make things a bit easier for her. Fitzgerald himself knew he had been given an impertinence, but as with all impertinences aimed at him by females past the age of twelve, he did not know how to parry them. He looked about a room that was astonishingly neat for a college girl's, except for the pictures on the wall: they looked to him like the salvage out of a wastepaper basket.

"Do you live here alone, Miss Russo?"

"No, sir. I have a roommate but she went home for two days between examinations."

He nodded. "Tell me, when was the *last* time Dr. Bradley visited you?"

Even in her state Anne could not miss the weighty insinuation in his voice. "He never visited me, not in the way you mean it, Inspector."

"Oh? He was never in this house?"

"Not alone, I don't think." Anne tried to remember. "He was here maybe a month ago—but the whole group was—for drinks. Then I asked Peter—Dr. Bradley—to stay a few minutes. I wanted my roommate to meet him. I'd talked so much about him. He's really great..." She paused realizing that what she had said was no longer precisely so. Marks was convinced by that brief spontaneous burst of praise that the girl's relationship with Bradley was worshipful—and pure. The old man sat, his arms folded, like an Irish prelate sifting truth from circumstance. Anne went on determinedly: "Afterwards, Janet—Mrs. Bradley—met the three of us and we had dinner out together."

"But Mrs. Bradley wasn't here till... afterwards?" Fitzgerald said.

The girl seemed to miss that point and Marks was glad.

She said: "She wasn't home the first time we called her."

"So, young lady, that was the only time Dr. Bradley was in your house?"

"No. Last fall Janet—she's a professional photographer —was taking pictures in this neighborhood, and further down. Sometimes Peter insisted on going with her—this isn't exactly the safest part of the city, and Janet was leaving some of her equipment here..."

"All right," Fitzgerald said. "That was last fall. What do you think he was doing here tonight?"

"It doesn't make sense that he should have been here. We were waiting for him at the laboratory. I'd come home to get my glasses, and I supposed..."

Fitzgerald interrupted. "You were here in this apartment tonight?"

"Yes."

"What time?"

"It was nine twenty-five when I left here."

"Alone?"

"Yes."

"It would be to your advantage, Miss, if you could think of someone to corroborate that," Fitzgerald said.

Anne looked from one man to the other. There seemed to have been a direct threat in Fitzgerald's words. "We took a cab, five of us, at the corner of Twenty-third Street and Third Avenue. On the way I remembered my glasses. Bob Steinberg, Dr. Bradley's associate, and the boys were anxious to get to the lab so I said they were just to let me out on my corner and go on. I'd come along on my own. That must have been a quarter past nine. I simply picked up my glasses, stopped in the bathroom, and left. I took the bus at Ninth Street . . ."

"And where was Dr. Bradley?"

"I don't know. We all assumed he was on his way. He always walked."

"This isn't much out of the way now, is it, Miss?"

Anne ran her long fingers rather desperately through her hair. "No, but he wouldn't even have been thinking of me. You've got to believe that, sir."

Marks, reasoning that people who need glasses in their work generally carry them with them at all times, and remembering that if Anne had come home she had not even paused long enough to open the windows, asked: "But would you have been thinking of him, Miss Russo? Did you think that perhaps you might meet him—say on Third Avenue—and then have the opportunity of walking the rest of the way alone with him?"

Anne shook her head. "Even if I'd thought that—even if I'd seen him I wouldn't have joined him. It's hard to explain, but I'd have known he wouldn't want company or he'd have come with us in the first place."

Marks accepted that part of it. Fitzgerald still looked skeptical.

"I'm terribly aware of being a woman in what's largely a man's world, Inspector, and sometimes I try maybe too hard not to get in the way. That's why I wouldn't ask them to wait in the cab for me."

This Fitzgerald understood. He shook his head in most fatherly fashion. "You'll never get a husband with that attitude, Miss. All right, let's go back to what you and the doctor were working on: tell me about the film he'd brought home from the Soviet Union."

Anne's eyes blazed. She wondered why he was being deliberately provocative. She could not believe it was stupidity. Carefully she distinguished herself as but one of six scientists working on the project, and then tried again to impress on the detective that Bradley himself had been but one of several physicists in Athens, not the Soviet Union, to whom the Russian scientist had given the film clips.

"I suppose the F.B.I. will be able to straighten me out on that," Fitzgerald said.

"Our research is not classified, Inspector."

"Isn't it?" He pursed his lips and then said: "But you scientists wouldn't have any of our secrets classified at all, would you now?"

"It was in all the newspapers," Anne said quietly. Now that she knew he was baiting her, it was easier to hold her temper.

Fitzgerald, as though he had all the time in the world and nowhere else to go, took a stick of gum from his pocket and unwrapped it. There was nothing the old man liked better, Marks thought, than to strain the temper of a witness.

Anne stared at the gum: something, some association . . .

"I'm sorry I don't have another stick," Fitzgerald said, seeing the look on her face and having put the gum in his mouth.

Anne met his eyes. "When I went out of here tonight—I heard someone's doorbell ring when I was at the second floor. I thought at first it was mine. Then when I got downstairs and there was a man waiting in the vestibule, I realized it was for Dr. Webb. I mean that's as much as I thought about him, but when I opened the door to go out, he got in without having to wait for the buzzer."

"Why did you assume he was waiting for Dr. Webb?" Marks asked.

"The Britts are in Europe, and the first-floor apartment is being done over before the new tenant moves in."

"We'd better have a description of the man," Marks said. "Was the light on in the vestibule?"

"Yes." Anne thought about the stranger and shook her head. She simply had not looked at him. "A dark hat, gray suit. He wasn't as tall as me. The only reason I thought of him just now—when he passed close to me I got a whiff of stale chewing gum."

The detectives looked at each other: the hopelessness of such identification.

"I expect we ought to have a word with Dr. Webb now if he's up there," Marks said.

Fitzgerald said: "For God's sake do. And send me up somebody to take down the young lady's information—such as it is."

Dr. Webb, a veterinarian, had been home all evening, but working in his study at the back of the house where there was a large fan in the window, he had heard nothing except his doorbell. He had expected no one and ignored it. He thought he heard the bell then in the downstairs apartment and was satisfied that the youngsters of the neighborhood were up to a not uncommon mischief. He could not even place the time. When Marks asked him then if it could have been nine thirty, he agreed that it might have been. This, it seemed, was as close as Anne Russo was to come to having a corroborating witness.

4

Marks thought he knew Manhattan well, having lived all his life in the city and having been a walker of its streets— until he joined the police force. Nobody could know the city like the cop who walked a beat. With this in mind he spoke to Precinct Captain Redmond and was assigned a young detective second-grade who had recently come out of uniform, a neighborhood product.

Marks introduced him to Anne in the car, "Detective Philip Pererro, Miss Russo."

"I used to meet Professor Bradley," Pererro said. "He'd look up if you spoke to him, but man, the way he'd walk with his head down, you'd wonder how he knew where he was going."

Anne sat stiff and numb. She had never been in a police car before. Nor would she remember much of this ride. She tried to think of the words with which to tell Janet.

Marks, as though reading her mind, said: "His wife is going to know why we're there the minute she sees us, Miss Russo. It's just going to be a matter of helping her through the shock."

He proved to be right. Janet released the door lock

downstairs before they had a chance to ring the bell. She was waiting on the landing, holding fast to the banister.

Anne, rounding the stairs and looking up, said just the name, "Janet . . ."

Janet sank to the floor, fainting for the first time in her life. Marks carried her to the livingroom couch and got her head down. Anne found some brandy.

Janet's first words when she regained consciousness were: "Peter's dead."

Anne nodded.

"I knew. When Bob did not call back, I knew then . . ."

Marks wandered softly about the room, leaving the burden of these moments to Anne Russo. For a man whose job it was to crowd the door of the bereaved, he felt utterly incompetent. There was no dignity in any death, much less the violent, but he was far less troubled looking at a naked corpse than into a face he should be watching that he might judge the true emotion from the simulated.

Pererro was better at it. His young face a mask of earnest concern, he stood at Anne's side, a glass of water in hand, his eyes never straying from the afflicted woman.

Marks picked up the dummied book, *Child of the City,* by Janet Hill Bradley. He opened it at random: a child on the city street bending over a dead cat. The child's expression seemed to say: why doesn't it get up? Marks felt a knot in his throat. God in heaven! What made him think he was a cop? He turned the page to another picture: the same child, now earnestly building a castle of beer cans on the pavement. But in the background was a young woman, photographed at the moment she had paused on the steps of a building to look down at him; her expression, anguished longing. Marks put the book down and studied the room itself, modern lines, the furniture probably Danish. Somewhere he had picked up the notion that most artists were conservative in their tastes in other arts than their own. He had no more grounds for it than for another of his assumptions: that all scientists liked Bach. But wandering to the shelf of records, he did find a preponderance of Bach.

He went to the window and looked down at the street below. It was not a well-lighted street. The haze caused a halo around the lamp across the street. Bradley had left the house after nine. If the attack on him had been planned beforehand, it had to have been carefully planned, and with considerable knowledge of Bradley's habits and his own plans for that night.

Anne came up behind him and said: "Mrs. Bradley thinks she can talk to you now, Lieutenant Marks. Could I call the Steinbergs? I ought to. They're really closer to Janet than I am. Louise would come and stay all night I think."

Marks looked at his watch. It was almost twelve. "Ask them both to come. You said there were three other students. Please give their names to Pererro." He did not suppose he would get to them that night unless a necessity for it showed up in the questioning of Mrs. Bradley or the Steinbergs. "Who else was here?"

"Eric Mather."

Anne's voice carried across the room. Marks thought he saw Mrs. Bradley's head bob up. He could not be sure.

"Another physicist?"

"He teaches literature I think," Anne said. "I don't know him very well."

Marks nodded. "I'll want to talk to Mrs. Bradley alone."

"I know. I'll be in the kitchen."

Marks drew up a chair next to Janet Bradley. She was still pale. He murmured his apologies for having to ask questions at a time like this. Pererro sat near Marks, his notebook open.

"I'll be all right," Janet said. "Just tell me what I have to know."

"I'm afraid it's the other way around," Marks said softly. "Your husband was attacked by a person or persons unknown either inside Miss Russo's building or very near by. You may speak freely. Miss Russo is in the kitchen."

"It . . . doesn't make sense," Janet said.

Anne Russo's own words, if Marks was not mistaken. "That he should have been there? Or that he was attacked?"

"Either. They were all going to the laboratory, including Anne." Janet moistened her lips and Marks offered her the glass of water on the side-table. She motioned that she did not want it. A little color was returning to her cheeks. She was very feminine, he thought, with a great deal of poise —and sensitivity. He thought of the book of photographs. He was not good at judging women's ages until they were past his own, but he supposed her to be not more than thirty.

"I'd like to start, if you don't mind," Marks said, "from the time Dr. Bradley came home this afternoon."

"He came directly from the air terminal," Janet said.

"You met him?"

"No. But I'd called and his flight was on time. He was home by five o'clock. He was very tired but, well, elated is a strong word for Peter. He had learned something . . ."

"In his work you mean?"

A flicker of a smile touched her lips. To Marks it was as though she had said on her husband's behalf: what else is there?

"Yes. I'd been a little uneasy as to how he would feel about people coming, but he was pleased."

"Forgive me if I interrupt you, Mrs. Bradley. If you felt he might not be pleased, why did you plan the dinner party? I don't ask that in criticism. I just want to get it clear who was here and why they were here."

"I understand," Janet said, but tentatively. It was borne home to her in that instant that everyone in the house that night was suspect to the police—suspect of Peter's murder. A little shudder ran through her. "Actually, I hadn't planned the party. Louise Steinberg—Peter's associate's wife—we're all good friends, you see—Louise called earlier and said she and Bob would like to have a few friends. I knew Peter would be tired so I suggested that we have it here."

"Who did the inviting?"

"Bob, I think, at the laboratory."

"Everyone who was here?"

"Everyone, I suppose . . . except Eric."

Marks waited.

"Louise must have invited him. He's a family friend. He went to school with Peter. He's not a scientist. Eric Mather."

Marks tried to weigh the significance of her adding, piece by piece, the information on Mather. It might simply be due, as she said, to his not being a scientist. Or it might be due to a personal need to justify his presence.

Now Janet was waiting. Marks said: "Was Dr. Bradley carrying much money when he left home tonight?" He had purposely broken the line of questioning to see if she would show a feeling of reprieve. He could not tell.

"It might have been a fair amount," Janet said. "He did not like to carry traveler's checks."

"And the film he had brought home, when did you first hear mention of that?"

"I'd already read about it in *The Times,* but from Peter, almost as soon as he got into the house. It was part of an exchange program very dear to Peter's heart. He had supposed at the beginning you see, that the Americans were going to have to give more than they received for a long time. There is nothing classified in Peter's work, you understand."

Marks nodded.

"This really isn't anything I'm qualified to talk about. Bob Steinberg could tell you better—or Anne."

"Please go on. I want to know what your husband felt about what he'd got."

"Well, as I understand it, the Russians who conducted the experiment were looking for something they wanted to know. But it occurred to—whoever it was—that there might be something in the film that would contribute to Peter's work. A Swedish physicist is onto the same thing. And somebody at California. They were also given prints. The Russians made great propaganda of it."

"At what point in the evening, Mrs. Bradley, was it decided that they would look at the film tonight?"

"I don't know exactly," Janet said after a moment's thought. "I didn't know about it until after dinner. Anne and the boys were washing up. They always do, and I was putting away. Peter asked me if I minded his going to the lab for an hour. He wasn't in the habit of consulting me but he'd been away." Again she qualified, as though anxious that Marks not think there were tensions between them: "By that I mean that long ago in our marriage, I'd come to know his way of pursuing an idea from the moment it occurred to him until he could use it—or throw it away."

"Anyone who knew him well would know that, wouldn't they?" Janet nodded and Marks went on: "You must help me work out a timetable, and tell me any suggestion you might have on the route he would ordinarily have taken. I understand he was accustomed to walking to the University?"

"Always, no matter what the weather. After Bob Steinberg called tonight, I remember thinking that Peter might have stopped at St. John's Church. He often did. Not to pray. It was just that sometimes he liked a Gothic darkness. And Athens is a very bright city. I don't even know what he saw of it . . ." She almost broke then. "He wanted me to go with him."

"Why didn't you?"

"It seemed like a great deal of money to spend for so little time, not even a week. And I needed to be here—or thought so then . . . a book that seemed important."

"Child of the City?"

Janet nodded.

"Do you have any children, Mrs. Bradley?"

"We had a son. He died."

"I'm sorry I asked."

Janet shrugged and then covered her face with her hands. "Oh, God. Will nothing make this real? Or would that be too much to bear?"

Marks glanced at Pererro. Notebook in hand, and pencil

suspended, he looked like an automaton. The clock rasped, and as Marks started to speak again, it struck twelve.

"Who, besides those present, would have known that Dr. Bradley was leaving the house at nine fifteen tonight?"

"I shouldn't think anyone else," Janet said.

"No one would have had to open the laboratory building?"

"Most all of the group had keys."

"After the others left—Miss Russo was stopping home," Marks said. "Did your husband mention stopping to pick her up?"

"No. He said simply that I should wait up because he wasn't gong to stay very long."

Marks asked then about Bradley's activity from the time he got home until the guests arrived. His only phone call had been to Professor Bauer, the chairman of the Physics Department.

A few minutes later the doorbell rang and Anne poked her head out the kitchen doorway. "Shall I go? It's probably the Steinbergs."

Janet moaned and turned away. "If only I could be alone . . . Where did they take Peter?"

"We'll let you know," Marks said. "There must be an autopsy." Anne had gone into the hallway. "Mrs. Bradley, there had to be some circumstance under which your husband would have gone to Anne Russo's apartment."

"Only if he were told that Anne was ill—or hurt. I can think of no other reason."

"You are absolutely certain?"

"I am. Peter had a very strong sense of propriety."

"That's all for now," Marks said, getting up. "I want to talk with the Steinbergs—in your kitchen if you don't mind?"

But Janet had withdrawn mentally. She sat very straight and looked almost prim and childlike, her hands in her lap folded tightly into one another. Marks remembered her husband's very young face—seemingly turned that way by death—which had no right to make its captives young—

and the remark of the Negro cop who had found him: "He looks like a preacher to me, a good man."

Marks and Pererro waited in the kitchen while the Steinbergs spoke to Janet. Pererro looked into the darkroom, the door to which was open.

"Jees," he said, "what a way to do up a pantry."

Marks looked into the room. A gallon bottle of acetic acid stood on the shelf near the door, the poison label clearly visible. "Makes you kind of thirsty, doesn't it?"

Steinberg joined them and tried his best to describe the kind of research Bradley and his group were engaged in. He was a heavy-built man who, Marks thought, like his work was a reservoir of latent energy. He wore thick-lensed glasses and probably wore them so much of the time that only his wife would immediately recognize him without them. He would be Marks's last candidate for a man likely to be involved in physical violence. Steinberg forgot everything else, talking of physics, even for a moment the death of the man with whom he had shared the enthusiasm. Marks, his attention divided, was unable to grasp the concept Steinberg had just said was so simple. He glanced at Pererro's suspended notes and was surprised at the three dots and an exclamation point representing Steinberg's testimony. He had learned something about Pererro if not about elementary particles. Finally Steinberg said:

"I'll loan you a book if you come round to the laboratory."

"Thank you," Marks said gravely. "I'd be interested. I want to ask you now about what happened at the laboratory tonight."

"Not a damned thing. We got there—myself and three of the graduate students working with us: we signed in at nine twenty, took about ten minutes setting up and then just stood around waiting."

"What time did Miss Russo arrive?"

"Twenty to ten maybe. It's in the check-in book. When

Bradley didn't show by ten thirty, I went out and called Janet."

Marks probed him on the business of Anne Russo's glasses. Steinberg's recollection of it was essentially the same as Anne had told.

"Does she wear her glasses regularly?"

"For work, yes. That's why she forgets them so much." It seemed a non sequitur to Marks but it satisfied him that there was not anything too unusual in the girl's having to stop for them that night.

"What's the connection?" Steinberg asked.

He had not been told, Marks realized, where Bradley was found. "Dr. Bradley was assaulted in the vestibule or just outside Miss Russo's building."

Steinberg's eyes blinked rapidly behind the glasses. "How did he get *there?*"

"That is our most difficult question at the moment. How or why."

Steinberg shook his head. "I don't get it. Why would he go there?"

"You can think of no reason?" Marks persisted, conscious of melodramatic overtones that made him sound like Fitzgerald.

Steinberg suddenly caught on. "Annie? She's one of the boys!"

Marks was reminded of one of his mother's favorite sayings: "The wisest men make the best fools."

It was Louise Steinberg who gave him the personality sketches he wanted of those present at the dinner party. Louise was the kind of woman Marks felt easy with: they had grown up in similar backgrounds, their parents early refugees from Hitler's Europe. They did not speak of this, but both supposed it of the other. Louise, the mother of three children, was getting plump, the tendency, Marks mused, in many a Jewish girl once she had snared or been snared by the man she wanted. He was extremely grateful to meet her at this stage of his investigation.

Louise had gone directly home from the Bradleys', taking a cab part of the way: she had calculated the distance she could walk, where by taking a cab then, she could arrive home in time to avoid paying the baby-sitter another hour's wage.

"Besides," she said, "my feet were hurting."

"I understand it was the original plan for you to have the dinner party at your house."

"I guess it was," Louise said. It all seemed a very long time ago. Then she remembered and amended: "Actually it was Eric Mather's idea. He called me this morning—yesterday now, isn't it? Anyway, he said he'd like to throw a little party for Peter the day he got home. I told him he'd better get to it. Peter was on his way. Then, typically Eric, he began fussing—all the things he had to do that day. I shouldn't say this, especially since I wound up doing the same thing in a way, letting Janet do the work."

Marks offered her a cigarette. "About Eric," he said easily, "What's 'typically Eric?'"

Louise shrugged. "He's a kook in lots of ways—I've audited some of his classes. Way out. But he's very charming and good company unless he's in a mood. Anyway, he's a bachelor, and it generally winds up that somebody else gives his party for him."

"But tonight's party was his idea?"

"Yes, but everybody was glad Janet and I'd taken over. When Eric does give a party, you don't get anything to eat until ten or eleven, and our boys don't live that way. You know, come six o'clock..."

Marks grinned. "If Mather had given the party, would the same people have been invited?"

"The Bradleys and us anyway, and Anne maybe."

"He likes Anne?"

"I wouldn't say that, but... I don't really know what I'd say, Lieutenant, so maybe I'd better not say anything."

"Please do," the detective said. "If there isn't any connection with what happened to Bradley, I won't see any of these people again. And if there is a connection, it might be important."

Louise nodded and brushed a swatch of hair from her forehead. "I want to help, but I have a bad habit of adding two and two up to five."

Marks chanced a direct question: "Would you say there was any private relationship between Anne Russo and Dr. Bradley?"

"Absolutely not. Outside of science they'd have had about as much attraction for one another as two neutrons. I think that's right."

Marks leaned forward, lowering his voice: "Mrs. Bradley and Eric Mather?"

Louise shook her head as though determined to convince herself as well. "No!"

Marks waited.

"He might have been helping her with her book," Louise supplemented. "Janet's a photographer, but really a photographer."

"I know," Marks agreed.

"They were going over the book last night while the rest of us were yakking."

Marks got the party picture at once: the scientists apart, Mather and Janet Bradley in a huddle. Louise, who would never be an outsider at any party, drifting to where the talk most interested her. "Who was the first to leave?" he asked.

"Eric."

Curious, Marks thought, if there was anything between him and Mrs. Bradley.

"But we were all ready to go by then. The boys were itching to look at their goddamn film. I asked Janet if she wanted to go to a movie. I guess in the last five years Janet and I have seen more movies than any two people in New York."

"Why didn't you share a cab with Mather? You live in the same direction, don't you?"

"He didn't ask me," Louise said. "Besides, he wouldn't have been going home. I don't think he ever does these days if he can help it."

"Do you like him?" Marks asked. He felt as though he had known Louise for a long time and hoped she felt the same about him.

She shrugged, something a little pitying in the gesture. "Sort of, I guess. I'm a real *Yiddishe* mama."

5

Nothing Mather had done that night, no part of his wanderings, his encounters with the wits of the Village, his sudden plunges into and withdrawals from barroom arguments and coffeehouse debates, not even his exultant sobriety in the post-midnight hours when poets fumbled for the lines they had bled into being and accepted his extemporaneous suggestions as the same—flattering whom?—nothing had assuaged his restlessness. Often he had fought down the temptation to call the Bradley house on some pretext—had he left his cigarette lighter? Peter's temper would have cooled by bedtime. The fools! he would say. The bloody idiots. Mather was sure he would not have gone to the police: it would take too much of his precious time. It would take a little of it to explain to the police in the morning how the lettercase came to be in a public mailbox.

Mather turned into Perry Street shortly after two in the morning. He dreaded solitary confinement in his own apartment. To have one's part in a conspiracy cut off at its critical moment was like asking an actor to play the lead in a badly constructed play, the climax coming when he was off-stage. It was not until he saw the car parked in front of his building, two men sitting in it, that he admitted to himself the true basis of his distress: fear. His legs were rubber. His eyes, however, searched the familiar street for the nearest police call-box. Come humiliation, come exposure, no matter: his first instinct was to save himself.

The car rolled toward him and he forced himself to move on. But when the car was almost abreast of him, he flung himself to the ground and lay there, his face averted, the few seconds it took one of the men to reach him.

Lieutenant Marks sprang from the car to the side of the fallen man. "Are you hurt?"

Mather gathered himself into a sitting position. In the failure of attack upon his person, the absence of the bullets he had unreasoningly anticipated, he was appalled at his exhibition of weakness.

"Damned city pavements," he murmured. "I think I've broken my toe." He reached for his foot and held it, and such was the strength of his imagination, a pain actually shot through his foot.

Marks said: "Are you Eric Mather?"

Mather looked up at him. "Who the hell are you?"

By the light of the street lamp, Marks offered his identification, saying at the same time: "Lieutenant Marks, police department." He nodded toward his partner, now squatting beside them. "Detective Pererro."

Mather took advantage of his feigned injury to try for some sort of reorientation. He had wanted a policeman and one had appeared. Two of them.

Pererro said, as though Mather was unconscious: "What's the matter with him?"

Marks spoke to the man still hugging his foot. "See if you can put some weight on it, Mather. We'd like to talk with you."

"Where?" He was afraid he would pass out if he had to get into a car with strangers even if they called themselves police.

Marks straightened up. "In your own house or police headquarters. It's up to you."

Mather got to his feet, throwing off Marks's offer to help. He limped a few steps, putting his weight on his heel. His left foot, he must remember, his left foot.

"It's going to be all right," he said. He was shocked that Peter had created such a ruckus that the police were investigating at this hour. It was the juxtaposition of this rationale with his own wild fears of the previous moments that brought him for the first time in the whole compass of the scheme to concern for the physical safety of his friend, Peter Bradley.

He was putting the key in the door to his basement apartment. The semi-darkness there and in the apartment as he groped for the nearest lamp covered his dismay. The apartment smelled of its recent disuse. He had scarcely more than slept there since the first time Jerry and Tom had fouled it with their presence. He lit the lamps on either side of the sofa and then sat down to remove his shoe. The detectives watched him massage the foot.

"Sit down and tell me what this is all about," he said. "It must be damned important for you to come at this hour."

"What do you think?" Pererro said. He had been due to go off duty at midnight, and while it was great to work closely on a case like this, he felt that during the long wait for Mather, more important things were happening elsewhere.

Marks picked up the shoe Mather had removed and took it to the light. He could see nothing with the naked eye that looked like glass, but it was now some four hours since the attack on Bradley. He held the shoe in his hand and watched the man massaging his foot: that something was burning him up inside, the detective was sure, the gray eyes furtive, then daggerish. They might be the key to the whole man, Marks thought. Handsome in a long-haired way, he would go over great with the girls in the classroom and possibly with a few of the boys; something effete about him.

"Do you always stay out this late on a week night?" Marks asked.

"Often," Mather said. "I am my own master."

That was something Marks very much doubted. He said: "Peter Bradley was murdered last night. That's why we're here."

Mather leaned back on the couch, his mouth open. The back of his head had gone stone numb.

Pererro stared at him. He did not know what it was about the man, but he kept feeling that he wasn't really there, that he wasn't a real person. It was the damnedest feeling he'd ever had about a person. Again he spoke to Marks: "Should I get him some water?"

Marks shook his head. He was trying to measure this performance with the sprawl on the sidewalk. This, he thought, was the real thing. What then caused the sidewalk tumble? That it was sham he was certain. An attempt at misdirection by calling attention to himself? Had he wanted to get rid of something on his person? Narcotics crossed his mind as a possibility.

He waited for Mather to come out of the shock, taking the opportunity to measure the man further by the house he lived in. A study in red and black. The chairs were painted black, red cushions. The floor was painted red, with here and there a black throw rug. Neat as a chessboard. In no way ornate or fussy: he could have lived here himself. It seemed an unlikely nest for anyone who had taken such an untidy fall. It would be a great shame, he thought, if Mather were not involved: he looked like an interesting nut to crack.

Mather made a smacking noise with his lips, trying to speak, and finally said: "When?"

"Some time before eleven o'clock," Marks said.

Mather pulled himself up jerkily, like a spastic. "For God's sake, man, tell me the whole thing."

"If we knew the whole thing we wouldn't be here. Or at least we would not be sitting down to a quiet exchange of information."

Mather threw him a sidelong glance. "Peter was a close friend of mine. I was at his house tonight."

Marks said: "That's why I thought you would want to help us. Can we clear the air first by finding out how you yourself spent the evening from nine o'clock on?"

"Will you tell me then about Bradley?" he demanded. He could not believe that Peter was dead. He dared not believe it. A shudder ran through his body. He could smell sickness in his own cold sweat.

"Of course."

"I left the Bradleys' at a few minutes after nine," he started. "I'd promised to look in on a group of my students..." He tried to block out from his own mind the moment of watching beneath the lamp post and signaling: the kiss, the Judas kiss. He remembered now Janet in the window, and his idiotic hope that she had seen him. "Oh, God Almighty." He buried his face in his hands.

To Marks it was an understandable emotional break. He would give him that much. "Where was the meeting with your students?"

Mather took his hands away, the fingertips briskly wiping the tears from beneath his eyes. He blew his nose. "Sorry. They always meet at a place called the Red Lantern on Sullivan Street. I must have spent a half-hour with them. After that...I can't even give you the names of the places in order."

"We'll put them in order," Marks said. "Just name them as they come to mind. To start with, did you go directly to the Red Lantern?" Mather nodded. "Do you have a car?"

"No. I walked."

"Let's have the route so we can check it out."

That part was easy: he could walk it again in his own mind's eye, and know exactly what went through his mind, that first joyous sense of freedom...But the detective was listening for something that wasn't going to turn up on the list of streets his partner jotted down. He was measuring the whys of "I can't be sure...I think I went round Gramercy..." Mather remembered where he had stopped midway to buy a package of cigarettes, and at the end decided to mention it.

"Do you know what time you arrived at the Red Lantern?"

"I'd have to guess—about nine thirty."

He watched the younger, raw-boned detective making notes, and reeled off the names of a half-dozen places he had gone afterwards, winding up at Barney's Coffee House, less than three blocks from where he lived.

Marks wondered if he spent many nights like that. He had not been drinking, and he now doubted the use of narcotics. He remembered Louise Steinberg's saying he never went home if he could help it. But what kind of a teacher could he be to live so erratic an existence?

"How long have you been at Central University . . . Professor, is it?"

"My students call me Mister," Mather said icily. He sensed the line of Mark's reasoning. "I've been in the English Literature Department for three years, my first as a lecturer. Now I am an assistant professor. And to answer the question you did not ask, sir: I need less sleep than other people."

Marks smiled. "I wish I did. How long have you known Peter Bradley?"

"We were in college together—just after the war. Before Bradley switched to physics. For years then I didn't see him, not until I came East to Central University. Oh, once or twice. He'd come out to a conference in Chicago and call me. I'd kept up with his career of course. It was rather more to keep up with than my own. I suppose the fact that he was here may have influenced my decision to take the job at Central."

"And Mrs. Bradley, have you known her long?"

"I met her out here. They'd been married for some years by then." He would have liked to add something, a little more on Janet, a show of sympathy. Instead, he demanded: "You said you'd tell me what happened."

"I'll tell you what I can, Professor. He was assaulted by a person or persons unknown. First a blow on the back of the head, but the cause of his death was a knife wound in the back."

"No!" Mather cried out the word as though he had felt the wound.

Marks said carefully: "It occurred in the vestibule or just outside the door of Anne Russo's building."

"Why there?" Mather said after a moment. "They were all going to the laboratory the last I saw of them."

"Miss Russo's is not so much out of the way, is it?"

"I neither know nor give a damn where Miss Russo lives," Mather said.

Marks said: "She lives on the edge of a rough neighborhood."

"Who doesn't in New York City?" But Mather suddenly saw what might be the line of police investigation: if some sort of relationship were discovered between Anne and Peter, if in fact Peter's being at her place could be accounted for, the crime could be put down to assault for the purpose of theft, the random street attack on a well-dressed man. Could it possibly be the truth? The knife was a street weapon. Jerry would not have dared . . . He could feel his jaws working, his own feeling of relief was so intense. He must somehow cover himself with this cop in gentleman's clothing. He said: "I make it a point to see *my* students only in the classroom or in some public gathering place."

Marks digested that for a moment. "Do you know Miss Russo?"

"Only from meeting her at the Bradleys'."

Marks gazed at him, all innocence. "Yet she was on your guest list for the dinner party. Why?"

"Because Peter liked her," Mather said with a small bitter smile on his lips.

An interesting response: Mather was willing to admit his intention of inviting Anne; if someone had told the police it was his idea, he was not going to contradict it now. Marks wondered how far this Galahad would go to hide whatever it was he had to hide. Something, Marks was sure, but he was inclined to doubt that it had anything directly to do with Bradley's death. Nor did he think he was going to find it out at this stage in the investigation. It would take a little more sweat and tears.

"I wonder if I may have your other shoe also, Professor. For a routine laboratory check. They'll be returned."

Mather shrugged. As the detectives got up he fumbled at his shoe laces, waiting for the parting shot. He felt that one had to come, something held back for when he would be least expecting it.

Marks said: "Better see a doctor about that toe, Professor."

"It's nothing. Just my clumsiness." He handed over the shoe.

"I'd feel better if you saw one. The city does have a responsibility—as you yourself pointed out."

Mather knew then why he loathed the slick bastard: Marks was the kind of man he had feared and fled from all his life, a man he suspected of seeing right through him. In his stocking feet and without the limp, he saw them to the door. There he ventured to ask: "Was Bradley robbed?"

"Oh, yes," Marks said. "Cleaned out. Can you think of any other motive for his murder?"

"It's the worst possible motive," Mather said from an inner compulsion to pay a tardy tribute to his friend. "Peter Bradley would have given any man who needed it anything he owned."

Marks merely looked at him and nodded, and then went out the door, his strong and silent partner following him.

6

Mather, alone and hearing the outer door click behind the detectives, tried to confront himself with the reality of Peter Bradley's death. But nothing ever seemed real to him while he was alone, not until he could find the context in which he could see himself as he wanted other people to see him. No such context was now possible: he wanted nothing so much as to disappear altogether, above all from his own view. He had worshipped Peter Bradley—worshipped, admired, envied him. What better tribute to pay a friend than envy?

He slumped down on the couch and let his mind seek its only solace, the memory of his finest moment with Peter Bradley. Once, in their college days, they had been swimming off a boat in one of the Finger Lakes when Peter got caught beneath an abandoned fishing net. He had managed to surface long enough to cry for help before the weight of the net bore him down again. Mather was not nearly the swimmer Peter was, yet he had jumped to Peter's rescue with no thought of his own safety, and he had carried a fishing knife with which Peter cut himself free. Peter might have died that day. The net and the knife.

Eighteen years later, was it again the net and the knife?

How curious the repetition of weapon and symbol. A poet could find no better a concept. This then was the beginning between Peter and himself. For Peter it had ended alone, a knife in the filthy hand of a stranger put there by his friend Eric. He thought then of what it would be like, to drive a knife into the warm flesh. It was the way *he* should die now by his own hand.

Signifying nothing. He had not meant Peter harm: there was nothing in the scheme of things as he had planned them, as he had—so he had thought—been allowed to plan them to warrant violence. In a way it was to end a larger violence he had joined the conspiracy. But there had been no place in his lovely simple scheme for Anne Russo. He could truly say he had never in his life given Anne Russo more than a passing thought. Nor, he was sure, had Peter outside that tight little island of science.

If he were to tell the truth now as he knew it . . .

To start at the beginning, he could not, although to tell all the truth he would have to: it was to keep forever from his own mind that noisome incident—one incident in a lifetime!—and to do it he could not tolerate even Jerry's suggestion of it—that he had entered wholeheartedly into their conspiracy. There! That much of truth he had admitted. He pinned it on the wall, that first confrontation with the stranger: the pudgy face, the ferret's eyes, the pink tongue coming out to receive a stick of gum as though it were a communion wafer.

"It was to save my own skin!" he cried aloud, "to hide my filthy image. Call it blackmail, straight and simple. The rest is all delusion."

His mind however slipped away from the truth to still pursue the delusion: he had made of the problem posed him a game of chess such as might have been played by correspondence. He had anticipated, nay, contrived, his antagonist's every move. Never had he felt involved with people, only pieces, except for the incidental pleasure it had given him to use Peter Bradley, the man who prided himself above all else on being the pawn of no man, of no institution, of no party.

But Peter was dead. Possibly by chance. But if not by chance who could name his killer?

Mather began composing in his mind a note he might leave: The man I knew called himself "Jerry." I am sure it was not his name, for he had a partner I met later whom he introduced as "Tom." Tom and Jerry. No wonder, having no more originality than that, they willingly accepted my brain, my imagination. Or did they? They could themselves have been no more than messengers, well-trained lackies...

He pulled himself out of the reverie, trying to go back, back... Peter was the friend of his youth on whom in later years he had thrust his friendship and had it tolerated. Like the devotion of the buffoon he often played. Had Peter been utterly contemptuous of him? Was he *persona grata* to Peter only because Janet found a kind of liking for him? He would never know now, never really know. He would have forced the revelation had Peter lived. There would have come a time of reckoning. There always did between him and his attachments, a time when rejection became itself gratifying, for it left him the ultimate solace: even as a dog, he must lick his own wounds.

Exhausted but not remotely sleepy, he pushed himself up from the couch and started for the bathroom. He realized that he was hobbling, favoring an imagined injury. He lifted the shoeless foot, the impulse to kick it violently at something, but he caught his self-image in his mind's eye and was struck by the ridiculous figure it made of him, the man who even played his own clown. He began to laugh aloud at himself, the laughter rolling up in him irresistibly. Only when the tears came and he was reminded of the deeper need for tears was he able to control himself. He went on to the bathroom and presently took two sleeping pills. There were only two more left in the bottle, which forestalled temptation in that direction.

He stripped, turned out the lights and groped his way

through the apartment to open the window at the front. As he raised it he saw the two detectives; a few feet away— near the place where he had fallen—they were playing their flashlights over the sidewalk, searching the curb, the gutter, around the stoops. The big silent one picked something up, examined it under his light and threw it away.

Just then Marks shot the full beam of his flashlight on the window. Mather stood in the glaring light like a man pilloried. Marks clicked off the light and said: "Better put some clothes on. You'll catch cold."

Mather slammed down the window and fell away into the darkness within.

7

Marks read the morning newspapers in a cab on his way to Precinct Headquarters. He did not often allow himself the luxury of a cab, but he had not had much sleep. He lived alone in an apartment hotel just off Central Park West. He had grown up not far from there where his parents still lived in the building they had moved into when he was ten years old. He sometimes stopped to have breakfast with them. But not that morning. He would manage his coffee and Danish on the taxpayers' time.

Bradley's death had made the tabloid headlines. The paper made the most of the fact that the physicist had been found outside the apartment building of an attractive female student. It was to be expected, Marks thought. The old man himself had briefed the reporters at 3:00 A.M., and while he would not deliberately throw them what he knew damned well they wanted, neither would he go out of his way to throw them off that track. No mention was made of the film at all. The story read like a clandestine love tryst in which the parties to it had got their signals crossed. Marks threw down the paper in disgust, but he thought of one of his father's favorite dictums: As long as you've got an open case, keep an open mind. His father was a good lawyer, but a better human being. Fitzgerald was a good policeman.

Marks admired him in spite of himself: the Inspector divorced facts from people. Facts never lied. People almost always did, even when they did not know they were lying, and the old man was short of patience when it came to looking for subconscious motives. The last thing he had said to Marks the night before was: "I hope to God this turns out to be a nice clean street job." He had emphasized the irony, but he had spoken the truth of himself.

The old man was in a better mood than Marks had expected. His eyes were bloodshot and he had cut himself in a hasty and not very efficient shave, but something in the case had gone the way he wanted it. He took Marks's arm as they started up the deeply grooved stairs to Redmond's office.

"Wouldn't you think they could do something to brighten these bloody mausoleums?"

Marks knew what he meant: he said it of every precinct house in the city. This two-story building at Houston Street had remained virtually unchanged since the days of the Tong wars, a bleak stone edifice with iron-meshed windows the dust of which God's own eyes could scarcely penetrate. The pea-green walls were chipped along the way, showing the pinkish taste of the previous administration.

"They're all waiting for us up here," Fitzgerald said, "hoping to build a mountain on a pinhead. But mark my words: as I said last night, it's a police case, pure and simple. We got back his wallet and briefcase this morning, the only thing missing his money, and I dare say he was carrying a fair amount. Didn't his wife tell you that?"

"She said it might have been," Marks said. "Where were the things returned?"

"At a mail deposit box on Sixty-fourth and Park Avenue. Picked up at 5:00 A.M."

The two double desks in Redmond's office had been moved back, and a table usually used for a miscellany of reports and office supplies had been converted into a conference table. Six men were around it, quietly talking, smoking, laughing, except for the one Marks rightly supposed to be the University representative. He looked at his watch and then sat back staring at Bradley's case which lay in a plastic laboratory container in the middle of the table.

Marks took the empty chair next to him and introduced himself.

"Arnold Bauer, chairman of the Physics Department," the man said, shaking hands. "I should suppose we could get on now." Then he added, nodding toward the case, "It seems incredible, doesn't it?"

"Yes," Marks said, "it always does."

He rose to shake hands across the table with the man opposite, Jim Anderson of the Federal Bureau of Investigation. A big man of about fifty, well-groomed, with a quick smile, his handshake had the grip of an iron cuff.

Marks noticed the laboratory clearance label as Redmond picked up the bag and emptied its contents on the table. Out of the lettercase itself he took the wallet, the film box, and several pages of handwritten notes. "Missing, to our knowledge," Redmond said, "an unknown amount of money. Dr. Bradley did not carry traveler's checks." Redmond summarized the police case to that hour. He turned to Bauer. "Professor Bauer has examined the film with Mr. Anderson and his colleagues. Professor?"

Bauer gave a gentle and lucid account of the kind of research that Dr. Bradley was engaged in. Unlike Steinberg, whom Marks had talked with the night before, Bauer was accustomed to dealing with the non-scientific mind. The chairman of any university department, Marks knew, was primarily a liaison officer between ivory tower and market place. It was a pleasure to watch him dislodge the fixed concept of a man like Fitzgerald that nuclear physics was necessarily a highly secretive, war-oriented science.

"Actually," Bauer said, indicating the film box, "the findings of such experiment had been published for some time. Dr. Bradley and our people were looking to what we

might call a by-product in the film. We don't know of
course whether it will tell us anything we didn't already
know until we compare it with what we do know. Dr.
Bradley obviously thought it might. Otherwise he and his
colleagues would not have been so anxious to study the
film last night. Some of the notes he had made"—Bauer
indicated the handwritten papers—"suggest his high ex-
pectations."

"The film is intact now?" Marks asked.

"I should think so," Bauer said. "I shouldn't suppose it
to have been tampered with at all. It would mean nothing
except to a person interested in the Pi-meson."

"And there can't be many of them in the world," Fitzgerald remarked dryly.

The others laughed, including Bauer.

"Let's have another look at the container," one of the
federal men said.

Redmond handed him the box, roughly one by one and a
half by four inches. When he was through examining it
inside and out, he passed it and its contents on. Marks
observed the customs' stamp overlapping the label on
which Bradley's name had been written in block letters.
Inside were a half-dozen film strips of four frames each.
The film was protected by coarse tissue paper. The box
itself was much like that in which Marks kept color slides.

Anderson spoke last: "The customs' seal was broken, I
understand, but Bradley himself might have broken it, or
more likely the thieves, to see that they weren't missing
anything. Customs cleared the film on the spot, duplicates
of it having entered the country at Boston, and Washington, D.C., as well as via another New York flight, a set on
its way to San Francisco. Both the box and the film are
identical with those received at the National Laboratory.
We had them flown up this morning for comparison."

Anderson smiled, and Marks thought he was one of
those characters who promoted men on the basis of how
early they got up in the morning. He had the glow of the
cold shower about him.

"I want to say that the Bureau's full facilities are at your disposal, gentlemen," Anderson concluded. "We shall expect you to inform us of any development you feel might concern the national security. I myself am available for consultation at any hour of the day or night. But at the present stage of your investigation, I see no reason for us to enter the case."

More than forty detectives were assigned to the case, most of them to the hard, gritty work of door-to-door inquiry, of trying to track the victim from the moment he stepped out of his own house. The first pay-off came early: Bradley, walking alone, had stopped briefly to exchange a few words with the sexton of St. John's Church who was closing the gate for the night. The time was nine thirty: the sexton was sure since he was performing his last chore of the day and was understandably punctual about it. He had known Bradley to have been in Greece and their exchange ran something like: "How was Greece, Professor?" To which Bradley replied: "Hot and noisy. I felt right at home."

The sexton "was pretty sure" Professor Bradley had continued on toward the University.

Marks noted the name of the interrogating officer, Tom Reid, and laid the report aside. The conversation of Bradley with the sexton was certainly not that of a man aware of immediate jeopardy. Marks studied a city street map. Reaching St. John's, Bradley had passed by three blocks the street on which Anne Russo lived. At some point between the church and the University he had either turned back or was intercepted and driven back to the building on East Tenth Street.

The detective dug out Anne Russo's statement. She had left her apartment at nine thirty, admitting the unidentified gum chewer to the building. Marks returned to the map. If Bradley had been tailed from his own house—either on foot or by two or more men in a car—the man Anne had seen would have left the others at the corner of Tenth Street and Third Avenue. The time was right, and to Marks's

satisfaction, Anne's story was corroborated by Dr. Webb's
account of the doorbell ringing. Bradley at that moment
had been at the gate of St. John's, his "tail" not far behind
him.

Marks was about to put these dovetailing circumstances
before Fitzgerald when he realized that the old man could
say: *If* the little lady is telling the truth. If there was a man
in the vestibule. Find me the man or another witness who
saw him. Anybody can ring a doorbell, including our
missy.

Marks made a note of his deductions and for the moment kept them to himself.

Fitzgerald was studying the preliminary report of the
medical examiner. When he finished he handed it to
Marks. The blow on the back of the head was likely to
have done no more than stun the victim; no serious brain
injury. The mortal wound came from a knife, a neat thrust
with a small, very sharp blade at the most vulnerable point,
suggesting that it was inflicted while the victim was unconscious. Bradley's clothing had been impressed in the immediate area of the wound. The absence of blood stains near
the victim, the condition of clothing at the surface of the
wound, suggested that a cloth or handkerchief had been put
round the knife before it was withdrawn.

"I wonder what our chances are of finding that bit of
dirty linen," Marks said.

"If it was yours, what would you do with it?"

"Get rid of it quick—unless it had my monogram on it."

Fitzgerald agreed. "If it's a street job, we'll find it."

Marks then picked up a call from the police laboratory:
he could collect a size eleven pair of shoes any time,
findings negative. He hadn't expected them to be otherwise. He doubted Mather could use a weapon sharper than
his tongue. It was too early in the day to check out the
taverns and coffeehouses. Marks looked up the precinct
duty chart. Pererro would come on in time to pick up part
of that detail.

Marks was on his way out of the building when Walter Herring caught up with him. He was in civilian clothes.

"Promoted?" Marks said.

"No, sir, but they don't mind much what I wear on my day off. You know, Lieutenant, I got thinking this morning —you ought to get another man to check out that Mrs. Finney again, the woman with the dog. I hate to say this, boss, but a cop of a different complexion might get more out of her than I did."

Marks tried to remember her testimony. Herring explained that she had thought the victim drunk at first.

Marks, intending to prowl the scene himself, said: "Let's go."

"Yes, sir!" No nonsense about Herring. He was ambitious, and he liked the company of men in authority.

Mrs. Finney greeted them with less enthusiasm than did her spaniel who waddled from one to the other of them, the tail wagging a lot of dog. Marks remembered having heard once that dogs were color-blind.

"What's so important you'd come around before a woman's put her house in place?"

"Officer Herring and I were trying to narrow down the time of the attack on the victim. We knew you'd want to help us if you could." Marks said it with a straight face.

Mrs. Finney wiped her hands on her apron and led the way into a parlor that had never been out of order, the sterile look of which was strangely heightened by the vividly colored religious pictures. The spaniel hurtled himself into the best chair.

"A professor, by the morning paper," Mrs. Finney said. "And will you tell me please what decent young girls are up to, living alone in this part of the city?"

Marks cleared his throat. The question had been rhetorical.

"Sit down," she said, with a nod toward two straight-backed chairs. She tucked a strand of gray hair into the bun at the back of her head, and stood, her arms folded, measuring Marks with watery blue eyes. About to sit down, he waited then till she did.

"It was me that found the body," Mrs. Finney said, "but you wouldn't see him mentioning that, would you?" She jerked her head toward Herring.

"I'm sorry," Herring said, "but you gave me the impression that you were trying to avoid publicity."

She made a small noise of righteousness. "I'm always ready to do my civic duty, but like everybody else I like to get credit for it."

"Understandable," Marks murmured. "You were taking the dog out, I suppose, when first you noticed the man?"

"As a matter of fact I was," she said, admitting now what she had denied the night before. "It's terrible what happens to a person living in a neighborhood like this. The poor man was trying to get up, you see, and I thought he was drunk. I just gave Dandy a pull and got away as quick as I could."

Marks was very much afraid that this testimony was reliable: unless there had been some movement in the prone figure, she was not likely to have assumed Bradley drunk. It opened wide the possibility of two attacks, one in the vestibule of Anne's building, and the second on the street when he was perhaps recovering from the blow on the head. If that were the case, the motive of the first attack was not robbery. Either that, or the second attackers, taking turns, as it were, got nothing.

"Do you know what time it was when you first saw him, Mrs. Finney?"

"Not much past ten," she said. "Dandy just won't wait any longer. He's getting old, you can see. We always stop at Molloy's on Third Avenue for a glass of beer and to watch the television, but I didn't last night. I was thinking about that man, you see, in the back of my mind though I never knew it at the time myself. I got as far as Molloy's and turned back without going in."

Marks leaned forward, inviting her confidence. "You didn't tell anybody about him on the way, did you?"

"What do you mean?"

"Well, you've just said you were thinking about him, a little concerned perhaps that he might be hurt?"

She thought about that, calculating the best light in which to put herself, and then shook her head. "I thought if he was still there I might call the police when I got home."

"Of course you would," Marks said. "Now you and Dandy walked along Tenth Street to Third Avenue. There you would have turned north, going to Molloy's."

"Do you know Molloy's?" she said, her face cracking into its first smile. You'd have thought she had discovered a long lost relative. "It's a funny old place, but it feels like home."

Marks nodded. "Before you reached Third Avenue, did you meet anyone?"

"I didn't, you see, or I'd have stopped worrying."

Marks thought: witnesses always lied even when they thought they were telling the truth.

"I remember a gang of boys when I reached Third Avenue. But I don't know where they went. I'm scared of the gangs, I'll tell you."

"Is there anything you remember about them?"

"Well . . . they weren't . . ." She gestured vaguely and gave a flit of her eyelashes toward Herring.

"Black?" he prompted.

"Colored," she corrected him in a slightly reproachful tone.

"They were or they were not?" Marks said.

"They were not. I heard them laughing and talking. Some of them were shouting something like, 'oleh!' Spanish, I thought, but I didn't see any of them close, just a sea of faces in the night."

"One last question," Marks said: "As you passed the entrance to the building near which the man was lying, did you notice a light in the vestibule?"

"I wouldn't know whether there was or not, Officer, but I've got an idea that if there was one, I'd have been able to see him better. You mustn't think too bad of me for pass-

ing him by. A lone woman can get into a lot of trouble.
Look at the one he was supposed to be visiting. Mind, I'm
not saying anything against her."

"We're not yet sure," Marks said, getting up, "that he
was visiting her."

"Then they shouldn't put it in the papers," she said
piously.

Going down in the elevator, Marks said to Herring:
"There's a saying in Yiddish that fits her: she wouldn't
touch a horse on the wall."

Outdoors the two detectives stood on the sidewalk looking down the street toward the area still blocked off for
police search although no search was in evidence at the
moment. Someone had chalked "Viva Fidel!" on the sidewalk and on the side of Mrs. Finney's building. Marks
grinned, thinking how that sentiment would sit with her.
More soberly, he thought: a Spanish-speaking gang . . .

Herring was thinking how different the street looked in the
daytime from at night. There was a lumberyard across the
street which with the door closed at night looked like
any other two-story building in the block. In the daytime you
could see the courtyard within, the lumber piled up on either
side. The possibilities fascinated him; he did not admit
why to the Lieutenant, barely to himself: as a child he
would have thought this The Most in secret hiding places.

Marks was watching the approach, from far down the
street, of two detectives moving from trash basket to trash
basket. They were picking up in their wake a caravan of
tiny street Arabs, children too young to learn their alpha-
bets but old hands at baiting policemen.

Herring visited the lumberyard; Marks went on to meet
the search party, a couple of pretty sour cops. "How are
you doing?"

"Treasure, Lieutenant. Gold and frankincense and
myrrh. Smell it?"

Marks could smell over-ripe banana peel.

The young detective raised the back of his hand threateningly to a dirty-faced, black-haired midget who was chinning himself on the rim of the basket. "Get out of here, you little baboons! Go on home! You got homes, ain't you?"

Marks tapped one of the gang on the shoulder. "You and your pals, come over here and talk to me." He sat down on the steps of a brownstone not unlike that in which Anne Russo lived. "Know what happened on this street last night?" He looked into one suspicious pair of eyes after another.

One of the youngsters made a clicking sound with his tongue, a very nasty sound when combined with the motion of snapping a switch blade. They knew.

"Where do you live?"

Two of them lived in the big apartment house opposite Anne Russo.

"Do you know anyone who saw what happened?"

The eyes grew larger, the heads wagged slowly in automatic no.

"Let's go and investigate," Marks said.

The two youngsters went with him, but with no great enthusiasm. Finally one of them looked up at him. "You're a cop, ain't you?"

"I'm a detective cop," Marks qualified. If that impressed them they didn't show it.

He could have predicted the greeting of the first mother: "Oh, God, what have they done now?" She called up the flight of stairs: "Maria!" and in a stream of Spanish announced that Maria's son also was in whatever trouble had just brought a policeman to the house. Marks shook his head in vain. One of the youngsters shrugged philosophically. The other had just discovered the symbolism in the primitive art work scratched on the plaster walls. As he let out the gaseous sound of suppressed laughter, his mother picked him up by the thick, curly black hair and set him down inside the door. Marks edged his way into the apartment and crossed the room to the open window. A cushion lay on the floor beneath the sill. He was directly opposite Anne Russo's house.

Behind him the two mothers were exchanging *sotto voce* speculations about him, the curlers in their hair clacking like castanets. Marks decided to make a speech. He swung around, pointing at the same time to the street below. "A man was killed down there last night, a good man, an honest man, a teacher. Nobody behind this wall of windows saw or heard anything." He put his finger to his eyes, to his ears. The women were watching him intently. He put the question: "Do you believe that?"

Both shook their heads tentatively.

"Neither do I," he said, "but I need your help."

The woman to whom he had spoken first, in whose apartment they now were, came forward. She touched the cushion with her toe. "My mother-in-law," she said. "Always she is looking out—with one eye. Otherwise she watches television." She indicated the set across the room. The other young mother, coming timidly forward, nodded to confirm the mother-in-law's habits. She was a lovely, dark girl, no more than twenty, proudly bearing an early pregnancy. An association brushed through Marks's mind, too brief and fleeting to hold onto.

"What did your mother-in-law see?" he asked.

The girls looked from one to another, both evidently having heard the story.

"Two men outside the building. One of them, he says 'Come!' and pulls the other's arm. But the other, he don't want to go. Then somebody calls out, 'Doctor!' and they all go in. After that..." Marks's informant shrugged, "Mama looks at television. Later when the police all come she remembers and tells us." She looked to her friend who confirmed the story with a vigorous nod.

"Was there a car? Did the men come up to the building in a car?"

"Mama did not say. Maybe, but maybe the car drives away?"

The daughter-in-law, Marks thought, considered herself a reliable spokesman for Mama, and probably she was right. The testimony pleased him, a circumstance that put him on his guard. But Peter Bradley's presence outside Anne Russo's apartment building made a lot more sense if there was a doctor—or the pretense of a doctor involved. He could have been brought or persuaded there if he thought Anne Russo ill or injured.

"This is very important," Marks said. "Will your mother-in-law be able to tell us at what time this happened?"

"What time? I will ask her."

Until then he had presumed she was not in the house. He followed the two young women as they scurried, chattering with each other, to the stairway. The children, he realized, had disappeared. Marks's informant called up, cupping her mouth in her hands. "Mama Fernandez?"

It was, even for him, a most unorthodox interview. He found himself looking up the stairwell at an enormous woman two flights up, nodding to her as she nodded back at him, and all the while a three-way exchange going on in Spanish among the women themselves. And after it all, the younger Mrs. Fernandez turned to him and said: "She does not know."

"Ask her what was on the television?"

The older woman's gold tooth caught the sunlight. She understood his question herself. She did an effective pantomime of wrestling and then punctuated it by holding out two fingers as she leaned over the banister.

"The second match?"

"Si!" She wagged her head, delighted that they understood each other.

"*Gracias, señora. Buenos dias.*"

It got him out just in time. He could not have gone a word further. He went to the corner phone booth and called the St. Nicholas Arena. After two dimes' worth of transfers, he learned that the second match had gone on at

nine forty. It was all over at ten thirteen. But so were a lot
of other things.

He walked slowly back to where Herring had joined the
trash basket detail, the technical truck having pulled up
alongside them. Using a pair of large tweezers with the
delicacy of a surgeon, one of the technicians was lifting a
bloodstained handkerchief from among the debris.

8

Mather's first class on Tuesday was not part of the curriculum: he coached a group of male delinquents who were having to face up to final examinations after a semester devoted to basketball and female anatomy. He found them as impossible to insult as they were to teach. They might know a member of the faculty to have been murdered the night before, but the fact that he was a physicist removed him from their personal concern as surely as if he had been a Kashmiri rug merchant. They read newspapers from back to front, starting with the sports page and reaching the comics. After that boredom set in. The only book they read in order to learn something they wanted to know was *Fanny Hill*. Mather watched the clock through that interminable period no less assiduously than they did.

His second class was a different matter. Sophomores, they wanted to learn everything there was to learn at once. God help him on such days as this when he had come ill-prepared for class. But that morning they paid him the opening tribute of an awed silence when he entered the room. He reached his desk to learn that someone had placed *The New York Times* there, folded to the Bradley story. He caught his own name in the second column, listed

69

as among those present at the dinner party. He scanned the faces before him, solemn, expectant boys and girls. He called them men and women, speaking to them, but they were not really. To them this death was probably romantic. They did not believe in death; they could be anti-war and anti-capital punishment, they could Remember Mississippi and pass out ban-the-bomb leaflets. But to them death had no sting. Nor had it had for him at their age. He thought briefly of the day he had saved Peter: that he might die himself jumping off that boat had not entered his mind at the time.

He opened his briefcase and took from it a mimeographed review quiz.

"Mr. Mather," a silvery feminine voice requested from halfway back in the room, "would you read 'Adonais' aloud to us?"

He looked at the girl without raising his head: her face shone with cherubic innocence. There were others in the class who could not so successfully dissemble. They feigned busyness.

"I think not, Miss Adamson," Mather said blandly, "but I should like to hear your rendition since it must be a favorite of yours." Over the ocean-swell of protest from her classmates, Mather turned to the textbook index and said aloud: "Page one hundred seven: 'Adonais' by Percy Bysshe Shelley. Miss Adamson?"

The next half-hour was no less an agony for Miss Adamson than for the rest of the class. For Mather the hour was simply to be got through; now a discussion of elegiac poetry would save him the humiliation of giving a stale quiz.

As soon as he dismissed the class, Mather took the elevator to the Physics Department which occupied the entire top floor of the General Studies Building. He found Steinberg and the boys who had been at Bradley's in a student conference room. They greeted him with some small camaraderie. He glanced at the blackboard. The names of the four of them had been written in block letters:

ROBERT STEINBERG
MITCHELL HOYTE
ALVIN ROBBIE
JAMES L. O'ROURKE

"So the police could get them down right," one of the boys said.

Steinberg added: "They've just left." He gestured toward a small box lying on the desk. "There's the film we didn't see last night."

"It wasn't stolen?" Mather said carefully.

"It was returned along with his wallet—without the money—in a public mailbox this morning."

"They must've got scared," one of the boys said, "finding out who he was."

Mather did not say anything for a moment. There was no room left for doubt now that his original plan had been put into motion. "Where's Anne?"

"She's gone down to the police lineup—or rogues' gallery or whatever it is—to see if there's anybody she recognizes."

Mather took a chance on the boy's name: he was glad the names were on the board. He could never remember them. "Fill me in, will you, Robbie? I haven't had the stomach to read the papers."

"I'm O'Rourke," the young man said. "I don't know what's to tell, just that Annie saw a man going into her building when she went home for her glasses. The only thing she could remember about him was the smell of chewing gum when he went past her. But they took her down to the police station anyway."

Mather reached for his cigarettes, patting his pockets, anything to distract from his own dismay. Gum-chewing, idealistic, lovable Jerry. Let there be no more war!

Steinberg pulled himself out of a morose lethargy. "I'm going over there now to take Louise some things. Do you want to come?"

"I ought to see Janet," he said. "Thanks. I'd like to go along."

On the way Steinberg peered out the cab window. Seeing a cluster of police cars near St. John's Church, he asked the cab driver to stop. He motioned to one of the detectives, and asked him if he was working on the Bradley case. "You ought to have somebody question the news vendor on the corner of University and the park."

It was not that simple, the matter of giving a detective a lead: Steinberg had to identify himself and his connection with the case. He got out of the car. It gave the waiting cabbie a chance to tell Mather that the cops had already screened every cab coming into the area between 9:00 P.M. and 11:00 last night. "Don't it make you wonder what they're doing between murders, the way they're swarming all over the place now?"

"I can't say that it does," Mather said to shut him up. He supposed Jerry had a car; men in his profession were provided with what they needed.

The cabbie was not to be put off. "It should, Mister. People like us forget the cops are civil servants. That means they work for us. Did you ever think of that? We the people."

Which put Mather in mind of the two detectives who had been waiting for him the night before. *Better see a doctor about that toe. The city has a responsibility* ... They had taken his shoes. For what? Would they demand an X-ray of his toe? It occurred to him then that they had been searching the street afterwards for the knife, thinking he had taken the sprawl to get rid of it, to throw it away, the knife from Peter's back. Could they be looking for Peter's blood on his shoes? The thought of it made him physically ill. He rolled down the window.

Steinberg, at the door of the cab, said: "I'm coming now."

In front of the Bradley house Mather stood for a moment looking up at the second-floor windows.

"Come on," Steinberg said.

"I don't know what to say to Janet."

"Don't say anything. Or else say you're sorry and you'd like to get your hands on the bastard."

"If you could get your hands on him, Bob, what would you do?"

Steinberg shifted Louise's valise from one hand to the other. "Come on. This kind of talk doesn't get us anywhere."

Mather followed him up the steps. "In tribal times it was easy, wasn't it? You just cut him off and the world outside devoured him. And that was fine. Men didn't have to kill their own." In the vestibule, waiting for the release of the lock, he added: "That's one of the refinements of civilization, isn't it? the ability to kill one's own?"

"Nonsense," Steinberg said. "Men like to kill when they think they have to. There's no other explanation for it, war and the whole bloody bit. You'd think that the thought of their own mortality would hold them back. It's just the opposite. They live. Inside themselves killers live because they've killed."

The lock-release clicked and they went upstairs. Mather did not suppose Steinberg had ever spoken to him directly before. Louise hugged her husband sloppily and then gave Mather very nearly the same treatment. All emotion. Her eyes were red from weeping. Death had its intimacy for her—but so did life: the flesh was good. Louise lived with all her senses and from them evoked zest and joy and such pleasures, Mather was sure, as he had never known. Sometimes he was revolted by her, put off the more because she was one of the few people who accepted him for his own sake. He now returned her embrace with fervor, shutting out the brief insight to his own sickness.

There were a number of people in the livingroom, Peter's brothers who had flown out from Chicago, Louise explained. They would go back together for the funeral. Peter was to be cremated. And Janet's family had come from Bridgeport, and Dr. Bauer was there . . .

Janet came to them then, her hands outstretched, but her whole body straightened as in some invisible armor. The touch of her cold hands claiming, it seemed, the warmth in his, moved him profoundly. He rubbed them and lifted them to his lips, cherishing to his heart's depth the little throb of response he quickened in them. Not until she had withdrawn them did she allow her eyes to directly meet his. Whatever their message, he could not probe it, for his own eyes bleared.

Janet kissed Steinberg lightly and thanked him for his kindness, and for letting Louise stay with her. "I don't know what I should do without her."

It happened without Mather's knowing: a great sob escaped him, a cry that seemed the louder for his trying to cover it with other sounds. People turned from the far room to stare at him and their image froze in his mind, the disapproving faces peering round chairbacks, a Gothic starkness to them: it was as though the whole of his Puritan ancestry were pillorying him with their rebuke.

Janet did not look back; her body a little stiffer, she moved steadily toward the brethren. Mather turned and went out the door, moving quickly so that Louise might not follow him. He ran down the stairs. Solace would be more than he could stand, as was love—if that was what was rising in him above the dirge. If Janet loved him—could love him—and he could love. What did it mean, simply to love? Unashamed and unresisting, letting the heart's song soar?

Was it Saul on his knees, blind and humble, crying out: "I believe!"

9

Officer Walter Herring could not say why that lumber-yard so fascinated him. It was not simply that he liked the smell of new wood, though he did that. One of the things he longed most for was a house he could walk into that was all wood, new shining wood. No plaster, no steel foundations, no thousand other families moving in on the same day. Just a house made of wood and a yard with trees. Something nagged at him about the lumber-yard. The more he thought about it, the surer he was that he had known that it was there all the time but had forgotten it until this morning. Why that mattered he couldn't figure out either. He tried to explain to Marks the way the thing kept nagging at him.

"I guess it's what you call a hunch. What I'd like to do, sir, I got the address of a guy who does a watchman's job there nights—works some other places round here too—I'd just like to check him out."

"Go to it," Marks said. They were on their way back to headquarters, Marks driving a precinct car that seemed to be missing on at least two cylinders. "What's the address and I'll see if this old dog can get us there?"

Herring gave him the address. "Did you read about

the guy who bought the old police car at auction? Before he got it to the paint shop he'd been stopped by five patrol cars. Lieutenant, oughtn't I to check in the station first?"

"I'll check you in with Redmond when I get back. The Captain's a decent sort, isn't he?"

"They don't come any decenter than Captain Redmond. No, sir."

"Then get something," Marks said, "and do us all some good."

A half-hour later Herring had something. He brought Fred Bolardo in for questioning. Marks and Captain Redmond listened to the watchman give his statement, Herring handling the interrogation.

"About two weeks ago I was closing up the yard for the night. I always do that, checking in the last truck, sometimes as late as seven o'clock. Then I padlocks the door. I come around again about midnight after that, just checking up. Kids broke in there once. Stole a keg of nails . . ."

Herring sat, his arms folded, just letting the man talk. The testimony was feeding into a tape recorder. Herring even smiled a little when Bolardo, a melancholy string of a man with a fringe of white hair, added: "Little bastards only wanted the keg, dumped the nails in the driveway." Marks observed that Redmond was measuring his precinct cop.

"You were going to tell us what happened two weeks ago," Herring prompted gently.

"I don't get paid much . . . Hell, I told it to you once. I ain't going to get into any more trouble, telling it again, am I?" Herring shook his head. "This doctor came up to me and asked me if I couldn't let him park his car in the drive there nights. Just early nights—say seven o'clock till nine or ten while he was seeing patients in the neighborhood . . ."

Marks and Redmond looked at each other. Mama Fernandez's "doctor?"

Herring held the witness to his story:

"We worked it out. I got him a key made for the padlock, and he paid me ten bucks for the first month. I was chiseling, sure. But there wasn't any harm. I kind of thought I was doing good, giving a doctor a place to park. His car'd been broken into, and he was scared, the way the crazy kids these days are doing anything to lay their hands on drugs and things."

"Try and give us a description of the car, Mr. Bolardo."

"Like I told you at the house, I didn't look much at the car—a black sedan is all I can tell you. Four doors maybe."

Herring smiled. "That's something you didn't remember up till now."

"I remember him opening the back door for something. And I looked to make sure there was an M.D. on the license plate. You know the funny thing was, he almost scotched the deal talking about the drugs he had to carry. I got thinking maybe he was looking for some kind of a hideout, or maybe a meeting place."

"You didn't see the license number?"

"I seen it but I don't remember except it was New York and the M.D. on it."

"Do you think you could tell us anything about the man?"

"Not much more than I already did. Kind of skinny and sallow. Not much of a dresser. Like his car, a little rundown you might say. Never got a name for him either. I just called him Doctor and he called me doc."

Marks hated to do it to Herring, but he moved in. "Fred, tell us the truth now. Deep down, weren't you hoping that he was in fact peddling the drugs?" The witness began to shake his head. "Weren't you counting on that possibility as a way to get more than a measly ten dollars a month from him? Don't ask us to believe you'd have been willing to put your job on the line for a lousy ten bucks."

"You're wrong, Mister. Ten bucks may be lousy to you,

but that was going to bring up to thirty what I was taking home from the Eastside Lumber Company."

"Okay," Marks said. "We had to find out. Was he the conversational type? Did he talk much?"

"He was mighty careful how he talked, the words, you know? Like maybe he was a foreigner. I'm not saying he was, but I got the feeling."

"There's plenty of them in that neighborhood," Redmond said. "I suppose they got some of their own doctors among them."

"I don't figure he lived in the neighborhood," Bolardo said. "Don't seem he'd need a place to park like that if he did."

Herring, without looking at his superiors and having planned his own line of attack which he did not want broken, said: "Now about early this morning, Mr. Bolardo, the call from your boss. Tell us about that."

"Well, sir. I don't know what it means after what happened down the street . . ."

"Just tell it the best you can," Herring said. "Don't worry what it means."

"The boss called up at 8:00 A.M. He was mighty sore and I can't blame him none. That damn-fool absentminded doctor forgot to padlock the door last night. He closed it all right, but forgot to snap the padlock on it. The boss thought it was me, you see, and I'd just as soon he didn't find out."

The situation suggested just one thing to the policemen: whoever had taken the car out was in a hurry.

Herring snapped off the machine and rolled up the tape. He took it along to have transcribed for Bolardo to sign.

Redmond and Marks left the watchman with a hasp of "Wanted" flyers to see if he could find a familiar face among them. Redmond could think offhand of several known criminals who sometimes passed themselves off as doctors. A check was made to learn whether any M.D.

license plates had been reported stolen. The results on both lines of inquiry: negative.

Fitzgerald put his finger on what proved the most significant link between testimonies to the hour: the precision of the wound and the nature of the weapon. A surgical knife fit the description perfectly, and it would very nearly have required a doctor's hand to do so clean a job. There was no report yet on the bloodstained handkerchief.

"Surgeons don't ordinarily carry instruments out of the hospital, do they?" Redmond mused aloud.

"Only when they have homicide on their minds," Fitzgerald said, and curled his lip nastily.

Redmond colored to the roots of his dark red hair. He said nothing, but went to his desk and set noisily about the routine of his command. Marks sympathized with him. Technically in charge of the investigation, he was not really on his own until Fitzgerald let go, and this the old man showed no signs of doing at the moment. Marks put another yellow-headed pin on the area map, marking the location of the Eastside Lumber Company, and wrote the legend for it on a card for the chart.

Fitzgerald watched till he was through. "This one's got everything, Dave. Even spooks. What do you make of this?" He handed Marks the interrogation report on the news vendor at the corner of the University and the park. Hank Zabrisky's testimony read in part:

"Q. Do you mean Dr. Steinberg?

A. The one with the glasses, yes. He come by the stand about ten thirty and asks me if I'd seen Professor Bradley. I says at first I had. Then I remembered it was the young lady, Miss Russo, I seen. But there's something screwy about it. I don't remember seeing him and yet I felt at the time I did, you know? . . ."

Fitzgerald said: "Did he or didn't he?"

"It might be worth another try," Marks said. He wanted to go over the university ground himself anyway. He thought of asking Redmond for the use of a better car. The time didn't seem right somehow.

Marks took seven feet of bus stop in which to park. A young student leaning on the route sign, an open book dangling from his hand, watched him cynically. The boy's eyes wandered toward the corner restaurant: the cop enjoying illegal parking privileges. Marks wondered if he would ever get over the little twinges of guilt he felt at such moments. He had thought of lunch, seeing the restaurant. But not now. Go parse your nouns, sonny: he took a long slow look at him, and the boy moved away.

This was the corner at which Anne Russo had got off the bus. The newsstand was across the street. And across the street in the other direction was the public phone booth. The laboratory building was two blocks beyond the main university building, its entrance around the corner and out of sight from where Marks stood. He passed up the news vendor for the moment, and followed what he assumed to have been Anne Russo's route of the night before. From the park east, once you had passed the University, this became as tough an area as any in the city. It had been for over a hundred years. The Astor Place Riots of 1849 had been partially fought through here.

Marks went into the building, the ground floor a warehouse. An old man was sitting on a stool outside the elevator cage working over the day's entries at Aqueduct.

"The Physics Laboratory?" Marks asked.

"Nobody down there now," the man said.

Down. Somehow he had expected up. He consulted the sign-in book on the ledger stand. Steinberg and Bauer had signed in at seven forty that morning along with two other names Marks supposed to be government investigators. They had signed out again at eight ten; that was how long it would have taken them to look at the film.

He turned back the page to look at the sign-ins of the night before: Steinberg, Hoyte, O'Rourke, Robbie at nine twenty-five, Russo at nine fifty. The boys had been questioned that morning; they were due at the precinct house late in the afternoon when he would go over the dinner party with them himself. They had all signed out at ten forty-five the night before.

Marks went outside again. Up the street a group of teen-agers were playing cards on an open stoop. In the momentary lull of traffic he could hear the ping of coins on cement. A drunk was kibitzing the game, trying to connect with the winner for the price of a jug of smoke. The Bowery spilled its overflow into this particular stretch of off-Broadway. A truck driver, trying to get his ton of paving blocks past a game of stick ball had to pull up and wait the kids' convenience. Marks wondered that the youngsters were not in school and then realized that the day was getting on. The truck driver blasted away with his horn and the street became a tunnel of noise. Gristle and nerve against stone and machine. Marks noted the east to west pattern of traffic: one way.

He walked back to the newsstand. Its owner was garrulous and minus at least six front teeth. He would dart the tip of his tongue through the yellow archway of his molars by way of giving emphasis—or wit—to what he had to say.

"You're the third man what asked me this, you know, and all youse are doing is driving the whole picture out of my mind."

"*Do* you have a picture?" Marks said.

"Of course I got a picture. You don't think I'm making it up as I go along?" The tongue darted out and in. "I seen Miss Russo getting off the bus. Now mind, I didn't see her get off the bus, but when the bus passed, then I seen her cross the street. Then the truck came with the *Timeses,* and he shouts out the window to me ..." The tongue came to rest and the vendor just stared at Marks, a look of awe on his face. Slowly he nodded his head: he was remembering something hitherto forgotten.

"The window, the car window," he said with mounting

excitement. "I did see the Professor. I knew I'd seen him! He come by here in a car."

"Professor Bradley? Are you sure? Did he wave to you?"

"I'm sure but I wouldn't swear. It looked like him. But I never seen him in a car before. He always come walking by and reminding me to save him a *Times.*"

"Did he wave to you?" Marks repeated.

"No, nothing like that. He was just sitting and another guy was driving . . ."

"Coming toward you?" Marks interrupted, indicating the direction.

"Yeah, yeah."

"Against the traffic on a one-way street?"

"They must've been but there wasn't no traffic." Hank was holding fast to the picture in his mind's eye.

"Then you'd have got a good look at the car," Marks said.

Hank shook his head. "It was just over, you know, in a few seconds. I didn't even think about it till people started asking questions, just a plain ordinary sedan. Black maybe. I don't remember no color."

Marks studied the street. Whoever had picked Bradley up had probably done so directly in front of the laboratory, both of them having reached there by coming from the easterly direction. If Bradley had passed this spot, walking, Hank would have known it. "Was it before or after Miss Russo got off the bus that you saw the Professor, Hank?"

"If I *did* see him," Hank said, now full of doubts again, "it must've been before. Once the *Timeses* come in, you see . . ."

It was remarkable, Marks thought, driving away and once more forgetting lunch, how the events of the night seemed to dovetail. And as Inspector Fitzgerald would be the first to point out, it was amazing how Miss Russo had avoided bumping into Bradley himself. Hers had been the one unpredicted—unchartered—course so far as Bradley's assailants were concerned. Or had it been? Without stronger proof, no reasonable detective could eliminate her from complicity.

It now, more than ever, had to come down to motive.

10

By mid-afternoon Marks was able to compare the statements of all those who had attended the Bradley dinner. The physics group had been invited through Bob Steinberg whom Louise had called at the office just before lunch. "Janet wants us to come up for a drink and a bite to eat about six. Peter will be home." The wording of Steinberg's announcement to the group did not vary much from one man's version to another's. Nor indeed did any other testimony, including Anne's and Bob Steinberg's.

They had all known about the film, but until talking with Peter, they had tended to be suspicious of a gift the Russians were making such good propaganda out of. Peter, however, as young O'Rourke put it, had caught fire in Athens. He had a hunch they might have been given something worthwhile.

None of them had arrived for dinner thinking they would be going on to the laboratory afterwards. But none of them was surprised when it was decided to go. The curious thing was—and Marks had been particularly careful in his uniform phrasing of the question to each of them —no one was able to say positively who had brought the matter to a head. Anne thought it happened when Louise said: "You aren't going to the lab tonight, are you?" Steinberg assumed they were going from the moment Bradley himself said: "It wouldn't take long after setting up." O'Rourke had suggested that he and the other fellows would go along early and set up. Steinberg said they would all go together. It was understood that Bradley would come later, so thoroughly understood that not even a passing reference was made to the fact.

No one remembered Eric Mather to have been in on any part of their conversation. But then not one of the scientists mentioned Mather in his statement beyond listing him among those present, except Anne. Two of the boys could not even remember his name. Anne recalled having facetiously invited him to come along and see the film.

Marks probed her on why she had asked him.

Anne bit her thumb while she thought about it. She looked so earnest, Marks thought, so eager to help, he would turn in his badge if she were in any way implicated. "I guess I must have thought he would say something clever," she answered finally.

"And did he?"

"Not very. He said Russian movies were too hammy. Something like that."

Marks was also particularly careful in the way he asked: "If the dinner party had been given at Mather's, say, would you have gone?"

The answer was the same from all of them: if the party had been given for Peter Bradley, yes. But the three young men added that if it had been given there they did not think they would have been invited. Steinberg had been at Mather's place on a few occasions. He had had a couple of good chess games with Mather. Except for that, he said, he'd rather go to the Dean of Women's tea party. For one thing you got as much to eat there as at Mather's.

The three male students had not been out of each other's presence from the time of their arrival at Bradley's until they left the laboratory at ten forty-five. Marks saw no

need to involve them further in the investigation, and Fitzgerald agreed.

"They're a tribe to themselves, aren't they?" the Inspector remarked.

"They probably think the same of us." Marks called the
desk to see if Pererro had reported in. There was no question in his mind that Mather was the enigma in the lot.

"Yes, sir," the desk sergeant said. "I told him you were
busy so he went in to the Captain's round-up. I'll get hold
of him right away."

"Never mind," Marks said. "I'll come down."

Some twenty detectives had gathered around Redmond
in the squadroom. Seeing Marks, Redmond invited him to
join them. It was Marks's first real opportunity to see the
Captain in action with his men. He was halfway through
briefing them on the general background of the case, the
combined work of his department and homicide: the findings of the medical examiner, the nature of the assault and
its possible motive, the theft and return of everything on
the victim's person except his money.

Each man reported on his own detail, including Herring,
who afterwards told Marks he had been transferred to the
detective force with a second-grade rank. The admirable
achievement of what Redmond called his "round-up" was
that every man working on the case and not out on assign-
ment at the time, was made aware of the full picture.

Marks himself picked up certain information he had not
known:

Anne Russo's story of taking the Ninth Street bus had
been corroborated by the driver, a regular on the run.

Peter Bradley had purchased a package of cigarettes at
Third Avenue and St. Mark's, which left little doubt that he
approached the laboratory building from Astor Place, a
desolate stretch after business hours.

The preliminary report on the bloodstained handkerchief
had come in from the laboratory: it had undoubtedly been
used by the killer—the blood type checked with Bradley's;
no identification marks; mass laundered, the laundering

chemicals were now under analysis. The handkerchief had been disposed of in a trash basket half a block east and two blocks north of the scene.

Pererro and his partner, their findings not yet evaluated, merely so reported, and at the end of the session, gave Marks the rundown he had been waiting for. Mather's itinerary from the Red Lantern on pretty accurately checked out. The bartender at the Red Lantern was sure that Mather had been there by nine thirty.

"How could he be sure?" Marks demanded. "Did he look at his watch? Does he keep that tight a check on all his customers?" The apparent neatness of the timing in this whole operation was infuriating.

Pererro said: "This is how he knew, sir: at a quarter to ten there's an intermission break at the Triangle Theater across the street and a crowd comes in for a quick drink. Mather had to fight his way out through that crowd when he was leaving, and the bartender knew he'd been there fifteen or twenty minutes before that. He was a guy you couldn't miss, sir. He'd been reciting for the kids. You couldn't miss him any place he was last night."

"Okay, okay," Marks said, aware of Pererro's defensive "sirs." "'He had to fight his way out.' Is that how the witness put it?"

Pererro consulted his shorthand. "Yes, sir. His very words."

Marks grunted.

"The kids meet there every night almost, Lieutenant. They got a club they call the Imagists, whatever the hell that is."

Marks intended to find that out for himself. But first he wanted to pay another visit to the Bradley house.

11

Marks stood a few moments across the street from the Bradleys', studying the neighborhood, watching the children pass on their way home from school. There was a nineteenth-century atmosphere to the street—the graceful poplar trees, the fine old houses shoulder to shoulder, all well kept, their shutters neat and freshly painted. Most of the children went on, he noticed. This was not a street of large families. And to his back where he stood was the Armory, a city block of solid stone with high windows out of which no one ever looked. All day the police had sifted the area for anyone who might have seen Bradley leave the house. No one had yet been turned up who had seen him before he reached the gates of St. John's Church. People were moving to and fro within the Bradley second-floor apartment. There were lights on in the middle rooms. As he crossed the street he saw Louise coming along the Bradley side with an armful of groceries. He went to meet her and took the bag.

"Things I forgot to order. I don't know what it is between me and the telephone. I keep feeling it's trying to gyp me."

Marks held the outside door. "How's Mrs. Bradley?"

Louise shrugged. "Everybody's here. Family, I mean. There's going to be a service at St. John's tomorrow. Then Chicago for the burial." She glanced at the mailboxes in the vestibule while rummaging in her pocket for the door key. "Something this morning that really threw me: I came down for the mail and there was a postcard from Peter— mailed in Athens before he left there. I didn't show it to Janet. I hid it in my purse and I've kept thinking about it all day—like it was something alive in there."

"Could I see it?"

"It's upstairs. I just brought my change purse."

Marks and Louise went directly into the kitchen. It was like being household help, Marks thought, vaguely liking it.

"Sit down and have a cup of coffee," Louise said.

Marks sat at the table while Louise turned on the gas under the coffee pot. A feeling remembered from childhood came over him: coming home to something happening in the kitchen. A baked ham was cooling on the table, the glaze shining and mottled with brown crust, the juices seeping down to the plate. The aroma made his eyes as well as his mouth water. Louise surprised him staring at the roast.

"I didn't have any lunch," he blurted out.

Louise covered her mouth to stifle the laughter. She made him a sandwich, slicing directly into the middle of the ham.

While he was eating she brought the postcard, looking first to make sure that Janet was at the front of the house.

It was a colorful picture of the Plakka, the old section of Athens teeming with activity beneath the awesome white- ness of the Acropolis. The message read: "Even as two thousand years ago. I want to see more. And you with me next time."

"'I want to see more,'" Marks said, and gave back the card which Louise returned to her purse.

"That's the story of his short, short life. My God. You'd think he was a poet to die so young."

"Poets are living longer these days," Marks said.

"He could have been one, you know. Maybe he was in a way. Eric always called him the Renaissance man. Peter started in literature, switched to history his last year in college, and finally to science. He took a lot of math of course all the way."

"Did he ever consider medicine?" Marks asked, his mind returning to the involvement of "a doctor" in his death.

"He left that to the rest of the family. Both of his brothers are doctors." Louise put her purse in a cupboard. "He always wanted to do more, to see more, to understand better. Janet told me once that his journal was marvelous —a thousand questions. Even his answers asked questions." She refilled Marks's coffee cup and poured a cup for herself. "What tears your heart out now is that all there's left is the 'why?' Why did he have to die—that way?"

Marks said: "It isn't hard enough to give life meaning. You want death to mean something too."

Louise smiled ruefully, studied her coffee for a moment, then lifted the mug. "Skol."

"Skol," Marks said. "The truth is, Mrs. Steinberg..."

Louise interrupted him. "Nobody calls me Mrs. Steinberg, not even the milkman. Louise."

"Louise," Marks repeated. "We've reached the place where we're asking why, too. It wasn't the money in his wallet. I'm almost sure of that. There was a plan, and when there's a plan there's brains at work, and they work on something already known. I keep wondering if something went wrong with somebody's plan, if maybe it wasn't intended that he be killed. If there was a plan that didn't include death—what went wrong with it? Did he recognize someone? I could be completely wrong about this, Louise, but I can't help feeling that the most ruthless killer would still think twice before destroying a person of Dr. Bradley's stature. I'm sure the return of the empty wallet and the briefcase was an afterthought, something intended to throw

us off the track. Was somebody trying to frame him with
Anne Russo? If something went wrong, what was supposed
to have gone right?"

Louise was just looking at him. Finally she said: "I
don't know what to say."

"You don't have to say anything. I'm just thinking
aloud." Marks finished his coffee and got to his feet. "I
wonder if you would ask Mrs. Bradley if I might see her
husband's journal, if I might have permission to go over
her husband's papers?"

A few minutes later Marks sat alone in Peter Bradley's
study. Janet herself about to close the door on him turned
back to where he was sitting in the swivel chair at the desk.
"That chair squeaks terribly," she said. "Peter was always
going to oil it, but he never did."

Marks, knowing her thought to be that he never would
do it now, got up carefully from the chair when she was
gone and exchanged it for the straight one by the window.

There was a lot of the adolescent in him still, Marks
thought of himself, as he lifted and looked at one and another of the books on the desk and finally opened the notebook Bradley had used for his journal. In the atmosphere
of scholarship, he longed to be a scholar. Much of the
journal was incomprehensible to him, equations and mathematical symbols. The question marks he understood, but
not the questions. He remembered that Steinberg had offered the loan of a book. What he really needed was to start
school all over again. Then he lost himself in the nonscien-
tific entries, discovering Bradley the human being. Most of
his entries did end in questions. Marks was amused at his
remarks on a very successful modern composer:

"Discovered another of his sources tonight, Beethoven's
Violin Concerto. He *is* an original composer, using the
original as his source. But then, where did Beethoven pick
up that theme?"

He read on, looking for personal items, comments on
family, friends, colleagues, of which there were virtually

none, unless they were anecdotal, as for example the last entry in the book written in Athens three days before:

"After today's session, Grysenko and I walked through the Plakka and searched out the Byron monument. All the Russians I've ever met love market places. I do too. We sat for a while in the little park. I tried to explain that Byron, an English poet, had fought for the Greeks in their war of independence. G. was profoundly skeptical. 'An Englishman?' he kept saying and he would shake his head. 'I cannot believe that.'"

The house was all stillness when Marks had finished. He found Louise asleep in a wing chair, her shoes tossed aside. The others had all gone away, perhaps to the funeral parlor. He stooped down and put the shoes side by side beneath the chair, and then let himself out of the apartment, the door automatically locking behind him.

12

Mather prepared his next day's classes in the few cubic feet of space he called his office. It was actually a desk in the Department's common room, a room generally avoided by the faculty except as a place to drop off odd encumbrances picked up throughout the day, a belatedly returned book, a picture frame, a tie that should better have gone to the cleaner's. He put his lecture notes in comprehensible order for the substitute teacher who would take the Victorian Novel, a class scheduled for the hour at which he would be attending the memorial service for Peter Bradley.

His desk cleared, he rummaged through a drawerful of books for one that might fit his pocket and came out with a small volume of Auden's poems. Then, repeating a habit with him since childhood, he closed his eyes, concentrated for a moment—(his grandmother had taught him the practice in connection with Bible reading)—and opened the book at random. He had opened it to a poem in memory of Yeats which in itself seemed an omen. Or so his grandmother would have said. He scanned the page avidly seeking the deeper message.

"But for him it was his last afternoon as himself . . ."

Mather had found what he sought, a sort of poetic jolt

93

that enabled him to contact truth. The stabbing poignancy
of the words cut through him: death's denial of life's greatest gift, a personal, inviolate identity. He pocketed the
book and walked out through the building deep within his
own thoughts and with no consciousness of whom he met
or what that person thought of him, with no quip on his
tongue, no falseness.

He waited outside the laboratory building for Anne
Russo, having checked the sign-in book to know that she
was there. It was the last frantic hour of the business day
and he could feel the fire hydrant on which he sat reverber-
ate with the rolling, throbbing traffic. Why, he wondered,
had he ever allowed the city to prison him? He knew of
course: the search for anonymity, the attempt to lose himself. As though one were ever lost until entirely exposed
and beyond caring as only death could make him. He took
the book from his pocket and opened it. A police car rolled
slowly up to the curb. Aware of it at the margin of his
vision, he looked up and down at the book again. Detectives, he knew, though he had not recognized them. All
day he had been waiting, fearing, yet somehow craving
that next encounter with the liquid-eyed Lieutenant.

Two of the detectives got out of the car and went into
the building, scarcely glancing at him as they passed. The
car moved on. A moment later Anne came out of the building alone.

"Carry your books, Miss?" he said, getting up.

"Eric." Anne often vacillated between Eric and Mr.
Mather. Today there was no hesitancy.

He said: "Let me buy you dinner. I want to talk."

"I'm dirty," Anne said, "but I guess that doesn't
matter."

"We're all dirty," Mather said, "and it matters very
much, but the question is: what can we do about it?"

They walked to the corner and toward the park, the
cursed park that was his preserve on the ridge of hell. Anne
was carrying a shoulder bag of tightly woven wool, colors

as vivid as the Greek flag. If he were not mistaken, it was Greek-made. "Can I carry that for you?"

"It's fine really," Anne said. "I'm used to it."

"It looks new." Mather could have bit his tongue.

Anne's color flared up and her black eyes snapped. She said nothing. Then a few seconds later at the park gate she stopped. He took her arm and gently propelled her along. "Please don't say you've changed your mind. I too am under suspicion. The police still have the shoes they took off my feet last night."

"What would they want with them I wonder."

"They often tell the truth of where a man has been I should suppose. Or perhaps of where a man has not been."

He chose a small restaurant with decent food and very little early custom. He asked Anne if she would have a drink.

"You bet."

He ordered two very dry martinis. "Right?"

Anne nodded.

"Anne, when you went through the police files or whatever, did you find a face you recognized?"

She shook her head. "It was impossible. The more I think about him the less I remember what he looked like."

"Was there something terribly American about him?"

Anne looked puzzled. "What's terribly American?"

Mather shrugged. He had hoped to spark something, and he had not even bothered to cover himself. He offered Anne a cigarette and took it himself when she refused.

"I'm letting everybody down I know," Anne said. "But I'm no good at this free-association bit. I'm a simple-minded, up and down, black and white thinker. I only know what I see and I didn't really see him."

The martinis came. They touched glasses and Anne took a sip. "Why, Eric? Why did it happen?"

He just stared into the glass. A little golden bead of lemon oil was floating within the crest of rind.

"Because somebody was afraid?" she said.

"Why do you say that?"

Anne shook her hair back over her shoulders. "I don't know how anybody kills if he's not afraid. But how could you be afraid of Peter?"

"Weren't you ever afraid of him—intellectually?"

"No," she said with utter frankness.

Mather grinned wryly. "Let me not to the marriage of true minds admit impediments."

"What does that mean?"

"It's from Shakespeare . . ."

"I know that," she interrupted. "What do *you* mean by it? That's what I want to know."

"Are you always so devastatingly forthright?" Mather took a deep pull at his drink. He could feel it right down through his loins.

"I am direct," she said, somewhat subdued.

Mather laughed at the understatement. He said: "I think what I meant was that when one's mind is the match for another person's, the two people can make contact without all the hypocritical subterfuge in which we disguise inadequacy."

"What do you mean by contact?"

Mather threw up his hand. "Nothing dirty certainly!"

"That's exactly what I wanted to make clear," Anne said. "There was nothing like that between Peter and me."

"If there had been something, would you have thought it dirty?"

"That's a silly question, Eric."

"I don't see why you should think so."

"Any question based on a false assumption is pointless."

"Mathematically speaking," Mather said, "but the human heart is a vast hunting ground, and the only guide-posts are such hypotheses. Don't you forget it. Now finish your drink and we'll have another while we order dinner."

Anne grinned at him. "Gee," she said, "you're great."

And that reaction quite unnerved him. It was a straight and impulsive compliment from the girl. He had not sought it and he unquestioningly believed it to be sincere. The sadness he felt coming over him was unutterable: it was as though that which he had loved most had to die before he had been able to live. He thought then, looking at the blackening rind in the bottom of his empty glass, that his own sickness, like the ancient plague, had only death for its curative.

He leaned back in the booth, watching Anne, while he said: "He's about five feet, ten inches tall, stocky build, with a small round face going flabby in the cheeks. You can see the flesh wriggle about the jowls when he chews gum. His nose, flat at the nostrils, fleshy at the tip, looks as though he had been picked up by it as a child. He has two small black buttons for eyes and his eyebrows run together like a black gash across his forehead."

Anne, her eyes wide, moistened her lips. "Where did you see him?"

"Is that he?"

She nodded.

"Outside Bradleys' as I was leaving." He was there, Mather knew.

"Did you tell the police? I mean they could make a picture of him from a description like that, Eric. I didn't see him that well, but now it's just like you'd frozen him in front of me at that second I saw him."

"More live than life," Mather mocked.

"You must tell Lieutenant Marks," Anne persisted. "Or I will. Only I'd mess it up."

"Lieutenant Marks," Mather repeated. "He's a very clever fellow."

"He's great," Anne said. Then seeing Mather's look of pained distaste: "I mean he isn't square. He knows things in a way like you do—you know, starting from a hypothesis that makes people think out loud."

Mather smiled. "You'd better say it in algebra, Annie."

She sipped the fresh drink, glanced at the menu and then laid it aside. "Eric . . . I guess this is the martini talking, but when you asked if I'd have thought it dirty, you know, something between Peter and me?"

He nodded when she waited to see if he had followed

her. Then trying to proceed she faltered entirely and took a cigarette out of the package he had left on the table. "Forget it."

"For heaven's sake, Anne, don't string me up like a Chinese goose."

She put the cigarette back in the package. "You're fond of Janet, aren't you, Eric?"

He remembered Janet at the window as he gave the signal, the Judas signal, and he remembered Anne coming up behind her.

"You don't miss much, do you?" he said quietly.

"I'm sorry. I won't tell anyone."

"There is nothing to tell. There never was anything beyond what you could have seen with your own eyes. Except my fantasy and I demand the right of privacy in that domain."

"Only . . . Eric, it shouldn't just be fantasy, not now. Janet needs you. It'd be great really. She's not like us. She has to feel something and then she can say it in a deep and beautiful way." The girl leaned back, despairing herself of words. "You're right. I can only talk in mathematics."

"When you say 'she's not like us' . . ."

"That was a silly thing for me to have said."

"The martini?"

"Maybe."

"That, my dear, is what martinis are for, to sniggle out the truth," Mather said. "You are snobs, you know, the lot of you. Towered and walled, you see the scramblers after life like piteous ants beneath you, bearing one another gifts. I used to feel myself crawling up that endless hill . . ." Suddenly he was tired, bone tired of trying to relate. He did not want to talk about the way he felt. He did not care. "What will you do now? Will you have to start your doctorate over?"

Anne tried to adjust to his change of mood. She felt it might be the drink in him—or even in herself. She said: "I'm going to talk with Dr. Bauer over the week-end. I should think Bob might be able to take over . . . only . . . the light's gone out. You know?"

"I know."

She tried going back: "And it's not that we're snobs, not really, Eric. It's just that we're safe in that little world we know best . . ."

"In that little world of cyclotrons and megaton thrusts, of smashed atoms and hydrogen mixes. It sounds like a party, you know, like you're having a ball." He finished off the sentence with his old devastating sarcasm.

"Eric," she said, trying to reach him with her eyes, to convey to him at least her own humanity.

"Oh, to hell with all of you," he said, unable to admit to himself, much less to her, that his distress lay in his inability to cope, not with scientists, but with the intimacy of man and woman, with the thought she had tried to share with him of Janet and himself.

Anne gathered her bag. "I'm going to skip dinner if you don't mind, Eric. But thank you very much for the drinks."

He started to rise but she was gone. "I don't mind," he said, slumping down heavily. "I don't truly mind." But he picked up the half-empty glass she had left, turned it in his hand for a moment, and then drank from where her lips had touched.

13

At a few minutes past nine, refreshed after a couple of hours of badly needed sleep and a shower, Marks walked into the Red Lantern. He was first struck by the resemblance of the place to a calendar picture of an old English pub. A wheel of candle-shaped lights hung over the bar; the dark paneling, the solid benches, and especially the covey of costumed students gathered at a large table in the rear all fit in the Old World setting. Even the bartender, his shirt open at the throat, his sleeves rolled up, and his face a ruddy moon, belonged where he was. He was drawing dark beer for a couple of men in work shirts at the end of the bar.

Marks studied the youngsters and was impressed by the fact that while one of them talked, earnest, animated, the others were actually listening. He wondered if even the listening was an affectation. His own attention focused then on the one girl amongst them: she was playing her fingers through the long hair of the boy next to her. Her own hair sat like a red beehive atop her head.

The bartender came to him. His small blue eyes were round and sharp as steel. An Irishman, Marks thought, a canny Irishman. He ordered a beer.

"Let's see your identification," the Irishman said.

Marks obliged him. He would have shown it in any case, asking questions.

"That's what I figured," the bartender said. "A fellow named Pererro was round this afternoon." He nodded at the table of youngsters. "Them's your patsies."

"What's the costume?"

"Edwardian," the bartender said, the word lathered with sarcasm. "At the beginning of every year I think I've seen everything, and by the end of it I know I've seen nothing at all. Still, I'd rather have them than the lousy ones."

Marks realized he was being literal. "Were they all here last night when Professor Mather came in?"

"I didn't count them. It's the usual crowd."

"The young lady?"

"She was here. She's their mascot as near as I can figure. Not much up here," he tapped his head, "but more than enough in the places that count."

Marks grinned. "Did you talk with Mather last night?"

"No. He was on the run when he went out of here. I figured he'd got a bellyful of the kids and took off. He's like that, you know. He'll stand round talking with you for an hour and you'd think you were really into something with him—religion—the old ballads, he's got a fund of them, but you go down to draw a beer and look round and he's gone. An unhappy man, I've always thought."

"But a man?" Marks suggested.

"I've thought about that, and I'd give the nod in his favor."

"I want to talk to the young lady," Marks said. "Is she old enough for me to offer to buy her a drink?"

"She's old enough to buy you one," the Irishman said. "Take a seat by the wall there and I'll send her over."

The girl approached Marks with a saucy swing to her hips. If the boys were interested in either girl or detective, Marks observed, they failed to show it. Marks introduced himself and waited while the young woman settled herself in the booth. He had to ask her her name.

"Sally Nobakoff."

Marks arched his brows. With her red hair and freckles he was not prepared for the Nobakoff. He wondered which of the boys had given her the name. "Are you a student of Professor Mather's?"

"No-o-o," she said, an amiable growl.

"But you are a student?"

"Not exactly. I work in the Records Office."

"I see," Marks said, and with a slight nod toward the Edwardians, "you've got a boyfriend."

"A few," she said and sighed.

Marks cut bait. "What will you have to drink?"

"Johnnie knows—Dubonnet, please." She looked across to the bartender.

"Dubonnet," Marks repeated. "You won't mind if I stick to beer?"

"It's not good for your bladder."

Marks could think of nothing he wanted less to discuss at that moment than his bladder, but he was at a loss trying to figure out the girl: she was neither ingenue nor pickup. Fragments of the boys' talk floated across the room, a discussion of someone named Bergson. The name was remotely familiar, but he did not want to chance showing his own ignorance. "I'm keeping you from the wars," he said.

Sally laughed throatily. "They won't even let me talk. But I think they're cute anyway."

"And Professor Mather?"

"He's the most," she said.

"You like him?"

"Well...I don't know him very well and I bet he wouldn't know me if he saw me on the street. But the first time I met him...My friend—he doesn't come here much any more—but the night he introduced me to Mr. Mather, you'd have thought I was Queen Victoria, and him Sir Walter Raleigh, or somebody like that. Gosh, you know..."

"Queen for a day," Marks murmured.

"Exactly. The next time and ever after I even *presumed* to speak to him—drop dead! You know?"

"What's your friend's name, the one who introduced you?"

"Jeffrey Osterman. Isn't Jeffrey a lovely name?"

Marks nodded.

Sally took the Dubonnet off the tray as the bartender leaned down, about to serve them. "Johnnie is my darling," she said.

"That's 'Charlie,'" the Irishman said with a wink at Marks.

"No. It's Jeffrey," Sally said.

The bartender, moving away and out of Sally's sight, made the gesture of holding his nose, Marks presumed at the mention of Jeffrey.

Sally swilled half the wine at one swallow. Definitely the Dubonnet type.

"Last night," Marks suggested, "was Mather in good form?"

"Last night was the most," Sally said. "The boys were discussing something—I mean they're always discussing something—but all of a sudden just as though he was the only person there except me, he started reciting a poem. I mean I liked it—he was getting dramatic and more dramatic, and looking at me because he knew I was understanding it, you see? And the others didn't know what it was all about."

Marks grinned in spite of himself. "What was it all about?"

"Well, I don't know exactly, but it was very patriotic—all about tyranny and blood, and rape. Afterwards the boys said it was a joke he was playing on them. I mean they think Lord Byron is square. But *square.* I was the only one who knew, but gosh, the way he opened his collar, and ran his hands through his hair..."

"Professor Mather?"

Sally nodded, and Marks had been given something to think about: he was remembering the last entry in Peter

Bradley's journal, his trying to explain the poet Byron to the Russian physicist at the monument in Athens. How strange that on the night he died, at the very hour probably, his friend Mather should be spouting the rhymes of the same Lord Byron.

"Sally, how would you like to introduce me to the boys? Or would you rather I introduced myself?"

She nodded with heavy emphasis in favor of his self introduction. Marks, leaving her, signaled the bartender to give her another drink.

"Excuse me, gentlemen." Marks tried to keep the mockery from his tone: they were so young, so apple-cheeked young as their faces turned up to him. "I'm Lieutenant Marks of the police department." He saw one of the boys glance at his glass of beer. Under-age, Marks thought. Johnnie should watch that. "It's a routine check—you've heard about the homicide last night?" The boys nodded. "Mr. Mather was with Dr. Bradley earlier. I wonder if any of you remember what time he joined you here?"

God help Mather if his life depended on their awareness of time. For Marks it had merely been an opening gambit. "What was the subject under discussion here?"

"T. S. Eliot."

One of the young pups sniggered at the mention of Eliot to a cop.

Marks said: "Eliot was passé in my day, but the Hollow Men seem to have come into their own again."

A boy said then, and Marks took it as their acceptance of him: "It was the Sweeney poems we were talking about last night, sir."

"'Sweeney among the Nightingales,'" Marks murmured. He was not going to be able to go much further. "Tell me something: is Professor Mather really a Byron enthusiast?"

"No, sir. I know for a fact, he absolutely loathes Byron. I take British Poetry under Mr. Mather, and I know. He thinks Byron was an exhibitionist, a fraud, an adulterer and a bad poet."

Marks said: "That last is unforgivable, isn't it?"

The boys laughed.

"Why do you suppose he took off on Byron then last night?"

The boys glanced at one another. The one who had made himself their spokesman said: "We were wondering about that. We thought—well, he doesn't think much of Sweeney either, and we thought maybe it was his way of saying what Byron was in his day, T. S. Eliot is now."

"Eliot and Byron?" Marks said incredulously.

Their hearty agreement set them all to talking at once. Marks listened, amused at the mixture of erudition and pomposity. There was nothing sadder, really, than a pompous child.

Finally the under-aged youngster said to Marks: "He just wings it sometimes, sir, to purposely throw us off. Sometimes he's spoofy, you know?"

Marks supposed it was as good an adjective as any.

"The thing he said when he took off from here last night..."

"I think it's bloody unfair to tell that," one of the others interrupted. "Out of context it could mean whatever somebody wanted it to."

"It was said out of context, wasn't it? Agamemnon died tonight—what did it mean to you?"

"What he said was, 'Live, Sweeney. Agamemnon died tonight.' To me that meant we're living in a Sweeney's paradise, a society of ape-necks with money—the hero, the individual's been crushed, murdered by them." The youth's face flushed with the excitement of his own rhetoric.

"My dear fellow, you are winging," the protester said. "That isn't Eliot's meaning at all."

"But couldn't that be what Eric meant, couldn't it?" he appealed to the group.

Marks took advantage of the pause and gave his place to

Sally who was standing beside him, her empty Dubonnet glass in hand. "Poor old Sweeney," he said, and then nodded to them. "Goodnight, all. Thank you."

He moved quickly to the bar and paid his bill, getting out of the Red Lantern at about the hour Mather had the night before. Across the street the intermission doors were opening at the Triangle Theater.

He sat in the car for a few moments, thinking. Agamemnon died tonight. Fact? Prophecy? Guilt? Or complete nonsense with no reference to Bradley? It was time to see the one person who could tell him what it meant—or what he chose now to pretend it had meant. In any case Marks had a pair of shoes to return.

He radioed in to Communications, and on the "Over" picked up the information that Miss Russo had telephoned him, leaving her number.

Marks stopped at the nearest public phone booth and called her. She told him how Eric Mather had described a man he had seen near the Bradley's who, she was sure, was the same man she had met in her hallway.

14

"My dear Lieutenant, until I learned that Annie had been trying to describe him, I had no idea of the possible connection."

Tonight, Marks thought, he was overplaying the nonchalance. In velvet smoking jacket, he had even dressed the part. He sat, his long legs stretched, his feet slippered, one arm draped over the back of the sofa. No matter how you served him, Mather was not his dish.

"How's the toe?"

Mather described a circle with his foot and flexed the toes: completely healed.

"What time of the day was it, Professor, that you realized we might be interested in this man?"

"Annie and I had a drink this afternoon. Sixish."

"And she didn't impress on you how important it might be?"

"If it were important, I expected you would tell me, Lieutenant. I've been waiting here for you all evening. I knew you would come."

"Intuition?"

"Call it that."

Marks said: "Did your intuition tell you earlier last night

that Peter Bradley was going to be killed at, say, a little after nine thirty?"

Mather's high-boned face showed a twitch of tension. "No. I swear to God I had no intimation of that."

It was a very earnest protest to come from an innocent man who liked to play it cool. Marks said: "What did you expect to happen? Something. That was obvious from your behavior. Make it easy for both of us and tell me."

Mather shook his head and shrugged.

"I'll find it out in time. You can be sure of that."

"Then you must inform me," Mather said with a touch of the old bravura. In Marks's presence he reverted—and all the more quickly it seemed to him for not wanting to—to the kind of snide and supercilious fop he hated most. "As I told Anne today, none of us is altogether innocent."

Whatever that meant, Marks thought. He did not propose to be led down the garden walk by this phony. He leaned back and folded his arms. The ridge of his back struck the frame of the chair. He smiled to conceal the pain. "I'm an ignorant sort," he said. "Who was Agamemnon?"

Mather realized at once the source of Marks's question. "Why, in legend he was the leader of the Greeks during the Trojan Wars. When he returned he was murdered by his wife and her lover..." He stopped, catching the look almost of shock on Marks's face. "Oh, my God."

Marks stared at him and waited.

Mather said very quietly: "I am not Janet Bradley's lover."

For the first time Marks was touched as by the discovery of something human in the man. He said: "What did you mean in the tavern when you said, 'Agamemnon died tonight?'"

"It was in the framework of an Eliot poem..."

"I know that," Marks cut in. He had had enough of poetry for one night. "I'm asking what *you* meant."

"And I am not going to tell you. The boys didn't know.

I'm not sure I did myself—at the time. I could make up something now and you would have to accept it. It was personal, self-critical, and therefore no one's business. But I was not thinking of Peter Bradley when I said it. I was thinking of myself." Mather leaped to his feet. "Christ, man. I've told you all I'm going to. You're not my analyst. Nor my priest. Let me describe this, this beast I saw for you. Then get on with your work and leave me to mine."

Marks with deliberate casualness took his pen and note-book from his pocket.

Mather repeated to the best of his memory the descrip-tion of Jerry as he had given it to Anne, including the nose by which he might have been picked up as a child. "Or possibly," he added to Marks, "he was dropped on it."

It was, Marks thought, a remarkably vivid picture of a man, one that an artist could work with handily. "Now just where was he when you noticed him, Professor?"

Mather saw the trap he had almost walked into. On a dark street it was not possible to see a man that clearly. "As I was coming down the steps he was standing on the street looking up at the building. He put me in mind of one of the Russian diplomats—I've forgotten whom now. But simply in passing I wondered what he was doing in that neighbor-hood."

"Where did he go?"

"I wasn't that curious, Lieutenant, and I quite forgot him until Annie's description turned up." God knows, he had tried to forget Jerry in those few hours after leaving the Bradleys'.

"Just what in Miss Russo's description made you think of him?" Marks asked blandly. Anne's description had been remarkable only in its failure to describe the man at all.

Mather paused but an instant, then gave a short laugh. "I suppose it was the chewing gum. The fellow I saw was putting a stick of it in his mouth."

"Very Russian," Marks said dryly. There was no use trying to get at this man directly. He could lie with the truth, Marks suspected. It would be easier to pick up mercury than to pin him down until you had the goods on him. He had described a man in great detail. A stranger? To the detail of the knob of a nose? But if not a stranger, why conceal the fact? If in complicity with him, why mention him at all?

He put away his notebook and got up. "The first thing in the morning, Professor, come to the Houston Street station. We'll have a composite picture by then for you and Miss Russo to take a look at."

"Very Russian." Mather thought about the detective's disgusted comment after Marks was gone. He had the feeling that if it weren't for Anne's corroboration the detective would have torn up the description at that point and forgotten about it, convinced that Eric Mather was again making a play for attention.

Waiting for Marks to come earlier that night, and knowing that he would come, he had tried to prepare himself to tell the truth. But the sickening image he saw of himself as splashed in the public press in consequence made death seem much to be preferred.

That he would die because Peter had died he now believed with an almost religious fervor. How many times in his life he had wanted to die rather than live with the shame he felt. The trouble was that simply to die amended nothing: it was the final run from what should have first been faced. "Thou'dst shun a bear, but if thy flight lay toward the raging sea, thou'dst meet the bear i' the mouth . . ."

One had to face the bear. Finally, one had to face the bear. Or die signifying nothing.

He called the air terminal and reserved a place on a nine o'clock flight to Chicago. Then he composed a telegram to the chairman of his department. Let who would take his classes take them.

The telegram dictated over the telephone, it remained for him to somehow commit himself at the other end of his journey. His life was patterned with the escape routes he had allowed himself, all leading away from crises he should have faced. It was after eleven. He called the Bradley house and got Louise. He asked if he might speak to Janet. Blessed Louise, keeper of the shrine! Only she would have called Janet to the phone without any questions.

The receiver clicked and he knew Janet had picked up the phone in another room.

"Yes, Eric. How are you?" It was not meaninglessly asked. He could sense the concern in the quiet depth of her voice.

"Janet, I shall be in Chicago tomorrow. If there is any way I can be of help—or comfort to you, I'll be staying over at the Palmer House."

"You're very kind, Eric."

"I'm not!" he cried out. "I may need you!" Then: "Goodnight, my dear. God give us courage."

15

Walter Herring was not prepared to accept frustration his first night on the detective force. He had made his own breaks all his life, almost always by being competent. Seldom brilliant. Just competent and on the scene. Willing, never eager. The eager Negro was too often taken for an Uncle Tom. Herring didn't like a number of things about his life, including where he lived, but he wanted to do something about it himself. He didn't want prefab equality thrust upon him. Besides, he knew enough white people with whom he wouldn't change places. He said something to this effect when he called his wife to tell her about the transfer. Her first question was: how much more money would he get? It was the one question he had not asked Captain Redmond.

"Well, I'm glad if you're glad, Wally," she said with an undertone of long-suffering that infuriated him.

"I should've been a baseball player," he said, which as always finished off the conversation in great style. The next step was to buy her a present better suited to the salary of the ballplayer.

At ten o'clock that night he was sitting in an unmarked car watching the Eastside Lumber yard. His partner had gone around the corner for coffee. They had been on the stake-out then for three hours, three of the dullest hours of his life. Now even the kids had gone indoors. The only interesting thing: he was pretty sure he had spotted a numbers operation in the corner cigarstore. He was sure of it when he saw a patrol car pull up to the side door. One of the cops went in: the other, waiting in the car, switched on the light for a moment. It came as a hell of a shock to Herring to see that it was his some-time partner, Tom Reid. He wasn't sure how he felt about that—having been included out—except that he was grateful not to have had to decide for himself out loud. He didn't want the payoff, but he wanted—what? To have been included? What the hell, he was a member of the Patrolman's Benefit Association. Or was he now? Something—he could not say what—happened inside him when he saw the uniformed cop come out, a cigar box in his hand, and slip into the car. He felt a little sick. The thing was, he shouldn't have watched at all if he knew he wasn't going to do anything about it. And he knew he wasn't.

As soon as the patrol car pulled away he got out of the junkheap he was sitting in and walked down the street to the lumberyard. There was a small, diamond-shaped window in the door panel. He shone his flashlight inside: just empty space between the wood stacked on either side of the court. He shone the light then on the padlock. He jiggled it, tried the hasp, half-expecting something to give in his hand. He was wild for something to happen. If the doctor never showed again, where were they? No place. But Detective Herring wouldn't be getting any citation for a bright idea that hadn't paid off.

"You're covered, fella. What are you doing there?"

He recognized Bolardo's voice and sickened with sudden humiliation: half a detective, and a crippled old night watchman could get the draw on him.

"Detective Herring, Mr. Bolardo. Remember?" He turned slowly and let the light of his torch play up the torso of the watchman. Bolardo did not even have a gun. "Your doctor friend didn't come round tonight."

"I could've told you that," Bolardo said. "He called me up at supper time and said he wouldn't be using the place for a few days."

Herring was a second or two recovering from his violent reaction to the matter-of-fact information, I could've told you . . .

"He called you up. Where?"

"Same place you called me. I'm in the phone book."

"He could remember a name like Fred Bolardo, but you didn't even get his name?"

"Didn't figure I needed to, him being a doctor."

"What makes doctors so special?" Herring demanded, which was not what he wanted to say at all. To him also doctors were special.

"Just being doctors," Bolardo said.

"When he *did* leave the car here—suppose you'd had to move it—where would you have got in touch with him?"

"He left the keys in it."

"And then one night forgot to padlock the door. Oh, man, don't you see we're being played for fools, you and the whole police department?"

"Don't see as I am," Bolardo said doggedly. "I got my ten bucks."

Herring tried to hold his temper. Losing it would get him nowhere. "Mr. Bolardo, you say he called you on the phone. How did you know it was him?"

"Because he told me . . ." Bolardo took off his hat and scratched his head. The fringe of white hair shone like a halo in the darkness. "I guess he must've said: this is Doctor . . . but I didn't catch the name."

"And you didn't ask him to repeat it, knowing we were looking for him? You don't want us to find him, do you, Mr. Bolardo?"

"I'd just as soon you didn't. It's only going to make trouble for me."

"Man, you've already got trouble. Did you tell him the police wanted to talk to him?"

"No, sir. He didn't ask."

Herring was beside himself. It was hard to believe that Bolardo was straight. You couldn't be that dumb. But if you were playing dumb, that wasn't the way to play it either. Maybe even the doc was straight. He had to make allowances for how much he had wanted to have got onto something really important. "Okay, Mr. Bolardo. Next time you hear from him, get his name, huh? And let us know."

Herring waited for his partner and then went back to headquarters. Redmond was off duty, but Lieutenant Marks was in the chief's office. Herring told him the melancholy news.

"What does it mean, Lieutenant?" Herring wanted his own doubts settled.

They were. "It probably means the car is hot," Marks said. "We may not ever find it."

"And the doc himself?"

"He called the watchman at supper time?"

"That's what old Fred told me."

Marks shook his head. "Why? Why take a chance? Why not let it ride? Was he trying to pump the watchman for information?"

"No, sir. I asked him if he told the man the police were looking for him and Bolardo said, no sir, he didn't ask and I didn't tell him."

Marks looked at the notes in his hand, the description he had just dictated over the phone: the man Anne Russo might have seen but couldn't accurately remember until Mather filled it in. One man was stocky, the other skinny: they could not possibly be the same person. Yet he felt there was something in common, but he could not remember what it was.

Herring got out the transcript of Fred Bolardo's testimony for him. Marks glanced through it and then read aloud: "He was mighty careful how he talked, the words you know, like maybe he was a foreigner." He looked up at Herring, remembering Mather's final word on his man, his resemblance to a diplomat. He said: "A Russian?"

"The doc? In this neighborhood, Lieutenant?"

"You've only got his word to Bolardo that he was making calls in the neighborhood," Marks reminded him.

"I know," Herring said doubtfully. "I don't know why, but I keep thinking of him as Puerto Rican."

"Why? It's interesting, but why?" Marks tried to prime him.

Herring thought for a moment. "The car, I guess. You know the docs in Harlem, there ain't many of them driving Cadillacs." He began to pace restlessly, stopping to run his hand along Redmond's desk, then wiping the dust on the seat of his trousers. He stopped in front of Marks. "There's something else in the back of my mind, but I just can't get hold of it."

"Me too," Marks said. He got up and put away the Bolardo file himself. "It'll come to you in the middle of the night. Just hold it to morning, will you?"

Herring grinned.

Marks said: "The only lead we have to him now is the handkerchief, and that's about as identifiable as a diaper on a clothesline."

"I was thinking about that," Herring said. "Institution laundered, isn't that what the lab report said? But hospitals don't give out handkerchiefs, boss."

"They don't even use them," Marks said.

"That's what I mean, man. We're living in a time of disposable sanitation. It'd be an old-fashioned place that'd give out handkerchiefs. Maybe foreign even, and a small place like a mission—or an old folks' rest home, huh? That'd be a place where a foreign doc could make a few bucks. You know, visiting physician ..."

"And surgeon," Marks added grimly.

"Yeah, there's that," Herring said.

Marks was tired and his cigarette package was empty. He felt as though he had a lethal residue of poison in his

lungs. "That's as good reasoning as any of the rest of us
have come up with. Put it in the basket to start checking
out in the morning."

Herring went down to the squadroom to type his report.
He tried to keep his imagination under control, to shut out
new dreams of glory. The concentration it required for him
to use the typewriter at all helped.

Pererro, about to go off duty, paused and watched him
for a minute. When Herring looked up he said solemnly: "I
didn't know you could play the piano, Wally."

Herring went back to work. "Go away, man. I'm composing a symphony for two fingers."

16

Marks, determined to learn what he could of Mather as quickly as possible, went in the morning to the university president's office for permission to see the school's dossier on the teacher. But in order to make his inquiry seem a routine affair, he asked also to see the records of Robert Steinberg and Anne Russo.

A secretary deposited him in a small office adjoining that of the president, assured him that he would be comfortable there while waiting, and closed the door on him. There were three straight-backed chairs and a table on which lay a back issue of the *Journal of Education*. The room smelled of pencil sharpenings. A single picture hung on the wall, an ancient print of the then new administration building. No windows. Air reached the room through a foot-square grill near the ceiling. Marks speculated on whether it was large enough for a man to crawl through: a room not intended for claustrophobics. He opened the door and left it open, and then angled his chair so that he could watch the secretary-receptionist at her work.

A pretty girl, she sat at her typewriter very erect, and every paragraph or so without letting up work she stretched her neck, turning her head from side to side, her chin out.

Unaware that she was being observed or, more likely, unconscious of the gesture itself, she sometimes lifted her graceful fingers to caress with an upward stroke the plumpness beneath her chin. Marks grinned, suddenly realizing that double chins were part of the typist's occupational hazards.

A student-messenger brought a file to the reception desk. The girl directed him with it to the room where Marks was waiting. It was the admissions record of Anne Russo.

Marks soon found himself totally absorbed: Anne Russo, the daughter of an editor of an Italian language newspaper, had finished high school at the age of fifteen, standing first in a class of sixty-five, and college at the age of eighteen; she had slipped in class standing: second among fifteen hundred thirty. Her list of honors was frightening. He was glad he had met her before seeing her record and it was not to be remotely suspected from her unassuming if earnest manner. Marks thought about the differences among people, even within families. What turned the daughter of a literary man to science? How did her father feel about it? Would the pendulum swing back with the next generation? What would Anne want for her children? What did he himself want for his, assuming he would someday have some? Not the law. He had mistakenly followed his father, a man, he thought wryly, much stronger than himself . . .

There was a tap at the open door. Marks glanced up to see Sally Nobakoff standing there. She was almost as surprised to see Marks as he was to see her. Sally, away from the Red Lantern, was a different miss, direct and businesslike. She wore her auburn hair parted in the middle and braided around her head.

"I need your signature for these, sir." After the first startled look of recognition, she struck the attitude of total stranger.

"Are you in charge of them?" Marks asked, scrawling his name on the form she provided.

"Oh, no. I'm just a clerk."

"I'm curious," Marks said. "Are they kept under lock and key?"

"Yes, sir."

"And when my request reached your office, you got the key to the file, got them out and brought them up?"

"Not, not exactly," she said with a slight hesitation. "Miss Katz is in charge. She gave them to me and told me to bring them up to the president's office."

Marks looked at the form he had just signed: CONFIDENTIAL MATERIAL, CENTRAL UNIVERSITY RECORDS OFFICE. He gave it to Miss Nobakoff and received in return a large Manila envelope. He watched her to the door. In the very modern sack dress she revealed little of the qualities that made her stand out by the light of the Red Lantern. He opened the envelope.

Eric John Mather was teaching in his first university post. He had come to Central three years before after taking his doctorate here. He had been working toward the degree while teaching at St. Monica's College, just outside New York City. Before that he had taught at Albion Preparatory School for Boys in Albion, Illinois. Marks studied the record which by sheer weight seemed sparse compared to Steinberg's. He had received high recommendation from the headmaster of the boys' school and from the president of St. Monica's. The letters, part of the file, revealed more of the senders than the subject, the detective thought: there was in the nun's words a sort of weary resignation at losing good teachers to better-paying posts. The headmaster of Albion closed a letter of rather heady praise with a single-sentence paragraph that struck Marks not in what it said, but in its terseness, its isolation from the rest of the letter: "We very much regretted Mr. Mather's leaving us for further study abroad."

Marks referred back to Mather's record: the curious thing about the stint at Albion was that he had taught there for a year and a half; not one year, not two: he had left after the first term of his second year. It was to be supposed the headmaster would have had some difficulty replacing a man he had so effusively praised, midyear.

Marks glanced through Steinberg's folio. It was the

record of a solid citizen, building all the way, a record religiously kept up-to-date, documenting his research projects, papers read before learned bodies, experiments published. Compared to this, Mather's dossier was thin and fragmentary, a circumstance not entirely attributable to the differences between art and science.

Marks put both folders back in the envelope and carried it out of the room with him. He decided to return the files to Sally in person. He wanted to see her in her natural habitat. The coincidence of meeting her again outside the Red Lantern was simply too strong to ignore. The receptionist got up and tugged her dress down over that other of a stenographer's distress areas, and offered to guide him to the Records Office. Regretfully, he declined. It was on the first floor, on his way out. He gave her Anne's record to return for him.

The Records Office was as comfortably furnished as a police van, and about as cheerful. At the railing, surveying a wall of filing cabinets, Marks waited for the one woman in sight to finish a basketful of filing. She seemed to be adding to certain folders such supplements as he had seen in Steinberg's records. He remembered Sally's saying that Miss Katz had given her the file so that when the woman finally came to him, Marks said: "Miss Katz?"

The dreary, sun-starved creature sighed, "Miss Katz is out sick today. Can I help you?"

"Did she go home ill?" Marks asked.

"She did not come in at all. What is it you wish, sir?"

"I'd like to see Miss Nobakoff then," Marks said, although it was plain that she was not to be seen anywhere in that room at the moment.

"You must have the wrong department," the woman said.

"The girl with red hair—a braid around her head?"

"That's Miss Kelly. She's out for coffee."

"Thank you," Marks said. "These files were signed out to me about a half hour ago."

The woman fumbled through a box on the desk and came up with the card. "David Marks?"

"That's right."

She tore up the card without checking the contents of the envelope and then looked up to see Marks staring at her. "Yes?"

Marks said: "Do you know where Miss Kelly goes for coffee?"

"If it was me it would be the place across from the main entrance."

Marks caught up with Sally Nobakoff, born Kelly, as she was coming out of the restaurant. He took her by the arm and led her toward the park. "Now look, little lady," he said, reminding himself of Inspector Fitzgerald, "you have told me at least two lies. It's a serious matter to give a wrong name to the police."

"That's the name I use when I'm with the boys," she said with a graceless attempt at innocence.

"And why tell me that Miss Katz sent you up with the records? She's not even in the office today."

"She almost always is."

"That's beside the point. Why did you tell me she had given them to you?"

Sally shrugged.

"Shall I take you in to the station house? It's a much better place to talk."

"No, sir."

"Then spit out the truth for a change."

"I didn't want you to think I'd looked at them. I'm not supposed to, but I stopped in the washroom on the way upstairs."

"Why did you want to look at them?"

"Just Mr. Mather's. I think he's wonderful. I couldn't help myself."

Marks didn't buy it. The devil of it was there simply wasn't anything in the record of manifest interest to anyone. "Sally, have you shown Mr. Mather's record to anyone else?"

"Oh, no sir. Not to anyone unauthorized. That's the truth."

"To whom?"

"To the F.B.I. investigators."

"I see," Marks said, and indeed it did put things in a different light. "When was that?"

"A couple of months ago maybe, and then with you asking me questions last night, well you can't blame a person's curiosity." Sally was beginning to sound righteous.

Marks cut her off. The truth, he realized, had turned out to be remarkably simple — as was often the case with truth when you finally got to it. "You'd better get back to your desk or you'll have somebody else's curiosity to answer to."

"Miss Fritchie? Isn't she the worst?"

Miss Fritchie and Miss Katz, Marks thought, wondering what they did at night at the hour Miss Kelly turned into Miss Nobakoff.

He returned to headquarters to find Anne Russo with Redmond and Inspector Fitzgerald, trying to select among the police artist's sketches the one most resembling their gum-chewing suspect.

Anne made her selection reluctantly. "They're all a little like him. Mr. Mather would know better, I should think."

"Hasn't he been here yet?" Marks asked. It was ten thirty.

"A late riser," Fitzgerald growled. "Or maybe you didn't impress upon him that it was important."

"I'll impress it upon him now," Marks said, the anger springing up in him. His immediate thought was to have Mather picked up at the University.

But Anne said: "He'll be at the funeral, Lieutenant Marks—St. John's Church at eleven."

Fifteen minutes later Marks was at the church. Mather was not among either the mourners or the curious: the detective watched the arrivals. Then to be sure when the service was half over, he checked the side-chapels, every area. Finally he slipped into the pew next to Louise Steinberg. She had not seen Mather since the previous morning when he had broken down at the Bradley house.

"What do you mean, broke down?" Marks whispered.

"He started to sob and ran out of the house," Louise said.

Marks, leaving the church, thought about the words "ran out." He contacted the chairman of Mather's department at the University, who, after a noisy search of the papers on his desk, read Marks the telegram he had received from Mather that morning:

A MATTER OF URGENCY MAKES IT IMPOSSIBLE FOR ME TO TAKE TODAY'S CLASSES. SHALL TRY TO RETURN BY TOMORROW AFTERNOON.

Marks did not like to think what Fitzgerald would say to this development. First, the vanishing doctor. Now this. A matter of urgency: it was Mather's language all right, but he would use it if he were only going to the corner drugstore for aspirin. He had two men check out Mather's home, meanwhile putting through an inquiry to the F.B.I. following Sally's information. Not that he would be given access to anything in their records unless it proved pertinent to the present case, but at least it was covered. He decided then to do a brief search himself into Mather's background.

He was taken into the visitors' parlor of St. Monica's College by the portress, a round little nun, who hoped he would be comfortable there until Mother St. Ambrose, the college president, could see him. Marks assured her that he would be, although he doubted it. The room was beautifully furnished, one of the Louis's, he thought. It was not a period he liked. His mother would go into ecstasies—brocade and gilt, chairs a man wouldn't dare stretch his legs from. It had always seemed appropriate to him that the kings of that day were rather better remembered for what they did in bed than anywhere else.

But outside the tall open windows was what seemed to him the whole of spring: green grass, iris beds, lilac bushes weighted with bloom, and trees not yet in full foliage so that through their veil of brownish green the branches seemed to grope the sky. He turned at the sound of the nun's coming. He was short on experience with members of a religious community, but he quickly discovered that Mother St. Ambrose was long on knowledge of the world beyond her convent. A volatile, quick-smiling woman, she put him at ease from the moment they shook hands.

Marks explained that he had come to inquire about Eric Mather. Then he said: "While I am a detective, I don't think you'd call what I'm after routine police information. He may not be implicated at all in my investigation . . ."

The nun watched him with a frank, patient curiosity, a look almost of sympathy while he made his inquiry seem more ominous by trying to minimize it. "I'm just trying to dig the man!" he said finally.

"Colloquial and succinct. I understand," the nun said, smiling. She sat a moment in thought. "I will say this for Mr. Mather from the outset: he helped us bring St. Monica's into the second half of the twentieth century. There are some who would call that a dubious blessing, but I have always felt it sinful to dawdle in the past. Education, after all, is a two-way stretch." Marks heard the sharp intake of breath. The suppressed laughter as she realized the origin of her illustration made her eyes merry. "Yes, indeed," she murmured, and Marks enjoyed that rare human experience, entering a world which seemed alien and forbidding and finding there all the comforts of home.

"His manners and decorum with the girls were admirable," she went on, "and our girls can be a provoking lot, especially with a handsome teacher of the opposite sex. He was not a religious man, but one got the feeling sometimes that he wished he were. I don't suppose this is what you want to know about him at all."

"It is," Marks said. "Actually it is." Nothing in his own experience of Mather remotely contributed to such a picture. And yet he knew there had to be something in him to attract so sensible a person as Louise and the perceptive woman he imagined Janet Bradley to be.

"He had been abroad for a year when he came to us, studying in London."

"For a year?" Marks questioned.

"I'm quite sure, but we can check our records if you like." She waited for him to say the word.

"I'd understood it was a shorter period of time."

The nun got to her feet. "Well, let's clear that up. Shall we?"

Marks regretted having precipitated their coming to grips with facts so soon: it was like having Fitzgerald prod him in the back. "I hate to leave this room," Marks said, pausing at the window. Just outside, the lilac was in bloom, the scent of it wafting in with every faint stirring of the wind.

"I'm much too fond of it myself," the nun said at the door.

Marks followed her out and past the chapel entrance, an arched door delicately carved, the pattern dominated by the fleur-de-lis. The long hallway through which they walked echoed with Marks's footfalls and the faint swish of the nun's light-footed tread. Her long prayer beads were noisier. The smell of floor wax was pungent. Some of the classroom doors were open and as they passed, Marks heard fragments of lectures, a burst of feminine laughter. Mother St. Ambrose caught him glancing sidewise into the rooms.

"So many girls," he said, smiling.

She raised her eyes to the heavens.

In her office, Marks sitting at the side of her huge, cluttered desk as they waited for her secretary to bring the file, the nun said: "Is the trouble serious—which you're investigating? I suppose I shouldn't ask that."

"Peter Bradley, the physicist who was murdered the day before yesterday, was a friend of Mr. Mather's. Mather was one of the people with him less than an hour before his death."

"I see." The nun did not look at him, staring at the glass paperweight on her desk. Something, Marks felt sure, had occurred to her, the relevance of which she was now questioning in her own mind. She turned the weight around absently, stirring the snow scene inside it. The sunlight caught the glint of gold in the ring she wore on her wedding-ring finger, a small gold cross on a simple band.

"A tragic affair," she said then, looking up. "One wonders, I suppose stupidly, at the possible international implications—the exchange of film and all."

"Dr. Bradley was not working in what they call a classified area," Marks said.

"But he was a high-energy physicist?"

"Yes."

"It's so easy to classify work," the nun said, "it tempts us to classify the people as well."

"I'm not sure I understand," Marks said.

"I simply meant that a man like Bradley must have had an open, inquiring mind—to have been engaged in the pursuit of knowledge for no other reason than just to know. It's the pedants, the utilitarians, the classifiers among us who come along and package the scholars in with their work. I've never known a true scholar who didn't have a lively curiosity about many things. Their impatience, however, with people less precisely informed than themselves, hides this from the, shall I say, shallow observer." She smiled. "A gratuitous lecture. The girls call where you're sitting 'the stock.'"

Marks said: "Would you call Eric Mather a scholar?"

"No. Not quite. I'm afraid that despite his aspirations, I should have to call Mr. Mather a dilletante. But mind you, he's a good teacher . . . for undergraduates."

"Yes. I've been informed of that everywhere," Marks said.

"Well, shall we look at the record?" The file had been laid before her while she was talking.

"Has anyone else ever come to you for information about him?"

"Central University," the nun said.

"I mean an investigative body—the F.B.I. for example."

"No. You are the only one."

She opened the folder and glanced at the letter of application Mather himself had typed eight years before. "I thought so," she said. "He had taught at Albion Preparatory School for one year, and then studied abroad for a year before coming to us."

"Do you have a letter of recommendation from Albion?"

She drew it from among the several papers in the folder and gave it to him. It was virtually the same letter as he had read at Central University. It made no reference to his tenure at the school. Marks wondered if he was not making a mountain out of a molehill. But why the variation in the records of the two teaching institutions? Was the University likely to have checked into his study abroad where St. Monica's was not? Probably, if he had wanted to use that credit toward his graduate work. The question still remained, why had he left Albion midyear?

"I'm very grateful to you, Mother St. Ambrose," he said, returning the letter. "There's something I want to admit to you and I'd like your comment on it—if you don't mind. I've talked with Professor Mather a couple of times now, I've talked with some of his students, and the picture I had of him was considerably different than the one you've given, except for the dilettante part and him being a good teacher. Personally, I find him glib and wily, like quicksilver. I get the feeling that he's a master of improvisation, and that he's staying just a leap ahead of me and enjoying it—in spite of the fact that he's a very frightened man."

The nun raised her eyebrows. "Frightened of what?"

"That's what I'm trying to find out," Marks said. "It may or may not have anything to do with Bradley's death. If it doesn't, it is none of my business. But I've got to find out."

"When he first came to us," the nun said thoughtfully, "I remember having the impression that he was—I so dislike to use the word—disturbed. He was like a novice to the priesthood in that terrible period of not being sure of one's vocation. I'm trying to remember now just what it was about him—self-doubt? fear of unworthiness? the attempt then to lose oneself in God and work. These are unrealistic terms I suppose to a skeptical person. I wonder if you understand what I'm getting at?"

"I believe in belief," Marks said.

"There!" the nun cried. "You are exactly like Mr. Mather. He might have said that."

Marks assumed it to be a compliment, but he would not have said it described Mather at all.

"He spent a great deal of time with Father Dunne who was our chaplain at the time and who also taught metaphysics. Mr. Mather audited some of his classes. He seemed always to be searching. For what? Reality?"

"In metaphysics?" Marks said skeptically.

"Then—in physics?" the nun countered. Marks did not say anything. "Father died last year, at the age of forty-two. He was a great loss, and I think he had been very helpful to Mr. Mather who left us a much more confident man than he had come to us."

"Obviously he needed help," Marks said.

The nun threw up her hands. "The words we bash into images! Disturbed, needing help. Which of us does not, sir, in order to know ourselves, to live?"

"And you think that was what Mather was trying to do? To know himself? To live?"

She was slower to answer this time. "Yes. I think that was so."

Marks leaned forward. "Forgive me, but isn't it possible that he was only trying to make that impression on you—and the rest of the college—to create an image of himself as the ascetic scholar, happiest at the feet of a priest?"

"Possibly. In which case I would find it a little sad, perhaps, but nothing to condemn. For don't you see, Lieutenant Marks, it would mean that that *was* the person he most wanted to be. And to me it was an entirely admirable person."

17

Mather landed at O'Hare Airport shortly before ten o'clock Chicago time. He rented a car and headed northeast over a complex of tollways entirely strange to him. The highways familiar to his youth were long since obsolete. Only the sky was familiar, the vast openness of prairie still unbroken. Homecoming. For him, the original Wasteland. The little soil he cherished here was mingled round his grandmother's bones. Having the car, he thought he might visit her grave that afternoon . . . and not far from it, the graves of two people he had never known: his parents had been killed in an accident when he was two years old. He glanced at his watch and realized that in New York at that very hour, the memorial service for Peter Bradley was taking place. Tears and eulogy . . .

"Mr. Mather, would you read 'Adonais' aloud to us?" How brutally close to the mark his students had come in that estimate of him, thinking they would flatter him into wiling away the class exhibiting himself before an imaginary bier. He set his mind to following the road only; no more revisiting of past ignominies. And yet he was driving pell-mell toward the greatest of them all.

Albion had changed. The village which had taken its

name from the preparatory school built in what was then near-wilderness had become a common town within commuting distance of the city. A giant new post office stood in the center of what had been a village square. The tearoom, once the refuge of sweet-starved youngsters who could get their fill of neither food nor love within the campus grounds, had been turned into a tavern. He parked in front of it. How often he had trooped a half-dozen teen-aged boys inside, crowded them into a red-upholstered booth and watched them stuff their pimpled faces. He could see them now counting out their money in small change and looking in jealous awe at the amount he always added to the waitress's tip. It was in this shop, in a noisy, crowded booth that he had first become aware of the boy —his large, eloquent eyes full of articulateness while he stammered out the lonely boy's story: a watcher at his mother's wedding feast. But he spoke of the opposite of loneliness that day: he got the attention he sought by painting a picture of the hilarious good time he'd had, the champagne he'd got drunk on, the friend of his mother's who had cornered him in the bedroom . . . Mather could see the boy still, the veins standing out on his splendid forehead. The others had fallen silent, eager for the sex detail, then raucous with scorn when the boy suddenly covered his face with his hands and wept.

The palms of Mather's hands were wet. They left a mist on the chrome of the steering wheel which he watched through its slow evaporation.

He went into the tavern, ordered a drink, and waiting for it, went to the phone booth: he needed now to hold one continuity by starting another in its midst. He called the Albion School and asked for the headmaster's office.

It was the headmaster himself who answered: "Rossiter speaking." The clipped voice had retained its Olympian resonance.

"Eric Mather here, Clem." Even now he found himself fashioning his speech delivery to the master's pattern. "I'm driving up your way this afternoon. Could I drop in for half an hour?"

"By all means, Eric. I'll see what I can set aside. Where are you now?"

Mather was about to lie, to say that he was in Chicago. But he had come for the sake of truth. "In the village," he said.

"Then come along and I'll have lunch sent up."

Rossiter had been his friend. True, he had been saving himself and the school from scandal, but even so he had extended himself in the subsequent recommendations. If he had hoped by giving them to need never hear the name of Eric Mather again, no indication of it came through now in his voice. It was as cordial, he was sure, as Rossiter could be to any man who hadn't a son to give to Albion.

The headmaster met him on the steps. He looked to have changed no more than had the gray stone of Albion. A little settling weight at the girth, but nobly cloaked. His hair was still sandy and his hand, extended slowly, was still moist and soft to the touch as a plucked pigeon.

They walked along a pebbled path, past the dining-hall windows. The clamor inside was intense.

"Boys don't change much," Mather said, "one generation to the next."

"Nor does the menu, I'm afraid, at Albion. You weren't fond of it then. Now I suppose you're a gourmet—though I can't say it shows."

Mather was already aware of his own leanness, striding alongside the master. They reached the side door entering directly onto the master's office. Rossiter performed his ritual of selecting the key from numerous others attached on a ring at one end of a chain that crossed his vest to his watch pocket.

The office still smelled of sweet pipe tobacco and Old Spice shaving lotion.

"I've got a tutors' meeting at one thirty. That gives us a little time. None of that nonsense at the University, what —tutors and all that? You like it, Eric?"

"Yes, I like it." He took the leather-backed chair Rossiter indicated at the side of the window and watched the master pull up his rocker and take his binoculars from the bookshelf. He was a bird watcher. The boys of Mather's day, and no doubt still, thought the hobby a ruse behind which the master could spy on them.

"Then why are you here?"

Mather met the small gray eyes full on. It was Rossiter that looked away. "Because I think my offense at Albion has caught up with me."

"Oh, dear me," Rossiter murmured and busied himself with the adjustment of his binoculars.

The curious thing about being with Rossiter in Mather's days at Albion was that he had never felt so much a man as in the master's presence. Rossiter then, and presumably now, had a wife who, Mather suspected, had come with his appointment to the headmastership. She lived in what the boys called The Castle, on the bluff at the campus's edge overlooking Lake Michigan. The master, a turret if not a tower of authority throughout the day, ambled home to her in the dusk, burdened with books and a small brown leather bag in which he kept a change of linen, measuring the path before him as might a peddler who had to sell something of which he was not especially proud.

"I must know now everything that happened afterwards," Mather said, "and who knew about it."

"There were not many sources," Rossiter said, fussing still with the glasses. "You know, we have an oriole this spring. See that tamarack, the second one, next to the maple sapling? They dangle their nests like ladies' handbags. She's found a bit of Christmas tinsel and woven it into the nest." He put the glasses to his eyes. "I suppose you've been discreet yourself? Psychiatry and all that, too?"

"I'm in love with a woman, Clem," he said. He had not meant to say that. It evaded within himself the truth he was seeking. And Janet was worthy of more honor than it paid her, in his position. "But that has nothing to do with it," he added.

Rossiter looked at him. "Oh, I should think it might. I should think it might."

"I want to know who exactly knew."

"At the time?" Rossiter put the binoculars away. "She ought to have built a window in that nest if she meant to hold my interest," he said, obviously of the oriole. "Well, there was myself, the boy and his father—fortunately there was no mother—for you, that is, and our lawyer. He's still our lawyer by the way, Wes Graham. A good friend to Albion, but he did not send his sons here." Rossiter did not attempt to disguise the reproach implicit in the last sentence. "Still, I shouldn't think there would have been any . . . leak, shall I say, from that source. And surely not from the boy involved: they would have fervently wished to forget the incident. I meant two people were involved, weren't they? You would not say the boy was entirely innocent now, looking back, would you?"

"I would not say," Mather said quietly.

"No, you wouldn't," Rossiter said dryly. "I recall it was I at the time who silenced his father by *that* suggestion."

"'At the time'—you said that before, just a minute ago. Has anyone talked about it since? Have *you* talked about it, Clem?"

"I resent it very much, Eric, your challenging me this way. No man could have had a more understanding friend than I was to you then. I virtually perjured myself, recommending you without qualification—to St. Monica's, was it—that girls' school in the East?"

"I have never been ungrateful. Nor have I given you reason to regret it."

"You have done something, Eric, whether you were aware of it or not. At some recent time you have joined an organization—applied for a fellowship or some such activity that a discreet man, knowing his own record, would not have done."

Mather was wracked with sudden trembling. He could hardly trust himself to speak. "Why do you say that?"

"For what other reason would you have been investigated by the F.B.I.?"

He moistened his lips. "I didn't know that I was."

"Now that I tell you it is so, can you think of any reason?"

The fear was sickening him, striking in the way it had when the police had driven up to him outside his house— fear, mostly of the unknown, fear now that his complicity in what had led to Peter's death was better understood by others than by himself. Until now he had thought that there still was time, that he still had the chance to master himself and possibly in the end, what was to become of him. Deep in his own thoughts, he had lost the trend of Rossiter's question. "Any reason for what?"

Rossiter made a gesture of impatience. "For the F.B.I. to be interested in that particular aspect of your career?"

"When did they come to see you?"

"Early February. During term examinations."

"And they told you *specifically* what they wanted to know?"

"Directly," Rossiter said. "Those boys don't beat about the bush. They wanted to know if there were any incidents of perversion in your record."

Mather flinched at the word. But having heard it spoken, he was better able to think, to get outside himself and look about. Early February: that was before Jerry had spoken to him in the park. Why at that time would the F.B.I. have been seeking information on him? "Didn't they tell you why, give some reason for being interested in me?"

"My dear Mather, they never do. They ask all the questions, and completely ignore any you might ask of them."

"You told them the truth?"

Rossiter spread his pudgy hands. "I had to. They implied knowledge of a more recent incident."

"That's not so!" Mather cried, and then because he remembered something he had thought of small significance at the time, so quickly and, he then believed, effectively had he repulsed the boy, he added now: "Oh, dear God."

"You see," Rossiter said, almost smugly, "Big Brother's always watching you."

"But it was nothing, Clem! One of my students—I struck him."

"Oh, a splendid show of manhood! In a public place, no doubt?"

"I tell you, there was no one about. And it was over in a minute. He apologized and that was the end of it."

"Obviously," Rossiter said. "And all this took place in the classroom?"

"In the park," Mather said, and saying it he saw Rossiter's "Big Brother" image as a sinister reality. It was in the park after all that Jerry had approached him.

"The university park there—it's rather notorious, isn't it? I shouldn't think with your background you would go near it."

"God damn my background," Mather cried, a helpless blast. Rossiter's capacity for niggling provocation had remained unimpaired through the years. Yet he was to be thanked now. One squirmed being made his pivot, but one saw. One had to see.

Mather got up and wandered the room. A row of clocks of many styles sat on top of a glass-enclosed bookcase. They told the varying times throughout the world. Rossiter liked to say: "In Paris now..." They all ticked quietly at differing tempos, but told their times meticulously. Mather, his mind breaking off from his immediate problem, remembered that moment of stillness while Janet turned the pages of her book. It was that moment truly—to which he had had no right—in which he had begun to live. Or to die?

Rossiter, his chair eased round to where he watched the younger man, folded his hands across his belly and said: "You're still a handsome bastard, Eric."

Mather turned and glowered at him. He had scarcely heard the words, much less comprehended their content until Rossiter added, a little mocking smile at his soft red mouth, "I suppose if I were to get up, you would strike me also?"

Mather wanted to laugh: the master's mystique revealed. He shrugged and moved back to the leather chair, standing beside it. He looked down at the man rocking himself round again to the window, and felt for him a pitying contempt of the sort usually reserved for himself. The experience had drained off his fear. Rossiter reached up for the binoculars again. With or without them, a voyeur.

"The F.B.I. agents, Clem—what do you remember of them? What *did* they say? Spare yourself the trouble of finding delicate words for it. I just want to know. What were they like?"

"What were they like? One was tall and blond and silent—the all-American. The other—I remember his name, Edward N. Fleming. But take away the Edward, leave just the initials, and what have you? E.N. Fleming. Life mocking fiction, what? Or as the boys would say, how corny can you get?"

Mather felt the drumbeat of his quickened pulse. "What did he look like, this character called Fleming?"

"Heavy-set, a bulbous face, eyebrows like shoe-brushes . . ."

Mather interrupted. "They showed credentials of course?"

"Identification." Rossiter looked at him. "Are you suggesting impersonation?"

"I am. How could we find out? There must be a way to check on them—to find out if there actually is an agent by that name."

Rossiter eased himself out of the chair. "I should think Wes Graham could find out for us—if he's in the office, that is. I'd rather not call them directly. But really, Eric—it is too fantastic."

"Please call Graham," Mather said. Rossiter did not know Tom and Jerry. Or having met the chameleons, he knew them only for what they said they were. He had no doubts now himself. They had had to know their customer in him, and they had come to the best source.

Rossiter, reaching the lawyer on the phone, voiced his skepticism. "It's nothing really, Wes, but I just want to be sure. They were checking on one of our old instructors. The agent's name struck me as odd: Fleming, E.N. Fleming..." He paused, listening, and then said: "Is that a fact?"

After hanging up he explained to Mather: "Wes knows of an agent by the name of Spillane. So! The bard said it all, didn't he—what's in a name? Shall I ring for lunch? He'll call us back within the hour."

They had reached a lumpy dessert which would not have had taste for Mather under any circumstances when the attorney reported on his inquiry to the local office of the Federal Bureau of Investigation. No agent by that name had operated out of the district in the past five years.

Rossiter, on the phone, passed it off as lightly as he could. "I might have got the name wrong. In any case there was nothing damaging in my man's history." He lied with a practiced grace. "Thank you, Wes. Come up for golf first chance you have, what? The greens were never better."

Nothing damaging, Mather thought. Lord God in heaven!

"Well, there you have it, Eric, make what you will of it. I had no way of knowing."

"Of course you hadn't. The blame is mine all through. But it's what I had to know."

Rossiter scraped the last bit of custard from his plate. He washed it down with coffee. "Eric, are you being blackmailed? If you are, take some very ancient advice and go to the police. You can get the villains, you know. Impersonating law officials is a serious offense. And Eric...if there is no other way, I shall testify."

"Thank you, Clem, but I'll find another way."

18

Returning to the city mid-afternoon, Marks stopped at his parents' house for something to eat. His mother had gone to a recital at Carnegie Hall, but Willie Lou, who had worked for the Markses since he was a boy and called him "David" still, was prepared at any hour to sit him down to a good meal. "No fussing, just a little fixing," she said as always. "You go wash up."

Marks went into his father's study and called the precinct house. The only important message was the answer to his inquiry to the F.B.I.: *re Eric John Mather no record of investigation.* To be sure the language meant what it seemed to mean, Marks called James Anderson, the F.B.I. liaison man on the case. "Could it mean that Mather was investigated, but that you turned up nothing on him?"

Anderson laughed. "We generally turn up *something,* no matter what it comes to in evaluation. No, it means just what it says, Lieutenant, the Bureau has not initiated any such investigation."

So, Marks thought, Sally Nobakoff Kelly had told him yet another lie. But why? Why not say she had never shown the record? Why the garnish? She had used the story to justify her own curiosity, and, Marks realized, if she had worked in the Records Office for any length of time, she was bound to have become familiar with F.B.I. investigators. Professors, especially at Central University, had a way of participating in Causes . . .

Marks found himself staring up at a faded print on the wall alongside his father's desk: an allegory of the tree of good and evil. She was a great plucker of apples, our Sally, he thought, she was ever ready to hand them out to any damn-fool Adam gullible enough to try one.

"You can come now, David," Willie Lou said from the door. "Your mother didn't want much to go today. Now she's going to be spitting mad, not seeing you."

Marks, at headquarters an hour later, tried to write up the gist of his interview with Mother St. Ambrose. There was nothing to write really, and yet the nun's words had affected him deeply. He was annoyed as a result of the visit. With himself? He wasn't sure. He did not like Mather. Was this the reason he had allowed himself to get on the man's back? He had no evidence against him. Just his eccentricity and the Byron coincidence out of which he'd been trying to build his own allegory. He could see himself trying that on the Inspector. There was something to be said for dumb cops, he decided. Facts were facts, and fancies were for the birds. He went down to the squadroom where the day's round-up was breaking up. Redmond, standing with Pererro and Herring who had just come in, called out to Marks to join them.

"I don't know what we got," Herring said, "but we got a lot of something."

Redmond was trying to take the top from a container of coffee, the tab having broken off in his fingers. Marks suggested he use his pipe reamer.

"I thought we had a tough precinct," Pererro said. "I just got me a Harlem education."

"Spanish Harlem," Herring corrected. "That's special. Most of the docs are Spanish-speaking where we went looking. Some of them are refugees and most of them don't want to talk, period. Pererro and I figured out that's because maybe they're not all the way kosher. You know, maybe they're not licensed to practice everything? And man, in some of those places you got to practice everything. Captain, did you ever see rickets? We got 'em in these United States in the great city of New York. Kids with legs like this." He held up two skinny fingers.

"A humanitarian yet," Redmond growled. The container lid gave way and he splashed the coffee over his hands and the stack of flyers face-down on the table.

Marks, moving the flyers out of the way, picked up the top one. The ink was not dry, but it was the printed composite picture of Anne's and Mather's suspect, a pudgy face, dark brows . . .

"Some of these places don't have their doc's address even," Herring continued, "only a phone number where they can leave a call. And not one out of ten could tell us the kind of car their medic drove. But we got a list of twelve doctors and checked out three of them so far . . ."

"Why twelve?" Redmond asked.

"That's the number of places where that handkerchief could've come from. Oh, man! Twenty-four gross of them were given out last Christmas by the Hispanic Brotherhood."

"Twenty-four gross!" Redmond said, "oh my God."

"One of the brotherhood imported them from Czechoslovakia and by mistake got ten times what he ordered. They were given out to all the charitable institutions on their list, twenty homes, hospitals and orphanages. But wait, man: only eight out of the twenty send their laundry out. That left us twelve just to worry about. We got samples of their washing compound from every one of them."

"Good work," Redmond murmured.

Herring grinned. "Old Pererro, the soap sniffer. Just call him Sneezy."

"Twelve institutions and twelve different doctors?" Marks said.

"Yes, sir. We figured they split up the charity so's one man wouldn't have to take too much of it."

Marks said: "It just seems like a lot of doctors, doesn't it?"

"You know—about these foreign medics," Pererro said, "I heard once they're the guys who get tapped for patching up criminals—you know, plastic surgery."

The others looked at him blankly.

"I was thinking about the knife," he explained.

"If it was a surgical knife," Redmond reminded him. "It's not in our possession."

Pererro went on just the same: "How about this angle on the doc we're looking for: say he had a sideline, a hole down here with a coverup where he could do abortions?"

Herring's eyes were dancing. He was ready to jump on the new theory, to expand it, but all he got out was: "How about that, man?"

Redmond broke in: "For the love of God, stop playing the D.A.'s men and just bring in the doctor who parked his car in the lumberyard. What a hell of a combine you two make."

The younger men looked chastened, but not enough so. "I mean it," Redmond said. "I get paid for doing the thinking for this precinct. You two get paid for doing piece work. Now get all that jazz into report form. Get your samples to the lab, and I'll make the assignments from there."

"Yes, sir," Herring said. Then, glancing at his book: "How about the docs we didn't get to check out yet?"

"Mañana," Redmond said. "And maybe the lab can thin them out for you. Did you think of that?"

Herring didn't say anything.

"If your doctor is on that list you're going to give us, you could flush him too soon and we might never get him. You've done a good day's work, but you're just the line men in this team. Remember that."

Marks, the "Wanted" flyer in his hand, followed Redmond upstairs. "Did Eric Mather show up to verify this likeness, Captain?"

"Not to my knowledge, but we decided to run it anyway.

We can always run another one if we have to. It's good press relations—as your boss pointed out."

Marks said nothing. So far he had escaped the pressure which was obviously mounting on the men nearer the top.

Redmond sat down at his desk, got out his pipe and filled it. "You know," he said, "those two *did* do a hell of a job today."

Marks, his elbows on the desk opposite Redmond's, nodded. "Twelve doctors, twelve Spanish-speaking doctors. Where did they all come from?"

Redmond lit his pipe, pulling noisily at it. "Cuba? Herring said some of them were refugees. The Trujillo outfit's washed up now, isn't it—wherever they came from? I can't keep up with all their revolutions. But they're a rotten bunch to tangle with, I'll tell you that. We had to break up an anti-Castro rally down here one night. I got a finger damn near chewed off. A woman! Christ, the way she carried on I thought I was going to get rabies." He thrust his hand across the desk for Marks to look at, the little finger extended. "Eight stitches."

"A Spanish-speaking doctor?"

"Hell, no. I went to Bellevue." He had to relight his pipe. He paused, the match mid-air, and pointed the pipe at Marks. "That abortion angle Pererro started on? I was thinking of that myself today. There's some of it goes on down here. Only I couldn't figure any way to tie it in with Bradley."

Something clicked with Marks, but he couldn't quite catch it.

Redmond squinted at him through the maze of smoke he was now pumping out of the pipe. He knew he had started something.

"Something," Marks said, rapping his forehead with his knuckles. "What is it?"

Redmond said: "She's a good-looking dame, Bradley's widow, if you can judge by the picture in this morning's *Journal.*"

"That's it!" Marks cried, but almost at once he doubted

the significance of his association. "Janet Bradley is a photographer. She has a book about to come out—pictures taken along these streets. When she was taking them, she'd leave her equipment at Anne Russo's. Bradley himself used to go with her sometimes . . ."

"But where does the doctor come in?" Redmond said.

Marks took his time. It wasn't going to be easy to explain to Redmond his own reaction to one of the pictures in that book. And that really was all there was to the association. But Redmond was waiting. Marks had to try. He shook out a cigarette and lit it. "The book is called *Child of the City.* There's a little boy in most of the pictures, a grubby little kid, Italian or Puerto Rican. But there's one picture that tore my guts out—a young woman standing on the steps of a tenement building looking down at the youngster. The more I looked at it, the more I thought, this girl's in trouble. What a picture! You couldn't pose that— you just had to wait for it to happen." Marks half-expected Redmond to spout a sarcasm as he felt Fitzgerald would under the circumstances.

But the Captain said: "Is the building identifiable in the picture?"

"I don't know. I'd have to see the picture again. This part could be my imagination, remembering something that wasn't in it at all, but I seem to think now there was some kind of sign in the window above."

"Dr. So and So?"

Marks said: "That's what's running through my mind now."

Redmond sat back and smoked thoughtfully. After a moment he said: "So there's the possibility that Peter Bradley was able to identify one of his assailants—or at least the assailant thought so. Let's take a look now at what we've got and see if we can put together what happened to Bradley in his last hour, shall we?"

Marks nodded and both men started to speak at once. Redmond said: "You start it off."

Marks said: "Bradley left the house at nine fifteen,

tailed by this character." He indicated the flyer. "We'll call him A. A was probably in a car driven by B who could be our doctor. A dropped off at the corner of Tenth Street to set up things at Anne Russo's. B tailed Bradley all the way to the lab and drove up behind him just as Bradley reached the entrance. He'd have to do that to make it seem natural, his asking: 'Are you Dr. Bradley?' Then he persuaded Bradley that Anne Russo was hurt—or ill."

"But the girl had left Bradley's house with the others," Redmond said. "Wouldn't Bradley assume she was at the laboratory?"

"Actually she hadn't. Steinberg and the boys had gone downstairs ahead of her. She had to run to catch up with them. And even if she doesn't remember it, it's just possible she said within Bradley's hearing: 'I've forgotten my glasses. I'll have to go home for them.'"

"In any case," Redmond said, "Bradley seems to have got into B's car without much protest. Go on."

"By a quarter to ten, they were outside Anne's house— but the car seems to have gone on quickly. The old lady looking out her window—dividing her attention between the wrestling match on television and the street, didn't notice the car, just two men—and heard somebody call, 'Doctor.' Whether from inside the vestibule or on the street, we don't know. There has to be a Mr. C involved now. Maybe he drove the doctor's car and parked it in the lumberyard while the other two went inside with Bradley. A was already on the scene."

"The lumberyard—that's the stickler," Redmond said. "Why that elaborate preparation? Why not just park the car on the street for a quicker getaway? Was it a safe place to count the money they'd taken from Bradley?" He shook his head.

Marks said: "It wasn't his money they were after. Something bigger. Something that came with the film or in his notes. It has to be."

"I agree," Redmond said. He relit his pipe, long since gone out again. "Dave, suppose they didn't get what they were looking for? Suppose Bradley had—in effect—doublecrossed them? Suppose they did use the lumberyard as a place to examine what they'd taken. Maybe they needed light, strong light—for film? A lumberyard would have an outlet for power equipment. Say they didn't get what they were looking for. They then assumed Bradley had caught on . . ."

"That means he was carrying something he wasn't supposed to know about himself," Marks interjected. "A dummy carrier?"

"Right. At the time they were examining the film, Bradley was lying unconscious in the apartment hallway. A few minutes later the woman with the dog saw him struggling out among the ashcans. He was out there for anybody to see who looked. And *they* would have looked. If Bradley *wasn't* carrying what they expected, he was their enemy. And in his condition at that moment, a very easy one to put a knife in."

"That makes the doctor our hottest prospect, doesn't it?" Marks said after a moment.

"Hot and slippery," Redmond said. "He must have a damned good story ready for us or he wouldn't have left so wide a trail."

"Funny, how we started in one direction and came out another," Marks said.

"That photograph needs to be checked all the same," Redmond said. "We're a long ways from home."

There was no one at the Bradley apartment when Marks called. He knew that Janet had flown to Chicago for the interment there, but he had hoped Louise might be at the apartment. He found her at her own home, Anne Russo with her, as well as three of the wildest children it had ever been his misfortune to meet.

"They're always like this after they've been with Grandma Steinberg," Louise shouted over the din. "I just let 'em go till they're exhausted."

Anne, apparently on the theory that she could not lick them, had joined them. They had her tied to a diningroom chair from which she smiled up at Marks while the Steinberg Indians whooped around her.

"Joan of Arc or Pocahontas?" Marks shouted.

"Houdini!" Anne cried and broke the string in a burst of flailing arms and legs.

The adults retreated to the kitchen, Louise closing the door behind them. Steinberg, the scientist, it was plain to see, hadn't washed a dish during his wife's absence.

"Do you have a key to the Bradley apartment?" Marks asked.

"I put it in the mailbox," Louise said. "Why?"

"There's something I want to see—Mrs. Bradley's book."

"It isn't there. I packed Janet's suitcase for her and stuck it in. There was room."

Marks, astounded, said: "Why not the telephone book?"

Louise looked offended. "I thought she might need something like that, work—some distraction."

Marks was beginning to understand that Louise was one of those people who organized other people's affairs for them and her own not at all. "There's a picture in it I wanted to see again and to ask her about."

"She'll be home tomorrow."

"Mañana," Marks said.

Then Anne said: "There's an exhibit of Janet's pictures in Lowell Hall. Mostly trick stuff though, you know, nonobjective."

"Are there pictures from the new book in it?"

"A few, I think," Anne said.

"Where's Lowell Hall?"

Louise said: "Annie, why don't you take him there? He might have trouble getting in at this hour."

Louise, the matchmaker, Marks thought, but he was not displeased. "Do you mind?"

Anne made a futile gesture toward the dish-filled sink.

"Oh, no you don't," Louise said. "I've got to do something till the demons wear themselves out." She took them to the hall door. "Come back later for coffee. I'd offer you dinner, but not in this mess." A very subtle woman, Marks thought, but the least he was going to do was take things at his own pace.

It was almost six o'clock when they reached the University and they had to get the custodian to open the lecture hall and turn on the lights.

"Should I tip him?" Marks whispered.

Anne shook her head. "Dangerous precedent." She flashed the man a smile and Marks thought it would be a mighty poor man who wouldn't settle for that.

They walked solemnly along the walls hung with Janet Bradley's work: wisping trailing camera effects, light and shadow; then a group of surrealist designs started out of city skyscrapers. "I shouldn't be enjoying this," Marks said, "but I am." He was aware of a group of portrait photographs which they had not yet reached.

"Why shouldn't you?"

"I don't know," he murmured. "She makes this city beautiful, and it's not."

"But there's beauty in it if you look hard enough."

"In the right places," Marks said. "I don't often get to them."

The first portrait in a series came as a shock to Marks: it was of Anne Russo. Janet had caught her as she was looking up from her desk at home. Pencil in hand, she looked radiant, as though she had just made a marvelous discovery. Marks looked from the picture to the girl. She was almost his height, her face flushed now, self-conscious. "It doesn't flatter you, you know. It's just you at the right moment."

"You should see me at some of my wrong ones," Anne said, trying to edge him along. "I'd forgotten Janet was there that night. She was working. So was I. She didn't tell me. Afterwards she said she'd been watching me for an hour. Most of the time I'd been biting my thumb." Anne motioned toward a picture down the line. "There's one from the book I think."

It was the portrait of the dark, troubled girl on the steps

which Marks had remembered. But it was the insert only, an enlargement of her face, showing nothing of the background in which Marks was at the moment most interested.

"Did Mrs. Bradley talk to you about this picture, where she took it?"

Anne shook her head. "She doesn't talk about her pictures ever. If they don't speak, she said once, then I don't have anything to say either."

In the hallway, having told the custodian that they were through in Lowell Hall, Marks said: "Anne, would you have dinner with me?"

She nodded vigorously. "I'd love to."

A half-hour later they were sitting in the Bretagne, a restaurant Anne said she always went to with her parents when they came into town. They had the menus and a martini each before them.

Anne said: "I haven't had much to eat lately. I always seem *about* to eat. Then something happens and I don't want to any more."

Marks, glimpsing the prices of the entrees, said: "You'd better eat tonight."

"I don't want to forget, you see, and already I'm beginning to. All day today I kept thinking: I don't want to go on in science. I don't care enough, not deep down inside."

"What do you want to do?"

"I want to live, whatever that means." She turned the glass round with her fingertips. Marks noticed she had put on nail polish since last he had seen her. "I want to be like that picture Janet took of me!" She bit her lip then, Marks thought charmingly. "I'm very young, aren't I?"

"Sometimes."

"How old are you, David? Do you mind? I shouldn't want to be called Dave if I were David, I don't think."

"I'm thirty."

"Are you married?"

"No."

"I'm glad," Anne said. "I mean—I was raised a Catholic, you see."

"And taught not to go out with married men," he prompted.

"It isn't exactly going out, dinner just, is it? I mean that was presumptuous of me, saying what I did."

Marks said: "To me, it's going out—if there are table-cloths on the table. What do you recommend we have to eat?"

"Everything is good."

"Would you share the Chateaubriand? Rare?"

She nodded. "You speak French, don't you—the way you said that?"

"Waiter's French anyway," Marks said.

"Louise said your father is a judge."

"A lawyer."

"That's like Louise. She always pushes people a step ahead of themselves. Everybody's the greatest." After a moment she added: "I wish I thought Bob Steinberg was. I don't."

Marks lifted his glass. "You're comparing him with Peter Bradley. Not many men could stand up to that comparison."

"Most of them don't even try." She sipped her drink and watched Marks while, by an old habit, he took his pencil and lightly checked off items on the menu.

He said then: "Clams, onion soup, Chateaubriand and salad. How's that? And an inexpensive claret—if there is such a thing any more." He gave the order to the waiter.

"I wonder if Eric will now," Anne said.

Marks was a moment remembering the sequence of her remark.

"Try to measure up to Peter," she added.

"With Janet?"

Anne nodded. "I know he's terribly fond of her—at least I'm reasonably sure of it. Only he hates himself so. But now with Peter gone, maybe he won't feel so inferior."

Marks said: "Anne, didn't I ask you about this once before, the possibility of Mather and Janet Bradley?"

"No."

He had asked Louise, he realized, and considered her a better judge of relationships than Anne Russo.

"I probably wouldn't have told you anyway," Anne said. "I mean, I was guessing and there wasn't anything between them actually. Just what Eric called his fantasy..." She finished her drink, remembering the martinis she had had with Mather. It seemed years before. "I think Eric is one of the lost people in this world. He tries to hate, I think, because he's afraid of being hurt in love."

What Eric called his fantasy, Marks thought...And here was yet another woman presuming to understand him, making allowances. Why? Marks motioned for another round of drinks. He was no psychologist. But the man Mather was psychopathic. He, too, David Marks, policeman, had been making allowances, subconsciously condemning that catch-all scapegoat, society. Society was the people who composed it, the Eric Mathers along with the rest. Because a sophisticated group of people could accept him, he was not cured automatically! In fact, acceptance might compound his malady—if he had to strive too hard to get it.

Marks concealed his own uneasiness. He tried to make the question he now asked sound casual: "When did it first occur to you that Eric might be in love with Janet?"

Anne thought for a moment. "That night...the awful one. Only earlier. I was just going to leave. Eric had already gone. But I wanted to tell Janet how much I'd liked the show at Lowell Hall. She was at the front window looking down. Eric was crossing the street. I didn't see him at first, but—this all happened in a minute—I saw him turn under the street lamp there and put his fingers to his lips...you know?" Anne repeated the gesture telling it: the fingertips of both hands from her lips toward Marks. "And that wasn't anything really. I mean I wouldn't even have thought about—Eric's like that to everybody—except that Janet, well, there were tears in her eyes when she turned around—and the way she caught my hands and hung onto them for a minute." Anne looked down at her own hands now. "I'm not very good at a time like that. I run. I'm a funny sort to be an Italian. I'm supposed to be emotional."

Marks let her finish, putting her own construction to the incident. But he had to press her then for the picture on the street that night. Mather had initiated the party, maneuvered it, and had been the first to leave. He had described in great detail a man whom he should have seen as no more than a passerby. "Eric crossed the street, turned, and threw the kiss? Didn't he look up first to see if there was anyone in the window?"

"No," Anne said. "That's what I mean. I wouldn't have thought about it at all if Janet hadn't been so—so moved, I guess. David, we're making a mountain out of it. We shouldn't. I ploughed in and asked Eric—last night, was it? the night before—I forget. And I didn't ask really, I just said I thought it would be great, Janet's needing somebody now. That's when he said that there was nothing—except his own fantasy."

Marks thought about his first meeting with Mather, informing him that Bradley was dead. At the suggestion on Marks's part that there might have been a relationship between Bradley and Anne Russo, Mather had lent credence to the idea; at least he had tried to contribute to it by saying that he never met his pupils in private, the insinuation being that Bradley did. He was a desperate, cunning man that night, and he had been writhing in his fashion from the moment he left the Bradley house.

And what actually had happened in Anne's vestibule: if Redmond was right, the knock on the head should have been enough . . . Marks felt he now had another part of the story. With just a tinge of regret he realized that this dinner could now go on Investigative Expenses.

"I've started something, haven't I?" Anne said, watching him. He had crumbled a piece of bread, and was making neat little clusters of the crumbs.

"You had a drink with Mather yesterday. Where?"

"A place on Sullivan Street. He was waiting for me when I came out of the lab."

"Were you that friendly before?"

"No. I'd just known him from Peter and Janet's."

"Why do you think he looked you up?"

Anne did not hesitate. "To compare notes on the man I'd seen in the hallway."

"Whom he had seen near the Bradley steps?"

Anne nodded.

"Whom neither you nor any of the others coming out of the house saw there?"

Anne shook her head.

"Now let's enjoy our dinner," Marks said. "You do like clams?"

"I like food," Anne said, "and I'd better have some before I drink any more of this martini."

19

If he had not told Janet that he would be in Chicago that night, Mather would have returned to New York at once. The one thing he would not permit himself was fantasy, the dream of Eric Mather, hero, or in disgrace. The future must be no larger than the compass of his atonement, step by step. He would go as far as he could by his own resources and hope that it was far enough to partially redeem him. Jerry and Tom had tracked him back in time; they had tracked him, he was sure now, from an incident in the park. First, they had chosen him as the most likely prospect for their scheme among Peter Bradley's associates. They must have done a similar job on others until they settled on him as their man. To have used Anne Russo as they finally had when he had no more than mentioned her was proof enough. But how bitterly ironic that in his righteous strength that day, striking a would-be offender, he had exposed the very weakness they were looking for! Evil born of good.

And he had convinced himself that he was breeding good of evil, content in their conspiracy. Ah, but nothing was that simple: to be honest now he needed to remember his feeling of exultation as, string by string, he had manipulated his unwitting friend. To have had such envious hatred of a man whom he truly loved!

They had tracked him from the park; and he must now track them. His last contact: the day of Peter's return. By prearrangement with Jerry, he had posted a notice on the third-floor bulletin board in the General Studies Building: PUPPIES FOR SALE—CALL EL 7-2390 AFTER 9:00 P.M. It told them Peter Bradley would leave the house at that hour, carrying the film. The confirmation: a thrown kiss. He had with consummate skill and sureness carried out his plan. Even now he felt the prickle of pride, and his self-humiliation was the greater for instantly realizing it.

All afternoon he walked the stark and windy lake front beneath the Albion bluffs, composing in his mind the details of his "Confession." It must be told ruthlessly, without a word of self-justification. But the sands of the shoreline kept giving way beneath his feet. In the late afternoon he drove into Chicago, parked the car, bought a notebook, and checked in at the Palmer House.

In a high room, looking down on the elevated tracks below, he noted that the window was sealed, and then began to write. Presently: "... They would have been watching me for some time then. Or they may even have put the boy up to it. I rather think they got to him afterwards. This I propose to find out if I am given the opportunity. They had liaison within the University itself. The boy's name was Osterman. He dropped out of my classes at the end of the semester, but he used to turn up now and then in a group that called themselves the Imagists..."

It was after nine when Janet called him. He had long since told himself he had no right to expect that she would call. But all evening long he had been writing with an almost superstitious haste against the moment when the phone might ring. It was as though time were the measure of truth. The notebook pages were scarred with his deletions, for over and over again he had sought to justify himself and scratched out the words. A lifetime of such reflex could not be stilled at a sitting, especially by one who taking pen in hand had always fancied himself a potential Proust.

His voice showed the strain when he answered the phone.

"Are you all right, Eric?"

"Yes. And you?"

"I'm fine," Janet said. "It's over now . . . the ceremony. Just ashes. We put them beneath an oak tree in the place where all the Bradleys are . . . near his son."

He had known of course that there had been a child, but never before had either Janet or Peter spoken of him to him.

"Now there's the other," Janet went on, "why he died. It doesn't seem important when a man's reduced to a little box of ashes."

"Janet, don't."

But she went on: "I kept thinking all day of the places I hadn't gone with him because I wasn't always sure he wanted me. It seemed so indecent—so grotesque to have him all—like a trinket at my wrist."

"For the love of God, Janet . . ."

"Eric, there has to be some deeper meaning to a man. What did his death mean to the person who killed him?"

"I too want to find that out," Mather said quietly.

"Then tell me quickly. I can bear it."

Something in the way she said the words made him say: "Peter was pure, Janet. There was no corruption in him."

"I'm much aware of that. Eric, I can take a cab and come downtown—just for an hour. I want to leave this house for a while."

He looked at the key lying on the table beside the phone. "Room 723," he said.

20

By the time they finished dinner, Marks knew several things about Anne Russo which he had not known: that she had a brother, an archeologist now digging with the British in Egypt—an Egyptologist was in no way to be confused with a United Arab Republican—and that her father and mother had a farm in northern Connecticut to which they had retired when her father left the newspaper; he still wrote editorials when he got angry enough. But on the whole, the evening had not gone as Marks would have liked. His was too grim a business to mix well with pleasure.

"When all this is over..." he said when they reached the street, and then cut the sentence off: it sounded like a brush-off. "Anne, if you're not in a hurry I'd like your help in an experiment. It won't take long."

In the car he said: "We're going to the Bradley house."

"Not housebreaking?"

"No. It's the outside I'm concerned with now."

Anne sat silently. Traffic was light. A cold wind had come up and the side window was open. Marks offered to close it. "No. It's real," she said, "the wind. I was forgetting again."

"So was I," Marks said, "which is much worse." Her ungloved hand lay on the seat between them. Marks laid his upon it and Anne turned hers, palm to palm, and held it. They were both remembering when this had happened before, her holding hard to his hand: when she had had to identify Peter Bradley.

A few cars were parked along the street in front of the Bradley house. Traffic was very sparse. A light burned in the second-floor apartment, but low and deep within the room. It was to be supposed that it was left burning much of the time. All the lights were on in the first-floor apartment.

"I don't suppose you noticed that night if there were lights on there?" Marks said, indicating the first-floor windows beneath which they were standing.

"No," Anne said. "I was trying to catch up. I could hear the others down the street, but I couldn't see them. It's a dark street, isn't it?"

He looked up at the street lamp a few feet from the Bradley steps, a sharp light which nonetheless gave off very little illumination. They waited at the bottom of the steps for a man to pass. He murmured "good evening," and they answered. He turned in a few doors down the street.

Marks took off his hat and said: "Do you mind putting this on for a minute?"

"No," Anne whispered. She knew now what he was about.

He put the hat at an angle he wanted, and brushing her hair back with his hand, he saw her lips tremble. "Now just stand where you are—at the bottom step." He tilted her chin so that she would be looking up. "No one would believe that what I'm doing just now is in the line of duty."

Anne laughed nervously.

"Head up," he said, "as though you were looking at the door." He went up the steps. The vestibule doors were half-glass, smoked-glass with etched floral patterns around the frame through which the light from within was multi-colored, prismatic. Marks went into the vestibule and stood there a moment, letting the door close behind him. There was mail again in the Bradley box. He closed his eyes to make sure the afterglow from his having looked into the street lamp had faded. Then he opened the door. For a second or two he could not see anything, then Anne, but only as a figure until he started down the steps, walking very slowly. Even then he had to shade his eyes with his hand in order to see her well: the street light was blinding to anyone coming down the steps. Not until he was alongside her could he really see her features.

He posted Anne in several places, then on the sidewalk in front of the building while he observed her from the steps. He could not see her clearly from any of them. "And I have twenty-twenty vision," he said under his breath.

Across the street they stood for a moment and looked up at the Bradley windows. The floor lamp burned over an empty chair near the study door. The blinds had not been drawn, everyone having gone away in daylight. Marks put the fingers of both hands to his lips and then tossed them toward the house. "Like this?"

"Yes," Anne said, scarcely audible.

They walked to the car in silence.

"What does it mean, David?" Anne asked, in the car again.

"I don't know. But he could not possibly have described the man much better than you did from a chance encounter. There's something rotten in his story. But till we find out what it is, I'd ask you not to say anything."

"Of course," Anne said. "But why would Eric have described him at all?"

Marks shook his head. "He's an enigma wrapped in a dilemma. But it's my job now to find him and take off the wrappings."

"I don't think I'd like to be a detective," Anne said presently.

Marks, pursuing his own thoughts of Mather, said: "'For each man kills the thing he loves...'" He pulled himself up. "God Almighty, they've got me doing it now too. And that whole spiel is rubbish, rhymed, lisping, self-pitying rubbish."

"I don't believe Eric could kill anyone," Anne said.

"Don't bet your life on it," Marks said. "Nobody could tell you better than Eric Mather the ways there are of killing."

"You hate him, don't you?" Anne said, a sort of hurt surprise in her voice. "You really hate him. Why?"

"Because I have to. That's what it's like being a cop. You hate men for the rotten things they do and you can't afford the luxury of sorting out the sinners from their sins. In the last analysis, it's them or you."

"Which makes it terribly simple, doesn't it?" And after a moment when he said nothing: "I never knew a policeman before."

"And you often wondered why men joined the force," Marks said, hurting himself further on her behalf.

"No. I left that question to my father. He asked it often, being an Italian."

"What has that to do with it?"

"There being so many Italian gangsters."

"I would suppose," Marks said, "he sees very little difference."

"I've heard him wonder if they weren't both stems from the same root," Anne said. "But in the end, he feels, it depends on the man himself."

"It should," Marks said, "but it doesn't. A cop is a cop."

After seeing Anne inside her apartment door, Marks returned to the station house and put a round-the-clock stakeout on Mather's apartment. He was to be contacted no matter what hour Mather showed.

Marks went upstairs to find that not only was Redmond still in his office, but with him were Jim Anderson and another federal investigator named Tom Connolly. Connolly, Redmond explained, was an expert on Cuban nationals presently enjoying refuge in the United States.

Redmond and his men had narrowed the doctors to one

prime suspect, a Dr. Rodrique Corrales, the house physician of an orphanage uptown, one of the institutions from which the handkerchief might have come. He also had an office in Harlem and an interest in a "clinic" on East Eleventh Street. "You were right," Redmond said, and then explained to the federal men, "Lieutenant Marks saw a photograph Mrs. Bradley had taken outside the clinic. That's what helped us narrow it down to Corrales." He turned back to Marks. "He drives a black '59 Chevrolet sedan. We have the license number."

"And the doctor himself?" Marks said.

"Not yet." Redmond heaved a heavy sigh. "We can't pick him up and work him over like an ordinary suspect. Corrales, it turns out, is a big *macher* in the Cuban liberation movement."

"But an American citizen." Anderson went on reproachfully: "I wouldn't say you can't pick him up, Captain. But it would be wise to have the goods on him first. He's a man of some importance, and his friends are politically most useful to our interests."

"But if he's a murderer?" Marks said.

"If he murdered Bradley, he must of course be prosecuted," Anderson said, "I am only suggesting it will be difficult on the basis of such evidence as you have to date."

To Marks his words had suggested something else: he felt that Anderson had made a distinction when he said: "If he murdered Bradley..." It caused the Lieutenant to wonder whether other murders were permitted the doctor.

"Which is not to say you are on the wrong track," Anderson added, opening the briefcase he hoisted up on Redmond's desk. He took out what looked to be a news photograph of a crowd of demonstrators. "Could we have the magnifying glass again, Captain?"

Under the glass, he pointed to a good-looking young man, distinguished by a very flashy smile.

"Dr. Corrales?" Marks asked.

"That's the man," Anderson said.

Marks looked at the picture again. "Hey!"

"Very good! You're an observant man, Marks."

Next to Corrales was a face which bore striking resemblance to the portrait that had been drawn from Eric Mather's description.

"What was the occasion?" Marks asked of the crowd picture.

"The arrival of Castro's first ambassador to the United Nations. It was taken in the U.N. Plaza."

"Was Corrales for or against Castro then?"

"Against, and presumably he still is." He glanced at Connolly who was unwrapping a cigar. "We shall be anxious to evaluate anything you pick up on him. I suppose much will depend on who this gentleman turns out to be." He indicated the dark-browed suspect in Bradley's killing.

"You have nothing on him?"

"You haven't found out his name for us yet," Anderson said in his bland way which was every bit as biting as Fitzgerald's sarcasm. "However, Mr. Connolly assures me that out of—how many people, Tom, in this picture?"

"Thirty-seven."

"Out of thirty-seven people here on whom we have fairly complete information this man is not among them."

"And I'd like to add," Connolly said, "I don't think he is connected with Cuban affairs."

"Eric Mather said he reminded him of one of the Russian diplomats," Marks said.

"Interesting," Anderson murmured, turning the photo around for another look. "This Eric Mather—he's your specialty, isn't he, Marks?"

"I've been out of touch with him for twenty-four hours. I just put a stake-out on his home."

"And you expect him to return there?"

Marks met Anderson's eyes straight on. "Yes," he said, "I do."

Anderson nodded and proceeded to put the crowd photo back in his briefcase. Marks caught sight within the case of the box in which Bradley had brought the film into the country. Anderson surprised him staring at it. The F.B.I.

man laughed. "I didn't steal it, Marks. Captain Redmond will explain it to you." He closed the bag and held out his hand first to Redmond. "I'm sorry we had no more to contribute to your investigation. But you seem to be doing remarkably well on your own." To Marks he said simply: "Good luck."

It crossed Marks's mind then that Mather might just possibly be in federal custody already.

"I don't get it," Marks said when he and Redmond were alone. "Are they asking us to lay off this Dr. Corrales?"

Redmond knocked out his pipe in the empty wastebasket. "I see two possibilities, Dave. They're playing it cool till they find out what it's all about—Bradley probably did bring something into the country—on microfilm by as simple a means as a false-bottomed box." He drew four lines on a scratch pad. "The bottom of the box, the microfilm, the false bottom, the legitimate film strips. As I said, either they don't know yet and want to run even with us, or they already know more than we do and hope that our due process won't break open their international cover system. Connolly, by the way, is C.I.A."

"So where does that leave us, Captain?"

"Full speed ahead in the morning. Phone in before you come down, Dave. If Corrales is available uptown, we'll pick you up on the way."

21

Opening the door to his room ten minutes after Janet
called, he left it open, and every time the elevator stopped
he looked out to see if it were she, and every time when
she did not come he felt reprieved. The urge kept building
in him to leave the notebook on the bed—the door open—
and himself to flee. He could see her in this room, sitting
with the notebook beneath the reproduction of autumn
colors in Brown County—trying perhaps to decipher the
words he had scratched out.

The fact remained that he had not killed Peter. For all
the crossing out he had done, the unexpected truth pared
down to in his scrutiny of self was that the man he killed
was Eric Mather...who now was simply taking a long
time dying. Agamemnon died tonight: how aptly he had
spoken in that grandiloquent cry of self-recrimination!

Janet when she came took him by surprise. Deeply sunk
in his own thought, he had not heard the elevator. She
stood in the doorway, her coat open, purse and gloves in
hand, like a young girl who had been running. He leapt to
his feet and crossed the room. Then both of them just stood
facing each other as though a phantom wall rose up between them. He opened his arms, a gesture of helplessness,

but Janet crashed into them. He held her close then, freeing one hand just long enough to close the door behind her. He brushed her forehead with his lips. She smelled of fresh air, of cleanness.

"I am alive," she said over and over again, "and I want to live."

Finally she pushed gently away from him and studied his face—as he did hers. Her eyes were deeply circled, the more blue for the darkness under them.

"You too have suffered," she said, touching her fingertips to his cheek. "I hope Peter didn't." She looked away, saying it. "He could never bear pain. Sometimes I've thought you like it."

"It has served me—in the absence of other things." He turned and made a vague motion toward the corner chair. "Would you like a drink?"

"No."

"I haven't eaten," he said. "Not that I care."

She sat on the edge of the bed. "Why are you here, Eric?"

He shook his head and smiled a little.

"Why am *I* here—in this room?" she said then. "The family has gone to bed—except John. He's gone to see a patient. He dropped me off here."

"No questions?"

"None of the Bradleys ever ask that kind of question," Janet said.

"Pride?"

"Of a certain kind, I suppose."

He sat on the floor at her feet, his elbow on the bed, his hand where she could touch it if she wished. "I should always be asking questions of you, Janet, wanting you to tell me more, and again more."

She smiled, a little color creeping into her cheeks. "I needed that kind of love," she said quietly.

"I worship you, Janet. I haven't the worth or the right, but it is so nonetheless, and I'm too weak *not* to say it to you now."

"Do not worship me, Eric. I worshipped Peter . . . and it wasn't a satisfactory substitute for love." She leaned back and spread her hand on the bed. "I didn't want to hurt him, so I fought—myself—in every way I knew. I asked him not to leave me—the night he came home from Athens. But I knew in my heart it was false. I wanted him to go . . . and you to stay. If you had come back, Eric . . ." She looked down at him, through him, seeing the supposed lost moment, and then beyond it. "And worst of all, I'm not at all sure now he didn't know."

"No wonder he went so willingly then, God damn him!" Mather cried, embracing the insight she suggested, and with it bursting the bonds of guilt in which he had tried to bind himself.

"Eric, Eric." She tried to reach him, but he drew back from the touch of her hand.

"Didn't he laugh in your face?"

"He would have been too kind for that—too civilized."

"But he went all the same, didn't he? He had nothing to fear from his friend Eric—Eric the cripple!"

Her sudden fury matched his own. She struck him hard across his face. The sound of it seemed to linger in the after-silence. She said: "I have never allowed anyone to say that of you in my presence, and you will not say it either."

His anger fled and he knew he had again sought justification where actually there was none. One's guilt was one's own: nothing qualified it. "Oh, Janet, dearest woman. If only faith could make man whole." He leaned his head on the bed beside her. She stroked it gently, her hand cool where it lingered on his forehead, his cheek. It smelt faintly of cologne.

"We aren't any of us ever whole, Eric. It's only in love that we come close to wholeness—and even that takes two to make one whole."

"I don't think I have ever loved before," he said.

"Are you afraid?"

"No. Not at the moment."

"Then you won't ever be afraid again."

"You don't know," he said. "I wish you never needed to know."

"I don't. I've never been one who had to start things from the beginning. I think photography has taught me that the 'now' carries enough of the past to answer all we need to know." She rested her fingers at his temple. He seemed to feel her pulse in them. It was his own, beating against her touch.

They did not speak for a time. Then she said: "Will you go back tomorrow?"

"Yes."

"Can we go together?"

"No. I think not. I must go alone on the first flight."

"Will you come to me—or shall I come to you?"

"I'll come . . . as soon as I can."

"Eric?"

He raised his head and looked at her.

"You want to—don't you?"

"With all the soul that's in me."

She smiled. "Don't move now. Not till I've gone." And leaning down, her hand beneath his chin, she kissed him softly but lingeringly on the mouth.

22

Redmond, Herring and Pererro picked Marks up at a few minutes past nine the next morning, Pererro at the wheel.

"Who's minding the store?" Marks asked.

Redmond, whose mood was as gray as the sky overhead, said: "The Inspector himself came round to cheer us up."

"Yes," Marks said, "he cheered me up this morning too. I failed to turn him in a report on yesterday's business. But he's right on one thing. I've goofed on Mather. He might have broken if we'd sweated him early."

"Let's concentrate now on Corrales," Redmond said. "At most Mather is accessory to the murder, wouldn't you say?"

"Yes, to give the devil his due, I think that's about right. He didn't expect Bradley's death. I spent the midnight hours doing up my own dossier on him. It reads like a term paper in psychology. I can't wait to show it to the Inspector."

For the first time that morning Redmond laughed.

They drove north through Central Park, up Seventh Avenue and then across to Lenox through a bleak and angry slum. Pererro pointed out one of the children's homes he and Herring had visited.

"Rats and rickets," Herring said. "Uncle Sam, take it away. No hablo Español."

"I didn't think of that," Redmond said, reminded by Herring's remark. "For his own convenience Corrales may not speak English."

"He got through clear enough to old Fred Bolardo at the lumberyard except for his name," Herring said, "if he's the same doc." Then he added: "Man, he's got to be."

As soon as they got out of the car, one of the men on the stake-out joined them and pointed out the second-floor window of Dr. Corrales's office. The red brick building was roughly divided, first-floor shops, second-floor offices, and residential from there up to judge by the milk bottles, beer cans, and laundry in the windows.

"Any patients with him?" Redmond asked.

"No, sir. No morning office hours. He's been on the phone most of the time."

"Is the place bugged?"

"Yes, sir, but not by us."

"Tell me something I don't know," Redmond growled.

"Or that Corrales doesn't know," Marks added. "Where's his car?"

"The black sedan wedged into that no-parking zone." The detective pointed to the corner.

"Let's get the technical truck up here," Marks said. "The main thing: any fragments of glass that might have clung to his shoes, glass from an electric light bulb. There might just be a chance on the foot pedals."

Dr. Corrales looked startled as the four detectives walked through the shabby waiting room and through the open door of his office. Cutting his phone conversation short, he flashed them a smile. It was something he turned off and on easily, Marks thought, and his good looks came and went with it. He stood up to meet them. "Gentlemen of the police, I presume."

Redmond pocketed his identification. "You were expecting us, Doctor?"

"I am not exactly a stranger to the American constabulary. I am sometimes honored, sometimes reprimanded. Which is it this morning?"

No wonder Bolardo couldn't understand him, Herring thought: he spoke too good English.

Corrales motioned to several yellowing oak chairs. "Please."

Marks could not remember having encountered a revolutionary before, but from the quick intensity of the doctor's eyes, he could suppose him a vivid example. He was lithe and muscular despite the slightness of his build. Forty.

"We'd like to know your whereabouts last Monday, Doctor, from say six o'clock in the evening on."

"Monday the twenty-fourth." Corrales flipped the pages back on his desk calendar, studied his appointments of the day, tracing them with a well-manicured finger. A hand scarcely to be associated with rats and rickets. "You know I suppose that I sometimes work at a clinic on Eleventh Street?"

"Yes."

"I was there before six and until, perhaps, eight o'clock. Then I picked up my car and came uptown, stopping for my dinner at a favorite restaurant of mine—Las Palmas on Fourteenth Street. I sometimes meet with my friends there. I made two calls, yes—a child with pneumonia whom I moved that night from the Misericordia Orphanage on Lenox Avenue to the hospital."

"You moved the child yourself?"

"Certainly not. I arranged the ambulance."

"What time was this, Doctor?"

"It was well after ten when the ambulance got there. I was going to be late for a meeting."

"Let's back up, Doctor. You went to dinner at, say, eight fifteen?"

"Approximately."

"How long did you spend in the restaurant? We'll check this, you know."

"An hour? It must have been about that. It's my only relaxation."

"And what time did you reach the hospital?"

"A quarter to ten? I can't drive uptown in less than a half-hour."

"All right, Doctor. The other call? You said you made two."

"I stopped for a few minutes to pay my respects to the family of a friend—a funeral parlor on 108th Street near Lexington."

"What time, Doctor?"

"Ten thirty?"

"And the meeting, where was that?"

For the first time Corrales showed his impatience. "In the old Hispanic Hall on East Ninetieth. I spoke last—and it was unfortunate. I should have been on the program earlier as scheduled. They lost money having me wind up the meeting, you see. The collection suffered. I am assuming you know the cause, gentlemen? Cuban liberation?"

Herring had made notes throughout.

At this point Marks took over the interrogation. "Dr. Corrales, you drive a black sedan—a 1959 Chevrolet?"

"I do."

"May we have the keys to the car?"

"For what purpose, may I ask?"

"To examine the car."

"I understand that. But isn't it time I was informed of the purpose of your visit? I'm not sure I shouldn't have my lawyer present before we go any further."

"Suit yourself, Doctor. A man of some distinction was the victim of a homicidal attack—not far from your clinic."

"Ah, yes of course," Corrales said, leaning back slowly in his chair with the air of someone suddenly realizing graver implications than he had at first suspected. "And closer still to where I have made the arrangement to park my car." He took his car keys from his pocket and offered them.

Pererro took them and left.

"An unusual parking arrangement, wouldn't you say?" Marks continued.

"Not at all. I had been the victim of having my car broken into."

"Something of value was stolen, Doctor?"

Corrales hesitated. "Yes, Lieutenant, a case of surgical instruments."

Marks heard the sound, almost a snort, from Redmond: he had predicted that the doctor would have a story waiting for them. He did not take his eyes from Corrales, however, and leaning on the desk he asked: "And a handkerchief, Doctor?"

"There were several—two or three at least in the case."

"Did you report the theft to the police?"

"I did not—which is why I am now distressed. The physicist was knifed, was he not?"

"Beautifully," Marks said.

The doctor looked at his hands. "I am . . . distressed," he repeated.

Marks glanced at Herring: they were coming full circle now to his and Pererro's wild improvisations, the thing that had put him in mind of Janet Bradley's picture. "Why did you not report so serious a loss, Doctor?"

Corrales moistened his lips. "I am not licensed to practice surgery in the United States, Lieutenant. I was afraid of that kind of investigation."

Redmond said: "When was the surgical case stolen, Doctor?"

"Oh, it was two or three weeks ago."

"Have you replaced it?"

"Not as yet, no."

"Then why take such precautions in parking the car—after the fact?"

Corrales said: "Because in my other, my patriotic profession—you do not know what it means to have to be a professional patriot, sir—I am often the custodian of certain things I should prefer not to have to carry. I will speak plainly, for your men will soon discover—if the vandals who smashed the window of my car to get what they took from it had broken into the trunk that night, they would have discovered an arsenal."

The detectives digested that bit of information for a moment. Kid gloves, Marks remembered. The same thought must have occurred to Redmond. He said: "There will be charges growing out of such possession, Doctor."

But not of homicide, Marks thought, that whole theory seeming to crumble. They were back on the street where Fitzgerald had wanted them in the first place, looking for a gang of thugs who attacked Bradley in the moments of his recovery from the blow on the head; two separate crimes. And yet there was Mama Fernandez's testimony: the call out of "Doctor!" But wasn't Bradley himself very often called Doctor?

Herring spoke for the first time: "Dr. Corrales, have you been out of town at any time since Monday night?"

For the first time something happened to disconcert the man, Marks thought, something in his eyes changed. He recovered almost at once: "Ah, I see—the old watchman, Bolardo. I read the newspapers, Officer. Having certain things on my conscience—irrelevant to your investigation, but nonetheless—I did not want to risk such trouble as I am now in. I have not been in the neighborhood since. But neither did I want to call attention to myself by my absence. I telephoned Bolardo with the simple lie."

"The surgical instrument is not irrelevant to our investigation, Doctor," Redmond said coldly, and then because he was a man who at some point had to throw away the kid gloves, he added: "You didn't by any chance give the thief a short course in how to use it?"

Corrales smiled blandly. "I do not understand."

"Think it over. It may come to you." He led the way out, Herring and Marks following.

On the wall, near the door to the office, was a picture of

Corrales, younger, but with the same smile. He was in uniform. Marks lifted it from the nail. "May I borrow this, Doctor?"

"I would prefer not to have it in the newspapers. I do not wish to further jeopardize the work of our committee by my personal blundering."

"I don't intend to give it to the newspapers," Marks said, and took the picture with him.

On the street, a considerable crowd now pushing the police cordon around them, the technical men had arrived and commenced their work on the car.

A forlorn chance at best, Marks thought.

Redmond was instructing Herring and Pererro. "I want every goddamned step of his itinerary checked out and clocked to the minute."

Marks and he took a cab, leaving the car with the younger detectives. Neither of them said much on the way downtown. "What are you going to do with that?" Redmond indicated the photograph in Marks's hands.

"Have a couple of people look at it. Janet Bradley for one."

A few minutes later Redmond said: "Did you believe him?"

"I'll bet he could tell it the same way again," Marks said. "Letter perfect. You prophesied that yourself, remember?"

"So did Anderson," Redmond growled.

"I wonder if he rehearsed him," Marks said.

Redmond looked at him: something very close to the same thought had crossed his mind. Then he said: "I don't think so, Dave. One of our leading physicists is not an expendable. You and I have to believe that. Otherwise . . ." He left the sentence unfinished.

23

It was oddly comforting to contemplate other men's destinies when you fairly well knew your own. The plane could go down in a crash of course. Mather wondered briefly if in such a case his notebook were recovered from the wreckage what the investigators would make of it. They always looked for sabotage, the planted bomb, the suicide proposing to take with him the plane's full complement. A small item in the Chicago paper he was still holding in his hand by the time the plane was soaring over the Allegheny Mountains told of the burial at Moncton Grove of Peter Bradley's ashes, while the New York police were still investigating the circumstances of his murder.

This being the early flight, his companions were mostly business men, starting their day soon after the opening of the offices of their New York conferees. Their Chicago suburb families would expect them home for dinner, the children waiting up ... He had always been fond of children: with them he was—what he was, their make-believe his perfect dish. He wondered then what Janet's child was like and why there had been no others.

Moving through the terminal to the limousine he picked up a copy of the morning *Times*. On the second page he saw the likeness of Jerry, the police artist's re-creation from his description. It was remarkably good, he thought. But thinking about Jerry now, he regretted having given the description, its appearance in the papers. Until now Jerry would have felt secure. He would have supposed Eric Mather sealed within the conspiracy, doubly sealed by Bradley's death. Now he would not know how much Mather had told the police, how much he had been able to tell the police. Jerry might be on the run.

The limousine was bound in by the morning traffic, the whole of it oozing forward like a log-jam on a river, the people within the cars and buses as helpless as wood-worms. What an insignificant thing a man was truly.

He forced himself to read the *Times* story adjacent to the picture. Inspector Joseph Fitzgerald was a garrulous Irishman, a master at saying nothing with an air of profundity. His intent seemed to be to create the impression that the police were not telling all they knew. One might hope to God that this were so, Mather thought. He turned to the page where the story was continued. At the bottom of the column he read: "Professor Eric Mather, missing from his home for twenty-four hours . . ." And there, maddeningly, the story was suspended, cut off midsentence by the compositor at the column's end and continued nowhere.

But the possibilities were not numerous. He could himself finish the sentence easily: ". . . is being sought for questioning." He wondered if Jerry would put it together that way too.

If the police were actually looking for him, however, Mather felt that he dared not go home. They might take him into custody. He would have to tell them what he knew; he would want to. It was all written in the notebook he carried now in the valise along with his overnight things, all—up to this minute. But it was not enough by which to measure anything but ignominy.

He went directly to the University. Here too they would be alerted for him possibly. But he had promised his chairman to return in time for the afternoon classes: a little time of grace might still be left him if he hurried.

Mather entered the General Studies building by the side door, opposite the park. Two girls were talking with the door attendant, and none of them knew him by sight. A better place for anonymity than a city university would be hard to find. Now he had to take the chance of charming a giddy girl who, he knew, would recognize him. He had tried to remember her name. He had had to leave a blank in his "Confession" though he could see her vividly in memory, pawing her face, wagging her wild red head while he had spouted Byron in the tavern. Then suddenly, opening the door to the Records Office, he had it: Sally. *Sally in Our Alley. . .*

He was not sure that it was the same girl now sitting at the desk until she looked up and recognized him. She opened her mouth, but closed it again without saying his name when he put his finger to his lips. An older woman turned from the files where she was working. Mather smiled and bowed a little toward her. With a curt nod she returned to her work and Sally came to the railing, asking loudly: "Can I help you?"

Close to him she said, scarcely above a whisper: "Mr. Mather, the police . . ."

He deliberately became off-hand. The girl was far too eager to conspire with him. "I'm trying to help them—in a certain matter," he said.

"Oh." She was disappointed.

"Sally, the boy who introduced us, Osterman?" She nodded, pleased now by the language of togetherness. "Do you see him still?"

"I don't go out with him if that's what you mean. Actually, it's vice versa since that night—you know? I told you I worked in the Records Office?" Vaguely Mather remembered it now, but he had dug it sharply out of his memory needing to remember Osterman. "Common, you know. Unclean." Sally made a face saying it that in his present disposition and relieved of this pressure he would have cherished: the girl who, for all her phony aspirations, could say that of herself. "And I thought we had a future. I do love the name Jeffrey..."

"Sally..."

"Sh..." She rolled her eyes toward the other clerk. "That's Miss Katz. Gee, I wish I could help you, Mr. Mather."

"Could you find Osterman for me now? I must know where he is, whatever class he's in. I must talk to him."

"Gee..." Sally said again, once more casting the backward glance toward Miss Katz who was now banging the file drawers, opening and closing one, then another.

"He's an English major," Mather prompted.

Sally drew a deep breath and called out: "I'm going out for coffee, Miss Katz. Okay?" She was on her way, Mather opening the gate for her before the woman could make up her mind what to say.

In the hallway Mather said: "I'll watch for you here."

"Do you want me to tell him...?"

"Nothing. Don't even speak to him. Just come back and tell me where he is."

Mather spent ten minutes in a booth of the men's room halfway down the corridor. He was not a bathroom reader, but the time was interminable, the confinement with such literary examples of the college-educated as were to be read on the wall, nauseating. He took Carlyle's *Hero Worship* from his bag and read a few paragraphs. Legs came and went. He heard an occasional monosyllabic greeting at the washbasins. Then the bell rang for the change of classes. He looked at his watch. It was five minutes to eleven.

On his first trip back to the Records Office, Sally had not returned. The second trip he came out in time to catch up with her in the hallway before she reached her office.

"He just went into study hall—room 408. I waited, you see, to find out where he'd go at the change of classes."

"Bless you, Sally, you are intelligent and a princess."

"I won't tell anyone I saw you, Mr. Mather. But it said

in the paper this morning that the police were looking for you."

Mather wanted to go quickly. The hall was by no means deserted. But the girl put her hand on his arm to delay him, and when he stayed, she removed it quickly. "I've been thinking whether I ought to tell you. You know that picture of the man in *The Times* this morning?" Mather nodded. "I think I saw him once. Only I thought he was an F.B.I. man. He came in and asked for me, and then he wanted to see your record."

"I know," Mather said.

"But the thing I wanted to tell you—the reason I remembered him—it's two or three months ago, you see— but the man that was with him, his partner?"

Mather said: "A tall handsome young man . . ."

Sally nodded. "I saw him with Jeffrey Osterman. I was kind of following after Jeffrey in the park. He sat down and I was going to walk by him, you know, casual? But that man came up and put his arm around Jeffrey so naturally I went the other way."

24

Marks checked with the men staking out Mather's apartment building on Perry Street. Not hide nor hair. A second day's mail now crowded the box. He called the chairman of Mather's department at Central University. The chairman himself was at that hour taking Mather's class in the Victorian novel. He called Louise Steinberg. She had not heard from Mather.

"That morning when he broke down at the Bradleys' and ran out—what caused it? What did he say to Janet, or she to him? You were there, weren't you?"

"Yes, but they didn't say anything. They just stood there and when Janet turned away, he broke down. But, Dave . . ."

"Yes?"

"Eric called her that same night."

"The night before last," Marks said. "What time?"

"It must have been close to midnight. I wasn't going to call her to the phone, but she was still up . . ."

"Did you hear what was said by either of them?"

"No. Janet took the call in the bedroom and by the time I got back to the kitchen to hang up the phone they were already off the line."

Suggesting one thing, Marks thought: a date to meet, and presumably a place. "Louise, I asked you yesterday morning..."

"I know, but you asked me if I'd seen him. And it was in the church. I couldn't very well run after you when I thought of it."

"I don't always get across," Marks said, as angry with himself as with Louise. "Where can I reach Mrs. Bradley now?"

"I can give you the flight number," Louise said.

He was waiting at the ramp when Janet came off the plane. She was a moment recognizing him. "Lieutenant Marks," he said.

"I remember now," she said, and allowed him to take her suitcase. She had no other luggage. Her dark blue suit, the white blouse fluffy at her throat, became her as few widows could claim of their weeds.

"There are some questions I need to ask you. I can drive you home meanwhile." Then, because she said nothing and he felt some commiseration, not too lugubrious, was indicated, he added: "You must be tired."

"I'm ... nothing," Janet said, but smiled at him. A gracious lady, Marks thought, which was perhaps the most deceptive of feminine characteristics. He had known some mighty gracious bitches in his day.

He decided to tell her on the way into the city of Dr. Corrales, the fiasco he had seemed to make of the police case. He dwelt as little as possible on the weapon aspect. It could not be avoided altogether. The name was in no way familiar to Janet. "I'm reasonably sure Peter did not know him either. Peter was apolitical, you know. He had been in school when it was considerably less than fashionable. Too many of the scientists he admired got bogged down—and hurt."

Which attitude, Marks thought, made Bradley the better instrument for the plotters. Marks opened the glove compartment of the car and took out Corrales's picture. Janet looked at it carefully.

"I've never seen the man to my knowledge," she said, and for him returned the framed photo to the compartment.

Marks said: "The picture in your book, Mrs. Bradley, the woman on the stoop looking down at the child?"

"Yes."

"It's a terrific picture."

"Because the subject herself was," Janet said. "She was a girl in trouble."

"You talked with her?"

"Oh, yes. I gave her twenty dollars, supposedly for allowing me to use her picture. It made it easier for her to accept it."

"Did she tell you the trouble she was in?"

"It was not hard to guess," Janet said. "It was in her eyes, the way she looked—wanting the child."

Marks thought for a moment. Then he asked: "How did you happen to be there?"

"I was following the child wherever he wandered—photographing him—with his mother's permission. By that time he had become so accustomed to me, he no longer noticed."

"Where did he live, Mrs. Bradley?"

"On Eighteenth Street near Second Avenue."

"And he wandered all the way to Eleventh Street?" Marks said.

Janet looked at him, not understanding.

"Dr. Corrales's clinic is on Eleventh Street."

Janet shook her head. "I simply don't get the connection. The picture I assume you're talking about was taken on Eighteenth Street, no more than a half-block from the child's home."

"... No clinic there, no doctor's office?" Marks was trying now to dislodge his own fixed idea.

"I couldn't say positively," Janet said, "but I'm fairly certain. It was an ordinary tenement house like most of the buildings in that block."

"I could have sworn I saw a sign in the background of your picture," Marks said.

Janet, twisting round in the seat, getting on her knees, opened her suitcase on the back seat. "Louise had the quaint idea I'd want the book with me."

A moment later she had it open to the page in question. Marks pulled off the road to look at it. A little square of reflected sky shone in the window behind the girl. Plainly it was not a sign: it had simply become one in his imagination.

"I shouldn't be surprised," Marks said after a bit, "if the fixed idea has ruined more people than it's improved."

Janet smiled. "That sounds almost un-American."

Not until they drove up to her house did he put the important question. He asked it with no particular emphasis, but watched closely to see her reaction: "Have you heard from Eric Mather in the last day or so?"

Janet hesitated, then with a faint uplift of her head— pride? defiance?—she said: "I saw him in Chicago last night."

"He should not have left New York," Marks said quietly. "Do you know where I can reach him?" There was no urgency in his voice, and having met Janet at the ramp of the plane he knew she had not seen the New York papers.

"At his own apartment or the University. He returned by the first flight this morning."

Or so he had told her he was doing, Marks thought. "Was he in Chicago—because of you?"

Janet tried to be as honest as she could. "I think that's possible, Lieutenant, but I am not sure."

Marks got out and opened the door for her, then got her suitcase from the back seat. Louise was waiting at a discreet distance, standing in the vestibule doorway.

Janet offered Marks her hand. The handshake was brief, its pressure light. She insisted on taking her own suitcase.

"You have my sympathy," Marks said.

She looked at him sharply, startled. Then she turned to

meet Louise who was running down the steps, her arms open. If the words, spoken rather late to have reference to her husband, might in any way forewarn her of further shock ahead, Marks was satisfied. That Mather had made the trip to confide, to confess himself to her, the detective could easily believe. But if that were so, he could not believe that Janet Bradley would now conceal it.

25

Mather climbed the stairs to the fourth floor, avoiding the use of the crowded elevators. He would take his chances now, but no more of them than necessary. He found the study hall crowded, some of his own students at the tables. He nodded at those who noticed him and ignored the whispering that sometimes followed in his wake. He laid a firm hand on Osterman's shoulder, coming up unnoticed behind him. As the boy looked up, he said: "I want to talk with you. Come."

Without protest the boy got up, leaving his open books, and followed him. Mather led the way to the English Department's common room at the end of the hall. It was deserted as usual. Mather closed the door, and finding a key on the inside, turned it.

Osterman was at the age when his features changed, month to month. Mather had thought him a good-looking boy, rather virile, when he had him in his classes. That no doubt accounted for the fury with which he had struck him when the boy had put his hand in his—and after which, except for the night in the Red Lantern, he had determinedly not thought of him at all. Now the boy's face was soft and sallow, an effete corruption showing at his

mouth that sickened Mather. He did not want to know
more than his own instinct told him of Osterman's relationship with the big blond partner to his own conspiracy. He
wanted to know but one thing.

"How do I get in touch with Tom? Where can I reach
him?"

"Tom?" The eyes were insolent.

Mather kept his hands at his side, but the boy saw the
clenching of his fists and his own eyes strayed toward the
door. Mather had left the key in it.

"I have a witness who will swear to your association
with him."

"Mr. Mather, why do you hate me so much? I've never
harmed you. I've tried with all my might not to embarrass
either one of us. I even tried at first to do what you said I
should—to find a girl. Remember, after you hit me?" The
boy was pouting, whining like a righteous child in its own
defense.

"Or a psychiatrist, I think I said."

"Do you know what I did, Mr. Mather? I walked
straight across the park, into the building and asked the
first girl I met to go out with me that night. And in spite of
all the show *you* made over her in the Red Lantern, she
was the most vulgar, horrid, pretentious hag. Besides
which, she smelled."

"And so you went back to the park for fresh air. And got
picked up by Tom."

"You make it sound so vulgar."

"A pickup, man or woman, is vulgar," Mather said.

"Oh, you Puritan! You're a New England prude, if you
don't mind my saying it, Mr. Mather."

"I don't mind what you say—or to whom you say it,
Osterman. I want one small piece of information from you.
You took a notice from the bulletin board on Monday.
What did you do with it?"

"I read it to Tom over the telephone. He's been wanting to get a dog, one he wouldn't have to pay much
money for."

Dear God, Mather thought. The boy could not be that simple. "But you took the notice down from the board!"

"I didn't want them all to be gone before he could get there."

"What did he say to you? And when? How did you know to watch the board?"

"He asked me to. He said a friend had told him when the litter was old enough he was going to advertise it there. And last week-end when I saw him, he reminded me to watch for it and call him right away."

"What does Tom do for a living?" Mather asked. He had to know it all now. For the boy's sake, not his own.

"He's a construction engineer. He was working on the project south of the park. Now he's gone to Florida. He's promised to write to me."

"Has he taken the puppy with him?" Mather asked, sick to his bones.

"I didn't think to ask him. I shouldn't think so, but I'd have been willing to keep it for him."

Mather folded his arms. He was half-sitting on a desk. Someone rattled the door and then went away. "Jeffrey, just when did you meet him?"

"You want me to tell you that. All right. I met him when I needed him. When you struck me in the face. The next day—he'd seen it happen."

"So I'd supposed. He asked you about me?"

"Not really. He wanted to know more about me . . . and the red-headed girl. Do you know, she's had the nerve to keep going back to the Imagists? On her own!"

Mather realized that if he tried now to tell the boy what he knew of the man with whom he had taken up he would not believe him. "Don't you have any parents, Jeffrey?"

"My mother's in Boston . . . with a man."

"I see. That accounts for your knowledgeableness about New England prudes. Did you ever meet a friend of Tom's, a man he called Jerry?"

"No. We don't mix with other people. Just ourselves. He has another life to lead."

How true. "Did you see a police drawing of a man in this morning's paper, a man wanted for questioning in Professor Bradley's murder?"

"I don't read newspapers. Bradley taught here at Central, didn't he?"

"Tom and his friend and *I* myself assisted in Bradley's murder." The moment he said the words, Mather recognized the irony: his first overt confession was to this sick boy. He was the more vehement when he added: "Unless I'm able to locate Tom today, I shall tell your story as well as my own to the police."

The boy smiled a little, his round mouth unable to hold itself firm. He went deadly pale and Mather thought he was going to faint. He caught him by the arms and shook him. "You've been used, my boy, in more ways than one. Do you understand?"

"No! I'll hear from him. I know I will."

"What name did he give you? Tom what?"

"Jones. But I knew that was a joke."

"Where did you call him? That notice about the puppies —where?"

"I'll give you the number. I left the message for him."

Mather let go of him. Osterman fumbled in his inside pocket and brought out an address book, his hands trembling so much that he could scarcely open the cover, on the back of which the number was written.

Mather waited, pencil and a match packet open in his hand. The boy held the book where he could see it for himself, a Spring telephone exchange, far downtown.

"It isn't true what you said, is it?" Osterman whined. "You made it up to get Tom's number out of me?"

Mather just looked at him. He picked up his valise, took it to his desk and, removing the notebook from it, he left the case on the chair under the desk.

The boy watched him, not moving from where he stood. "I wish I'd never met him!"

"So do I," Mather said from the door.

Again he used the stairs, running down the four flights,

passing only a workman with his toolbox on the way. Reaching the main floor he decided against the trafficked corridors and went on to the basement and outdoors by way of the loading entrance.

He was on the south side of the building where the traffic was almost entirely commercial. Nonetheless, he went on for several blocks angling east and south into the hatters' district before he stepped into a public phone booth. He watched for a pause in the flow of buses and trucks, then deposited his dime and dialed.

After the second ring, a man's voice shouted above the noise at his end: "Margueritta Import Company," and when Mather did not respond at once: "Hello?"

"I must have the wrong number," Mather said and hung up. He looked up the address of Margueritta Import in the phone book. It was on DePeyster Street. He then searched for the nearest public library. The Ottendorfer branch was within walking distance.

There, in the midst of newspaper-reading derelicts, he brought his "Confession" up to date, the last words: The Margueritta Import Company, DePeyster Street.

The librarian was kind enough to give him an envelope and sell him two five-cent stamps. He addressed the envelope to Lieutenant David Marks, marked it urgent, and going out mailed it at the nearest box. Then he took the Lexington Avenue subway downtown.

26

Marks searched the study he had written of Mather the night before. In the margin of his pages was an occasional question mark, indicating a matter which at the time had seemed of dubious importance but which now remained unanswered. Finding the one he was looking for, he asked Redmond across the room, "Where's Albion, Illinois? What part of the state?"

"It's a Chicago suburb, on the lake."

Clement Rossiter refused at first to talk to him over the phone. "How do I know who you are, sir? Your telling me doesn't make it so."

Marks said: "I'll hang up. Then ask the operator to put through the call to me, David Marks, at the Houston Street precinct, New York City."

To his amazement Rossiter did just that, calling him collect. "I've been a victim once of an impersonation. I don't propose to make the same mistake twice."

"Eric Mather, a teacher in your employ at one time," Marks said briskly.

"I supposed that was why you were calling. I advised him to go to the police."

"When?"

"Yesterday," Rossiter said.

Piece by piece, Marks got the story from him.

"Do you mind telling me the offense Mather had committed?"

"He was never prosecuted, mind you. The charge was withdrawn . . . but I did not feel I could withhold such information from men I presumed to be F.B.I. agents."

"I understand," Marks said with more patience than he felt. "The offense, sir?"

"Violating a minor of the same sex."

It would be hard to find an offense more susceptible of blackmail, Marks thought. "Do you remember the bogus investigators well enough to give me a description of them, Mr. Rossiter?"

"Actually, I remember them the better for Mather's having described them to me yesterday . . ."

"The dark, pudgy one," Marks tried to propel him.

"And the tall, blond, all-American footballer."

"Right," Marks said, and thanking him, hung up.

Downstairs he picked up Detective Pierce, the most likely man available, and went directly to the University. Miss Kelly-Nobakoff was not his prime target, but because the Records Office was on the first floor, he got a newspaper from the corner vendor, and stopped off to see if Sally could identify the police composite in the morning paper. In one instance at least she had told him the truth, she had been visited by men she thought to be F.B.I. investigators.

Sally did not long withhold the story Mather had asked her to take to Lieutenant Marks. "Only I wasn't supposed to tell it unless something happened to him."

Marks assured her she might be saving her idol's life, telling it now.

"Jeffrey Osterman. Remember, I told you about him that night at the Red Lantern?"

Marks remembered. Jeffrey was another of his neat question marks in the margin of the Mather story.

27

Eric Mather left the subway at Wall Street and climbed aboveground into a wild melee of scurrying people. Lunch hour was almost over. Clerks and brokers' jobbers, stenographers and I.B.M.'ers rushed in and out of buildings and along the street like figures in accelerated motion pictures. Even conversations were thrown against him in bits and pieces: the familiar "So-ahs" punctuating everything. One phrase he caught and remembered: "You know, Michael the big noiser..."

Michael the big noiser, Mather thought, whom he would never know beyond that epithet. How often he had thought of following one conversation picked up on the city street or in a bus until its end. He was confused now in his directions. It did not matter for the moment. He had postponed a purchase until reaching "The Street." Its affluence prospered the kind of store he was looking for. He walked along Broadway until he came to Billings' Sporting Supplies. He surveyed his own reflection in the plate-glass window. He had never thought of himself as the sporting type. He went inside and asked to see a fishing knife.

"For cleaning fish?" the attendant asked.

"For killing them," he said, a smile twitching at the corners of his mouth.

"What kind of fish, sir?"

Mather could feel the sweat starting at the small of his back. He could not think of the word. The clerk played with a tuft of hair in his ear, waiting. Mather did not want to say the word "big." He had it then. "Game fish," he said.

The clerk showed him a knife with an exquisite blade, having carefully removed the shield.

"Fine," Mather said, and watched him wrap it.

On the street again, his purchase in hand, he looked up trying to gain his direction. The towering buildings swayed against the fast-rolling clouds. Rain was about to fall again. At the corner newsstand he asked the way to De-Peyster Street. A few short blocks toward the waterfront, but such a difference; glass, marble and steel giving way to brick, wood and plaster. In an alleyway he removed the knife from both paper and shield and plunged the blade through the lining of his pocket to secure it, the leather hilt available to his hand. He threw the wrappings and shield into the first trash basket.

DePeyster Street was short, ending at the waterfront, where Mather could see the cargo ships lying in their slips, their funnels and derricks obscured by the elevated highway. There were not many people, and all of them, he realized, observing from a metered parking area, were about the final tasks of closing up their businesses, stacking crates, lowering grills, hosing down platforms and loading zones. He approached one of the workmen. "You're closing up?"

"We sure are," the man said without looking up. He was sorting fruit baskets by sizes. "We open at 2:00 A.M. Twelve hours is enough."

"More than enough," Mather murmured, going on.

The name Margueritta Import Company was lettered in flaking gold on the black wooden canopy over a loading platform. At his back as he looked across the street were the walls of a vast brick warehouse. That side of the street all the way to the corner was abandoned except for a cat worrying a fish head in the gutter. Traffic on the highway rumbled constantly. Foghorns had started their rhythmic braying in the bay. Mather studied the building for a long time. Someone remained in it. He saw the shadow moving between the office light and the window. Next door was a grill-fronted fish market, hosed and locked up. Further down was a seaman's home. He saw old men come out of the glass-paneled door. Invariably they moved toward South Street and vanished along the docks. A panhandler ambled past him, reconsidered and turned back to ask him for a quarter. Mather gave him fifty cents and a "drink hearty!" The old lush shambled on. A spitting rain began to fall.

Mather drew a deep breath and crossed the street. He picked up the smell of rotting fruit as he neared the building, and remembered Jerry's asking him what kind of work he thought he did. "You sell fruit." Mather the psychic!

Baskets and crates were stacked neatly at either side of the platform. Near one of the dusty windows a pale light hung from overhead, throwing its faint rays over a cluttered desk. Mather shielded his eyes and tried to see the room better. An inside door opened on the hallway. He could see no one.

The outside door opened soundlessly to his hand. The hall beyond the office door led to what looked like a vast storage room. The smell of fruit was pungent here, no longer fetid, the sweet fresh fragrance of orange and lemon. Mather stepped into the office where a battered leather valise sat on the floor a few feet from the door. He heard voices from the storage room, faintly as from a caverned distance, droning on in conversation.

He moved quickly across to the desk and removed the phone from its receiver. He listened, thinking the voice he heard might be talking on the phone. "All right, my friend." And after the clicks the buzzing signal. He had caught the last words in a conversation, but both the phrase and the voice he knew to be Jerry's. To Jerry everyone was "my friend." He left the receiver off the hook and returned to the door to listen. He could still hear voices.

Mather knelt down and tried the valise clasp. It was locked, but the bag when he took it by both handles and wrenched them apart burst open. Underwear and socks, a striped shirt . . . He groped through it wildly, sick, despairing of finding what he sought, the identity of the owner. He listened again for the voices. They seemed to have stopped. His own heartbeat was too loud in his ears for any but the throbbing sound. He heard a laugh then.

In a zipped side-pocket of the bag he found seaman's papers and a passport. They belonged to Thomas Gregoris, a naturalized American, born in Greece. Even the passport photo had not disguised his good looks. The tall, blond, Anglo-Saxon-looking all-American was a Greek. Mather thrust the papers and passport into his own breast pocket and closed the bag. It refused to catch; he had to leave it open. At the desk he put the phone back in the cradle.

"Good luck, my friend!"

He heard the words ring down the hall and hard upon them the clack of approaching footfalls. Mather concealed himself the only place he could, behind the office door. Through the crack he watched, his hand on the hilt of the knife.

The big blond man came into the office and went to his knees at once to examine the open bag. Just as he called out, "Jer . . ." Mather in one high swift stroke drove the knife with all his power into the stooped back just beneath the left shoulder blade. The man's cry died in mid-air. He toppled over the bag to the floor.

Mather left the knife where it was and ran into the corridor. Jerry was coming from the storeroom. Mather waited. He wanted to be seen. Then he ran toward the street, waiting again outside the window that Jerry might see him. A flash of light and an explosion splintered the glass. But Mather had begun again to move. He leaped from the platform and ran, crouched, to the end of the building. He squeezed through an opening beneath the platform and waited, his stomach revolting at the stench there.

He heard Jerry's footfalls pounding overhead, then running back to the other end of the platform. He crawled out and poking his head above the platform called his name.

Another shot rang out, then another. Mather crouched down in momentary safety. Two men were watching now from the storehouse window across the way. And on the street beneath them a man had reached the police call-box. Mather sprinted toward the open street. He heard the singing bullet almost simultaneous to its report. He hit the ground, lay there a moment and began to crawl, trying to draw fire again. People were aware now: that was all he demanded. He wanted to die in the open with witnesses to his killing. A car, approaching from around the corner, had to stop suddenly or run over him. He heard the brakes. But instantly he felt a small sharp pain at the back of his head. Just for an instant he thought of a bee-sting and of his grandmother's orchard. He could hear the humming from the hive, louder and louder. Then nothing.

28

Marks had already started for DePeyster Street and had himself called Communications for the deployment of cars already in the area when the "All Cars" command came through. The narrow streets of the old city north of Wall Street were filling with people who responded in ever greater numbers as the police cars converged. Marks had to abandon his car a block from the scene and push his way on foot through the crowd.

Mather lay, face down, covered by a police raincoat. Marks lifted the coat for a moment and then spread it again. The sprawling legs protruded. No chance whatever now, Marks thought, of a mere stubbed toe. He had seen the wound at the back of Mather's head.

The officer in charge gave Marks the passport and papers. "Not his, sir. His own wallet was in his hip pocket."

The Margueritta Import Company was cordoned by police. Witnesses who had seen the killer firing from the platform were repeating their testimony...a stocky man with heavy eyebrows...The three entrances to the building were sealed off. Marks passed the word that the man was to be taken alive. Through the splintered glass of the office window Marks first glimpsed the blond prone figure on the floor there. Inspector Fitzgerald sirened his way through the crowd, not leaving the car till it reached the police cordon. Briefed by Marks, he took command.

The crowd squealed with awe, delight, whatever it is that moves a mass instinct in the presence of tragedy that is not their own, when Fitzgerald's voice boomed out over the bull horn:

"Hear me, wherever you are in there! This is Police Inspector Fitzgerald speaking. Come out, your hands in the air! You have five minutes. In five minutes we'll fill the building with a gas that will bring you out!" He repeated the ultimatum and then looked at his watch. "How many are in there?" he asked.

A uniformed sergeant said: "One dead and one alive— to the best of our knowledge, sir."

Marks selected a team of three men to go in with him. The gas threat was a device only. Contaminating the building, the police would not themselves be able to enter it for hours, perhaps to then discover that their man had escaped before their arrival. Marks and the others put on armored vests beneath their coats.

The crowd fell silent as time passed, men here and there among it clocking the countdown on their own watches.

The detectives moved cautiously into the building, the others waiting, covering Marks as he went into the office to examine the victim there. He was easily identified by the passport found on Mather. The knife in his back had its own grim eloquence.

Marks rejoined the men in the hall and they moved along it, spaced to cover one another, Marks in the lead. From the door to the storage room he saw the man he wanted, and holstered his own gun. Jerry was slumped over a desk, his hand dangling at his side, the revolver on the floor.

Marks moved quickly. He was sick of the sight and smell of blood, but he wanted to know the name of the man. His wallet yielded the identity: Jerome Freeman, born

in Boise, Idaho, forty-seven years before. Marks returned
the wallet to the owner's hip pocket. He briskly searched
the jacket pockets—a package of chewing gum, a ring of
keys, and one small key, loose, that might fit a mailbox or
a bank deposit box or a locker. He took that with him,
leaving the rest to be inventoried at the morgue.

29

"I tell you, Captain, if that doc's straight I'm crooked as a boomerang," Herring said.

Pererro added: "It was a mighty slippery story to check out, sir."

"And look, man—the knife, his story how he lost it."

"Forget the knife!" Redmond exploded. "We don't have the knife. We can't prove the murder weapon was a surgical knife."

"Yes, sir. All we got's a might-have-been. And that's the way his story checks out too. It might've been the way he told it to us this A.M. And then again it might not."

"Let's have it, point by point," Redmond said. "Then you can add this to it." He shoved the technical report on Corrales's Chevrolet across the desk. Findings: negative.

Pererro gave Dr. Corrales's statements, Herring the check-out on them.

"I was there (at the Eleventh Street Clinic) until eight o'clock."

Herring: "Corroborated by Dr. Moore at the clinic. He came on duty when Corrales left. Corrales, by the way, didn't join the clinic staff until two months ago."

"Go on," Redmond said.

"Las Palmas Restaurant on Fourteenth Street."

"Dr. Corrales ate a full-course dinner, Mexican style. Nobody clocked him, but the waiter says it took an hour at the very least."

"That's nine fifteen, give a few minutes either way," Redmond said. "Bradley had left his house by then."

"Next stop," Pererro said. "Misericordia Children's Home, Lenox Avenue and 103rd Street."

"A half-hour's drive," Redmond said. "A quarter to ten. Bradley was in Miss Russo's vestibule."

Herring said: "Miss Juanita Franco, age sixty-nine, on night duty at the children's home, quote: 'Dr. Corrales comes, he looks at the child, then he goes and calls the ambulance. Then he curses me for not doing it sooner. But I am not a doctor.'

"Question: 'Did you go to the phone with the doctor?'

"Answer: 'I stayed with the child.'

"'So that you did not actually hear him make the call?'

"'That is so.'

"Question: 'What time did the doctor arrive, Miss Franco?'

"'I do not remember. By eleven o'clock everybody was gone. I went back upstairs to clean the room.'"

Redmond grunted. "He was falling behind schedule, wasn't he?"

Herring said: "The call for the ambulance was made at ten fifteen."

Redmond said: "Bradley was dead by at least fifteen minutes."

"The ambulance rolled at ten twenty. It took them eighteen minutes to get there."

"Where's the Reid Hospital?"

"On York Avenue."

"But God's teeth, man. The Harlem hospital is virtually next door to that orphanage."

"Yes, sir," Herring said. "They get more customers than

most, but we checked, and Monday night they could have answered immediately if Corrales had called them. That child didn't last the night, Captain. Maybe that's why I'm on him. But I think he's lying to us all the way."

Redmond said: "All right. Let's hear your version of what happened."

"I got to start from the beginning. The doc says he picked up his car at the lumberyard. I say he walked to the restaurant straight from the clinic. The other boys picked up his car and used it to tail and pick up Bradley. Corrales had plenty of time to enjoy his dinner, man. He wasn't needed at Miss Russo's apartment until half-past nine. It was only a five-minutes walk. He did his 'good deed' there and drove his own car north. He was moving then, but he took time at Park and Sixty-fourth Street to throw Bradley's wallet and briefcase in a mailbox. And here's the thing, Captain: I say he called for the ambulance before he ever got to the orphanage. Maybe one of the other partners even called. Corrales must've known all day how sick that child was. He'd seen her in the morning."

Redmond shook his head. "I'm not saying it couldn't be that way, Wally. But we can't use it, not without witnesses."

"Give us time and we'll get 'em. I swear we'll get 'em."

Redmond said: "Go on with Corrales's story."

"The rest checks out. The funeral parlor on 108th Street and the Liberation meeting. Just like he said."

"It seems odd," Redmond said, "when he was late for a meeting where he was scheduled to speak that he'd stop at a wake on the way."

"I don't think you exactly call it a wake, Captain." Herring grinned. "This was one of the old-time Latin American revolutionaries, eighty-nine years old. He's been here since 1927, but they've shipped him back to Mexico for burial."

Redmond looked at him sharply. "When?"

Herring glanced at Pererro. They had in that small particular failed to check. "We'll have to find out, sir."

"Get onto it."

The phone was ringing on Redmond's desk when the two detectives left his office. When they reached the squadroom downstairs, the report was coming in on the killings in DePeyster Street.

30

Marks was not likely ever to forget the ride back to Houston Street with Fitzgerald. The targets of the Inspector's abuse were as wide as the range of police officialdom, from the Commissioner and his bright young men to the bright young men themselves. "I'll take a cop with his nose to the ground over one with it in the air any day. Wasn't it crime prevention you were interested in, Lieutenant? And look at the bloody slaughter back there. If corpses were blessings, we'd be lined up now for all eternity."

Marks, his eyes straight ahead as he took the lashing, saw young Detective Pierce's ears turn from pink to a dark glowing red. Marks knew he had failed badly on Eric Mather, trying to think his way through the man. There had been a point, he remembered, where he had himself thought of the virtues of so-called dumb cops. That Fitzgerald was right made the situation that much more uncomfortable. But that one reason for his failure lay in the fact, he was sure, that Eric Mather had wanted to die was something he could not tell Fitzgerald, certainly not in the old man's present mood.

They reached the station house and pushed through the

reporters and photographers, and over the wires and cables servicing the sound media.

"I'll be up in a few minutes, Inspector," Marks shouted.

Whether or not Fitzgerald heard him, or whether he cared if Marks ever came up, he did not know. The old man, his stone face moving like a wedge before him, was saying over and over again: "Not now, boys. Nothing for now."

Marks picked up Herring in the squadroom and went back to the car where he had asked Pierce to wait. "Tenth Street. Go up Third Avenue."

In the car he asked Herring how Corrales's story had checked out.

"Lousy by me, Lieutenant, but we can't prove it, not till we go over it with a fine tooth comb. By me you could drive a Mack truck through it."

"Or a Chevy sedan? Anything in the car?"

"Negative," Herring said.

"We got to it several days late," Marks said. "Still . . ."

"Look, man, that doc wouldn't have been in the hall after the light bulb was broken, not according to my way of seeing it. He was gone by the time they busted it."

"You're probably right," Marks said.

"You know, don't you, Lieutenant, the feds are in this up to here?" Herring indicated eye level.

"Yes," Marks said, "we may not see them, but they're in it."

Herring told him of Redmond's orders to track down the casket destined for Mexican burial. "You know how far I got? The Baltimore and Ohio freightyard. No information. Then the Captain calls me up and says we're to make no further inquiries into it. How do you like that, man?"

"They must have their reasons," Marks said, "but what I don't understand is their failure to act in the case themselves."

"It's like they wanted to get things botched up."

"If that's what they wanted," Marks said, "they got it."

Herring said: "We just got to tie the doc in now, and we got to do it ourselves."

"Is the stake-out still on him?"

"Yes, sir. Captain Redmond don't like him any more than I do."

They had reached Tenth Street and turned east. As they passed Anne Russo's apartment, Marks said: "Are you a praying man, Wally?"

"Like most of us, on occasion, Lieutenant."

"We aren't going to have a better one." Then to Pierce, Marks said: "Pull up at the lumberyard there where the gate's open."

Two men were working in the yard with a power saw as Marks and Herring got out of the car. Marks took out the key he had removed from the suicide Jerome Freeman's pocket and gave it to Herring. "Try this on the padlock while I speak to the men in back."

Marks walked through the yard, and when one of the men turned off the saw, Marks said: "It's all right. I just wanted to check the electrical outlet." It was at the side of the wall, available to anyone with access to the yard itself.

As he turned back, Herring came to meet him, the padlock and key in his hand, a wide grin on his face. "They fit, man. They were made for each other."

Marks put his arm around Herring. "Like you and me, Wally. Get yourself a warrant and bring in Corrales."

When Marks walked into Redmond's office a few minutes later it was to an unexpected silence. Men were moving in and out, and the noise from downstairs could not be shut out, but Fitzgerald and Redmond were sitting side by side at Redmond's desk, reading the same material.

Fitzgerald glanced up. "We're reading your mail, Lieutenant." He indicated the envelope on the desk. "It wasn't marked personal."

Marks picked it up, the envelope Mather had addressed to him from the public library.

31

Corrales had not talked by eight o'clock that night, at which hour the police principals in the case as well as the district attorney met with Jim Anderson in his Manhattan apartment. They met there for the simple expedient of avoiding, for the time being, the understandably clamorous press. One reason Corrales had not talked was because Anderson had requested that he not be questioned until the security picture could be put before the police.

Anderson's wife served coffee, then took her purse and gloves and went out, putting Marks in mind of Louise Steinberg's remark that she and Janet had probably seen more movies over the years than any other two women in New York.

In the middle of the highly polished diningroom table, around which the men gathered, lay several Xeroxed copies of Eric Mather's confession.

Anderson started by saying that Jerome Freeman's true identity had not yet been established. He had not been born in Boise, Idaho, as his identification papers showed. Apparently he had manufactured an American identity which had served him for at least eleven years. Of his death Anderson said: "A man in his business kills himself for one of two reasons: he is afraid he will crack under interrogation, or he knows that the government he served—and failed—will deal as harshly with him as would the enemy if he had succeeded."

"I take it you don't mean the produce business," Fitzgerald said dryly.

"I don't, though I understand he ran a profitable American enterprise in the Margueritta Import Company. An excellent cover, afternoons and evenings free, accessible to the waterfront . . . As for the Greek, on whom we have no file either—the Immigration Department does have a record. But that is all. I think you have another lead to him in this . . ."

Anderson picked up a copy of Mather's confession. "Gentlemen, I say it sadly, believe me, but to us this document is virtually worthless, though I must say it reads like a work of art. It was largely fantasy, the part Mather thought he played in their conspiracy. I don't mean they didn't set him up and use him: they did. And we may suppose that they followed his program—the identification in Athens of Bradley as their man by his visit to the Byron monument. But they would not have left it to chance that Bradley would go there because his friend Eric Mather had suggested it.

"The scene at that end would have gone something like this: Grysenko would have said to each of the American physicists to whom he was to give a copy of the experiment film—casually of course: 'There is a monument to the poet, Byron, which I should like to see while I am in Athens.' In fact, we know he did say just that to Sylvester of Boston. Sylvester's response was: 'Better ask the hall porter how to get there.' Bradley, on the other hand, would have said: 'A friend of mine told me to be sure to see it.' The reverse, you see, of Mather's plan. But to Grysenko it established Bradley as the 'carrier.'

"But as for the story they told Mather—intercepting vital Soviet secrets intended for transmission to the United States—for *their* evaluation here—is that how he put it?

Only a very naive man would believe that—or one who felt he had to believe it because he was hooked anyway. To risk sending into this country such valuable information as we spend fortunes supporting an apparatus to obtain? And what was the scheduled courier supposed to do? To *intercept* such information means it was intended for someone else. Presumably this contact would inform his superiors at once. Or dead, his death itself would be expected to start the grisly wheels of the C.I.A. in motion." He smiled at Connolly, sitting in the background.

"No, gentlemen, Mr. Mather did not think out that part of the game at all. But he played his own part admirably, as Lieutenant Marks has documented for us. He knew his people and their habits. In that house that night five eager scientists were determined to see the film of the Soviet experiment before the night was over. I should say, from reading this colorful confession, that up to this point, Mather enjoyed himself."

Anderson cleared his throat. "I can see that you feel the same is true of me at this moment."

"You have the clandestine microfilm in your possession now, don't you?" Redmond asked. His face showed the lines of weary tension.

"Yes. I can tell you now that we do have it. We were not playing cat and mouse with you, Captain, as I'm pretty sure you and Marks thought.

"The point at which the Bradley case became significant to us occurred Wednesday morning. The State Department passed along the intelligence that Vassil Grysenko had been arrested shortly after his return to the Soviet Union, charged with Stalinist activity. We were with you from then on, and sometimes, forgive me, ahead of you.

"When your investigation veered toward Corrales, it opened up the whole vista to us. Because of his political activity, we had kept a close check on Dr. Corrales's travel plans. We did not interfere, we just watched. He had booked flight to Mexico for Tuesday morning, and at midnight Monday, he canceled that flight. As soon as you tied him into the Bradley case, we wanted to know why he had changed his plans. As Captain Redmond suspected, he had simply found another, safer way, he supposed, to transmit the microfilm—the fortuitous burial plans for an all-but-forgotten revolutionary. The shroud, as I needn't tell you, is an ancient hiding place for small treasure.

"It was most important to United States interests—I might say to world interests—that the microfilm brought from Athens *appear* to go over the border. Sufficiently convincing film was substituted in the casket, and it did go over the border at 7:05 last night.

"The microfilm which came in with Bradley does indeed contain vital, secret Soviet information—information on how to produce high-energy explosives. It probably contains nothing we have not ourselves achieved, but you see, gentlemen, it was destined for a Chinese Communist courier.

"Dr. Corrales has posed from the early days of Castro's Cuban take-over as an anti-Castro man. And perhaps he is—in the larger scheme of things. That will depend on which side Castro is on if it comes to a showdown between Soviet and the Chinese-Stalinist Communism. But in bringing him to trial," Anderson glanced at the district attorney, "you will undoubtedly gain sympathy in his having betrayed the anti-Castro movement."

"Do you think we will need sympathy, sir?"

"In the absence of powerful evidence, it is possible. Yes."

"Mr. Anderson," Marks said, "do *you* believe that Dr. Corrales murdered Bradley?"

"I should say it is extremely likely. But we must not underestimate the significance of their diversive tactics. In order to see my point, you must try to understand the working of such minds: they cover themselves and cross-cover, and sometimes use a third highly developed alternative. They protect themselves, perhaps above all else, against one another. Certainly against a man whom they had converted as easily as Mather. Miss Russo was the keystone of their first cover. May I remind you of the headlines Tuesday morning: 'Physicist Murdered Near Apartment of Attractive Student?'"

Anderson moistened his mouth with the last of his coffee and went on: "It must have been in their plans from the beginning that Dr. Bradley would die. But not until they knew whether he had brought the microfilm they expected. He had to live long enough to be available to them for questioning and the lumberyard was the ideal place for such questioning. He would have died in any case.

"I very much doubt that Corrales tried to view the microfilm there. He would not be trained in its evaluation. He simply went there to make sure the film had come through, that it was in the box. If it had not been, Bradley would have been brought to the lumberyard and cross-examined. Perhaps Corrales himself will clarify some of these things. But I doubt it."

"He's not even mentioned in Mather's confession," Fitzgerald said.

"Undoubtedly because Mather had no knowledge of his existence, much less his complicity. And if it had not been for a little key to a padlock—and a routine photograph in the F.B.I. files of an anti-Castro demonstration, you might have difficulty in bringing him to trial. I understand he built himself a solid alibi for the night of the crime."

"You underestimate a couple of young detectives on my squad when you say that," Captain Redmond said. "I think Herring and Pererro can break that alibi, given time."

"I deeply hope that is so," Anderson said. "And that, by the way, is all we ask also—a little more time. You see, Dr. Corrales is not aware that the microfilm he took from Bradley has been intercepted. He still believes his mission was accomplished. Tuesday morning he telegraphed Mexico City that business here detained him. He detailed what he had hoped to accomplish by that trip to Mexico: it reads like a legitimate précis of anti-Castro activity. We have not yet broken the code beneath that message, but it is to be supposed it directed his contact to the casket of the old gentleman sent home for burial. We may even have to wait for the next move to come from the midnight ravagers of the grave. But when it comes, our people are prepared. There is no telling of course how deeply within the ring this will lead: before the film itself is evaluated at its true worth, it may pass through a number of hands, some quite as lethal as Dr. Corrales. That is something you and I, gentlemen, are unlikely ever to know. In fact, from the moment the casket crossed the border, I became no more than Stateside liaison. But as that liaison, I now ask you to delay, for the time being at least, disclosure of our possession of what we may call the shrouded film—the film Corrales concealed in the casket."

"But, Lord God Almighty," Fitzgerald exploded, "we have to arraign the man within twenty-four hours. What do we use as motive?"

Anderson waited a moment. Then he said quietly: "Why not this—for the arraignment?" He picked up a copy of Mather's confession. "There was a sort of latent decency in this poor bastard. He deserves to have been of some use to his friends and country. You will have ample time to prepare then for the Grand Jury.

"And you may just find yourselves with an easier case ultimately, for having used it. Corrales, you see, may admit to participation in a 'conspiracy' such as Mather describes here. The details are familiar to him—and to him it would represent the perfect protection for the microfilm he now believes on its way to the Eastern World."

The latent decency . . . It was a phrase that haunted Marks throughout the night. He found himself, leaving Anderson's lower Fifth Avenue apartment shortly after ten o'clock, walking south alone. He wanted to call Anne Russo, but he didn't: only Anne would know that Janet cared enough for Mather to suffer a new bereavement with his death. But it was something she would have to suffer through. And his own desire to see Anne again would also have to wait for days to pass, perhaps weeks, until the final story could be told.

He did not go into the Red Lantern, passing it, but he went into the bar across the street and ordered a double Scotch, and wondered while he drank it if the Edwardians were still disputing Sweeney's presence among the nightingales.

BAD KiTTY

vs THE
BABYSITTER

Previously titled Bad Kitty vs Uncle Murray

NICK BRUEL

ROARING BROOK PRESS
NEW YORK

Published by Roaring Brook Press
Roaring Brook Press is a division of Holtzbrinck Publishing Holdings Limited Partnership
120 Broadway, New York, NY 10271 • mackids.com

ISBN 978-1-250-76784-4
Library of Congress Control Number 2020912112

Our books may be purchased in bulk for promotional, educational, or business use.
Please contact your local bookseller or the Macmillan Corporate and Premium Sales
Department at (800) 221-7945 ext. 5442 or by email at
MacmillanSpecialMarkets@macmillan.com.

First edition, 2010 • Full-color edition, 2020
Color by Crystal Kan
Printed in China by 1010 Printing International Limited, North Point, Hong Kong

1 3 5 7 9 10 8 6 4 2

To Neal

• CONTENTS •

• CHAPTER ONE •
PUSSYCAT
PARADISE

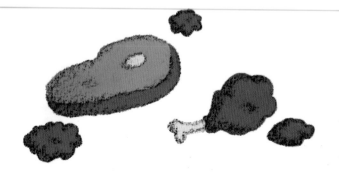

WELCOME, KITTY!

Welcome to Pussycat Paradise, where everything you see is made entirely out of **FOOD**—food for your belly!

The mountains are made out of kibble. The trees are made out of sausages and bacon. Cans of cat food grow out of the ground. And the grass is made out of catnip.

Yes, Kitty! Eat! EAT! Food is everywhere! The rocks are made out of turkey and giblets. The dirt is made out of tuna fish. Even the rivers flow with beef gravy.

And the best part, of course, is that YOU are the only one here! No dogs to hound you. No people to make you take a bath. There is no one else here. Only you.

Be careful, Kitty. Don't touch that can. It's the only thing holding up that gigantic chicken liver.

14

OH NO! TOO LATE! The gigantic chicken liver is going to fall! Look out, Kitty! LOOK OUT!!

WHOOPS!

Sorry, Kitty. I hope I didn't wake you when I dropped the suitcase.

That's right, Kitty. We're going on a little trip. We'll be gone for a while.

Sorry, Kitty. You're not going with us. You'll have to stay home with Puppy.

Oh, don't be like that, Kitty. We'll be back in just a week. And when we get back, we'll have a REALLY BIG SURPRISE for you!

That's right, Kitty. **A REALLY BIG SURPRISE!** You like surprises, don't you?

In the meantime, Kitty, you won't be alone. We found someone who's going to stay here and feed you and take good care of you and Puppy while we're gone.

In fact, that must be him!

Where did Kitty go? Oh, well. At least Puppy is excited to see who's here.

There you are, Kitty. Don't you want to say "Hi" to good ol' Uncle Murray?

GET IN MY MOUTH SO I CAN BITE YOU AND TASTE YOU AND CHEW YOU WITH MY BIG, SHARP TEETH!

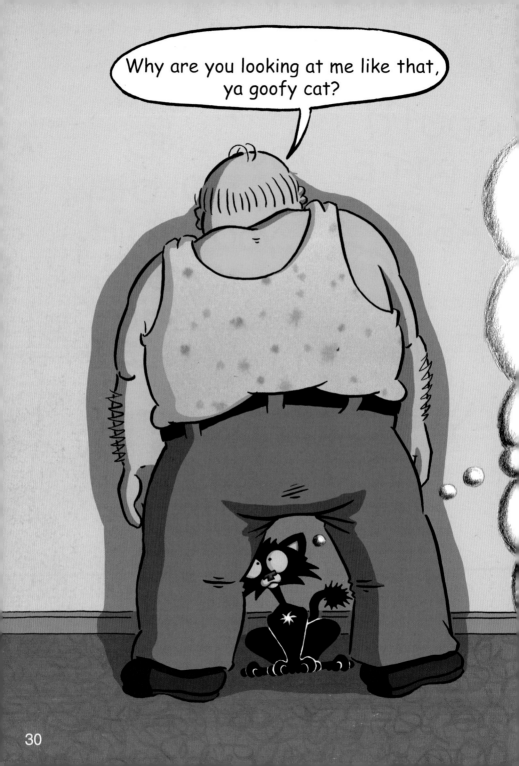

AND THEN I WILL SWALLOW YOU AND YOU WILL BE IN MY BIG, FAT BELLY!
MWAH-HAH-HAH-HAH!

32

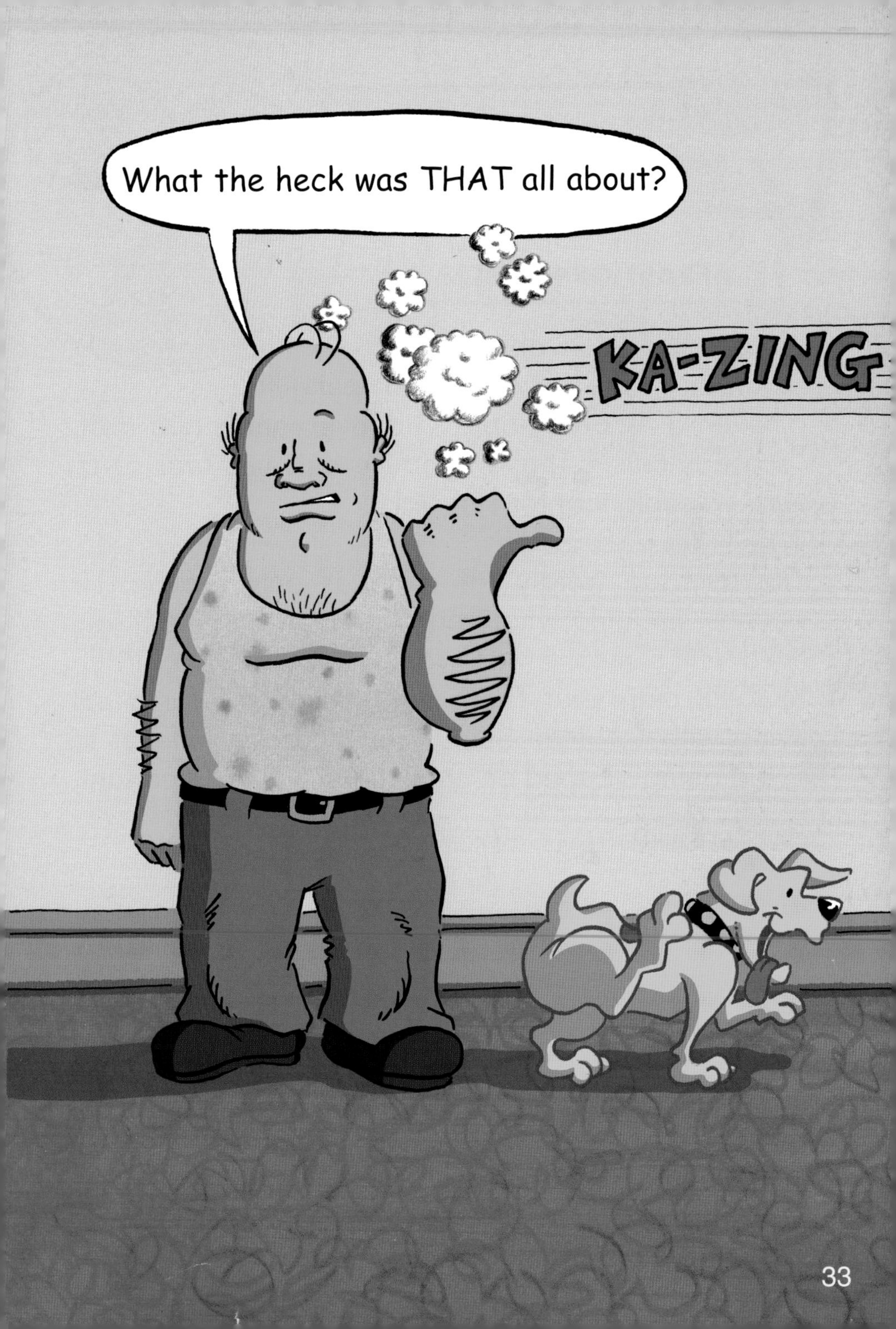
What the heck was THAT all about?
KA-ZING

UNCLE MURRAY'S FUN FACTS

> I was just wondering about that.

WHY ARE SOME CATS AFRAID OF PEOPLE?

No one ever talks about a "scaredy-giraffe" or a "scaredy-penguin" or even a "scaredy-dog," but everyone's heard of "scaredy-cats"! That's because cats use fear as a very valuable tool for survival.

The average weight for a cat is only around 10 pounds. Imagine what your life would be like if you lived with someone who was almost TWENTY TIMES BIGGER than you! That's what life is like for a cat living with a human being. Having good reflexes to avoid being stepped on or sat upon is very important.

CAT: AROUND 10 POUNDS.

BIG, FAT, GOOFY-LOOKING AUTHOR OF THIS BOOK: 185 POUNDS.

> REALLY? DOES THIS BOOK MAKE ME LOOK FAT?

But sometimes a cat's fear of people can become exaggerated. Sometimes this happens when a kitten is raised without any human contact. It can also happen if a cat or a kitten has had a bad experience with a person.

But I'm a nice guy! I wouldn't hurt a fly, much less a dog or a cat, no matter how goofy it is.

It doesn't matter. A cat's instinct always tells her to be careful around people, especially strangers. The best way to get a cat to grow used to you is to be patient, be gentle, be quiet, and try not to take the cat's reaction to you too personally.

And one more thing . . . Try not to make any sudden, loud noises. Cats hate that.

No loud, sudden noises. Got it! What kind of jerk do you think I am? Everybody knows that!

Bye, Uncle Murray! Thank you for taking care of Kitty and Puppy while we're gone. We'll see you in a week!

By the way, you have to really push hard on this door to close it. If you don't, it won't really shut properly.

Okey doke! Goodbye! Good luck!

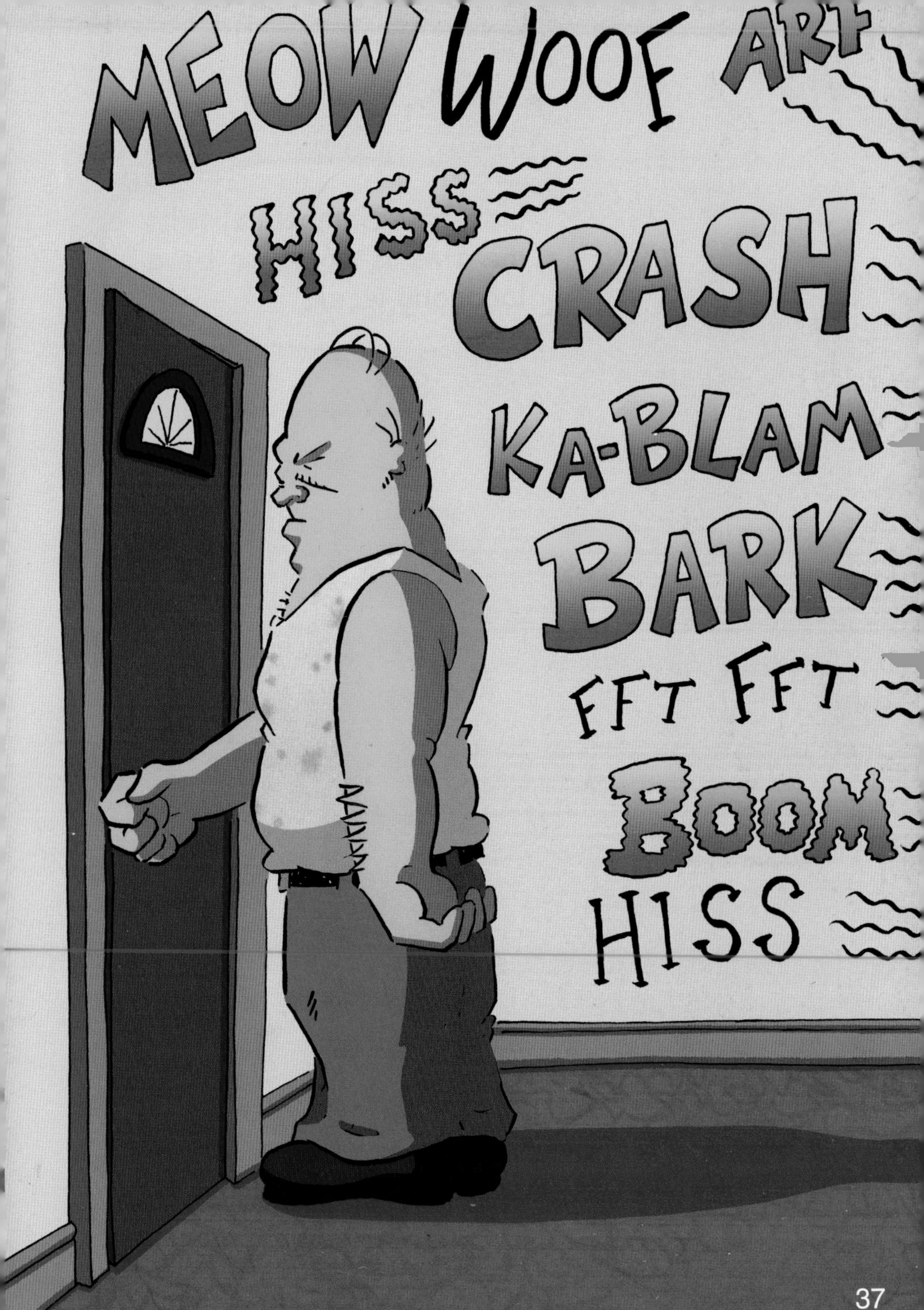
MEOW WOOF ARF
HISS
CRASH
KA-BLAM
BARK
FFT FFT
BOOM
HISS

· CHAPTER TWO ·

HIDE!

You know what, dog . . . I think the best thing to do right now is to sit down, relax, have some lunch, and maybe watch a little . . .

41

45

49

• CHAPTER THREE •
THE KITTY DIARIES

No FOOD. No WATER.
MONSTER IS STILL
OUT THERE. IT HAS
BIG FEET.
DOG SMELLS BAD.

SIX MINUTES . . .
TWO DAYS WITHOUT FOOD. SO HUNGRY. I CAN STILL HEAR MONSTER. DOG REALLY SMELLS BAD.

FIVE DAYS NOW. DOG STILL
SMELLS BAD. DOG IS UGLY,
TOO. DOG DROOLS A LOT.
SO THIRSTY. MAYBE I COULD
DRINK DROOL..... NO. I
WOULD RATHER MONSTER EAT ME.

61

63

64

·CHAPTER FOUR·
UNCLE MURRAY STRIKES BACK

GOBBLE CHEW
MUNCH MASTICATE
GNAW SLURP
GULP
CHEW
YUM
MUNCH
EAT
KITTY
GOBBLE GNAW

73

Y'know, dog . . . when I was just a kid, I had a pooch a lot like you. He was a good dog, too.

I named him Sam, and I found him lost and hungry in an alley near where I lived. He was all white except for some black spots on his face and one of his back legs.

Anyways, I still had half a sandwich on me from lunch so I tossed it to him. Boy, oh, boy was he happy to get some food into his little dog belly. You'd think he hadn't eaten anything in a year. It was just baloney, after all. No mustard, even.

I used my belt as a leash and put it around Sam's neck. At first I thought he'd go crazy when I started to pull him, but he didn't. In fact, he barked and licked my hand the whole way home.

But there was a problem. My mother wouldn't let me keep Sam in the house 'cause my baby sister was real allergic to dogs. I guess it was true, 'cause she still is. I told my mom I would keep Sam only in my room, but she told me that wouldn't really work. She was right.

So I did the only thing I could think of . . . I took little Sam to a dog shelter where they'd feed him and take good care of him.

They were real nice to Sam there. He had his own little cage, and there were lots of other dogs there for him to talk to. But the best part was that they said I could come visit him every day after school. So I did!

I went to visit Sam every single day, and each time he saw me he'd jump up and lick my face and wrestle me to the ground like he was sayin' "Gee, I'm really happy to see you! Where've you been?"

Each day, I taught
him a new trick.
I taught him to
sit and to stay.
I taught him to
beg and to roll
over. I even
taught him
geography.
NAHHH! I'm just
kidding about that
last one. But he
really was smart.

K-CHOO!

Gee, Sam and I
had a lot of fun
together. Then one day
I walked in and didn't see him there.

A lady who worked at the shelter told me a family had come in just after I left the day before, fell in love with Sam, and took him home. She said they were real nice people and promised to feed him and take good care of him. But that didn't help. I started crying like Niagara Falls. He may not have lived with me, but Sam was <u>MY DOG</u>!

I thought for sure that I'd never see little Sam again.

But then, one day, about a year later, as I was walking through the park, I looked over and saw a little girl playing with a dog that looked a whole lot like my Sam. He was all white except for some black spots on his face and one of his back legs. It <u>was</u> him! And they were having a swell time. Sam was even doing some of the same tricks that <u>I</u> taught him.

It hurt me so much inside to see this little girl playing with my dog. <u>MY DOG</u>. But then I looked at how much fun they were having and how happy he looked, and I thought to myself . . . all I ever really wanted for that lost, hungry dog sitting alone in that alley was for someone to take him home and feed him and take good care of him. Right? And that's what I got.

I loved that dog, and now I knew that someone else loved that dog as much as me.

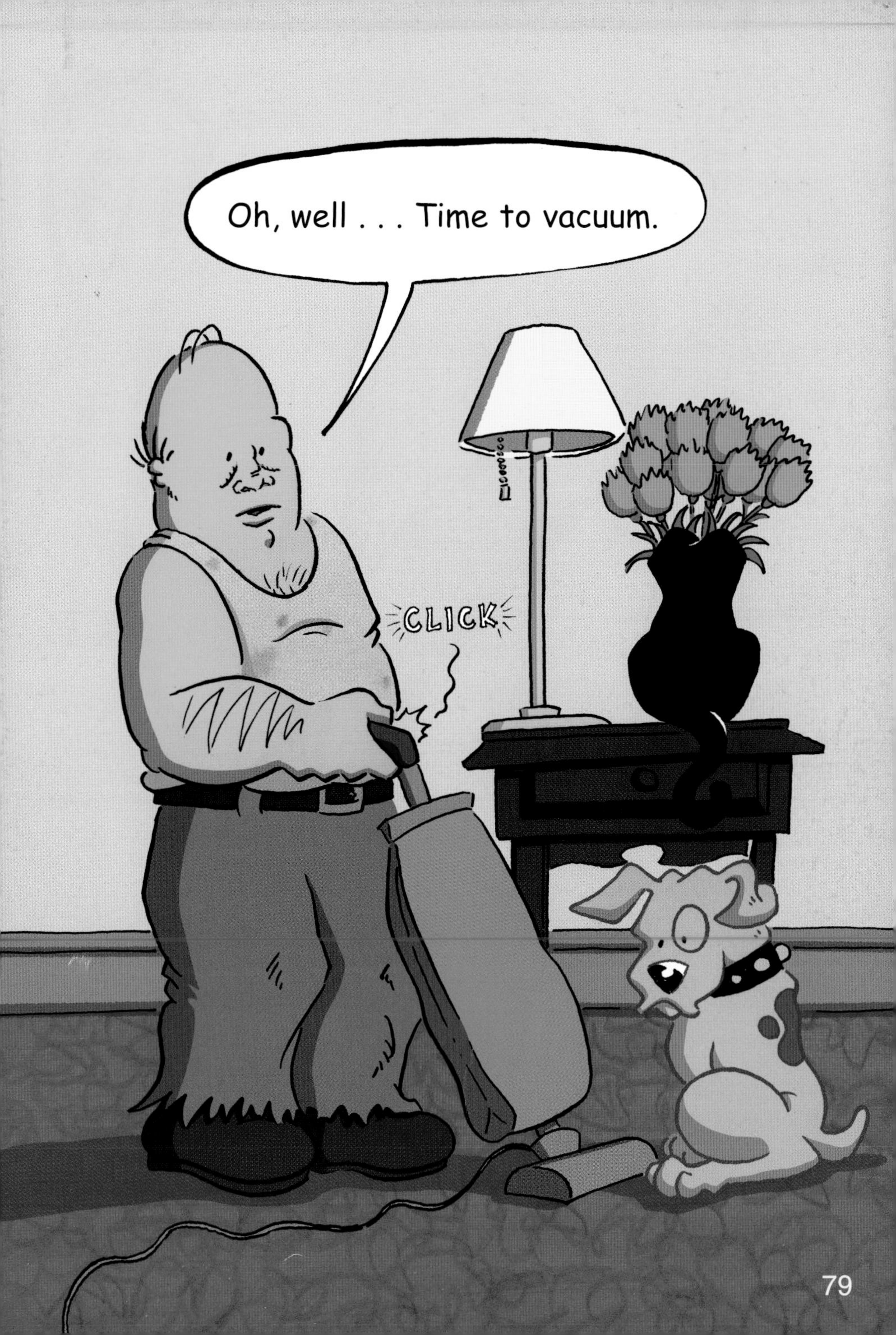
Oh, well . . . Time to vacuum.
CLICK

81

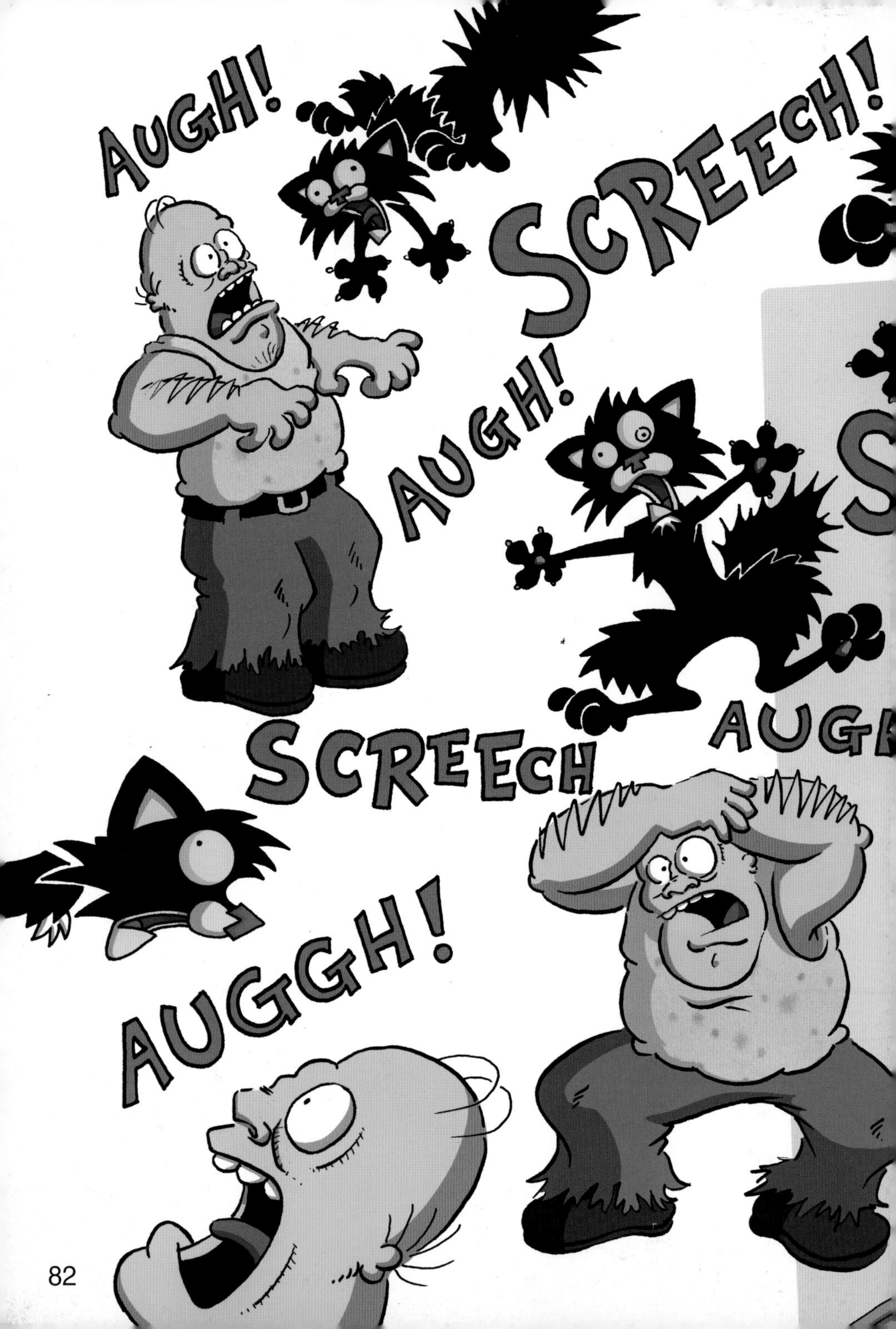
AUGH!
SCREECH!
AUGH!
SCREECH
AUGGH!

83

UNCLE MURRAY'S FUN FACTS

WHY ARE CATS AFRAID OF VACUUM CLEANERS?

It's not the vacuum cleaner that frightens cats so much as the sudden, loud noise it makes. Most cats will react quickly to any sudden, loud noise like a car horn, or a firecracker, or someone yelling.

Cats can hear very, very well—even better than dogs. In fact, a cat can hear three times better than a human being. That's why a cat can hear a mouse rustling through the grass from 30 feet away. But it's also why loud noises are particularly painful for cats. And that's what inspires their fear.

Fear of loud noises is another survival tool for cats. If a little noise is a signal that something to eat might be nearby, then a very loud noise acts the same as a fire alarm held up next to their ears. And that means DANGER. And that means FIGHT or RUN AWAY.

When a cat is frightened, running away or hiding is a common response. But sometimes if a cat feels trapped or cornered, she'll stand still while unusual things happen to her body.

First, all of the fur on her body will stand on end. Then the cat will arch her back up using all sixty of her vertebrae—humans have only thirty-four, by the way. This will make the cat look much bigger; a tactic it uses to intimidate its enemies. But the sign to be very aware of is when a cat has turned its ears back. A cat will do this when it feels like fighting back and wants to protect those sensitive ears. That is a clear sign to back away from a VERY angry cat that could attack you.

•CHAPTER FIVE•
CATCH THAT KITTY

88   *Hark!

89

MEANWHILE, IN THE SECRET BASEMENT LAIR OF STRANGE KITTY . . .

DO YOU HEAR THAT, OLD CHUM? I DO BELIEVE I HEAR PLAINTIVE CRIES FOR HELP FROM OUR OLD FELINE FRIEND WITH THE BLACK FUR AND REBELLIOUS ATTITUDE!

HOLY CATNIP, S.K.! WE CAN'T IGNORE A PLAINTIVE CRY FOR HELP!

RIGHT YOU ARE, OLD BEAN! ONCE AGAIN, THE WORLD IS IN NEED OF . . .

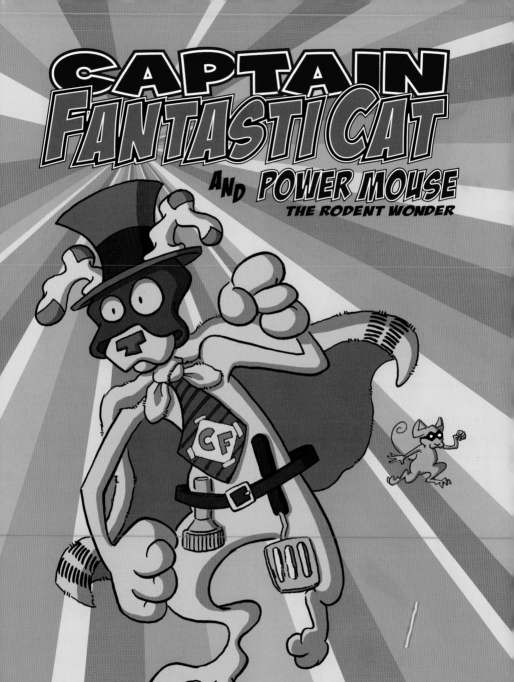

94

HOW ABOUT...

"UP, UP, AND AWAY!"

IT'S BEEN DONE.

"ON YOUR MARK, GET SET, GO!"

IT DOESN'T FEEL QUITE RIGHT.

"I'M DREAMING OF A WHITE CHRISTMAS!"

TOO SEASONAL.

CHEESE POPCORN?

HMMM... WILL IT REALLY STRIKE FEAR IN THE HEARTS OF OUR MOST BITTER AND DANGEROUS ENEMIES?

• CHAPTER SIX •

KITTIES TO
THE RESCUE

103

*Let us in, and I mean RIGHT MEOW!

111

LOOK OUT FOR THE SPATULA!

Huh?

121

125

128

129

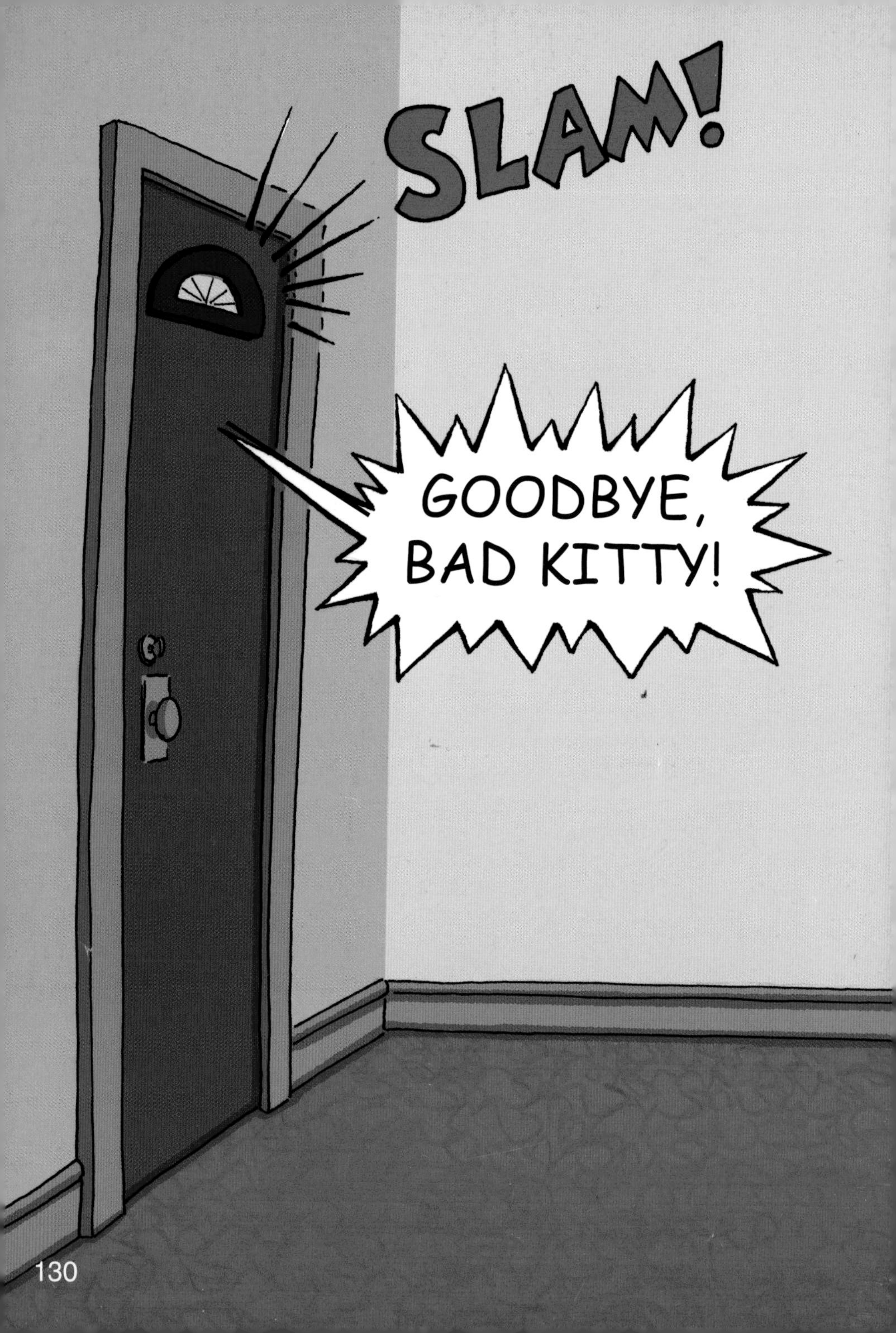
SLAM!
GOODBYE, BAD KITTY!

• CHAPTER SEVEN •
KITTY ON HER OWN

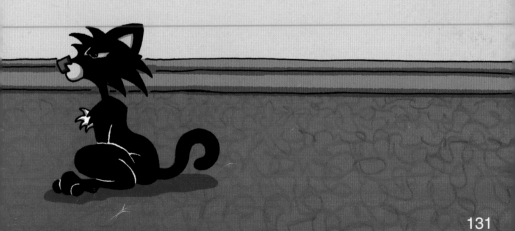

133

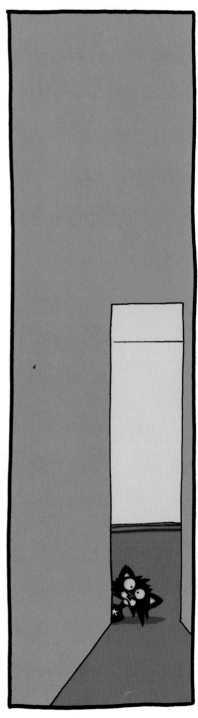

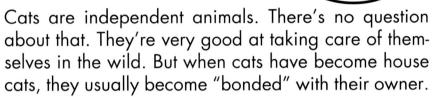

UNCLE MURRAY'S FUN FACTS

WHY ARE SOME CATS AFRAID OF BEING ALONE?

Cats are independent animals. There's no question about that. They're very good at taking care of themselves in the wild. But when cats have become house cats, they usually become "bonded" with their owner.

When a cat becomes very close, even dependent on a human being for food or protection, that's called "bonding."

MEOW?

And sometimes when that bond is broken, even for just a little while, some cats might exhibit "separation anxiety." Have you ever seen a baby begin to cry just because her Mommy has left the room for just a few seconds? That's a good example of "separation anxiety," and even cats can get it.

Leave cats alone for too long and they'll start to cry out to see if anyone is in the house, just like a baby. Sometimes they'll even lose their appetite and not eat. The most anxious cats will even pull out clumps

of their own fur because of nervousness.

The solution for all fears is to let the cat gradually grow used to whatever scares them. Cats can adapt very quickly.

If a cat is afraid of people, keep your distance and step a little closer day by day while also letting her come to you under her own power. If your cat is afraid of loud noises, try to keep the sound down at first if possible, and then increase the exposure a little bit each day.

And if the cat is afraid of being alone, give her time to adjust as she learns that you'll eventually return. She'll hate being alone at first, but in time she'll learn that there's nothing to be afraid of once you keep coming back.

139

141

142

143

145

• EPILOGUE •

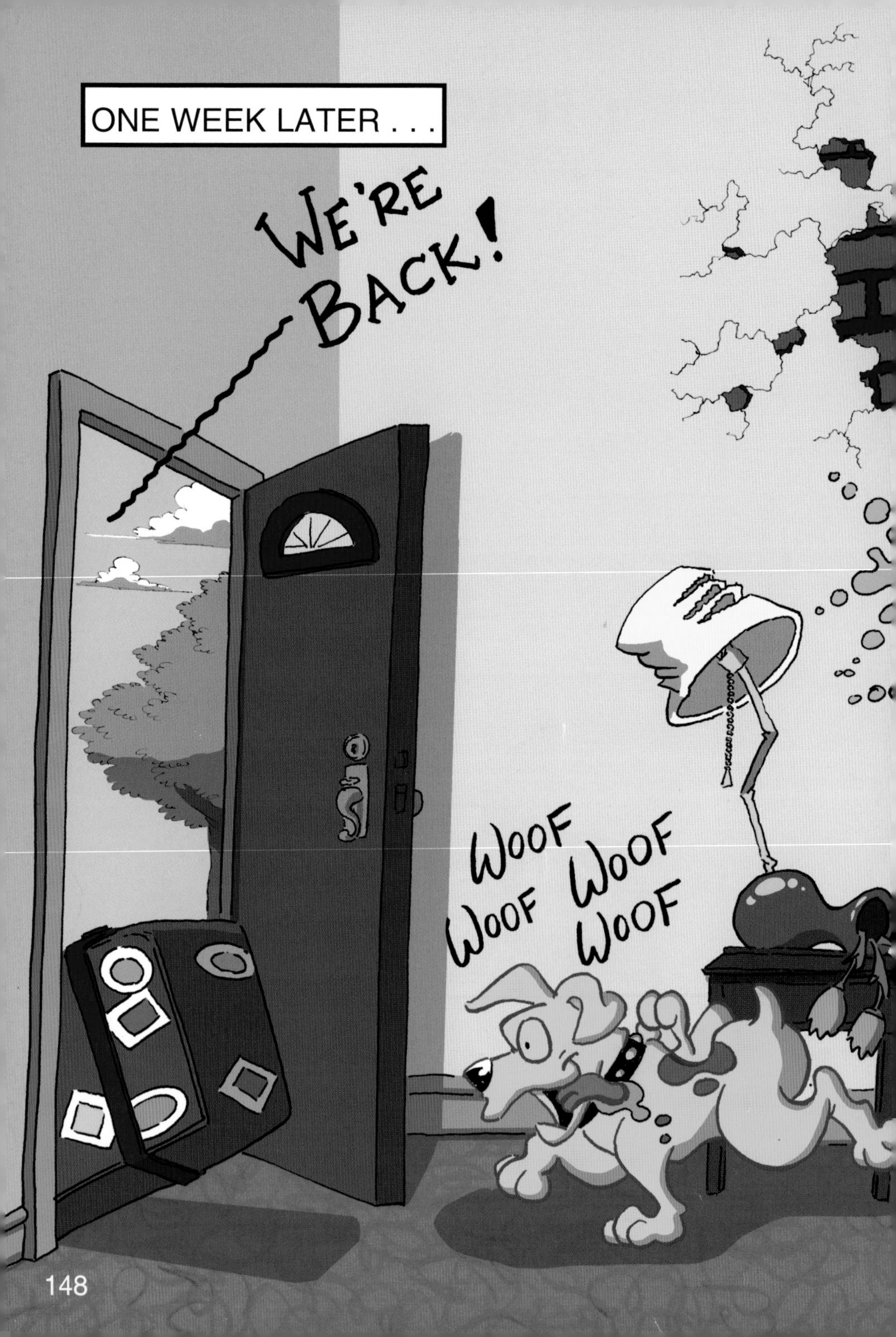
ONE WEEK LATER . . .
WE'RE BACK!
WOOF
WOOF WOOF
WOOF
WOOF

Thank you so much, Uncle Murray, for taking such good care of Kitty and Puppy. I know they can be a real handful. I hope they weren't too much trouble.

What did you say, Uncle Murray?

Fish don't bite or scream or chase you around the house or hit you on the head with a spatula. All they do is swim around and make nice little bubbles that don't hurt anybody. And they're pretty. Pretty like little rainbows. Fish.

Fish don't bite or scream or chase you around the house or . . .

Hmmm . . . Oh, well. Goodbye, Uncle Murray. And thanks again.

HI, KITTY!
Did you miss us?

HMPF

Awwww! We missed you, too, Kitty!

HEY! Do you remember that REAL BIG SURPRISE we promised you? Do you? DO YOU?!

Well, here she is!

To be continued . . .

• APPENDIX •

A SELECTION OF PHOBIAS

A "phobia" is a strong fear of a specific object or a specific situation. Most of the time the fear is irrational, meaning that the person who has the phobia really has nothing to fear. For instance, a boy might be afraid of worms (Scoleciphobia), but that doesn't mean the boy has any real reason to be afraid of worms, other than he thinks they're scary and doesn't want them anywhere near him.

Ten percent of the people who live in the United States have a phobia. That's over thirty million people! This means that phobias are very common and nothing to be ashamed of.

We've seen a lot of different examples of fear in this book. The following is a small selection of the more than five hundred known phobias.

Agrizoophobia—Fear of wild animals.

Ailurophobia (also, Elurophobia)—Fear of cats.

Amychophobia—Fear of scratches or being scratched.

Cynophobia—Fear of dogs.

Ligyrophobia (also, Phonophobia)—Fear of loud noises, also, fear of voices or one's own voice.

Lilapsophobia—Fear of hurricanes or tornadoes.

Monophobia (also Autophobia)— Fear of being alone.

Olfactophobia (also, Osmophobia)— Fear of smells or odors.

Peladophobia—Fear of bald people.

Phagophobia—Fear of swallowing, eating, or being eaten.

Pnigophobia— Fear of being choked or smothered.

Teratophobia—Fear of monsters.

NICK BRUEL is the author and illustrator of the phenomenally successful Bad Kitty series, including *Bad Kitty Meets the Baby* and *Bad Kitty for President*. Nick has also written and illustrated popular picture books, including *A Wonderful Year* and his most recent, *Bad Kitty: Searching for Santa*. Nick lives with his wife and daughter in Westchester, New York. Visit him at **nickbruelbooks.com**.

1997 $24.95

Decorating Gift Baskets, Boxes & Bags

Decorating Gift Baskets, Boxes & Bags

Amanda Knight

Sterling Publishing Co., Inc. New York
A Sterling/Chapelle Book

FOR CHAPELLE LTD

Owner
Jo Packham

Editor
Amanda McPeck

Staff:
Malissa Boatwright
Sara Casperson
Rebecca Christensen
Amber Hansen
Holly Hollingsworth
Susan Jorgensen
Susan Laws
Barbara Milburn
Pat Pearson
Leslie Ridenour
Cindy Rooks
Cindy Stoeckl
Ryanne Webster
Nancy Whitley

Designers:
Holly Fuller
Sharon Ganske
Amber Hansen
Mary Jo Hiney
Kristin Kapp
Susan Laws
Cookie Lyday
Jo Packham
Jamie Pierce
Cindy Rooks
Edie Stockstill
Kelly Valentine-Cracas
Nancy Whitley

Photography:
Kevin Dilley for Hazen
    Photography

Photography Styling:
Cherie Herrick
Susan Laws
Jo Packham

If you have any questions or comments or would like information on specialty products featured in this book, please contact:
Chapelle Ltd., Inc.
PO Box 9252
Ogden, UT 84409
(801) 621-2777
(801) 621-2788 (fax)

Library of Congress Cataloging-in-Publication Data

Knight, Amanda.
    Decorating gift baskets, boxes, & bags / Amanda Knight.
        p.   cm.
    "A Sterling/Chapelle book."
    Includes index.
    ISBN 0-8069-4275-4
    1. Handicraft.   2. Gifts   3. Baskets.   4. Ornamental boxes.   5. Bags.   I. Title
TT157.K533   1996
745.593--dc20   95-46284
                                                                                                                        CIP

10 9 8 7 6 5 4 3 2

Published by Sterling Publishing Company, Inc., 387 Park Avenue South, New York, N.Y. 10016
© 1996 by Chapelle Limited
Distributed in Canada by Sterling Publishing, c/o Canadian Manda Group, One Atlantic Avenue, Suite 105, Toronto, Ontario, Canada M6K 3E7
Distributed in Great Britain and Europe by Cassell PLC, Wellington House, 125 Strand, London WC2R 0BB, England
Distributed in Australia by Capricorn Link (Australia) Pty Ltd., P.O. Box 6651, Baulkham Hills, Business Centre, NSW 2153, Australia
Printed and Bound in China

Sterling ISBN 0-8069-4275-4

CONTENTS

GENERAL INSTRUCTIONS

Decoupage

Combine one-part water and one-part white craft glue, or use ready-made decoupage glue. With paintbrush, paint back of art with glue. Lay art on item. Press down with fingertips and remove any air bubbles. Brush over art with several light coats of glue. Let dry. Apply several thin coats of water-base varnish on piece to protect it from water.

Laminating

(1) Prepare a wet rag and a dry rag for constant hand cleaning. Place or tape brown paper bag onto work surface. Pour enough thin-bodied tacky glue into a disposable plastic or tin dish to cover bottom of dish. Place cardboard onto paper bag. Place fabric wrong side up on work surface. (2) Roll glue onto paint roller in dish. Completely cover roller's surface; then roll off extra glue in dish. Paint entire surface of cardboard with glue. Make sure to follow any instructions regarding which side should be laminated if the cardboard is scored.

(3) Place glued cardboard on fabric by flipping cardboard over onto wrong side of fabric and pressing in place.

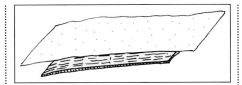

(4) Flip fabric and cardboard over and smooth fabric completely. Eliminate any wrinkles immediately. Pay special attention to edges. Fabric should adhere to cardboard everywhere, especially at the edges.

(5) Turn laminated cardboard over again. Use roller to paint edges of cardboard and fabric with glue.

(6) Trim out bulk from each corner; then wrap extended fabric over onto glued edges. Double-check corners for fraying fabric, and dab frays with glue if necessary. Let dry for 10 minutes.

Painting Tips
Base Coat

Gesso, a base coat artists use to treat canvas, can also be used on other surfaces. When painting on surfaces such as wood, which tends to soak up paint, paint the surface with gesso following manufacturer's directions. Doing so will save both time and paint. Gesso can be used as a base for watercolors, but it will create a blotchy effect.

Wet and Dry Painting

(1) Painting with a dry brush on a dry surface creates a rustic look. (2) Painting with a wet brush on a dry surface creates a clean, precise look. (3) Painting with a wet brush on a wet surface creates a loose, "smudgy" look.

Each style is good, depending on what the finished product should look like. Some instructions specify what kind of brush to use. If no brush is specified, feel free to experiment to create the desired look.

Mistakes

Most mistakes can be corrected by simply going over the mistake with more paint after the original paint has dried. However, some mistakes can only be fixed by sanding or stripping the paint. Try fixing the mistake with more paint before taking drastic measures!

GENERAL INSTRUCTIONS

Finishing

Sealers or varnishes come in matte, clear, and gloss. Use the kind of sealer specified in instructions. For projects that will be outside, use waterproof varnish. Several light coats of sealer are better than one thick coat.

Have Fun

Remember that patterns are not coloring books–you do not have to stay in the lines! Be creative with the paint. Sometimes "mistakes" look better than what was originally intended.

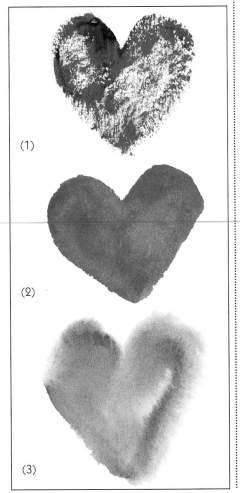

Ribbon Embroidery

Ribbon Tips

Always keep the ribbon loose and flat while working stitches. Untwist ribbon often and pull ribbon softly so that it lies flat on top of fabric. Be creative with the stitching. Exact stitch placement is not critical, but make sure any placement marks are covered.

Needles

A size 3 crewel embroidery needle works well for most fabrics when using 4mm ribbon. For 7mm ribbon, use a chenille needle, sizes 18 to 24. As a rule of thumb, the barrel of the needle must create a hole large enough for the ribbon to pass through. If ribbon does not pull through fabric easily, a larger needle is needed.

To Thread Ribbon on Needle

(1) Thread the ribbon through the eye of the needle. With the tip of the needle, pierce the center of the ribbon ¼-inch from end.
(2) Pull remaining ribbon through to "lock" ribbon on needle.

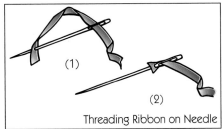

Threading Ribbon on Needle

Knotting End of Ribbon

(1) Drape the ribbon in a circular manner to position the end of the ribbon perpendicular to the tip of the needle.
(2) Pierce the end of the ribbon with the needle, sliding the needle through the ribbon as if to make a short basting stitch.
(3) Pull needle and ribbon through the stitch portion to form a knot at end of ribbon.

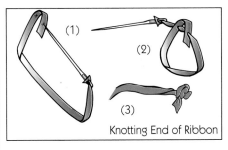

Knotting End of Ribbon

To End Stitching

Secure stitches in place for each flower or small area. Do not drag the ribbon from one area to another. Tie a slipknot on the wrong side of needlework to secure the stitch in place and end ribbon.

GENERAL INSTRUCTIONS

Ribbon Stitches

Folded Leaf

(1) Cut ribbon to desired length. Overlap ends of ribbon and gather-stitch at bottom edge. Gather tightly.

(2) Wrap thread around stitches to secure. Trim excess ⅛-inch past stitching.

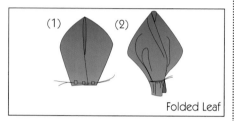

Folded Leaf

Free-Form Flower

(1) Use a 2" piece of ribbon. Fold each end under about ⅛-inch. Baste along one long edge of the ribbon with one strand of sewing thread or floss. Gently gather ribbon to create a petal the desired length. Knot to secure ruffled effect. Stitch ribbon in place along the gathered edge.

(2) Ribbon can also be gathered tightly to create a flower.

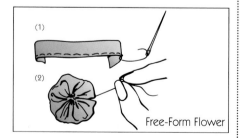

Free-Form Flower

French Knot

(1) Bring needle up through fabric; smoothly wrap ribbon once around needle.

(2) Hold ribbon securely off to one side and push needle down through fabric at the starting point.

(3) Completed French Knots.

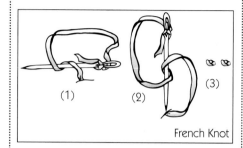

French Knot

Japanese Ribbon Stitch

(1) Come up through fabric at the starting point of stitch. Lay the ribbon flat on the fabric. At the end of the stitch, pierce the ribbon with the needle. Slowly pull the length of the ribbon through to the back, allowing the ends of the ribbon to curl. If the ribbon is pulled too tightly, the effect of the stitch will be lost. Vary the petals and leaves by adjusting the length, the tension of the ribbon before piercing, the position of piercing, and how loosely or tightly the ribbon is pulled down through itself.

(2) Completed Japanese Ribbon Stitch.

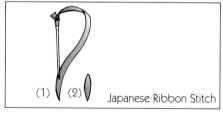

(1) (2) Japanese Ribbon Stitch

Lazy Daisy

(1) Bring the needle up at A. Keep the ribbon flat, untwisted and full. Put the needle down through fabric at B and up through at C, keeping the ribbon under the needle to form a loop. Pull the ribbon through, leaving the loop loose and full. To hold the loop in place, go down on other side of ribbon near C, forming a straight stitch over loop.

(2) Completed Lazy Daisy.

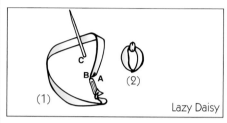

Lazy Daisy

Morning Glory

(1) Cut one 2½-inch length and one 4½-inch length of same color of ⅝-inch-wide wired ribbon. Overlap and glue raw edges together, forming a tube.

(2) With one tube, gather lightest edge and pinch and glue closed, forming a cup.

(3) With other tube, gather lightest edge slightly and glue around top edge of cup.

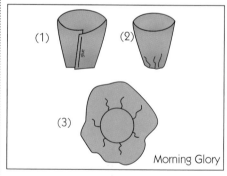

Morning Glory

Morning Glory Bud

(1) Cut two 1¼-inch lengths of ⅝-inch-wide wired ribbon. Glue top raw edge under ⅛-inch on each ribbon.

(2) Place wrong sides together and pinch and glue bottom edges.

GENERAL INSTRUCTIONS

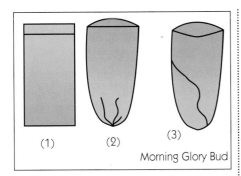

(1) (2) (3)

Morning Glory Bud

(3) Twist bud.

(4) For leaf cap, cut ⅝-inch-wide green iridescent wired ribbon into a 1½-inch length. Glue each raw edge under ⅛-inch.

(5) Place bud in center and bring bottom wired edge up to top edge. Glue.

(6) Tuck bottom corners inside forming a triangle, and glue.

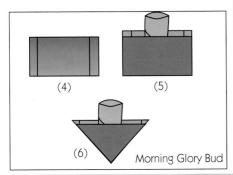

(4) (5)

(6)

Morning Glory Bud

Morning Glory Leaf

(1) Cut ⅝-inch-wide green iridescent ribbon into a 1-inch length. On one raw edge, fold and glue corners back to make a point. Fold opposite end under ⅛-inch and glue.

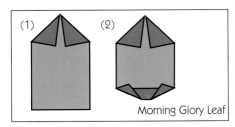

(1) (2)

Morning Glory Leaf

(2) Glue each bottom corner back slightly and pinch center to make indentation.

Folded Pansy

(1) Cut two 1¼-inch lengths of purple 1-inch-wide ribbon. Tacky-glue top raw end of one ribbon length forward ⅛-inch. While glue is still pliable, place a round toothpick at an angle against one corner of the glued edge. Roll ribbon around toothpick between thumb and forefinger one or two revolutions. Repeat with other corner.

(2) Glue and pinch opposite end, forming a petal. Repeat with other piece of ribbon.

(3) Overlap petals and glue at pinched ends.

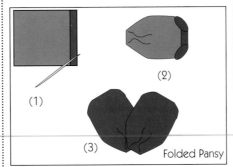

(1)

(2)

(3)

Folded Pansy

(4) Cut two 1-inch lengths of yellow 1-inch-wide ribbon and repeat petal process. Glue these petals, overlapping each other, on top of other petals.

(5) Make a ½-inch hook on one end of a 6-inch length of stem wire. Place and glue hooked end in center of petals. Cut one 1¼-inch piece of yellow 1-inch-wide ribbon and make a petal. Glue this petal, right sides together, to

other petals. Pull this petal forward and down. With fabric pen, make fine lines from center of flower outward.

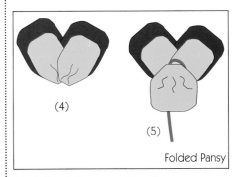

(4)

(5)

Folded Pansy

Folded Pansy Bud

(1) Make two petals from 1¼-inch lengths of 1-inch-wide ribbon and glue pinched ends wrong sides together.

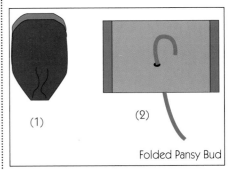

(1) (2)

Folded Pansy Bud

(2) Cut a 1½-inch length of 1-inch-wide green ribbon. Put a thin bead of glue along one raw end and fold forward ⅛-inch. Repeat on other end. Poke a small hole through center of ribbon with stem wire and make a hook.

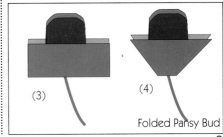

(3) (4)

Folded Pansy Bud

9

GENERAL INSTRUCTIONS

Folded Pansy Bud continued.
(3) Glue bud on wire. Fold bottom wired edge of ribbon up to top edge and glue. (Bud should be poking out.)
(4) Tuck bottom corners inside and glue to form triangle shape.

Folded Pansy Leaf
(1) Cut a 1-inch length of 1½-inch-wide green ribbon. Fold and glue each raw end under ⅛-inch. On top wired edge, fold and glue each corner under slightly.
(2) Insert hooked stem wire in other end, pinch and glue.

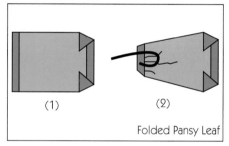

(1)   (2)

Folded Pansy Leaf

Gathered Pansy
Note: Project instructions will indicate dimensions for making specific pansies.
(1) Fold one long edge down. Pin to hold. Mark intervals.
(2) Fold on marks. Gather-stitch.
(3) Pull thread as tight as possible, secure thread. Join petals together.

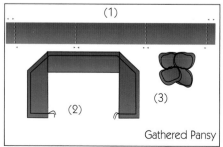

(1)

(2)   (3)

Gathered Pansy

Large Pansy
(1) Cut one 5-inch piece and four 4-inch pieces of 1-inch-wide purple ombré wired ribbon. Gather-stitch dark edge of 5-inch piece of ribbon.
(2) Pull tightly and shape into petal.
(3) Gather-stitch dark edge of two 4-inch pieces of ribbon, pull tightly and shape. Gather-stitch light edge of two 4-inch pieces of ribbon, pull tightly and shape. Stitch petals together to form pansy. Stitch five Japanese ribbon stitches with yellow 7mm silk ribbon in center of pansy to cover edges and tack in place .

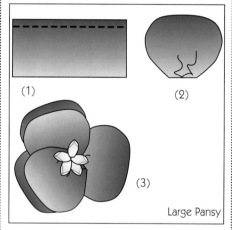

(1)   (2)

(3)

Large Pansy

Rosette
For ⅛-inch rosette, cut 5-inch ribbon length; for ¼-inch rosette, cut 9-inch length. Mark center of ribbon length.
(1) Beginning at one end, fold end forward at right angle.
(2) Fold vertical ribbon forward at right angle. Continue folding ribbon forward at right angles. Roll to center mark. Secure, leaving needle and thread attached.

(3) Gather-stitch on edge of remaining ribbon length. Gather tightly. Wrap gathered ribbon around bud.
(4) Secure and fluff flower.

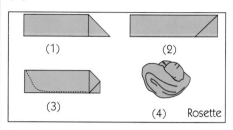

(1)   (2)

(3)   (4)   Rosette

Squared Petal or Leaf
(1) The interval of the gathering stitches must be greater than the width of the ribbon to make a squared petal or leaf.
(2) Pull thread to gather and secure. Shape as desired.

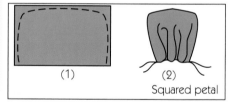

(1)   (2)

Squared petal

Straight Stitch
This stitch may be taut or loose depending on desired effect.
(1) Come up at A. Go down at B, keeping the ribbon flat.
(2) Completed Straight Stitch.

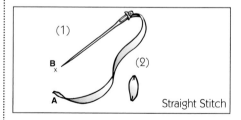

(1)

B
x

(2)

A

Straight Stitch

GENERAL INSTRUCTIONS

Stuffing Ribbons

When decorating with dried naturals like pinecones, holes can be easily filled with ribbon.

First, fill the hole with hot glue. Fold ribbon leaving desired length on tail. Then using a pencil or blunt needle, stuff the ribbon inside the hole at the fold. Loop the end of ribbon to desired size and stuff end into hole.

Continue looping and stuffing ribbon inside the hole until desired look is achieved.

A long length of ribbon can be used and spread throughout the design, if desired. Fold ribbon in half and stuff in the center of design. Then loop and stuff one tail along one side of design, followed by the other.

Unique Handles

To attach a unique handle to an unhandled basket, first wrap desired handle with wire twice to hold in place. Then thread a heavy-duty needle with doubled twine. The needle has to be long enough to go through the basket.

Pull needle through basket and wrap twine around handle. Pull twine tightly and push needle through basket. Wrap twine again, pulling tightly. Continue sewing handle onto basket with twine until it is secure. Secure twine with a firm knot and stitch one more time through to hide end. Clip twine.

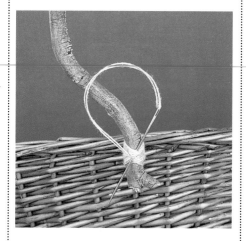

A Few More Tips . . .

◆ Collect decorations as you go. An autumn walk is the perfect time to collect pinecones, acorns and other dried naturals to decorate a basket, box, or bag.

◆ Crafts store sales are great for collecting small items for decoration. Almost anything can be used for decoration. Keep your eyes open for them!

◆ Most of the projects in this book are designed to be used after they hold your gift. Suggestions for use are noted next to the pictures of the projects.

◆ Never throw anything away! Old jewelry can be taken apart, old Christmas ornaments can be recycled, even some toys can be an unexpected delight. Anything can look new and different if used in a new and different way. Don't be afraid to experiment.

BASKETS BASKETS BASKETS BASKETS

use it . . .

◆ Use the SPRING basket as a garden planter.

◆ This basket makes a cute and convenient keeper for cotton balls and swabs.

◆ This WAGON is perfect as a child's toy.

◆SPRING   ◆WAGON   ◆BABY

need it . . .

One shallow basket (model is
   16"-diameter and 5"-deep)
Wild flower sod
Stuffed bunny
3 or 4 wire nests
Wooden eggs
Medium blue and tan acrylic paint
Paintbrush

make it . . .

1. Plant sod in basket. Water as
needed.

2. Decorate basket with stuffed
bunny, wire nests, and wooden
eggs painted medium blue and
tan.

change it . . .

◆ Plant grass sod and
decorate with miniature
gardening tools or a
miniature lawn mower.

◆ Plant ground cover and
decorate with a miniature
wooden house.

◆ Plant ivy and decorate
with small baskets filled
with bird seed.

need it . . .

Small unfinished wood wagon
24" of 1½"-wide sheer lavender
   ribbon
24" of ¾"-wide light blue wired
   ribbon
Blue, light lavender, orange, periwinkle, pink, turquoise, white,
   and yellow acrylic paint
High-gloss acrylic spray
Glitter spray
Paintbrushes

make it . . .

1. Paint body of wagon yellow
and top edges periwinkle. Paint
handle blue. Paint one wheel
orange, one light lavender, one
blue, and one pink. Let dry completely. Thin a small amount of
periwinkle paint with water. Paint
a wavy plaid design on body of
wagon. Add narrow white lines
over periwinkle plaid. Add small
pink dots randomly.

2. Decorate wheels as desired
with painted swirls, dots, squig-
gles, ovals, crosses, zigzags and
circles. Let dry. Spray wagon with
glitter spray and finish with a coat
of high-gloss acrylic spray.

3. Tie a double bow with
lavender and light blue ribbon to
wagon handle.

need it . . .

Small white basket
Card stock
Assorted pastel acrylic paints
   (optional)
Tissue paper or Easter grass
Decoupage glue
Hot glue gun and glue sticks
Paintbrushes
Pinking sheers

make it . . .

1. Using design below and on
page 61 as patterns, paint card
stock with acrylic paints, or color
copy designs onto card stock.
Hot-glue card stock designs onto
basket. Coat card stock with
decoupage glue.

2. Cut out pink and blue dotted
card stock (painted or color
copied) with pinking sheers. Hot-
glue to inside of basket.

3. Fill basket with tissue paper
or Easter grass.

Pattern full size.

use it . . .

◆ Hang this wire basket above your sink to store fresh vegetables.

◆ Use the steamer to cook vegetables from the garden, and put the magnets on your refrigerator.

◆ Use the larger flowerpot as a cheerful centerpiece that doubles as a silverware holder.

◆POTS

need it . . .

4½"-tall terra-cotta flowerpot
Five 1¼" terra-cotta flowerpots
5 brightly colored napkins
Green, pink, purple, red, and yellow acrylic paint
Matt spray sealer
Drill with ½", ¾" and 1" bits
Paintbrushes
Scrap of lumber or 2" x 4"

make it . . .

1. Set a 1¾-inch terra-cotta flowerpot upright on lumber or 2 by 4. Drill ½-inch hole in bottom. Change to ¾-inch bit and repeat. Change to 1-inch bit and finish hole for napkin ring.

2. Paint each napkin ring with a different acrylic paint, inside and out. Paint small diamonds in the other colors randomly on each napkin ring. Let dry. Spray all napkin rings with matte spray sealer. Let dry.

3. Paint outside of 4½-inch-tall terra-cotta flowerpot with red acrylic paint. Paint small diamonds in the other colors randomly on flowerpot. Let dry. Paint inside of flowerpot with green acrylic paint. Spray entire flowerpot with matte spray sealer. Let dry.

4. Slip napkins into napkin rings and place in 4½-inch-tall terra-cotta flowerpot.

◆TURNIP

need it . . .

Metal basket with wire handle (model is 6"-diameter and 3"-deep)
Green, lavender, and white acrylic paint
Yellow spray paint
Water-resistant primer
Sealer
Paintbrushes

make it . . .

1. Paint basket inside and out with primer. Let dry. Spray-paint basket yellow. Let dry.

2. Paint turnips on basket with acrylic paints using pattern below as a guide. Let dry. Spray with sealer. Let dry.

Pattern full size.

◆VEGGIE

need it . . .

Small metal vegetable steamer
1 package of ½"-diameter magnets
1 package small plastic vegetables
2 yds. of ½"-wide orange ombré wired ribbon
1 yd. of ½"-wide sheer yellow ribbon
Industrial-strength adhesive
Masking tape

make it . . .

1. Glue magnets to flat side of plastic vegetables with industrial-strength adhesive. Let dry.

2. Open small metal vegetable steamer until sides are lined up with holes along top edge. Wrap ends of ½-inch-wide orange ombré wired ribbon with masking tape to thread through holes in steamer. Thread one end of ribbon through steamer and wrap through holes along one-half of steamer. Repeat with other end of ribbon. Trim tape. Tie ends into a bow with ½-inch-wide sheer yellow ribbon in center.

3. Attach magnets to sides.

use it . . .

◆ The BARN basket makes a cute napkin holder.

◆ Use the DREAMS basket to keep bedtime accessories close at hand.

◆ Place a hurricane lamp and an orange candle inside the CARROT basket.

◆DREAMS

need it . . .

Oval wooden basket with handle removed (model is 8"-wide by 5"-deep)
Three 2½", seven 2", and nine 1" wooden stars
3" wooden sun
3" wooden moon
Bright blue and metallic gold acrylic paint
Wood sealer
Spray gloss sealer
Wood glue
Paintbrush
Natural sponge

make it . . .

1. Arrange sun, moon, and stars on a flat surface in the shape of a handle. Pieces should overlap and the distance at base should be the same width as basket. Glue together with wood glue and let dry. Seal basket and handle with wood sealer and let dry.

2. Paint basket with two coats of bright blue paint, letting dry between coats. Paint handle with two coats of metallic gold paint, letting dry between coats.

3. Sponge paint with metallic gold around top and bottom edges of basket.

4. Glue handle to basket and let dry completely. Spray entire basket with gloss sealer.

◆BARN

need it . . .

Wooden crate (model is 10"-long by 5"-wide by 4"-high)
2 wooden barn shapes
Wooden cow
Miniature cow bell
Small amount raffia
8 tongue depressors
Black, brown, dark green, light green, red, off-white, and golden yellow acrylic paint
Clear acrylic spray
Wood glue
Handsaw

make it . . .

1. Paint crate and both sides of tongue depressors brown. Paint front and back of barn shapes as desired, referring to photo for color scheme. Glue barn shapes to each short side of crate.

2. Saw cow in half and paint front half off-white with black spots. Thread cow bell through raffia and tie around cow's neck. Glue cow to barn door.

3. Break tongue depressors into various sizes and glue to sides of crate to resemble fence posts.

4. Spray entire surface with acrylic spray.

◆CARROT

need it . . .

Small pot-shaped basket without handle (model is 5"-diameter and 4½"-deep)
Orange twisted paper ribbon
4 yds. of yellow to orange ombré wired ribbon
Green raffia
18" jute
Stuffing
Hot glue gun and glue sticks
Pencil

make it . . .

1. Untwist paper ribbon and cut into about fifteen 5-inch lengths. Fold each piece into a cone shape and glue edges. Fill cones with stuffing, pushing down into point with pencil.

2. Cut raffia into fifteen 3½-inch bunches. Cut ribbon into fifteen 9-inch lengths. Stuff each bunch of raffia into tops of carrots and tie with ribbon.

3. Glue jute around bottom and top of basket. Glue carrots around basket.

change it . . .

◆ Glue candy canes to basket and fill with treats.

◆ Glue colored pencils or fat crayon's around basket and fill with fun art supplies.

use it . . .

◆ Keep pool accessories in this FISHNET basket.

◆ Bath soaps and bath crystals are just right in the SHELLS basket.

◆ The BEACH bucket will be your child's favorite toy at the beach.

◆FISHNET ◆SHELLS ◆BEACH

need it . . .

Wire basket with handles and
    woven bottom (model is 10"
    x 8" and 12"-tall)
Fishnet
4 wooden fish
Black, rust, and white acrylic paint
Hot glue gun and glue sticks

make it . . .

1. Paint woven bottom of basket white. Let dry. Dilute a small amount of rust paint with water. Wash diluted paint over white paint. Let dry. Paint wire portion of basket with undiluted rust paint.

2. Paint fish as desired with acrylic paints, following any design carved into fish. Wedge fish into wire and glue in place.

3. Wrap fishnet around basket and glue in place as desired.

Note: Any wired basket may be used as long as the wire is loose enough to wedge wood cutouts in.

change it . . .

◆ Any theme of cutouts may be used. Wrap basket with coordinating material.

need it . . .

Wire basket (model is 8"-diameter
    and 12"-tall)
Assorted small shells
Sand
3 yds. of ombré 7mm silk ribbon
White acrylic spray paint
Hot glue gun and glue sticks
Spray adhesive

make it . . .

1. If basket is not already white, paint with white spray paint following manufacturer's instructions. Let dry.

2. Spray entire basket with adhesive. Roll basket in sand. Let dry. Repeat if necessary.

3. Glue shells randomly on each side of basket both inside and out. Glue shells up handle. Tie ribbon in bows and glue between shells to fill gaps.

need it . . .

Plastic beach bucket
Blue, red, white, and yellow
    contact paper
Transfer paper

make it . . .

1. Measure around the base of the bucket. Enlarge pattern below 200%. Transfer wave pattern onto blue contact paper, continuing the pattern to fit around bucket. Cut out the waves. Remove backing and adhere to bucket.

2. Transfer boat, sail, and sun patterns below to appropriate color of contact paper. Place on bucket as desired, smoothing out any bumps or wrinkles.

3. Fill with Sandpile Surprise ice cream (see page 62).

Enlarge patterns 200%.

use it . . .

◆ Keep the ANTLER basket next to the fireplace filled with wax dipped pinecone fire starters.

◆ The western basket makes a perfect planter for a cactus.

◆ Store magazines in this masculine G.Q. basket.

◆ANTLER

need it . . .

Natural basket without handles
(model is 15" x 12" and 6"-
deep)
Discarded antler to fit across basket opening
1 yd. of burlap ribbon
Heavy twine

make it . . .

1. Tie antler to basket with
twine to make handle. Make sure
to secure as tightly as possible.

2. Cover twine with ribbon.

*Note: If a basket without a handle
cannot be found, the handle may
be removed with wire cutters.*

change it . . .

◆ **Use an interesting tree
branch for a handle. Or,
barbed wire–but be care-
ful carrying it!**

◆ **Use PVC pipe as a handle to make a unusual gift
for a builder or plumber.**

◆YAHOO

Need it . . .

Basket with tall handle (model is
8"-diameter by 5"-deep)
5 ft. of rope
2 red bandannas
1 horseshoe
9" of barbed wire
Hot glue gun and glue sticks
Pliers

make it . . .

1. Tie a loose knot in one end
of the rope and glue to one side
of handle. Hold tightly until glue
cools. Continue to glue rope
around handle, letting glue cool
at each interval. Wrap any excess
rope around basket.

2. With pliers, twist barbed
wire around top of handle. Slip
horseshoe through loop. Place
bandannas in basket.

change it . . .

◆ **Use a miniature pirate
flag in place of a ban-
danna and hang a pirate's
hook from the handle.**

◆ **Use waterskiing or sail-
ing rope and fill basket
with suntan lotion.**

◆G.Q.

need it . . .

Wicker basket (model is 10"-wide
by 10"-deep)
4 yds. of ¼"-wide leather strips for
loops (model basket had
loose weave, so making loops
was not necessary)
3 old ties
2 suspender clasps
Belt buckle
Navy blue acrylic paint
Hot glue gun and glue sticks

make it . . .

1. If necessary, weave leather
strips through basket so that loops
are 1-inch-wide and 1-inch-apart.
Create two rows of loops.

2. Weave a tie through each row
of loops and secure with hot glue.

3. Paint handle navy blue and
let dry.

4. Glue suspender clasps to
each end of handle, facing front
of basket. Center belt buckle over
ties on front of basket and hot-
glue in place.

5. Tie a tie onto the handle.

use it . . .

◆ This basket-covered tray makes a perfect organizer for the office, sewing room or kitchen.

◆ This beautifully decorated glass jar is a wonderful alternative to a money tree at a wedding or graduation party.

◆ Bar accessories like a corkscrew and cocktail napkins can be stored in this grape basket.

◆NAPA

need it . . .

Wicker basket with green wire
   handle (model is 6"-diameter
   and 4"-deep)
2 plastic green grape sprays
2 yds. of narrow purple braid
Brown, metallic antique gold, and
   dark green acrylic paint
Spray gloss sealer
Industrial-strength adhesive
Paintbrushes

make it . . .

1. Dry-brush grapes with gold
paint. Dry-brush leaves dark green.
Dry-brush edges brown. Spray
grapes with sealer and let dry.

2. Loop purple braid around
fingers and tie a knot in center to
make a bow.

3. Glue grapes down one side
and across top of handle. Glue
bow between grape sprays.

◆BUFFET

need it . . .

Wood tray with handles
Enough small baskets to fill tray
Hot glue gun and glue sticks

make it . . .

1. Glue small baskets to tray.
Line with napkins and fill.

change it . . .

◆ Use different shapes
and sizes of trays and
baskets to make practical
and beautiful organizers.

◆REJOICE

need it . . .

Large round glass bowl
Metallic gold paint pen

make it . . .

1. Using patterns below as a
guide, write words on outside of
glass bowl with gold paint pen.

*Note: A calligraphy pen may also
be used, but it is more difficult to
handle and may smear. Bowl may
be gently hand-washed but is not
dishwasher safe.*

Pattern full size.

use it . . .

◆ The folk angel basket makes a wonderful poinsettia planter for the holidays.

◆ The drum-shaped basket with a nutcracker is a cute—and practical—nut bowl at Christmastime.

◆ Fill the twinkling Christmas basket with elegant stuffed animals or Christmas gifts as a holiday decoration.

◆TWINKLE

need it . . .

Large basket with handle (model is 12"-diameter and 10"-high)
One string of Christmas lights
Artificial pine garland
Crystal bead garland
Gold wire garland
Dove
Large tapestry bow
Gold thread
Thin wire
Snow
Hot glue gun and glue sticks

make it . . .

1. Wire Christmas lights around top of basket and up over handle, making certain that the plug ends up in back. Twist pine garland to cover lights. Secure with wire.

2. Drape gold and crystal garlands as desired. Secure bow to basket side with hot glue or wire.

3. Glue dove in place. Decorate with snow and drape gold thread.

change it . . .

◆ Use decorative chili pepper lights and decorate with southwestern miniatures for a Southwestern basket.

◆ Use white frosted lights and wedding flowers for a bridal shower gift.

◆DRUM

need it . . .

7"-diameter papier-mâché drum
5" painted wooden nutcracker
2 berry and pinecone sprays
9' brown twisted paper ribbon
Thin wire
Blue, metallic gold, and red acrylic paint
Spray gloss sealer
Paintbrushes
Hot glue gun and glue sticks

make it . . .

1. Paint drum blue and red with trim metallic gold. Let dry. Spray with sealer. Let dry completely.

2. For handle, cut three pieces of paper ribbon 2-feet long. Untwist ribbon. Wire all three pieces together at one end and braid tightly. Wrap wire around other end to secure. Cut remaining paper ribbon in half lengthwise. Make two bows for each side of handle.

3. Glue handle to drum and glue bow to each side. Glue nutcracker to center back of basket with sprays on each side.

◆ANGEL

need it . . .

Willow basket (model brim is 18"-wide)
Wooden angel ornament (model is 8"-high)
Gold star wire trim
Thin gold wire
1 yd. of 2"-wide burgundy wired ribbon
Hot glue gun and glue sticks

make it . . .

1. Wrap gold star wire trim around brim of basket, curling loosely. Secure trim with thin gold wire at 3-inch intervals.

2. Glue angel to one side of handle and tie ribbon to other side of handle.

change it . . .

◆ Use a red heart garland for Valentine's Day.

◆ Twist greenery around the edge of the basket and use a garden angel.

◆ A gold bell garland makes this basket perfect for a wedding gift.

◆ Use baby's breath and a nursery angel to celebrate a baby's christening.

use it . . .

◆ Put decorative Christmas soaps or hand towels in this cute basket.

◆ Fill this basket with mistletoe and hang it in a surprising spot.

◆ The chimney basket is ideal to hold firewood and kindling.

◆ST. NICK   ◆HOHOHO   ◆SANTA

need it . . .

Oval basket with rounded handle (model is 7"-wide by 4"-deep)
⅜ yd. of red wool fabric
One ⅝"-diameter wooden bead
Two ⅜"-diameter wooden beads
Wire glasses
Small amount of quilt batting
Spanish moss
Black and light peach acrylic paint
Hot glue gun and glue sticks
Paintbrushes

make it . . .

1. Cut red wool from bottom of one corner to top of other corner, forming a long triangle shape. Starting at center front of basket, glue widest part of triangle to basket, pleating as necessary. Wrap fabric snugly up around handle and continue until reaching center. Trim off any excess fabric and hot-glue in place.

2. Leave a 1½-inch space on front of basket and glue the moss in the same pattern as hat on opposite side. Paint the 1½-inch space light peach for face.

3. Paint small beads black and larger bead light peach. Glue "eyes" to face. Twist a small piece of moss and glue below eyes for "moustache." Glue "nose" and wire glasses in place. Glue a strip of quilt batting across hat above eyes and a ball of quilt batting to top center of handle.

need it . . .

Large white basket (model is 15"-diameter and 12"-deep)
Large stuffed Santa
Barn-red and brick-red acrylic paint
Snow texturizing medium
Paintbrushes

make it . . .

1. Paint brick shapes onto basket, alternating red paints. Leave space in between bricks for "mortar."

2. Following manufacturer's instructions for snow texturizing, paint between bricks.

3. Paint over top edge of basket with snow texturizing to create "drifts." Refer to photo if needed.

change it . . .

◆ Make a smaller chimney basket and hot-glue a miniature Santa sleigh and reindeer across the top of the handle. Fill with presents.

need it . . .

Round wicker basket (model is 9"-diameter and 4"-high)
Flat painted ceramic Santa head
Black, green, red, and off-white sculpting clay
Red acrylic paint (to match red clay)
Spray gloss sealer
Industrial-strength adhesive
Paintbrushes

make it . . .

1. Paint basket with red paint and let dry.

2. Roll red clay on a hard surface to make arms. Flatten slightly. Place on basket to shape. With a small amount of off-white clay, shape two sleeve cuffs and press onto bottom of arms. From green clay, shape two mittens and press onto place on cuffs. From black clay, shape two shoe shapes. Press Santa head onto the center of arms lightly to indent clay. Remove head and clay from basket. Taking care to retain shape, bake clay according to manufacturer's instructions.

3. Glue clay pieces and Santa head to basket, referring to photo for placement. Spray entire basket with gloss sealer.

use it . . .

◆ The cow basket filled with decorative dish towels is a nice addition to a country kitchen.

◆ Fill the sparkling basket with pretty potpourri or freeze-dried fruits.

◆ A basket with a clothesline is perfect in the laundry room!

◆HANG IT

need it . . .

Wicker laundry basket
Assorted Barbie doll clothes
Small clothespins
Twine
Assorted buttons
Green ricrac
Sky-blue and white acrylic paint
Hot glue gun and glue sticks
Paintbrushes

make it . . .

1. Dilute sky-blue paint with water and brush onto basket. With white paint, add clouds (see photo).

2. String twine from both handles.

3. Along bottom edge of basket, create flowers from buttons and glue into place. Add green ricrac for stems and grass.

4. Hang doll clothes from twine with small clothespins.

change it . . .

◆ Hang small quilts or quilt blocks from the line and use basket to hold quilting material.

◆ Hang Christmas cards or stockings from the line and fill basket with Christmas decorations.

◆MOOO

need it . . .

Shallow basket with handle (model is 14"-wide by 4"-deep)
Small wooden letters—M, L, K, C, O, O, K, E, and S
8 small wooden milk bottles
Cow bell
9" of jute
18" white ½"-wide cording
Black, blue, red, silver, and white acrylic paint
Fine-point black permanent marker
Paintbrushes
Sponge
Hot glue gun and glue sticks

make it . . .

1. Paint entire basket white and let dry. Sponge black spots onto basket and handle.

2. Paint letters red. Paint milk bottles white with silver lids and blue caps. Paint a thin red stripe around necks. When dry, write "milk" on bottles with black marker.

3. Glue letters and milk bottles to top of handle referring to photo for placement. The "I"s in milk and cookie are milk bottles.

4. Attach white cording to one side of basket and tie a knot in end for tail. With jute, tie cow bell to other side of handle.

◆WINTER

need it . . .

Round basket with handle (8" x 12½")
Vine of Christmas flowers
Angel icicle ornament
2 yds. of 1"-wide ombré ribbon
"Jewel" beads
Assorted pastel acrylic paints
Glitter snow
Hot glue gun and glue sticks
Spray adhesive

make it . . .

1. Dilute a small amount of pastel paint with water. Stain rows of basket randomly with diluted paint. Let dry.

2. Glue "jewel" beads on basket. Hot-glue vine of Christmas flowers around handle of basket. Wrap and glue ribbon through vine of flower and handle. Tie angel icicle ornament to handle.

3. Spray basket with spray adhesive. Sprinkle heavily with glitter snow.

change it . . .

◆ Paint basket dark blue and use gold glitter for a sweet dreams basket.

◆ Use multicolored glitter and party decorations for a birthday basket.

use it . . .

◆ This metal basket with painted flowerpots is an elegant planter.

◆ A bright sunflower TEACUP holds sunflower seeds for anytime snacks with style.

◆ The hanging basket is an elegant fruit bowl.

◆TEACUP   ◆CHERRY   ◆PLANT

need it . . .

7"-diameter Styrofoam ball
Small pie tin
Blue, crimson, gold, green, and
    white acrylic paint
Masking tape
6" piece of heavy wire
Papier-mâché
Paintbrushes
Knife and spoon

make it . . .

1. Cut off top quarter of
Styrofoam ball. Scoop out center
with spoon. Trim bottom of ball
to resemble cup bottom.

2. Mix papier-mâché according
to manufacturer's instructions and
cover outside of ball, trying to
create a smooth surface. Let dry.
Cover inside of ball and let dry.

3. Bend wire for handle and
cover with masking tape. Stick
ends of wire into Styrofoam to
form handle. Papier-mâché handle, overlapping onto Styrofoam.
Let dry.

4. Papier-mâché inside of pie
tin and let dry. Cover outside and
let dry.

5. Paint cup and saucer according to patterns on pages 62 and
63 and photo. Enlarge patterns as
desired.

need it . . .

Wire round basket (model is 14" x
    25")
Round wooden bowl to fit in wire
    basket (model is 8" x 10½")
Checkered stencil
6 bunches of artificial cherries
Red acrylic paint
Green spray paint
Hot glue gun and glue sticks
Sandpaper
Stencil brush
Paintbrush

make it . . .

1. Spray-paint wire basket
green. Let dry. Paint bowl green.
Let dry. Using checkered stencil,
paint red checks on bowl. Let dry.
Distress bowl with sandpaper.
Dilute a small amount of green
paint with water and "wash" entire
bowl with diluted green paint.

2. Glue cherries randomly on
wire basket handle. Place bowl in
wire basket.

need it . . .

Metal basket with wire handle
    (model is 6"-diameter and 3"-
    deep)
Clay pots—3"-high and 4"-high
Assorted acrylic paints
Water-resistant primer
Sealer
Hot glue gun and glue sticks
Paintbrushes

make it . . .

1. Paint both pots and basket
inside and out with primer. Let dry.

2. Paint metal basket desired
color. Paint 4-inch pot desired
color. When dry, paint flowers on
metal basket if desired. Paint all
with two coats of sealer.

3. Glue 3-inch pot to center of
metal basket, upside down. Glue
painted pot to other pot, bottom
to bottom.

4. Fill both basket and pot with
dirt and potted flowers or ivy.

◆ The tool box is a fun way to organize nails, nuts, and bolts or any other tools.

◆ This basket is an elegant container for dried herbs or cinnamon sticks.

◆ A basket in a wreath is a unique wall decoration.

◆RUSTIC

need it . . .

Basket with tree handle and base—see step 1 (model is 12"-diameter and 4"-deep)
Carved wooden Christmas ornament
Assorted dried naturals: pods, pinecones, apple slices, orange slices, artichokes, cinnamon sticks, pomegranates
Assorted miniatures: 3 birds, 1 frog, and 1 basket
4 yds. of hand-dyed ribbon in natural colors
Hot glue gun and glue sticks

make it . . .

1. If a basket with tree handle and base cannot be found, use a round shallow basket with no handle. Find two 1-inch-diameter sticks long enough to bend over basket for handle. For the base, use two 1-inch-diameter sticks about 2-inches wider than the basket diameter. Soak the handle sticks in water until they are flexible. Bend tree handles over basket and secure with twine on both sides and in middle. (See diagram to right.) Cover twine with raffia. Attach base sticks to front and back bottom of basket with twine and cover with raffia.

2. Glue drieds, ornament, and miniatures to basket as desired. Tie a looped bow with ribbon and glue to top of handle. Attach additional ribbon bows randomly throughout drieds.

◆ACORN

need it . . .

Grapevine wreath (model is 17"-diameter)
Wall basket with handle to fit middle of wreath
Assorted dried items, e.g., pinecones, pods, nuts, etc.
2 metal acorn bells
2 yds. of ombré 7mm silk ribbon
Bead strings
Hot glue gun and glue sticks

make it . . .

1. Glue basket into wreath.

2. Glue dried items randomly around bottom of basket where it meets the wreath. Tuck ombré silk ribbon and bead strings randomly through dried items to fill gaps.

3. Tie acorn bells to basket handles with ombré silk ribbon.

RUSTIC diagram.

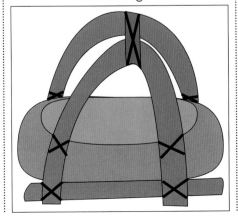

◆TOOLS

need it . . .

Small wooden toolbox (model is 5½"-tall, 20"-long and 7"-wide)
3 small empty paint cans
Light gray, dark gray, peach, and white acrylic paint
Acrylic base coat
Matte spray sealer
Paintbrushes

make it . . .

1. Paint base coat onto toolbox and paint cans according to manufacturer's directions. Let dry.

2. Paint toolbox dark and light gray and white. Paint paint cans peach and white. Mix colors on the surface of toolbox and paint cans for a textured look. Let dry. Using pattern below and on page 63, paint screws, nails, and nuts and bolts on paint cans. Let dry. Using dark gray paint, write "TOOLS NAILS SCREWS NUTS BOLTS" on side of toolbox. Let dry. Spray toolbox and paint cans with matte sealer. Let dry.

Pattern full size.

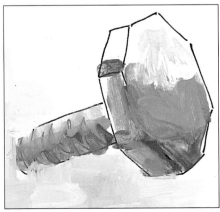

use it . . .

◆ Fill this basket with fresh bread, jams, and honey and use for your family and guests.

◆ This PANSY basket is a lovely towel holder.

◆ Put glazed breads in the BAKER basket and hang him in your kitchen.

◆WHEAT

need it . . .

Large basket with unusual handle
Metal wheat ornament
25½" x 24" loosely woven fabric;
    matching thread
2½ yds. of 1½" textured ribbon
Industrial-strength adhesive
Wire or twist ties

make it . . .

1. Tie a bow in the center of ribbon. Glue to basket handle. Cascade ribbon on handle, gluing about every 3 inches.

2. Glue wheat on top of bow. Use wire or twist ties to hold in place until glue dries.

3. Using a very small zigzag stitch, sew around all four sides of loosely woven fabric 1-inch from outside edge. Pull away loose threads of fabric to create fringe. Place inside basket.

change it . . .

◆ Use real wheat instead of metal ornaments for a truly rustic bread basket.

◆ To make a country bread basket, use a red-and-white checked cloth and decorate handle with kitchen utensils and clay bread dough sculptures.

◆PANSY

need it . . .

Small laundry basket
Five 2" velvet leaves
1½ yd. of 2"-wide sheer purple
    ribbon
1 yd. of yellow 7mm silk ribbon
2 yds. of 1"-wide purple ombré
    wired ribbon; matching
    thread
2 yds. dark green cording
Lavender, brown, and medium
    green acrylic paint
Matte spray sealer
Hot glue gun and glue sticks
Paintbrush

make it . . .

1. Dip dry paintbrush into lavender acrylic paint. Wipe off excess paint. Lightly paint over entire basket. Repeat process to dry-brush velvet leaves with medium green acrylic paint. Brush around edges with brown acrylic paint. Spray basket with matte sealer.

2. Make three large pansies.

3. Tie a bow in center of 2-inch-wide sheer purple ribbon. Glue to center of basket, 2 inches from bottom of basket. Glue leaves above bow. Glue pansies in center of leaves (see photo).

4. Loop dark green cording around fingers, leaving 18 inches at each end. Tie in center of bow. Cascade through purple tails. Glue tails to basket (see photo).

◆BAKER

need it . . .

Round hanging basket with flat
    back side
32" x 15" piece of ¼"-wide
    plywood
2½" x 24" strip of white canvas
Black, country-blue, peach, pink,
    and white acrylic paint
Hot glue gun and glue sticks
Sandpaper
Saw

make it . . .

1. Trace pattern from page 61 onto plywood and cut out. Sand all edges.

2. Paint baker according to photograph and pattern. Let dry.

3. Attach basket to front of baker with hot glue.

4. Cut canvas in half and paint arms on each piece using photo as a guide. Glue canvas to back of baker, bringing arms to front. Glue hands to basket.

use it . . .

◆ This is an elegant—yet practical—FRUIT basket.

◆ The WATERMELON slice basket is designed for picnic or party supplies.

◆FRUIT

need it . . .

Unfinished round wooden basket
Medium-size greenery spray
3 plastic fruit sprays
6 plastic grape clusters
Assorted plastic cherry sprigs
Golden oak stain
Metallic gold, dark green, medium green, and light green acrylic paint
Hot glue gun and glue sticks
Medium round stiff paintbrush

make it . . .

1. Stain basket with golden oak stain. Let dry.

2. Dip stiff paintbrush in metallic gold acrylic paint. Wipe off excess paint. Lightly paint over all plastic fruit, grape clusters, and cherry sprigs.

3. Using same method as step two, paint leaves, starting with dark green, then medium green, and then light green acrylic paints.

4. Spacing evenly, glue fruit sprays around top outside edge of basket. Glue two grape clusters between each spray. Fill in with greenery. Glue cherries randomly between fruit sprays and grape clusters.

◆WATERMELON

need it . . .

Two 12" wooden rings
⅝ yd. green cotton print fabric; matching thread
⅛ yd. pink cotton print fabric; matching thread
½ yd. burgundy cotton pin-dot fabric; matching thread
⅓ yd. fleece
24" each of green and burgundy wired ribbon
Two ⅜" wooden beads
About 30 black glass pebble beads
Black embroidery floss
4" craft stick
Green acrylic paint
Hot glue gun and glue sticks
Embroidery needle

make it . . .

1. Paint wooden rings and beads green. Let dry. Cut green cotton print fabric into 1½-inch-wide strips.

2. Place one 12-inch wooden ring on top of the other. Wrap one fabric strip around top of rings, making a 3-inch-wide handle. Secure end of strip inside wrapping with hot glue. Wedge a ⅜-inch wooden bead between rings on each end of wrapping. Glue in place and let dry completely.

3. Pull rings apart at the bottom and glue 4-inch craft stick between rings. Let dry.

4. Sew four green fabric strips together to make one long strip. Fold in half lengthwise and hot-glue one end across center bottom. Wrap in a figure eight manner through rings and halfway up one side. End by wrapping over last two crosses, tying a knot and tucking down inside weaving. Repeat for other side.

5. Enlarge patterns on page 61 400%. From large pattern, cut two fleece and four green cotton print fabric pieces. From medium pattern, cut two fleece and two pink cotton print fabric pieces. From small pattern, cut two fleece and two burgundy cotton pin-dot fabric pieces.

6. Layer two green fabric pieces with fleece in between and blanket-stitch with black floss around curved edge. Repeat with two remaining green pieces. Layer fleece and pink fabric on top of green fabric, matching straight edges. Blanket-stitch curved edge. Layer fleece and burgundy fabric on top of pink fabric, matching straight edges. Blanket-stitch curved edge. Blanket-stitch top, going through all layers.

7. Sew black glass pebble beads randomly on each watermelon slice. Glue a watermelon slice to each side of basket. Tie a double bow with wired ribbons to handle.

use it . . .

◆ This pretty bear with her basket will be wonderful as a little girl's treasure basket.

◆ The NOAH'S ARK basket is a perfect decoration for a nursery.

◆LOVE U

need it . . .

Plush bear (model is 14"-tall)
Small basket to fit in bear's arms
1½ yds. of wide lace
1 yd. of 2"-wide ribbon
1 yd. each of 5 colors 4mm silk
    ribbon
Heavyweight thread
6" square of mat board
Spray adhesive
Doll sculpting needle
Hot glue gun and glue sticks

make it . . .

1. Make a color photocopy of "Bear's my love" design below. Mount design onto mat board with spray adhesive.

2. With 2-inch-wide ribbon, tie a bow around back of bear's head and up around ears.

3. Handling all silk ribbons as one, tie a small bow with long tails and glue to one side of basket.

4. From lace, make a collar for bear's neck.

5. Using doll sculpting needle and heavyweight thread, stitch through bear's paws to firmly attach basket. Place sign in basket.

◆NOAH'S ARK

need it . . .

Ark-shaped basket with handle
2 pieces of plywood, each cut to
    the length and half the width
    of basket
1 package dollhouse shingles
Assorted soft sculpture animals in
    pairs
Noah soft sculpture doll
2" x 24" fabric scrap
Light blue, dark brown, cream,
    and tan acrylic paint
2 craft sticks
Paper towels
Paintbrushes
Hot glue gun and glue sticks

make it . . .

1. Cut ends off craft sticks at an angle. Glue craft sticks across each end of handle with angled edge up. Position plywood pieces together across handle and hot-glue to center of handle and to craft stick braces.

2. Glue shingles to roof in rows, overlapping rows. Paint basket and roof with tan paint. Let dry.

3. Thin dark brown paint with water. Brush onto basket and roof, small sections at a time, wiping off excess paint with a paper towel.

4. When roof is dry, use cream paint to write "Rain Rain Go Away. . ." Paint raindrops with light blue paint.

5. Glue animals randomly to inside of basket. With fabric scrap, tie a bow to one side of handle.

LOVE U art full size.

41

use it . . .

◆ Fill this basket with birdseed and hang in the garden for the birds.

◆ Fill baskets with Easter eggs or candy for a springtime celebration.

◆GARDEN ANGEL

need it . . .

Long-handled basket
8" square of ⅛"-thick plywood
Pre-cut wooden sunflowers,
    apples, bird, and birdhouse
10" of heavy wire
Dried moss
Brown, light brown, cream, gray,
    moss green, light peach, red,
    tan, yellow, and light yellow
    acrylic paint
Fine-point permanent brown
    marker
Light brown water-base wood
    stain
Paintbrushes
Hot glue gun and glue sticks
Wire cutters
Scroll saw

make it . . .

1. Angel and watering can patterns are on page 60. Enlarge patterns 200%. Transfer onto plywood square. Cut out with scroll saw.

2. Paint angel's face and hands light peach; hair and shoes light brown. Paint wings cream, apron and legs tan, and dress moss green. Thin a small amount of red paint with water and paint cheeks. Make dots on dress with cream paint and crosses on wings with tan paint. Paint watering can gray. After angel and can are dry, outline features with brown marker. Make dots for eyes with brown marker.

3. Paint centers of sunflowers brown and petals yellow. With brown, light brown and light yellow paint, dip end of paintbrush into paint and make dots around sunflower centers. When completely dry, outline details with brown marker.

4. Paint one apple red and one apple red with a cream center. Paint leaves moss green, and stems and seeds brown. When completely dry, outline details with brown marker.

5. Paint birdhouse tan with a red roof. Paint bird cream. When completely dry, outline details with brown marker.

6. Brush wood stain on all pieces and let dry for one hour.

7. Glue sunflowers, apples, birdhouse and bird to basket referring to photo for placement. Glue on moss as desired.

8. Cut wire into a 4-inch and 6-inch length. Poke a hole through both hands and through watering can handle. Thread 4-inch wire through bottom hand and handle. Wrap ends of wire around a paintbrush to curl. Thread 6-inch length of wire through top hand. Wrap one end of wire around a paintbrush to curl and wrap the other end of wire around center of basket handle.

◆TRAIN

need it . . .

Unfinished wooden train engine
    (model is 4½"-long by 3½"-tall)
8 wooden wheels
4 wooden 3"-long axles with
    hubs
2 small baskets without handles
    (models are 3½"-wide by 1½"-
    deep)
8" of red ribbon
Blue, green, purple, red, white,
    and yellow acrylic paint
Paintbrushes
Hot glue gun and glue sticks

make it . . .

1. Paint each part of train engine a different color, using white to accent with polka-dots and stripes. Paint one basket yellow with white polka-dots and the other basket red with purple stripes. Paint two wheels yellow, two purple, two blue, and two green. Paint axle hubs yellow, purple, blue, and green.

2. Thread an axle through front and back bottoms of both baskets. Pushing a pencil or a paintbrush through weave first is helpful. Place wheels and hubs onto each end of axle. For a more secure hold, glue wheels in place.

3. Glue ribbon to back underside of train engine and to underside of each basket, spacing baskets evenly.

use it . . .

◆ Fill the snowman bas-
ket with popcorn for a
snowy day.

◆ This pumpkin basket is
the perfect candy server
for Halloween.

◆FROSTY ◆JACK-O-LANTERN

need it . . .

Round white wicker basket with-
out handle
Black top hat
Strip of fabric for hat band
Plastic carrot
7 black buttons
6 or 7 assorted green buttons
3 red wooden beads ⅝"-diameter
Brown acrylic paint
10" of twine
Hot glue gun and glue sticks
Paintbrush

make it . . .

1. Dilute brown paint with
water and brush onto basket to
soften whiteness. Wipe off excess.

2. Cut carrot so that a 4-inch
portion of tip remains. Glue onto
front center of basket.

3. With twine, stitch an "X"
through holes in two black buttons. Glue into place for eyes.
String remaining black buttons
onto twine and glue into place
for mouth.

4. Cut fabric strip to fit around
hat. Fold raw edges inside and
glue band to hat.

5. Overlap and glue green buttons into two rows to resemble
"holly." Glue three red beads,
"berries," and "holly" onto hat
band.

need it . . .

Large round basket without handle (model is 10"-diameter
and 10"-deep)
1 yd. black fabric with gold stars
24" square of quilt batting
Black thread
3 yds. of thin wire
6" square of black paper
Orange and dark yellow acrylic
paint
Decoupage glue
Spray gloss sealer

make it . . .

1. Paint basket orange and let
dry. Trace stars and moon from pattern below onto basket in the position of eyes and nose. Paint stars
and moon dark yellow. Let dry.

2. From black paper, cut out
cat patterns below. Decoupage
into position on basket, referring
to photo for placement. Spray
basket with gloss sealer.

3. From pumpkin hat pattern on
page 60, cut two from fabric and
one from quilt batting. From stem
pattern on page 60, cut one from
fabric on fold.

4. Lay quilt batting on flat surface. Place fabric pieces with right
sides together onto quilt batting,
matching shapes. Sew around
edges, leaving a 4-inch opening
to turn. Lay thin wire over stitched
edges and go over wire with a
zigzag stitch. Turn right side out
and stitch opening closed.

5. Fold stem pattern in half with
right sides together. Sew the seam
up the side. Easing stem top
around top opening, sew into
place. Turn right side out and stuff
with batting. Hand-sew into place
in center of pumpkin top.

Enlarge patterns 200%.

45

use it . . .

◆ Fill this basket with wooden eggs and sit him on a shelf in the kitchen.

◆ This basket with a gardener crow is just right for holding vegetables fresh from the garden.

◆CHICKEN SOUP

need it . . .

White round wire basket (model
    is 8"-diameter and 7"-high)
20" x 4" piece of ¾" wood
Blue, red, and yellow acrylic paint
2 buttons for eyes
Yellow feathers
Black wire hanger
Double-sided tape
One sheet white paper
Hot glue gun and glue sticks
Tacky glue
Paintbrushes
Sandpaper
Wire cutters
Saw
Drill with small bit
Broomstick

make it . . .

1. Enlarge feet, beak, comb,
and gobbler patterns at right
200%; then trace onto wood and
cut out. Sand edges. Paint feet
and beak yellow and comb and
gobbler red. Let dry.

2. Cut two 12-inch lengths of
black wire and wrap around
broomstick to curl. Drill a hole in
the top of both feet and insert
wire. Twist closed. Attach other
end of wires to basket bottom.
Repeat with a 6-inch length of
black wire and curl tightly. Drill
hole in bottom of comb and
insert wire. Attach other end of
wire to top center of basket.

3. With double-sided tape,

attach button eyes, beak, and gobbler to front of basket. Hot glue
may be needed for more stability.

4. Enlarge wing pattern below
400% and cut two wings from
white paper. Paint wings with yellow, red, and blue paint, blending
blue on tips, then red, and finally
yellow. When dry, brush a thin
layer of tacky glue to back sides
and press firmly to each side of
basket. Hot-glue feathers onto
wings and on back for tail.

Enlarge Wing pattern 400%.
Enlarge all other patterns 200%.

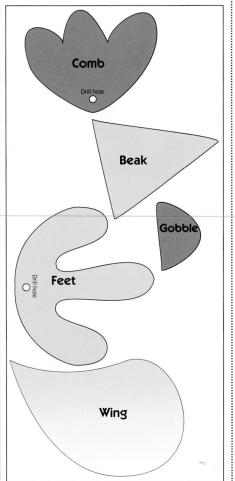

◆FRESH

need it . . .

Large shallow basket with handle
    (model is 14"-diameter and
    5"-deep)
Crow doll
Miniature garden utensils
Miniature clay pot
⅔ yd. of garden print cotton fab-
    ric; matching thread
4 yds. of green to rust ombré
    wired ribbon
12" of twine
Green acrylic paint
Paintbrush
Hot glue gun and glue sticks
Drill with small bit

make it . . .

1. Dilute green paint with
water and brush over entire basket. Let dry.

2. Wrap ribbon around handle.
Make a large looped bow with ribbon and secure to top of handle.

3. Glue garden utensils into
crow's "wings" and hot-glue crow
to center of bow.

4. Drill a small hole in upper
portion of pot and insert twine
through hole. Hang pot from
handle.

5. Cut a 24-inch-square of garden print fabric and hem edges.
Place fabric into bottom of basket.

use it . . .

◆ Fill the mouse toy with catnip and your cat will play all day!

◆ This basket holds yule logs stylishly as well as being a doggy bed.

◆HERE KITTY KITTY

need it . . .

Large round basket with handle
    (model is 14"-diameter and
    7"-deep)
1¼ yd. of cat print cotton fabric
Matching thread
1 yd. of ⅛"-wide elastic
Stuffing
Cat toys (mouse, ball, etc.)

make it . . .

1. Cut two 15-inch-diameter pieces of fabric for cushion. Place fabric circles wrong sides together and sew a seam ¼-inch in from edge, leaving a 5-inch opening. Stuff cushion firmly and sew opening closed. *Note: Raw edges should be on outside of cushion.*

2. For sides, cut two fabric pieces measuring 6-inches by 27-inches. Hem 6-inch edges. For ruffles, cut two fabric pieces measuring 4-inches by 45-inches. Fold each piece in half lengthwise and press. Sew a gathering stitch along raw edge. Pull gathering thread until each ruffle is 26-inches-long. Pin ruffles to side pieces with right sides together. Sew ruffles in place. Cut elastic in half. Sew elastic around same seam.

3. For ties, cut four fabric strips, each 20-inches by 4-inches. Fold each strip in half lengthwise with right sides together. Cut a 45-degree angle off one end of each strip. Sew a seam around long edge and angled edge, leaving short edge open. Turn right side out and press. Sew a tie to each end of side pieces just above ruffle.

4. Pin side pieces around cushion edge with right sides together. *Note: Side pieces will overlap about 1½-inches on each side.*

5. Place enough stuffing in basket bottom so that cushion can rest on it. Place cushion in basket. Wrap side pieces over sides and tie bows around handles. Tear a scrap of fabric and tie toy mouse tail to handle.

change it . . .

◆ Use an extra bed sheet as fabric and you and your cat will have matching beds.

◆ Use bird or fish fabric and tie an appropriate tie to the handle for a different look.

◆DOGS

need it . . .

Large, loosely woven basket
1 yd. plaid flannel
Four 2" x 4" leather swatches
Four 18"-long leather ties
Large eyed needle
Hot glue gun and glue sticks

make it . . .

1. Cut fabric into 1¾- by 20-inch strips. Thread fabric strips through needle so that a small amount of fabric is in needle. Randomly insert fabric strips around basket and tie into bows. Continue until basket is covered.

2. Tie a fabric strip onto bottom of one handle and stuff end down inside basket. Wrap strip around handle and tie off on other side, hiding end down inside basket. Repeat with opposite handle.

3. Wrap leather swatches around bases of each handle and hot-glue. Wrap leather ties around leather swatches several times and tie in knot.

change it . . .

◆ Choose a bright red basket, use red, white, and blue ribbons for bows and fill with fireworks for a patriotic gift.

use it . . .

◆ After using this sun hat as a gift basket, wear it!

◆ Use the MAYPOLE as an Easter egg holder and put on display during the celebration.

◆MAYPOLE

need it . . .

6 small baskets
4½"-diameter wooden plaque
13½" length of ⁵⁄₁₆"-diameter dowel
1" wooden knob
3"-diameter doily
1⅓ yd. each of light blue, lavender, peach, light pink, teal,
  and yellow 7mm silk ribbon
Beige acrylic paint
Spray gloss sealer
3 tea bags
Hot glue gun and glue sticks
Tacky glue
Drill with ⁵⁄₁₆" bit

make it . . .

1. Drill a hold in the center of wooden plaque. Glue dowel into hole.

2. Paint baskets, dowel, plaque, and knob with beige paint. When dry, spray with gloss sealer.

3. Place tea bags in one cup boiling water for three minutes. Dip doily into tea until completely covered. Remove doily and gently wring out excess liquid. When dry, cut a small hole in center and slide over dowel. Glue to plaque with tacky glue.

4. Cut 20-inch lengths from each color ribbon. Hot-glue one end of each ribbon to top of dowel and twist ribbons around pole for 2-inches. Hot-glue ribbons in place so that they will not unwind.

5. Tie one ribbon to each basket handle. Cut 10-inch lengths from each color ribbon and tie a bow with each. Glue to each coordinating basket handle.

6. Tie a bow with remaining ribbons and hot-glue to top of pole. Hot-glue knob on top of bow. Fill maypole cups with beads, strings, and threads so party members can each make their own party bracelet.

change it . . .

◆ Use bigger baskets and put spring flowers or plants inside each basket.

◆ Use the maypole as a centerpiece and fill with party favors.

◆ Make a red, green, and white maypole for Christmas celebrations or for any other holiday.

Pattern full size.

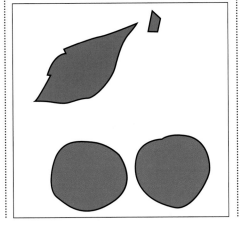

◆SUNNY

need it . . .

Straw sun hat
2 yds. of dark green ribbon
Plastic stencil sheet
Brown, green, red, and white
  acrylic paint
Masking tape
Pencil
Small sponge
Flat paintbrush
Thin paintbrush
X-acto knife

make it . . .

1. Photocopy stencil pattern below. Place stencil sheet over pattern on work surface and masking-tape in place. Trace pattern at left onto stencil sheet. Cut pattern out with X-acto knife.

2. Using red paint for cherries and green paint for leaves, stencil cherries with sponge randomly across both sides of brim. With thin paintbrush, hand-paint stems brown. Let dry. With flat paintbrush, paint a red strip around edge of brim on both sides. Let dry.

3. With flat paintbrush and white paint, paint a strip about 1 inch in from edge on underside of brim. When dry, paint green squares on white strip in checkerboard fashion. Let dry.

4. Cut ribbon in half and tie through holes on each side of hat.

use it . . .

◆ This watermelon basket is perfect for a picnic!

◆ A basket with silky carrots is a wonderful—and unique—centerpiece.

◆IN GOOD TASTE

need it . . .

Oval wicker basket with handle
   (model is 12"-diameter and
   5"-high)
Two 12" squares each of 3 shades
   of silky orange fabric
Matching thread
1 yd. of ombré orange 1⅛"-wide
   wired ribbon
2 yds. of avocado green 2"-wide
   sheer ribbon
2 yds. of peach 2"-wide sheer
   ribbon
Thin gold cord
Potpourri
Gold metallic craft paint
12"-square heavy cardboard
4 push pins
Paintbrush

make it . . .

1. Enlarge pattern below 200%
and cut one from each square of
silky fabric.

2. Place silky carrot on piece of
cardboard and secure with push
pins. With gold metallic paint,
paint along top edge of carrot to
prevent fraying. Paint freehand
designs on carrot as in photo.
Repeat with remaining five carrots.
Let dry.

3. With right sides together, sew
back seam along dotted line. Turn
and fill with potpourri to about
1½-inches from top. Tie each carrot off with gold cord. When all
carrots are complete, tie gold
cords together and attach to one
side of basket handle.

4. Brush gold accents onto ribbons. When dry, tie bows around
handle between carrots and wrap
handle with sheer peach ribbon.

Enlarge pattern 200%.

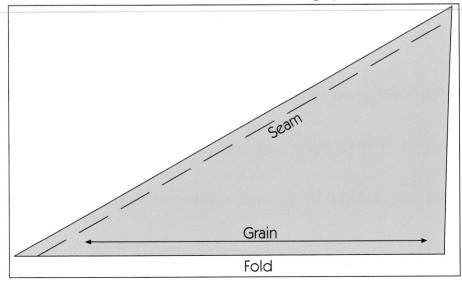

Seam

Grain

Fold

◆PICNIC

need it . . .

One basket with lid (picnic style)
Black sculpting clay
Assorted miniatures: utensils, gar-
   dening tools, and pot
One small straw hat
18" of dark green 1⅛"-wide ribbon
12" of red ½"-wide sheer ribbon
5 shades of green acrylic paint
Red acrylic paint
Spray sealer
Hot glue gun and glue sticks
Sponge
Paintbrush

make it . . .

1. Paint bottom of basket with
green stripes to resemble watermelon rind. Paint basket lid and
handle red. Sponge-paint straw
hat with five shades of green to
resemble leaves. Let dry.

2. Following manufacturer's
instructions, make seed shapes
from black sculpting clay.

3. Decorate hat by using red
sheer ribbon for hat band and
gluing utensils to brim.

4. Glue pot and gardening
tools by handle and seeds randomly on top of lid. Spray basket
with sealer.

5. Tie dark green ribbon into
bow around handle.

use it . . .

◆ Fill these hand-made doily baskets with pot-pourri or perfume bottles.

◆ This elegant basket is perfect for the boudoir.

◆SOUTHERN CHARM

need it. . .

Flower gathering basket with handle (model brim is 20"-wide)
3 mesh butterflies
4 small round ivory doilies
Lightweight 4"-wide lace (twice the circumference of basket)
Heavyweight 5"-wide lace (twice the circumference of basket)
2 yds. of ¼"-wide peach organdy ribbon
2 yds. of peach 4mm silk ribbon
1½ yds. each of peach and ivory braid
4 bunches of peach wedding flowers
Assorted pearls in peach and ivory
Ivory thread
Peach acrylic paint
Gold spray paint
Fabric stiffener
Sewing needle
Hot glue gun and glue sticks
Paintbrush

make it . . .

1. Sew a gathering stitch around one edge of 5-inch-wide lace. Pull thread to gather and fit around top edge of basket. Hot-glue lace in place. Repeat with 4-inch-wide lace and hot-glue along basket edge with lace pointing inside, overlapping outside lace at top edge. Follow manufacturer's instructions and brush fabric stiffener over both laces. Let dry.

2. Wrap handle with braid, alternating peach and ivory. Glue in place.

3. Sew pearls randomly over lace.

4. Gather each doily in the center and secure with thread. Glue one bunch of wedding flowers in the center of each doily. Glue or stitch doilies randomly around basket.

5. Paint butterflies lightly with peach paint. When dry, glue pearls on wings. Glue butterflies randomly around basket.

6. Tie small bows with organdy and silk ribbon. Glue bows randomly around basket.

7. Lightly spray basket inside and out with gold paint. Edges of lace will catch some of the gold spray paint.

change it . . .

◆ Use white flowers and lace for a wedding basket or a bride's gift.

◆ Red and white flowers and hearts make a Valentine's Day basket.

◆ Use black lace and satin for a "noir" basket.

◆LACY

need it . . .

12"-diameter doily
Lace or doily for handle
Styrofoam shape (models used a 2½"-square and a 3½"-diameter cylinder)
Assorted flowers, ribbons, and charms
Fabric stiffener
Large zip-top plastic bag
Plastic wrap
Rust proof straight pins
Hot glue gun and glue sticks
Stiff paintbrush

make it . . .

1. Place doily in plastic bag and pour in enough fabric stiffener to saturate. Squeeze bag to thoroughly cover doily.

2. Cover Styrofoam shape with plastic wrap. Stretch doily over plastic wrap and pin in place. Use fingers to mold curves around top edge. Let dry. Gently remove from shape and use stiff paintbrush to remove any flakes or residue from stiffener.

3. Handle ideas: Cut a strip of doily or lace that ribbon can be woven through. Stiffen as in step one. Shape and let dry. Weave ribbon through "handle" and sew or glue to basket. Twisted paper ribbon may also be used and wrapped with desired ribbon.

4. Embellish basket with flowers, ribbon, and charms.

use it . . .

◆ This basket is the perfect centerpiece for a tea party.

◆ The picket FENCE basket holds bath oil beads and bath salts beautifully.

◆TEA FOR TWO ◆FENCE

need it . . .

White basket
Blue-and-white china teacup and
  saucer
White linen tea towel
1 yd. blue and white teapot-and-
  cup print cotton fabric
3 yds. of 1"-wide yellow iridescent wired ribbon
½ yd. each of 1"-wide purple, yellow, green, peach, and rose
  iridescent wired ribbon
½ yd. each of ⅝"-wide lilac, yellow, and green iridescent
  wired ribbon
Nine 6" lengths of stem wire
Fray preventative
Hot glue gun and glue sticks
Decoupage glue
Shredded paper
Black fabric marker

make it . . .

1. Cut out motifs from teapot-
and-cup print fabric. Dab all
edges with fray preventative.
Using decoupage glue, glue a
teacup motif to tea towel.

2. Decoupage strips of fabric to
outside of basket following manufacturer's instructions.

3. Slightly gather 1-inch-wide
yellow ribbon by holding wire at
one edge and pulling ribbon.
Glue ribbon around edge of basket with hot glue.

4. Make three folded pansies
out of purple and yellow ribbon;
one large pansy out of peach and
rose ribbon; and one large pansy
out of yellow ribbon. Make a bud
out of yellow and green ribbon.
Make three leaves out of green
ribbon. Gather pansies, bud and
leaves together to form bouquet.
Fill tea cup with shredded paper
and insert bouquet.

5. Make two small lilac pansies,
one small yellow pansy and one
small purple and yellow pansy.
For small pansies and leaves, follow instructions for folded pansies using ⅝-inch-wide wired ribbons. Do not insert stem wire in
pansies or leaves. Hot-glue into
tea cup on tea towel.

6. Fill basket with shredded
paper and place cup, saucer, and
tea towel inside.

need it . . .

White picket fence basket
36" green rattail cording
21" each of ⅝"-wide pink ombré,
  blue ombré, and ivory wired
  ribbon
12" of ⅝"-wide green iridescent
  wired ribbon
Tacky glue
Hot glue gun and glue sticks
Green shredded paper

make it . . .

1. Weave cording through
"pickets" and over handle, making
a vine. Secure with hot glue in
several places.

2. Make three morning glories
of pink ombré, blue ombré, and
ivory ribbon. Hot-glue randomly
onto vine.

3. Make several morning glory
buds and hot-glue onto vine.

4. Make several morning glory
leaves. Hot-glue leaves randomly
onto vine.

5. Fill basket with green shredded paper.

use it . . .

◆ Use these holiday buckets as candle holders or fill with holiday treats.

◆BUCKETS OF FUN

need it . . .
Santa Pail

Aluminum pail
Small wooden plug
⅛" yd. red plaid fabric
4" natural twine
2 yds. of #72 4-ply natural jute
Natural-colored wavy wool hair
Cream, light gray, forest green,
    mauve, light peach, dark red,
    red, tan, white, and yellow
    acrylic paint
Paper towel
Hot glue gun and glue sticks
Fine-point black and brown per-
    manent markers
Paintbrushes

make it . . .

1. Paint pail cream. Paint Santa face onto pail using pattern on page 60 and photo as a guide. Lightly sponge light gray and tan paint with a small section of paper towel onto hat. Let dry. Add detail to bell and hat with black permanent marker. Make a small bow out of twine and hot-glue above bell. Paint plug light peach. Dip dry paintbrush in mauve paint. Blot off excess paint. Lightly dry-brush plug. Dry-brush mauve on Santa's cheeks. Draw eyes on Santa with black marker. Hot-glue nose to face.

2. Trace star and tree patterns randomly all over pail and paint according to patterns. Let dry. Add detail with brown perma-nent marker. Paint a plaid pattern on bottom of pail with diluted red and tan paint. Let dry. Make stitch marks on red cross sections with brown marker.

3. Cut wavy wool into various lengths and glue randomly to make beard and moustache. Cut small pieces for eyebrows and hot-glue in place.

4. Starting at one end, wrap and glue #72 4-ply jute around handle very tightly. Tear red plaid fabric into strips and tie in bows on handles.

need it . . .
Stocking Pail

Aluminum pail
2" strip of fabric 36" long
Black, light blue, cream, dark
    green, light green, red, tan,
    and yellow acrylic paint
Pencil
Fine-point black and permanent
    markers
Paintbrushes

make it . . .

1. Paint pail tan. Let dry. With pencil, draw stocking shapes around sides of pail. Paint tops of stockings with cream paint. Paint stockings as desired with patch-work and stripe designs. (Thin paint as desired.) When dry, out-line stockings and designs with a fine-point black marker.

2. Thin red paint and paint a stripe around top and bottom of pail. With pencil, write "I've been very good!" around sides of pail. Paint over pencil lines with a thin paintbrush and black paint.

3. Tear fabric strip so that edges are frayed. Secure one end of strip to one end of handle and wrap tightly around handle to cover. Secure at other end.

need it . . .
House Pail

Aluminum pail
1 yd. of thin white rope
Light blue, cream, light gray, navy,
    dark red, red, tan, and dark
    yellow acrylic paint
Snow texturizing medium
Hot glue gun and glue sticks
Fine-point black permanent
    marker
Paintbrushes

make it . . .

1. Paint pail using patterns on page 60 and photo as a guide.

2. Thin snow texturizing with a small amount of water and apply to pail with paintbrush. Let dry one hour.

3. With black marker, add detail. Wrap handle with rope and secure with hot glue.

Enlarge JACK-O-LANTERN Hat pattern 400%. See page 45.

Hat
Cut 2

Enlarge GARDEN ANGEL pattern 200%. See page 43.

Enlarge House Pail pattern 200%. See page 59.

Top
Cut 1

Enlarge JACK-O-LANTERN Top and Stem patterns 400%. See page 45.

Top

Stem
Cut 1

Seam

Fold

Enlarge Santa Pail pattern 200%. See page 59.

Enlarge WATERMELON pattern 400%. See page 39.

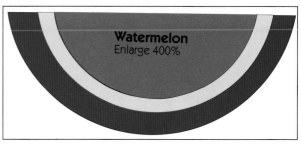

Watermelon
Enlarge 400%

Enlarge BAKER pattern 400%. See page 37.

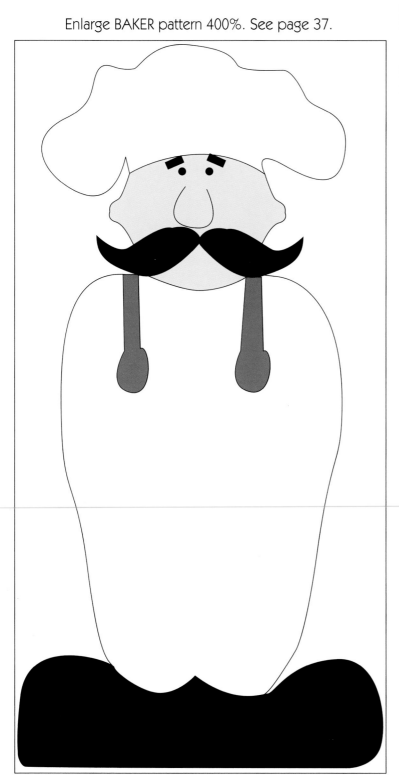

BABY patterns full size. See page 15.

See BEACH on page 21.

Sandpile Surprise

Ingrediants: 1/2 gallon icecream, Lg. box Vanilla wafers

1. Let your favorite icecream soften at rm. temp.
2. While icecream softens, place cookies in a resealable plastic bag.
3. Crumble Cookies until the texture looks like sand.
4. When icecream is soft, (not melted) scoop a 2" layer into bucket, followed by a thinner layer of crumbled cookies. Continue until your final layer is cookies and meets the top of the bucket.
5. Place in freezer for an hour. Remove half an hour before serving.

Enlarge TEACUP cup pattern as desired. See page 33.

Enlarge TEACUP saucer pattern as desired. See page 33.

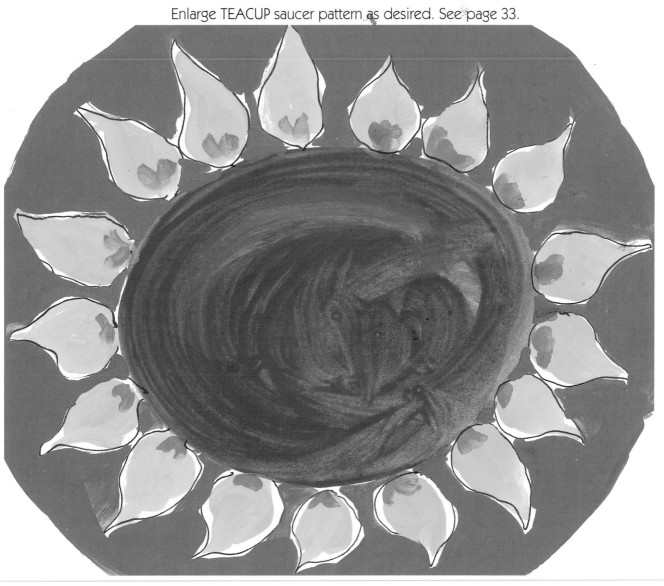

TOOLS pattern full size. See page 35.

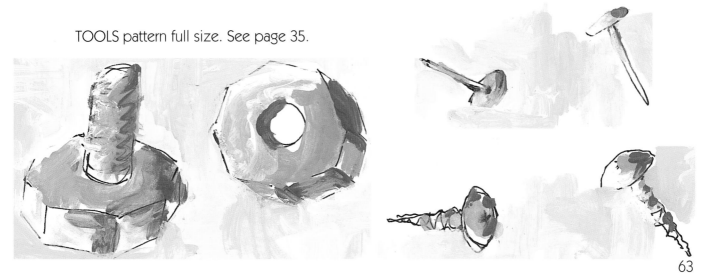

At times
I can almost feel
The presence of
My ancestors ~

A gentle,
Guiding touch
From those
Who've gone before

use it . . .

◆ Store seed packets or gardening notes inside this seed box.

◆ Fill this hat box with doll hats and clothes.

◆ Fill this box with little earrings and other petite accessories.

◆GARDEN

need it . . .

8" square cardboard box
Craft stick
Gardening tool charms
Package of small plastic vegetables
1⅝" x 2¼" piece of card stock
7" square vegetable-print fabric
Raffia
Decoupage glue
Hot glue gun and glue sticks
Pinking sheers

make it . . .

1. Trim all edges of 7" square vegetable-print fabric with pinking sheers. Center fabric on lid of box and decoupage. Let dry.

2. Make a color photocopy of art below. Decoupage onto card stock. Hot-glue to craft stick.

3. Tie a bow with raffia and hot-glue to lid. Hot-glue gardening tool charms, plastic vegetables, and seed sign to lid as desired.

Art full size.

◆HATS

need it . . .

10"-diameter round shaker-style box
10 miniature hats
3 large craft sticks
2 small craft sticks
Charms for hats
Ribbons for hats
22" of ⅝"-wide ribbon
Brown acrylic paint
Clear spray sealer
Hot glue gun and glue sticks
Paintbrush
Wire cutters

make it . . .

1. Dilute brown acrylic paint with water. Lightly wash box with diluted paint.

2. Make a notch in middle of two large craft sticks with wire cutters. Hook sticks together to form an "X". Make a notch on one end of remaining large craft stick. Hook in middle of "X". Cut two small craft sticks in half. Cut a notch on cut end of each half. Glue to large craft sticks on a slant. Let dry. Wash entire craft-stick hat rack with diluted brown paint to match box. Let dry.

3. Glue hat rack to box lid. Spray entire box with clear spray sealer. Let dry. Glue ⅝-inch-wide ribbon around edge of lid. Decorate miniature hats with charms and ribbons. Arrange and glue on box and hat rack as desired.

◆PETITE

need it . . .

Triangle-shaped cardboard box with 3½" sides
Small piece of button-print fabric
12" of natural string
Large antique button
Decoupage glue
Hot glue gun and glue sticks
Pinking sheers

make it . . .

1. Cut a triangle with 2½-inch sides out of button-print fabric with pinking sheers. Center fabric on lid of triangle-shaped box and decoupage to box.

2. Thread doubled natural string through antique button. Tie a bow on top. Hot-glue button and string to center of lid.

change it . . .

◆ Decoupage a magazine photo to the lid and glue make-up brushes on top.

use it . . .

◆ Use this black CROW box as a nut or seed box.

◆ Put your favorite recipes inside this cute cherry RECIPE box.

◆ This teatime box is just right for keeping buttons.

◆CROW   ◆RECIPE   ◆BUTTON

need it . . .

Octagon-shaped cardboard box
   with 2½" sides
4 small fabric sunflowers
Miniature resin crow
Small piece of country-print fab-
   ric
6" of 1"-wide dark green sheer
   ribbon
6" of black textured 7mm ribbon
Black acrylic paint
Semigloss spray sealer
Decoupage glue
Hot glue gun and glue sticks
Paintbrush
Pinking sheers

make it . . .

1. Paint box with black acrylic
paint. Let dry. Spray entire box with
semigloss spray sealer. Let dry.

2. Cut an octagon with 2-inch
sides out of country-print fabric
with pinking sheers. Center fabric
on lid of octagon-shaped box
and decoupage.

3. Tie a bow with 1-inch-wide
dark green sheer ribbon. Hot-
glue to center of lid. Tie a bow
with black textured 7mm ribbon.
Hot-glue to center of sheer bow.
Hot-glue miniature resin crow to
center of ribbons. Randomly hot-
glue small fabric sunflowers
around bow.

need it . . .

5¾" x 3¾" wooden recipe box
Acrylic paints (optional)
Decoupage glue

make it . . .

1. Make color copies of designs
below and on page 99. Decoupage color copies onto sides of
box using photo as a guide.

2. If different colors are
desired, use designs below and
on page 99 as a guide and paint
box with acrylic paints.

need it . . .

8"-diameter cardboard box
6 ivory buttons
Assorted brown and yellow
   acrylic paints
Clear acrylic spray sealer
Hot glue gun and glue sticks

make it . . .

1. Paint lid and sides of box
with light yellow acrylic paint. Let
dry. Trace teacup pattern on page
101 to lid of box. Trace zigzag
pattern on page 101 to sides of
lid and box. Paint as desired. Let
dry. Spray with sealer. Glue buttons randomly on lid.

Art full size.

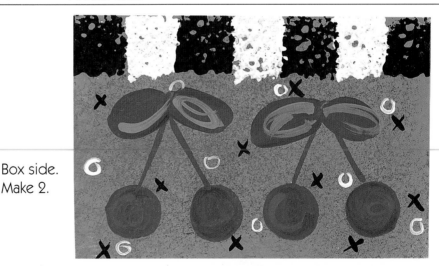

Box side.
Make 2.

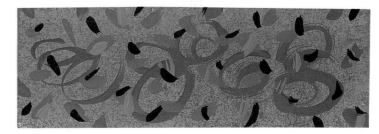

Lid side.
Make 2

◆ This box with cattails is just right for storing fishing lures and flies.

◆ A FISHY birdhouse will be a welcome accent in any fisherman's garden.

◆ This box is just the right size to put napkins in for an autumn dinner party.

THE ONE THAT GOT AWAY WAS AS BIG AS THIS HOUSE!

◆GOLDEN

need it . . .

Small square cardboard box
3 silk maple leaves
Dried eucalyptus
1½ yds. of ⅞"-wide gold wired
    ribbon
Gold enamel paint
Sponge brush
Paper towels
Hot glue gun and glue sticks

make it . . .

1. Stir gold enamel paint well. Using sponge brush, paint one silk maple leaf with gold enamel paint, not too thickly but cover surface of leaf. Press on box, cover with paper towel and press, making sure that all of leaf has been pressed on box. Lift off. Repeat, placing leaf randomly on box. Use a new paper towel for each leaf press. For a lighter look, leaf can be used twice before repainting.

2. Paint remaining two leaves with gold enamel paint. Let dry.

3. Tie ⅞-inch-wide gold wired ribbon around box. Make a bow and shape tails as desired. Cut small tops of dried eucalyptus off. Glue eucalyptus and painted leaves under ribbon bow.

change it . . .

◆ Use a holly leaf as a stamp and glue poinsettias to the top of the box.

◆FISHY

need it . . .

Wooden birdhouse
Dark blue, gray, green, peach,
    teal, and white acrylic paints
Matte spray sealer
Paintbrushes
Sponges

make it . . .

1. Paint birdhouse with dark blue acrylic paint. Lightly sponge over dark blue with teal and green paint. Let dry. Spray with matte spray sealer. Let dry.

2. Make a color photocopy of fish on page 100. Decoupage fish to side of birdhouse, wrapping around all four sides. Paint desired saying on top of birdhouse with peach paint. Let dry.

3. Splatter-paint entire birdhouse with all colors of acrylic paint. Paint inside of hole with white paint. Let dry. Spray entire birdhouse with matte spray sealer. Let dry.

change it . . .

◆ Decoupage cat motifs on the birdhouse and write "Here birdy birdy" on the lid.

◆STREAM

need it . . .

Cigar box
Small dry cattails
2 small resin or plastic fish
Moss
½ yd. dark green velvet
Fishing-print wrapping paper
1 yd. of ¼"-wide jute
Metallic copper acrylic paint
Decoupage glue
Hot glue gun and glue sticks
Tacky glue
Paintbrush
Rag

make it . . .

1. Decoupage fishing print wrapping paper to outside of cigar box. Do not smooth paper completely so that the box has a wrinkled look. Let dry. Coat again with decoupage glue. Let dry.

2. With rag, rub box and two small resin or plastic fish with metallic copper acrylic paint to antique. Let dry.

3. Measure inside of box. Cut dark green velvet to fit inside of box. Tacky-glue fabric to inside of box.

4. Hot-glue ¼-inch-wide jute to lid and front side of box (see photo). Hot-glue small dry cattails diagonally across lid. Hot-glue moss to bottom of cattails. Hot-glue small resin or plastic fish on top of moss.

use it . . .

◆ Fill this little frog box with fish food.

◆ Keep road maps to favorite fishing spots and your fishing license inside this outdoorsy box.

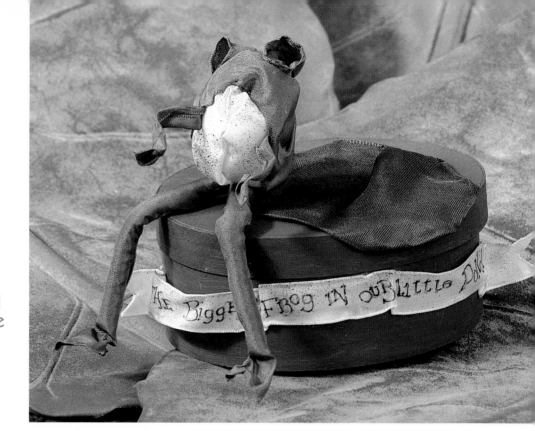

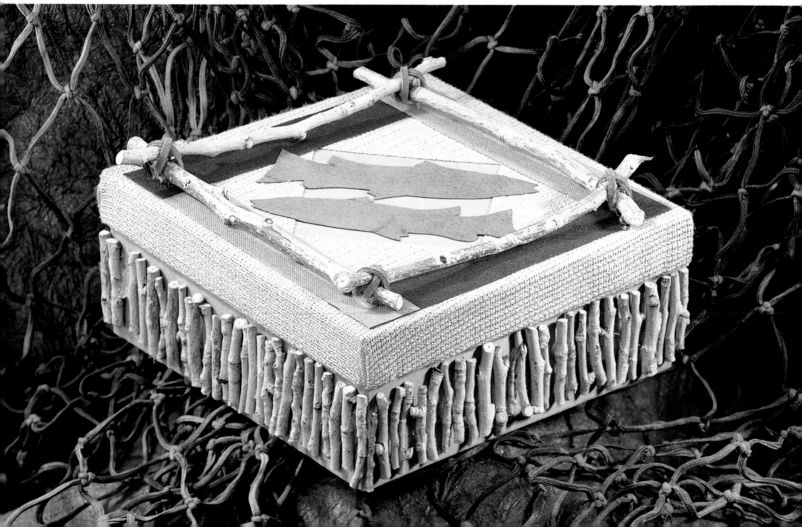

◆LILY PAD

need it . . .

Small oval shaker-style box
½ yd. of 1"-wide green iridescent ribbon
9" of ½"-wide white wired ribbon
6" each of 1½"-wide white and green iridescent wired ribbon
5" of ⅝"-wide green iridescent ribbon
4" of 2⅝"-wide green iridescent ribbon
8" of ¼"-diameter cord
Dark green and brown acrylic paint
Stuffing
Hot glue gun and glue sticks
Tacky glue
Stiff toothbrush
Black and brown fabric markers

make it . . .

1. Paint oval shaker-style box with dark green acrylic paint. Splatter all white ribbon with brown acrylic paint using stiff toothbrush.

2. Put a bead of tacky glue along one raw end of 2⅝-inch-wide green iridescent ribbon. Fold forward ⅛-inch. Put a drop of tacky glue on folded corners and fold forward slightly, making a blunt point. Repeat with opposite end. On one end pinch, forming a round shape. Hot-glue ribbon to box, making lily pad.

3. Cut a 6-inch length of 1½-inch-wide green iridescent rib-bon. Overlap and tacky-glue raw ends of ribbon length, forming a tube. Gather and tacky-glue one edge of tube together, forming a cup. Repeat process with 1½-inch-wide white ribbon. Put green cup over white cup and stuff. Hot-glue together to form frog body. Stuff.

4. Cut two 2-inch lengths of ⅝-inch-wide green iridescent rib-bon. Make tubes, then cups. Hot-glue to frog body for eye sockets.

5. Cover 3½ inches of ¼-inch-diameter cord with 4 inches of 1-inch-wide green iridescent ribbon. Tacky-glue in place. Use last ½ inch to make webbed feet by turning under raw edge and shaping. Repeat process to make another leg. Hot-glue legs to frog body.

6. Cut two 2-inch lengths of 1-inch-wide green iridescent rib-bon. Overlap and tacky-glue long edges of ribbon, forming a tube. Leave ¼ inch open. Fold top corners on one raw end in, making a point. Hot-glue to frog body.

7. Hot-glue frog to lily pad. Make a 1⅜ inch cut in each raw edge of ½-inch-wide white wired ribbon. Fold ends under to make a notched end. Tacky-glue in place. Hot-glue ribbon banner style to side of box. Write desired saying on banner with black and brown fabric markers (model says "The biggest frog in our little pond").

◆TWIGS

need it . . .

8" square box
Twigs cut to fit around bottom side of box (about 2"-long)
Four sticks about 8"-long
12"-square natural textured fabric
Two 1¼" x 7½" strips each of navy and brown fabric
5" x 7" piece of leather
12" leather tie
Fusing material
Hot glue gun and glue sticks
X-acto knife
Iron
Scissors

make it . . .

1. Apply fusing material to 5-by 7-inch piece of leather, 12-inch-square natural textured fabric and two 1¼- by 7½-inch strips each of navy and brown fabric following manufacturer's instruc-tions. Cut 3½-inch square dia-mond on the diagonal in center of natural textured fabric with X-acto knife. Iron fabric to box and wrap around edges to inside of box. Iron on fabric strips, overlapping each other (see photo).

2. Cut out two fish shapes from leather. Iron fish over diamond cut out in natural textured fabric.

3. Attach sticks together with leather ties and glue on top of box (see photo). Glue twigs all around bottom sides of box.

use it . . .

◆ Keep antique hankies or dried flowers in this floral box.

◆ Use this surprising box as a pin keeper.

◆WISH ON A STAR ◆FLORAL

need it . . .

Poster board
½ yd. of gold-star-print cotton
   fabric
8" square of fleece
2½ yds. of 1"-wide gold mesh
   wired ribbon
Hot glue gun and glue sticks
Tacky glue
Old paintbrush
Craft knife
Straightedge ruler

make it . . .

1. Trace patterns below onto poster board and cut one base, one lid, four inside flaps, and one inside lid (enlarge pattern 400%). Score dotted lines by gently cutting part way through using craft knife and straightedge ruler.

2. Trace patterns onto fabric and cut the following, adding 1 inch around all edges: one base, one lid, four inside flaps, and one inside lid. From fleece, cut four inside flaps to exact pattern size.

3. Place fabric base, wrong side up, on work surface. Brush scored side of cardboard base with a thin layer of tacky glue and press onto fabric. Clip corners, wrap and glue edges to other side. Cut two 13-inch ribbon lengths. Place one ribbon across fabric-covered base and the other ribbon going down. Hot-glue in place in center, wrap and glue ends to the other side.

4. Brush cardboard inside flaps with tacky glue and press a fleece insert in place. Cover fleece with fabric flaps; wrap and hot-glue edges to other side.

5. Lay cardboard base with fabric side down. Tacky-glue remaining fabric insert to center of base, trimming corners if needed. Hot-glue padded flaps to base flaps.

6. Cover outside lid with fabric; wrap and tacky-glue edges under. Pull corners together and hot-glue in place. Cut two 8-inch lengths of ribbon and hot-glue across and down lid top, wrapping and gluing ends under. Cover inside lid with fabric and tacky-glue in place.

7. Make a looped bow with remaining ribbon and hot-glue to lid. Pull flaps of base up and place lid on box.

need it . . .

8½" x 11" box
18" x 13" piece of flower-print
   fabric
Assorted silk flowers and leaves
1½ yd. of 1" teal ribbon
Hot glue gun and glue sticks

make it . . .

1. Wrap lid with fabric. Glue in place on inside of box. Place a piece of ribbon across top and glue to inside of box. Repeat, running the ribbon the other direction. Make a bow with remaining ribbon and glue in place at cross.

2. Glue silk flowers and leaves on top of bow at center. Put lid on top of box.

Enlarge patterns 400%.

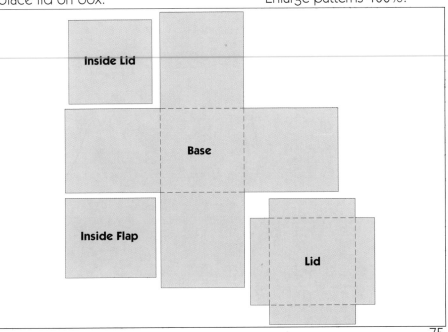

use it . . .

◆ Use the little bird's NEST with ribbon eggs as a Christmas tree ornament.

◆ Put little earrings and other jewelry in these little Battenburg lace boxes.

◆NEST

need it . . .

Small box
Small forked twig
Gold floral hair
Egg-patterned tissue paper
1 yd. of 2"-wide blue/brown
    ombré wired ribbon
5" of 1"-wide white wired ribbon
Stuffing
Brown acrylic paint
Gold spray paint
Hot glue gun and glue sticks
Stiff toothbrush

make it . . .

1. Fill box with gift. Wrap box in tissue paper. Wrap 2-inch-wide blue/brown ombré wired ribbon around package. Tie bow and shape. Make a 1-inch cut in each raw edge. Fold edges down to create notch; glue.

2. Paint small forked twig with gold spray paint. Glue to center of bow. Shape gold floral hair into a 2½-inch-diameter nest. Glue nest to bow over twig.

3. Cut 1-inch-wide white wired ribbon into two equal lengths. On one length, overlap and glue raw ends, forming a tube. Gather and glue one long edge, forming a cup. Stuff lightly. Gather and glue remaining long edge, forming egg. Repeat to make another egg. Splatter eggs with brown acrylic using stiff toothbrush. Glue eggs in nest.

◆LADY LOVE

need it . . .
(Large Box)

2 oval Battenburg doilies
½ yd. of 2½"-wide Battenburg lace
Assorted silk ribbons
Assorted dried flowers
12"-square Styrofoam
Plastic wrap
Fabric stiffener

make it . . .

1. Place oval Battenburg doily right side up. Starting at center back, hand-sew edge of 2½-inch-wide Battenburg lace to edge of design on doily. Cut off excess lace, leaving ½-inch to turn under. Turn ends under and hand-sew ends together. This forms the bottom and sides of box.

2. Cut two pieces of Styrofoam to fit center of box and stack together. Cover shape with plastic wrap. Using fabric stiffener, stiffen constructed box and remaining oval doily. Follow manufacturer's instructions. Stretch over Styrofoam shape. Lay additional doily flat to dry (this is the lid).

3. Using assorted silk ribbons and dried flowers, embellish top of box. Use two 18-inch-long pieces of silk ribbon for box hinges. Tie lid to box. Tie ribbons in a bow at back.

need it . . .
(Small Box)

2 heart-shaped Battenburg doilies
⅓ yd. of 1¼"-wide Battenburg lace
Assorted silk ribbons
Assorted dried flowers
6"-square Styrofoam
Plastic wrap
Fabric stiffener

make it . . .

1. Place heart-shaped Battenburg doily right side up. Starting at center back, hand-sew edge of 1¼-inch-wide Battenburg lace to edge of design on doily. Cut off excess lace, leaving ½-inch to turn under. Turn ends under and hand-sew ends together. This forms the bottom and sides of box.

2. Cut two pieces of Styrofoam to fit center of box and stack together. Cover shape with plastic wrap. Using fabric stiffener, stiffen constructed box and remaining oval doily. Follow manufacturer's instructions. Stretch over Styrofoam shape. Lay additional doily flat to dry (this is the lid).

3. Using assorted silk ribbons and dried flowers, embellish top of box. Use two 12-inch-long pieces of silk ribbon for box hinges. Tie lid to box. Tie ribbons in a bow at back.

◆ A box covered in pot-pourri is the perfect container for—what else—delicate sachets!

◆ This harlequin box is just the right size to hold you favorite romance novels.

◆SWEET SCENT

need it . . .

7"-diameter lined box with lid
Crushed potpourri
¾ yd. of 1½"-wide rose velvet
   ribbon
1⅛ yd. of 1½"-wide sage green
   organdy ribbon; matching
   thread
13" of 1½"-wide iridescent
   magenta and gold wired ribbon; matching thread
30 medium-sized velvet and satin
   leaves
20 small velvet and satin leaves
11 small rosebuds, silk or dried
5 velvet pansies
Bits of fern, eucalyptus and other
   assorted dried textures
Tacky glue
Hand-sewing needle

make it . . .

1. Glue 1½-inch-wide rose velvet ribbon around side edge of
box lid. Cover a small area of outside box side with thick tacky
glue. Flatly press crushed potpourri into tacky glue. Continue
thickly gluing until box side is
covered with potpourri. Let dry
one-half hour. Press potpourri flat.
Repeat same process for lid.

2. Trim bottom edge of box
with medium velvet and satin
leaves, fern, eucalyptus, and other
dried textures.

3. Glue small velvet and satin
leaves and rosebuds to top edge
of lid. Glue velvet pansies to lid
so that pansies sit about 1-inch
above lid. Fold three loops with
1½-inch-wide iridescent magenta
and gold wired ribbon, each 2-
inches deep. Gather-stitch bottom edge of loops, pull thread
tight and secure thread. Glue in
back of pansies, on right side.
Fold a five-looped bow with 1½-
inch-wide sage green organdy
ribbon, each loop 2-inches deep.
Gather-stitch center of loops, pull
thread tight, and secure thread.
Glue bow in back of pansies on
left side. Knot ribbon tails. Glue
small velvet leaves and a ribbon
leaf from 1½-inch-wide rose velvet ribbon around pansies.

change it . . .

◆ Use dried herbs and
leaves for an autumn box.

◆ Cover a box with
crushed spices and cinna-
mon sticks for the
kitchen.

◆ A box covered in
sweet lavender would be
lovely in a bedroom.

◆JEWEL

need it . . .

Wooden box
4 amber teardrop flat beads
Cream, mauve, and yellow acrylic
   paints
Matte spray sealer
Hot glue gun and glue sticks
Masking tape
Paintbrushes

make it . . .

1. Paint entire box with yellow
acrylic paint. Dilute cream and
mauve paint with water. Wash
entire box with diluted paints.
Let dry.

2. Place a piece of masking
tape diagonally across front of
box. Crisscross with another
piece of tape. Continue making
diamonds with tape. Paint inside
of diamonds with yellow paint.
Shadow and highlight with
diluted mauve and cream paints.
Let dry. Repeat process on other
sides of box and lid. Let dry. Peel
off tape.

3. Paint yellow dots next to
each corner of diamonds (see
photo). Shadow and highlight
with diluted mauve and cream
paints. Let dry. Spray entire box
with matte spray sealer. Let dry.
Glue four amber teardrop flat
beads on top of dots randomly.

◆ A baby girl's hair bows and barrettes could be stored in these little boxes.

◆ Keep antique thimbles in this tiny thimble box.

◆PASTEL

need it . . .

3 small nesting shaker-style boxes
1 yd. of 1¼"-wide pale pink wired
    ribbon
Pale green, pale blue, pale pink,
    and white acrylic paints
1¼-diameter sponge paintbrush
¾-diameter sponge paintbrush
Narrow paintbrush

make it . . .

1. Paint largest shaker-style box pale green, next-largest box pale pink, and smallest box pale blue. Let dry.

2. Using narrow paintbrush, paint freehand white plaid lines on the blue box.

3. Using 1¼-inch-diameter sponge paintbrush, dot blue spots on pale green box. Let dry. Using ¾-inch-diameter sponge paintbrush, dot pink spots on green box. Let dry. Fill boxes. Stack boxes on top of each other and tie together with 1¼-inch-wide pale pink wired ribbon. Tie a bow in ribbon and shape tails as desired.

change it . . .

◆ Use red, white, and blue boxes for a patriotic gift.

◆ Tie green and red boxes with Christmas-print ribbon for a yuletide gift.

◆SEW SMALL

need it . . .

Two 3½"-diameter wooden bases
Forty-two ⅝"-tall wooden spools
Fourteen ½"-tall wooden spools
Small scissor charm
3 small gold pins
20-30 assorted colors of embroi-
    dery floss
1½"-diameter button
Light wood stain
Matte spray sealer
Tacky glue
Wood glue

make it . . .

1. Stain all wooden spools and both wooden bases with light wood stain according to manufacturer's instructions. Let dry. Spray with matte sealer. Let dry.

2. Place a small dot of tacky glue on one wooden spool. Wrap embroidery floss around spool, keeping the strands even. Dot end of floss with tacky glue and secure. Repeat with all spools, varying the colors as desired.

3. Place base right side up on work surface. Take fourteen ⅝-inch-tall spools and arrange in a circle on base (spools should touch each other). Turn each spool so that the glued end of the floss is on the inside on box. Glue each spool in place with wood glue. Repeat for next two rows, staggering the spools on the second row like bricks. Let dry completely.

4. Arrange all fourteen ½-inch-tall wooden spools on top of remaining base as desired. Glue in place with wood glue. Embellish with scissor charm and gold pins. Let dry completely. This is the lid.

5. Glue button to center inside of lid with wood glue. Let dry. Place on top of box.

change it . . .

◆ Make a box out of thimbles to keep small antique buttons.

◆ Use tiny Christmas ornaments or nutcrackers lined up in a circle for a small Christmas present.

◆ A box made out of bells and filled with catnip would be perfect for a cat lover.

◆ Baby blocks or miniature bottles would make a great pacifier holder.

use it . . .

◆ Store fine teas in this elegant box.

◆ Use this as a jewelry box or treasure keeper.

◆TEA SET ◆TREASURE CHEST

need it . . .

7"-diameter fabric or paper cov-
ered box with lid
8" Battenburg doily
Miniature tea set and cakes
1½" wooden bead painted black
Four 2" wooden finials painted to
match box
Small bouquet silk flowers
Industrial-strength adhesive
Tacky glue

make it . . .

1. For legs, glue finials to bottom of box with industrial-
strength adhesive.

2. Apply a thin layer of tacky
glue to top and sides of lid. Press
Battenburg doily onto lid and
around sides, smoothing out
wrinkles.

3. With industrial-strength adhesive, attach tea set and cakes onto
lid as desired. Glue flowers into
wooden bead for vase and glue
to top of lid.

need it. . .

Wooden hinged box (model is
7" x 4" x 5")
Floral paper napkins
⅓ yd. of matching craft velvet
1½ yds. of ½"-wide matching dec-
orative cording
Batting (to fit top and bottom of
box)
Heavy cardboard (to fit top and
bottom of box)
Matching acrylic paint
Clear acrylic finish
Decoupage glue
Hot glue gun and glue sticks
Paintbrushes

make it . . .

1. Paint the inside edges
around lid and base with acrylic
paint. Let dry completely.

2. If napkins are double-ply,
remove back layer. Tear napkins
into random size pieces. With a
paintbrush, apply a thin layer of
decoupage glue to a section of
the box. Layer and overlap napkins onto glued area and smooth
into place with paintbrush and
more decoupage glue. Repeat
until top and sides of box are
covered. Let dry completely.

Apply clear acrylic finish to box
and let dry.

3. Cut two pieces of cardboard
slightly smaller than bottom of
box and inside lid. Using cardboard as a pattern, cut two
pieces of craft velvet, adding 1-
inch around all edges. Cut a piece
of batting to fit each piece of
cardboard. Spread hot glue onto
one side of cardboard and press
batting on. Cover with craft velvet, wrapping and gluing edges
to back.

4. Cut strips of velvet to fit
around inside box and lid sides.
Hot-glue into place at each corner. Press fabric into crease with a
butter knife. Hot-glue padded
box bottom and lid into box by
putting glue in bottom of box and
lid and pressing wrapped cardboard inside.

5. Measure around inside box
and cut cording accordingly. Hot-
glue cording around inside top
edge of box. Repeat around
inside lid edge.

6. Cut a piece of craft velvet to
fit outside bottom of box. Hot-
glue into place.

use it . . .

◆ Keep tea biscuits or tea bags in this tin.

◆ This tin is perfect for storing lacy cookies.

◆LADY OF LIGHT

need it . . .

8"-diameter tin
7"-tall glass dome with wooden
    base
4½"-tall plastic flocked tree
Very small porcelain doll head
    and arms
2" x 8" piece of pink satin fabric
20" of 1¾"-wide gray gathered
    ribbon
27" of ¼"-wide ribbon to match
    gray gathered ribbon
2 yds. each blue, gray, green,
    rose, purple, and yellow 4mm
    silk ribbon
2 yds. of 1"-wide flat white lace
4" of ¼"-wide flat white lace
Iridescent beads, star, and icicles
1" acrylic crystal ball
Small silver filigree bead cap
Stuffing
Rose acrylic paint
Spray gloss sealer
Spray primer
Drill with ¼" bit
Epoxy glue
Hot glue gun and glue sticks
Industrial-strength adhesive
Wire cutters

make it . . .

1. Spray tin with primer. Let dry.
Paint tin and wood base with rose
acrylic paint. Let dry. Spray with
gloss sealer. Let dry.

2. Drill a ¼-inch hole in center
of wooden base. Glue base to
center of tin with industrial-
strength adhesive. Remove base
of tree. Cut 1½-inch from top of
tree with wire cutters. Glue tree in
drilled hole with industrial-
strength adhesive. Let dry.

3. Fold short ends of pink satin
fabric under ⅝-inch. Sew ¼-inch
from fold. Fold in half, long sides
together with right sides facing.
Sew a ¼-inch seam on unfinished
edge, 2¼-inch from each end,
leaving center open. Cut a slit in
the center 1¼-inches. Turn right
side out. Hot-glue slit area around
doll's neck with the slit in back.
Stuff arms with a small amount of
stuffing. Hot-glue raw edges
under doll base. Slide arms in
sleeves. Tie small bows tightly
around doll wrist. Hot-glue doll
to top of tree.

4. Hot-glue a few iridescent
beads and star to doll's arms (see
photo). Hot-glue beads and icicles on tree. Sew a gathering
stitch on flat edge of ¼-inch-wide
flat white lace and hot-glue
around neckline. Clean inside of
glass dome. Glue into wood base
with industrial-strength adhesive.
Hot-glue crystal ball into small silver filigree bead cap. Glue to top
of dome with epoxy glue. Let dry.

5. Hot-glue 1¾-inch-wide gray
gathered ribbon and ¼-inch-wide
ribbon to sides of tin and wooden
base (see photo). Hot-glue 1-inch-
wide flat lace around wooden
base and ribbons. Tie a bow with
all 4mm silk ribbons. Hot-glue to
top of dome. Cascade tails and
secure with hot glue.

◆TEA TIN

need it . . .

7¾"-diameter tin with lid
³⁄₁₆" x 4" x 24" piece of basswood
5 teapot gift tags
8" white paper lace doily
Decoupage paper or stickers
    (Victorian tea pattern)
2 magnets
Acrylic paint for tin and gift tag
    background
Primer spray
Decoupage glue
Tacky glue
Paintbrushes
Band saw

make it . . .

1. Spray tin with two coats of
primer, letting dry between coats.
Paint tin with desired color of
acrylic paint. Let dry.

2. Cut out images from
decoupage paper. Glue to sides
of tin using decoupage glue.
Decoupage doily to lid of tin and
brush a thin layer of decoupage
glue over entire tin.

3. Glue gift tags to basswood
with a thin layer of tacky glue. Cut
around gift tags with band saw.
Paint edges and backs with coordinating acrylic paint. Brush a thin
layer of decoupage glue over
pieces.

4. Tacky-glue three teapots to
top of can. Tacky-glue magnets to
remaining teapots.

use it . . .

◆ Fill the FINIAL jar with oil or vinegar and the box with dried herbs and keep in the kitchen.

◆ MAKE A WISH and light one of the candles in the box each day. You can also keep a special journal of wishes and dreams inside.

◆FINIAL

need it . . .

Glass jar with cork lid
Wooden box
2 wooden finials
Assorted wood cutouts
Assorted acrylic paints
Matte spray sealer
Hot glue gun and glue sticks
Wood glue

make it . . .

1. Paint wood cutouts and finials as desired with acrylic paints. Let dry. Spray with matte sealer. Let dry.

2. Hot-glue half of wooden cutouts and one finial to jar lid and front of jar. Glue other half of wooden cutouts and one finial to wooden box with wood glue.

◆MAKE A WISH

need it . . .

Cigar box
Small matchboxes
Small jar candles
⅔ yd. of black satin
12" of black decorative trim
2" tassel
Shades of pink, purple, and blue watercolors
Black acrylic paint
Acrylic base coat
Spray matte sealer
Poster board
Tracing paper
Hot glue gun and glue sticks
Fine-point black permanent pen
Paintbrushes

make it . . .

1. Paint base coat onto sides of box, matchboxes, and lids of jar candles. Let dry. Paint sides of box with purple watercolor. Paint matchboxes and lids in coordinating colors. Let dry.

2. Make a color photocopy of art on page 98. Decoupage to top of box. Using patterns below, write "Wish Box" on top of box, and wishes on matchboxes and jar lids with black permanent marker. When dry, spray box, matchboxes, and lids with matte sealer.

3. Cut a piece of poster board to fit inside lid of box. Cover poster board with black satin. Glue to inside lid of box, inserting tassel in between at front center.

4. Cut a 1-inch-wide strip of cardboard long enough to fit around all four sides of inside box. Cut a piece of black satin to fit around inside box sides and bottom. Attach satin to cardboard strip following step 2 for "Mi-Lady" on page 93. Attach lining to inside box by gluing cardboard strip around top of sides. Glue black decorative trim across hinge on outside box lid.

Patterns full size.

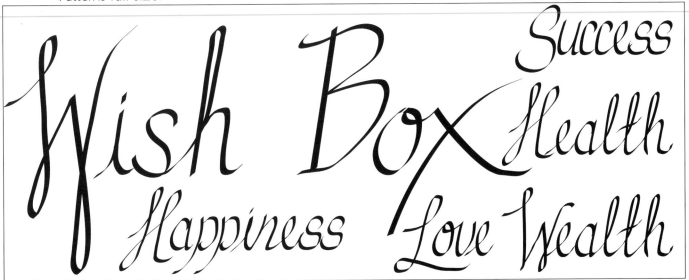

use it . . .

◆ This box is ideal for storing old photos.

◆ A gingerbread house is just right for gingerbread-men cookies.

◆FAMILY

need it . . .

Wooden hinged box
Photocopies of old family
   photographs
⅓ yd. of craft velvet
1½ yds. of decorative cording
Batting (to fit top and bottom of
   box)
Heavy cardboard (to fit top and
   bottom of box)
Matching acrylic paint
Clear acrylic finish
Decoupage glue
Thin-bodied tacky glue
Hot glue gun and glue sticks
Paintbrushes

make it . . .

1. Paint the inside edges around lid and base with acrylic paint. Let dry completely.

2. Make a photocopy of poem at right. Arrange photocopied photographs and poem on box as desired for placement. With a paintbrush, apply a thin layer of decoupage glue to a section of the box. Layer and overlap photos onto glued area as previously determined and smooth into place with brush and more glue. Repeat until top and sides of box are covered. Let dry completely. Apply clear acrylic finish to box and let dry.

3. Follow steps 3–6 for "TREASURE CHEST" on page 83 to finish inside of box.

◆GINGERHOUSE

need it . . .

Wood or cardboard house with
   removable roof
2 small wooden gingerbread men
Small silver ball beads
Small red oval beads
Frosted ball beads in assorted
   colors
Frosted star beads in assorted
   colors
4 small black beads
2 striped plastic candy sticks
2 red-and-white swirled beads
Light brown acrylic paint
3-D white paint pen
Industrial-strength adhesive

make it . . .

1. Paint house and gingerbread men with light brown acrylic paint. Let dry.

Pattern full size.

*At times
I can almost feel
The presence of
My ancestors ~
A gentle,
Guiding touch
From those
Who've gone before.*

2. With 3-D white paint writer, scallop roof to look like icing and outline edges. (You may want to lightly sketch design first in pencil.) Press frosted ball beads across top of roof while paint is still wet for "gumdrops." On each side of roof, glue a garland of frosted star beads.

3. On front of house, paint door and windows with 3-D white paint writer. Paint along corners and press silver ball beads into paint. Let dry.

4. Cut plastic candy sticks to fit on each side of door and glue in place. Top each with a red-and-white swirled bead.

5. Glue red oval beads along bottom edge of house.

6. Outline gingerbread men with white paint pen and make two dots for eyes. Press small black beads into paint dots. Glue beads down front. Glue a gingerbread man under star garland on each side of house.

◆JACK-IN-THE-BOX

need it . . .

6" x 6" decorative box with lid
3" x 3" decorative box with lid
8"-tall, 3"-diameter cylinder
  (empty can)
4" x 8" piece of Styrofoam
¼" dowel
3 small brass bells
Star charm
½ yd. of black fabric with stars
⅓ yd. green fabric
¼ yd. red fabric
12" x 12" piece of muslin
6" x 6" piece of peach fabric
12" x 12" piece of fusing material
Black sewing thread
1¼ yd. of 2½"-wide green iridescent wired ribbon
1¼ yd. of 2"-wide green sheer
  ribbon
2 yds. each assorted silk and
  sheer ribbons for bow
14" elastic
Stuffing
Gold glitter spray
Hot glue gun and glue sticks
Wax-base colored pencils
Fine-tip permanent marker

make it . . .

1. Using patterns on page 101, trace each section of Jack in the Box's face on fabrics indicated on pattern. Transfer markings for face. Following manufacturer's instructions, bond fusing material to fabric. Cut along lines. Place pieces right side up onto muslin. Adjust as needed to make Jack's head. Press, following manufacturer's instructions.

2. Layer muslin on top of green fabric. Cut along edges of Jack to form head. Outline face features with fine-tip permanent marker and color in with wax-base colored pencils. Stitch along lines and edges with black sewing thread, leaving an opening in Jack's chin to stuff. Stuff lightly. Insert ¼-inch dowel. Sew on bells. Sew opening closed and glue dowel into place.

3. Pull wire from one edge of 2½-inch-wide green iridescent wired ribbon. Gather edge without wire. Pleat wired edge. Pull gathers tight. Slide gathered ribbon on dowel in Jack's head to make collar. Secure with glue.

4. Gather-stitch 2-inch-wide green sheer ribbon along one edge. Set aside. Cut a 11- by 20-inch piece of black fabric with stars. Fold in half lengthwise. Sew ¼-inch seam along long edges of fabric. Turn right side out and slide over cylinder. Glue at both ends. Glue sheer ruffle to top edge of tube. Slide Styrofoam into center of tube. Cut edges to fit as needed.

5. Glue tube to inside center of 6- by 6-inch box. Push dowel in Jack's head through center of tube into Styrofoam. Tack collars together with glue. Tie ribbons and charm around neck.

6. To make arms, cut two 4- by 45-inch strips of black fabric with stars. Fold one strip in half lengthwise. Sew ¼-inch seam along long edges of fabric. Turn right side out. Cut elastic in half and thread elastic through. Repeat for other arm. Glue arms to side of Jack. Cut one hand pattern (see page 101) from red fabric and one from green fabric. Glue hands to arms. Spray entire box with glitter spray. Place Jack's hands on 3- by 3-inch box.

Note: This box can easily be made into a music box. Simply purchase a small music-box kit and follow manufacturer's instructions.

◆ Use this as a jewelry box or to store family heirlooms.

need it . . .

Book-shaped papier-mâché or
   bentwood box
Lightweight cardboard (enough to
   form four ½" strips around
   inside of box)
1 sheet of wrapping paper
Decoupage motifs
1 special paper picture to center
   on box top
⅓ yd. lining fabric (lavender silk
   floral print)
Quilt batting–enough to cover
   bottom of box
25" of 1"-wide pansy shaded
   wired ribbon; matching
   thread
½ yd. of ⅝"-wide pansy shaded
   wired ribbon; matching
   thread
7½" of 1½"-wide pansy shaded
   wired ribbon; matching thread
10" each of 1"-wide dark and light
   green wired ribbon; matching
   thread
45" of variegated 7mm ribbon;
   matching thread
6" of bud and bow garland, or
   other small trim
12 small velvet and satin leaves
Brass charms
Other embellishments as desired
Decoupage glue
Hot glue gun and glue sticks
Industrial-strength adhesive
2" sponge brush
Hand-sewing needle

make it . . .

1. Cut wrapping paper to cover
outer surfaces and inside lid of
box. Glue wrapping paper to box
with decoupage glue and sponge
brush, finishing all edges. Coat
with two layers of decoupage
glue, letting dry between coats.
Cut out small decoupage motifs
to cover visible seams. Coat with
two layers of decoupage glue.
Glue special picture to center top
of box. Coat with two layers of
decoupage glue. Let dry in
between coats.

2. Cut lining fabric 2½-inches
larger all around than box bottom.
Cut ½-inch-wide strips from lightweight cardboard to fit inside
each side of box. Glue batting to
inside bottom of box. Finger-
gather lining fabric, right side up,
onto each corresponding side
strip while gluing in place. (An
alternative is to gather-stitch
around the outer edge of lining
fabric, ⅛ inch from edge.) Adjust
gathers to fit lining strip. Glue in
place. When all fabric has been
glued to strip, the strip becomes
circular and inside out. Flip lining
strip, fabric right side out. Turn
down cardboard strip so that lining has a finished edge. Glue
wrong side of strip to inside of
corresponding box sides at top
edge, thoroughly flattening glue.
Begin gluing a corner of the strip.
Where cardboard edges meet,
you will be able to adjust lining
strip larger or smaller as needed,
depending on fabric weight.
*Note: If you prefer, you may sim-
ply paint inside of box.*

3. Stitch five gathered pansies
from 1-inch-wide pansy shaded
wired ribbon. Use 5½-inch-
lengths of ribbon, folded down ⅜
inch. Intervals are ¼-inch, 1½-inch,
2-inch, 1½-inch and ¼-inch. Stitch
three gathered pansies from ⅝-
inch-wide pansy shaded wired
ribbon. Intervals are the same as
above. Stitch one gathered pansy
from 1½-inch-wide pansy shaded
wired ribbon. Use 7½-inch length
of ribbon, folded down ⅝-inch.
Intervals are ¼-inch, 2-inch, 3-
inch, 2-inch, and ¼-inch.

4. Cut 7mm variegated ribbon
into five lengths, each 9 inches.
Stitch a rosette with each length
of ribbon. Stitch three folded
leaves with 1-inch-wide dark
green wired ribbon. Cut 1-inch-
wide light green wired ribbon
into two lengths, each 5 inches.
Gather-stitch as squared leaf. Pull
thread as tight as possible. Secure
thread. Fold leaf in half and join
ribbon ends together. Cup top
edge of leaf. Pinch bottom edge.

5. Refer to photo for placement.
Hot-glue velvet and satin leaves,
pansies, ribbon leaves, brass
charms, bud and bow garland,
and other embellishments around
center picture. Use industrial-
strength adhesive for applying ribbon flowers, charms and beads.

use it . . .

◆ Place this log cabin box by the fire to house matches and fire-starters.

◆HOME IN THE WOODS

need it . . .

30" x 6" piece of ⅝"-wide wood
⅝"-diameter willow sticks (see step 1 for lengths)
½"-diameter willow sticks (see step 1 for lengths)
Green acrylic paint
Two small hinges
Small nails
Wood glue
Paintbrush
Hammer
Saw

make it . . .

Note: The cabin may be put together with wood glue, nails, or both. If using wood glue, allow time for glue to set up between steps.

1. The ⅝-inch diameter willows need to be cut in the following quantities and lengths: six 1¼-inch, four 2-inch, two 2¾-inch, fourteen 3-inch, four 3⅜-inch, four 3½-inch, six 4-inch, two 4⅝-inch, eight 5½-inch, forty-four 6¼-inch, seven 7-inch, six 8-inch, and twenty-two 9¾-inch. The ½-inch diameter willows need to be cut in the following quantities and lengths: two 2-inch, two 7¼ inch, two 7¾-inch, and one 11½-inch.

2. On four 3½-inch lengths, cut both ends at a diagonal. See diagram below. Repeat with four 3⅜-

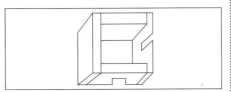

inch lengths, two 3-inch lengths, two 4⅝-inch lengths, and two 6¼-inch lengths. On forty-two 6¼-inch lengths, cut one end at an angle.

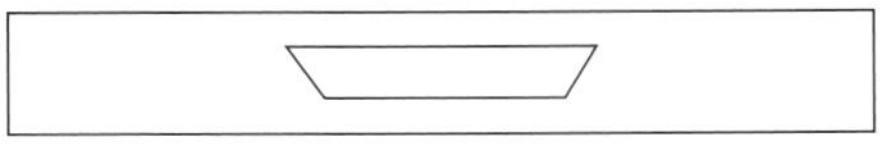

3. Cut patterns on page 96 from wood. Secure fifteen 9¾-inch sticks together "raft style" for cabin floor. Set aside. Assemble wood walls as in diagram below.

4. Starting at bottom front of cabin, attach a 4-inch stick to one side of doorway. Alternate 3-inch, 4-inch, 3-inch, and 4-inch sticks, keeping one edge flush with doorway. Repeat for other side of door. Top with an 8-inch stick, then a 9¾-inch stick. Front of cabin should now be completely covered.

5. To cover the window side of cabin, start with a 5½-inch stick along bottom and alternate 7-inch, 5½-inch, and 7-inch sticks to reach bottom of window. On each side of window, alternate 2-inch, 2¾-inch, and 2-inch sticks.

6. To cover back of cabin, start with a 9¾-inch stick along bottom and alternate 8-inch, 9¾-inch, 8-inch, 9¾-inch, 8-inch, and 9¾-inch sticks.

7. To cover other side of cabin, start with a 5½-inch stick along

bottom and alternate 7-inch, 5½-inch, 7-inch, 5½-inch, 7-inch, and 5½-inch sticks.

8. Secure cabin to floor. Turn cabin over. Using ½-inch-diameter sticks, attach two 7¼-inch sticks about ½-inch in from side edges and two 7¾-inch sticks to top and bottom.

9. Assemble roof frame as in diagram below. Around edge of

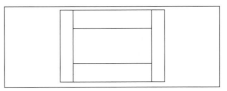

roof frame attach 8-inch sticks to long sides and 7-inch sticks to short sides. See diagram below.

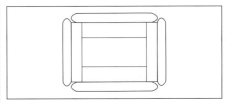

Lay roof frame flat. On one of the sides, attach a 5½-inch stick on top of the 7-inch stick. Next add a 6¼-inch stitch with angled ends, a 4⅝-inch stick with angled ends and a 3-inch stick with angled ends. Secure a 2-inch piece of ½-inch diameter stick to inside of roof side as a brace. Repeat on other side. Attach a 9¾-inch stick to the top of the 8-inch sticks on the front and back of the roof frame. Secure the 11½-inch length of ½-inch diameter stick across the roof braces. Beginning at one end, start attaching the roof sticks, butting angled edges together to form a point. See diagram below.

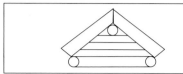

Join two 3⅜-inch angled sticks together for first row. Next join two 3½-inch angled sticks. Using forty-two 6¼-inch angled sticks, make twenty-one rows joined together. Finish with two 3½-inch angled sticks and two 3⅜-inch angled sticks.

10. To make chimney, place two 3-inch sticks about 1½-inches apart on flat surface. Attach two 3-inch sticks across bottom sticks in opposite direction. See diagram below. Repeat twice more.

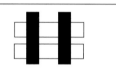

Wedge and secure the six 1¼-inch sticks in between spaces. Secure chimney to top of roof.

11. Attach hinges about 2½-inches in on each side of back of cabin and roof.

12. Thin green acrylic paint with water. Brush paint over cabin surface.

13. Make folk angel to attach to cabin (see next column).

96

Folk Angel

need it . . .

5" x 5" piece of ⅝"-wide wood
5" x 3" piece of ¼"-wide wood
1" of ¼"-diameter wood dowel
Small wooden star and heart
8" of thin silver wire
Black, light blue, dark brown, cream, dark green, light green, metallic gold, mauve, purple, light peach, dark red, tan, white, and dark yellow acrylic paint
Small checkerboard stencil
Pencil
Paintbrushes
Sandpaper
Paper towel
Thumbtack
Hot glue gun and glue sticks
Drill with ¼" bit
Scroll saw

make it . . .

1. Using pattern at right, cut out wood with scroll saw (enlarge pattern 400%). Cut angel out of ⅝-inch and wings out of ¼-inch wood. Paint crown dark yellow and face light peach. Paint dress dark green and shoes metallic gold. Paint wings cream. Let dry.

2. With metallic gold paint, paint dots on crown. Dry-brush mauve paint onto face for cheeks. Dip tip of pencil into black paint and make dots for eyes and mouth. Stencil white checkerboard pattern along bottom of dress. Paint swirls on dress with dark red. Paint a purple heart on dress and add "stitch" marks with black paint. Add detail to shoes with black paint. Paint "cloud" shapes on wings with light blue paint and shade with light green. Paint small tan crosses on wings. Paint wooden heart dark red and wooden star metallic gold. Paint 1-inch wooden dowel with flesh paint. Let dry. Sand all edges.

3. Drill hole in top of body and bottom of head. Glue head onto dowel and glue into body. Glue wings to back of body.

4. To antique angel, thin dark brown paint with water and paint over entire surface. Wipe off excess paint with paper towel.

5. Cut silver wire into a 3-inch length and a 5-inch length. Wrap each piece around a pencil to curl. Glue star and heart to wires. Push a tack into top of head to make two small holes. Glue curly wires into holes.

Enlarge pattern 400%.

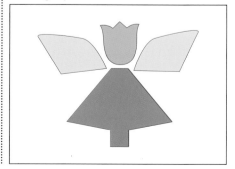

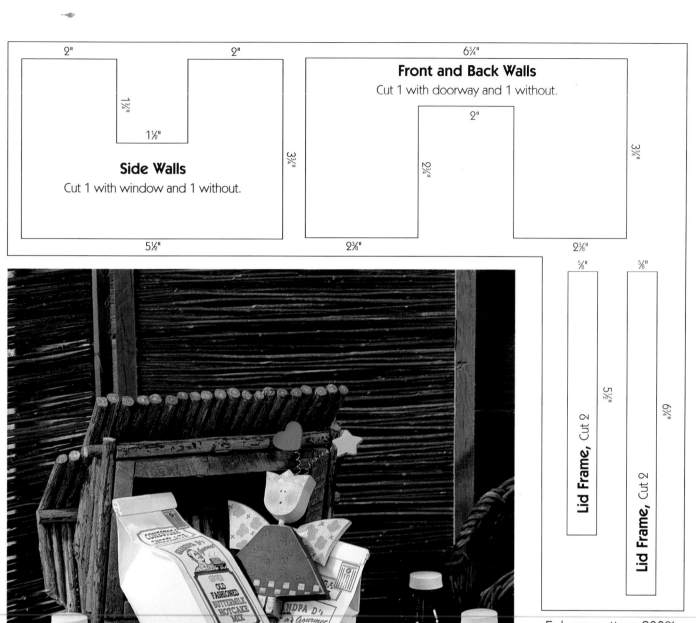

Side Walls

Cut 1 with window and 1 without.

2"   2"

1¾"

1½"

5½"

Front and Back Walls

Cut 1 with doorway and 1 without.

6¾"

2"

2¼"

3¾"

2⅜"   2⅜"

3¾"

⅝"   ⅝"

5½"   6¾"

Lid Frame, Cut 2

Lid Frame, Cut 2

Enlarge pattern 200%.

Opposite page (98): MAKE A WISH art full size. See page 87.RECIPE art full size. See page 69.

Lid back.
Make 1.

Lid top. Make 1.

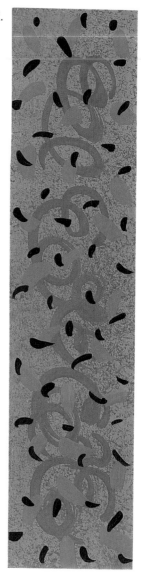

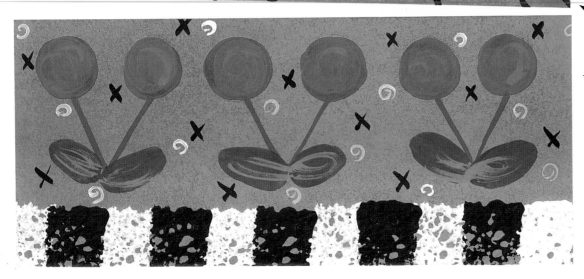

Lid front.
Make 1.
Box front
and back.
Make 2.

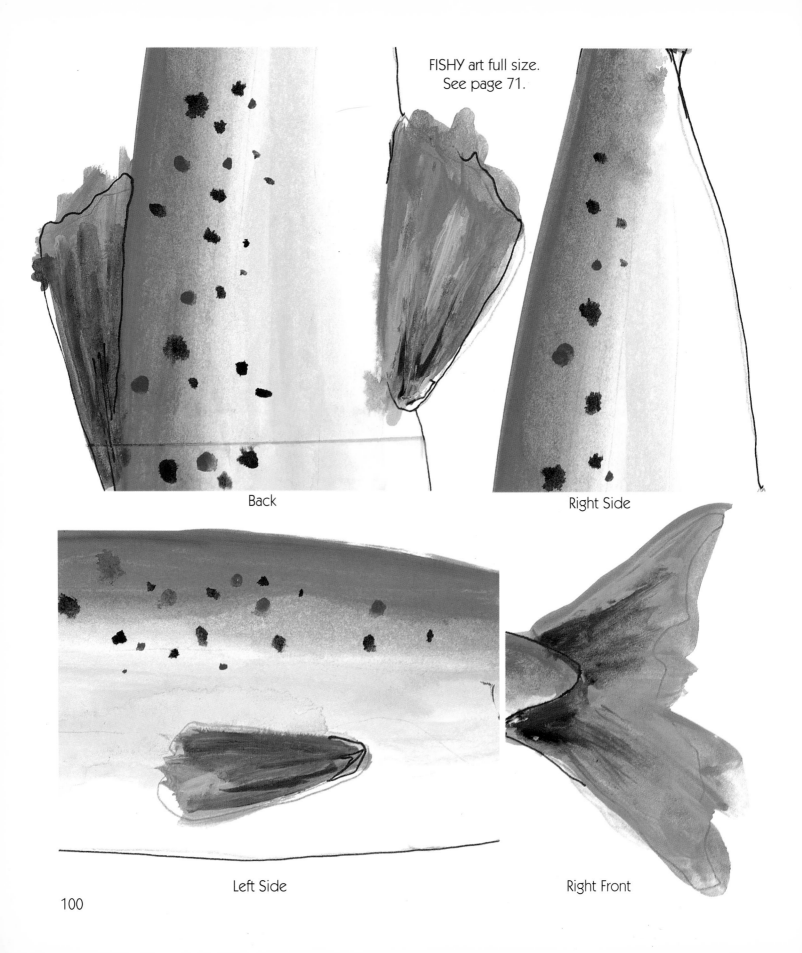

FISHY art full size.
See page 71.

Back

Right Side

Left Side

Right Front

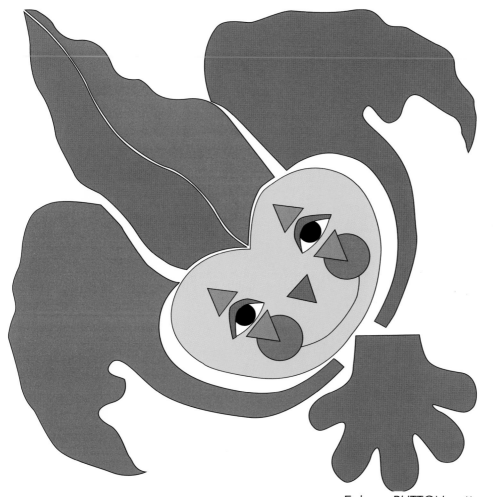

Enlarge JACK-IN-THE-BOX
pattern 400%. See page 91.

Enlarge BUTTON pattern 200%. See page 69.

FISHY art full size. See page 71.

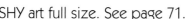

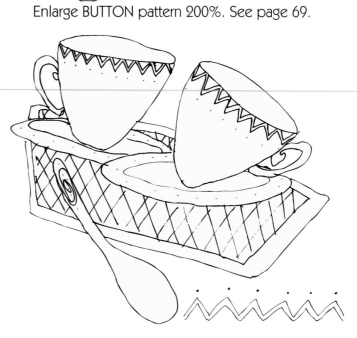

Left Front

101

use it . . .

◆ Use the beeswax snowman attached to this bag as a Christmas tree ornament.

◆ This mitten bag is a perfect door decoration at Christmastime.

◆ Fill this bag with cocoa mix and marshmallows.

◆FOREST ◆FRIENDS ◆SNOMIT

need it . . .

Beeswax
Santa pressed cookie mold
Large brown bag with handles
1 yd. of 1"-wide gold ribbon
1 yd. of raffia
Black, green, red, and white
    acrylic paints
Gold enamel paint
Nonstick cooking spray
Potato
Paper plate
Toothpick
Knife
Paintbrushes

make it . . .

1. Spray cookie mold with non-stick cooking spray. Heat wax in can in double boiler. When melted, pour into cookie mold. Let harden. (Placing in freezer will quicken hardening time.) Pop out molded wax. While still warm, make small hole in top with toothpick. Wipe off any cooking-spray residue. Let cool. Paint Santa as desired with acrylic paints.

2. Cut potato in half. Sketch a tree shape (see pattern on page 124) in potato and cut away excess. Pour green paint onto paper plate and stamp potato in it. Test stamp before decorating bag. Randomly stamp bag and let dry. Paint small gold dots with gold enamel throughout trees. Loop raffia and tie onto one handle. Tie on Santa ornament and ribbon.

need it . . .

8" x 24" flannel fabric; matching
    thread
4 red bells
4 tiny pom-poms
Scraps of 4 different fabrics
Black, light blue, blue, lavender,
    orange, purple, white, and
    yellow felt
Fusible iron-on adhesive
18" plaid ribbon
Red embroidery floss
Needle
Pinking shears

make it . . .

1. Bring right sides of fabric together matching short edges. Sew a seam up both sides. Turn. Cut across top with pinking shears.

2. Iron fusible adhesive onto fabric scraps and felt following manufacturer's instructions. Cut out patterns on page 124 from scraps and felt, and iron on front of bag. (See photo.)

3. Sew pom-poms onto mittens and bells in corners. With red embroidery floss, stitch across hat and mittens.

4. Tie bag with plaid ribbon.

need it . . .

12" x 18" heavy canvas fabric
5" x 18" white looped fur
6" of plaid ribbon
Red thread
2 small twigs
Black, brown, dark green, light
    green, orange, white, and yel-
    low acrylic paint
Tracing paper
Tacky glue
Paintbrush
Sponge

make it . . .

1. Trace mitten pattern on page 124 onto canvas and cut two.

2. Place mittens together and sew ¼-inch seam around edge, leaving top open. Do not turn inside out–leave flat.

3. Paint both sides of mitten red. Use two coats of paint and let dry after each coat.

4. Transfer pattern on page 124 for snowman onto front of mitten. Paint as desired. Paint a crooked pine tree with a star on top. Paint small snowflakes and sponge white paint along bottom for "snow." Glue on twigs for arms and ribbon for the scarf.

5. Fold fur in half lengthwise and glue to the top of mitten, starting at one side.

use it . . .

◆ Unpick the placemats and use for everyday.

◆ Use the oven mitt to hold wooden spoons—or to protect your hands!

◆ Use this bag to store napkin rings.

◆DINNER

need it . . .

4 placemats
4 matching cloth napkins
Matching embroidery floss
Needle
Straight pins

make it . . .

1. Place two placemats together with right sides out. With six strands of embroidery floss, sew a large basting stitch around side and bottom edges.

2. Roll up remaining two placemats and insert side by side into one end of bag. With a pin, mark how much space the placemats take. Remove placemats and sew a wide basting stitch from the top to bottom along this mark, forming a pocket.

3. Repeat for napkins on the other side of bag. Since the napkins will be shorter, make a vertical basting stitch across bag for proper depth of pocket.

4. The center pocket may be as deep as needed for silverware, napkin rings, etc.

5. Enclose a note with this gift explaining that the stitches can be easily removed so that the placemats can be used.

◆TIE IT

need it . . .

4 cloth napkins
4 napkin rings (or silk flowers)

make it . . .

1. Lay one napkin face down. Place another napkin on top at an angle so that all eight corners are showing. Fold the remaining napkins and place in the center along with three napkin rings. Bring corners of outside napkins up to center, forming a bag. Slip on the remaining napkin rings. Pull the corners out like flower petals.

change it . . .

◆ Make napkin rings from silk flowers by twisting stems into circles.

◆ Use bandannas for napkins and chicken wire or straw for napkin rings.

◆ A lady's scarf or set of hankies would be elegant with a beaded scarf clasp.

◆HOT!

need it . . .

Oven mitt
Hot pad
2 plastic cookie cutters
Plastic measuring spoon set
Wired ribbon
Thread
Large-eyed needle

make it . . .

1. Thread desired length of ribbon through needle and insert in top center of oven mitt. Tie a cookie cutter on with ribbon. Insert another cookie cutter through ribbon tail. Tack in place.

2. Thread another length of ribbon through top of hot pad. Tie on measuring spoons and make a bow. Spread spoons apart.

change it . . .

◆ Fill a bath mitt with sponges, a washcloth and a back-scrubber.

◆ Use a pair of wool winter gloves and put ski-passes inside.

◆ A miniature bat and ball would be perfect inside a baseball glove.

use it . . .

◆ Use these bags as a pretty alternative to brown paper lunch bags.

◆ This cute diaper is perfect for holding baby wipes and diaper pins.

◆ Use this bag for pajamas or as an overnight bag to Grandma's house.

◆BAG IT   ◆BEAR IT   ◆WET IT

need it . . .

Cardboard box for pattern
   (choose box size to corre-
   spond with desired bag size)
Wrapping paper
Tacky glue
Pinking shears

make it . . .

1. Cut a piece of wrapping
paper as if wrapping box. Cut off
top edge with pinking shears.

2. Center box on paper. Fold
sides of paper in and glue, turning outside edge under for a finished look. Wrap bottom like a
present and glue paper to paper.
Be careful not to wrap too tight so
that box may be removed. Crease
edges with fingers for crisp look.
Remove box.

need it . . .

Purple sweatshirt
5" x 8" pink gift bag
Lavender poster board
2 iron-on appliqués
Silver and gold glitter fine-line
   paint writers
Tacky glue
X-acto knife or small sharp scissors

make it . . .

1. Cut poster board 2-inches
larger than iron-on appliqué.
Following manufacturer's instructions, transfer designs to sweatshirt
and center of poster board. Cut
around design on poster board,
leaving ¼-inch around sides and
top. Leave bottom edge straight.

2. With silver and gold glitter fine
-line paint writers, randomly outline motifs and outside edge of
iron-on appliqué. Let dry for 24
hours.

3. Apply a thin layer of tacky
glue to one side of bag. Center
poster board lining up bottom
edge evenly. Lightly press out any
air bubbles.

need it . . .

Cloth diaper
2 diaper pins
4-ounce bottle fabric stiffener
Large plastic bag with zip-top
   closure
2 or 3 plastic garbage bags

make it . . .

1. Cover work surface with
garbage bag and tape edges.

2. Lay diaper flat and drizzle
half of the fabric stiffener onto diaper. Start at one end and roll.
Unroll and put in plastic bag. Pour
in other half of stiffener. Squeeze
bag until diaper is saturated, remove diaper and wring out excess liquid.

3. Fold diaper as you would for
a baby and pin corners. Stand diaper up and stuff plastic bags inside to shape. Let dry. Take out
plastic bags and fill.

use it . . .

◆ Fill this bag with birdseed or old bread to feed to the birds. Hang it on your door so you that won't forget it.

◆ Use this bag to keep buttons or old letters. Or use it to store seeds.

◆EARLY BIRD

need it . . .

12"-square burlap; matching thread
18" of tan cording
12" of 2"-wide brown to blue ombré wired ribbon
12" of 1½"-wide brown wired ribbon
4" of ½"-wide ivory wired ribbon
Small feather
Black fabric pen
Tacky glue

make it . . .

1. Cut burlap in half and place both pieces together. Sew around sides and bottom, forming a bag.

2. Cut brown to blue ombré ribbon into 6-inch lengths and place side by side with dark edges out. Draw a 1½-inch circle in center. Cut out half circle from each ribbon. Clip curves, fold, and glue curved edge under. Fold and glue bottom raw edge of each ribbon under ⅛ inch. Fold and glue top outside corner back to make a pointed roof. Glue ribbons, side by side, onto burlap bag about 1½-inch up from center front.

3. Fold and glue raw edges of brown ribbon under. Fold in half at an angle, making a roof. Crimp ribbon with thumb and forefinger and glue on top of house.

4. Print "Early Bird" with fabric marker in center of ½-inch-wide ivory wired ribbon. Make a small cut in each end of ribbon. Fold and glue ends under, forming a "V". Glue to house above opening. Glue small feather at bottom of opening. Tie cording around top of bag.

Enlarge pattern 200%.

◆4 YOU

need it . . .

13" square of light brown wool fabric; matching thread
1 yd. of brown twine
Black, dark green, and yellow yarn
3 assorted buttons
Large-eyed needle

make it . . .

1. Cut wool square in half. With black yarn, use a straight stitch to stitch the words "Just for you" 3-inches down from top edge of one wool piece. With yellow yarn, make three Lazy Daisy flowers and sew buttons in centers. With dark green yarn, make running stitch stems and Lazy Daisy leaves. (See diagram.)

2. Place wool pieces right sides together. Stitch up both sides and along bottom. Turn. Tuck top edge 1½-inch down into bag.

3. Thread needle with twine, starting at one side, and baste around top of bag, catching the edge that was turned under. Knot ends and tie a bow.

use it . . .

◆ Use this as an evening bag or as a sachet for a lingerie drawer.

◆ Fill these envelopes with stationery, pens and stamps for love notes and other correspondence.

◆FINERY

need it . . .

Two 9"-diameter lace doilies
Silk ribbons (see Stitch Guide on
    page 125)
3 tea bags
Beige thread
Size 3 crewel embroidery needle

make it . . .

1. Heat two cups of water to boiling and add tea bags. Steep for two minutes and remove bags. Place doilies in tea until completely covered. Let set one minute. Remove and squeeze out excess liquid. Lay flat to dry.

2. Stitch embroidery design onto one doily, following Embroidery Chart and Stitch Guide on page 125.

3. Place embroidered doily on top of other doily. Hand-sew a circle around edges, leaving a 6-inch opening at top.

4. Thread one yard each of two colors 7mm ribbon onto needle. Weave through top of doilies for drawstring. Knot ends.

Note: Bag can be embroidered to match doily design, if desired.

◆SPECIAL DELIVERY

need it . . .

½ yd. of muslin
16" square of fusible iron-on
    adhesive
Cherub charm
4 yds. each of 3 colors of silk
    ribbon
Fabric stiffener
Extra-fine black permanent marker
Fabric color marking pens
Hot glue gun and glue sticks
Paintbrush

make it . . .

1. Cut two 16-inch-squares of muslin. Follow manufacturer's instructions and bond both squares together with iron-on adhesive.

2. Cut out envelope pattern on page 124 from muslin square. Transfer all markings.

3. Pleat bottom of envelope along dotted fold lines. With sewing machine, tack both ends to hold pleats in place. Fold both sides in and press folds. Fold bottom flap up and press fold. Glue edges of flaps together and let dry.

4. Using paintbrush, coat the outside of the envelope with fabric stiffener. Shape as desired and let dry completely. Repeat on inside.

5. With black marker and color marking pens, decorate the front of envelope following pattern below.

6. Glue ribbon lengths at an angle across envelope and tie a bow in bottom corner. Add cherub charm.

Enlarge pattern 200%.

113

◆ Use this bag to send home Thanksgiving or family dinner leftovers.

◆ Use these bags in the car as garbage bags.

◆FALL

need it . . .

Large brown bag with handles
Tissue paper
2 silk maple leaves
Raffia
Gold ribbon
Gold enamel paint
Paint thinner (for clean-up)
Newspaper
Paper towels
Hot glue gun and glue sticks
Sponge brush

make it . . .

1. Follow instructions for decorating with leaf design on page 71 and decorate bag and tissue paper as desired.

2. Loop raffia and tie onto one handle. Tie gold ribbon around raffia and hot-glue leaves on for decoration.

change it . . .

◆ Make hand stamps all over the bag and hang a glove from the handle.

◆ Make dog or cat paw prints all over the bag and hang toys and a collar from the handle.

◆TWIGS & THINGS

need it . . .
Pinecone Tree

Solid-color gift bag
3 twigs in various lengths
Pinecone
Moss
Hot glue gun and glue sticks

make it . . .

1. Glue twigs vertically onto front of bag. Glue small clumps of moss to base of trees.

2. Pull apart pinecone. Create trees by gluing smallest pieces at top of twig and larger pieces at the bottom.

need it . . .
Knotty Pine

Solid-color gift bag
Scrap of brown fabric
Scrap of green "woodsy"-print fabric
Scrap of brown "autumn"-print fabric
Skinny twigs
Hot glue gun and glue sticks

make it . . .

1. Tear fabrics into long strips about ½-inch-wide. From "woodsy" strip, cut into 5-inch, 4½-inch, 4-inch, 3½-inch and 3-inch lengths. From "autumn" strip, cut into 4½-inch, 4-inch, 3½-inch and

3-inch lengths. From brown strip, cut a 10-inch length and an 8-inch length.

2. Place longest brown strip vertically on table. With longest "woodsy" strip, tie around center with a square knot. Move up the tree with next-largest strip. Tie three knots in bottom tree trunk. Repeat with "autumn" strips to form smaller tree. Glue trunks only on front of bag.

3. Break twigs into pieces to form the words "Knotty Pine." Glue to top front of bag.

need it . . .
Log House Bag

Solid-color gift bag
10" of country fabric border
2 houses cut from house-print fabric
Skinny twigs
Hot glue gun and glue sticks
Tacky glue

make it . . .

1. Cut border to fit along bottom front of bag. Apply a thin coat of tacky glue and press border in place. Glue fabric houses to front of bag in same manner.

2. Break twigs to fit around house lines and chimney. Hot-glue in place. Hot-glue two long twigs across border.

115

use it . . .

◆ Keep this bag and blanket in your car or in the living room.

◆ Undo the sewing and wear the T-shirt.

◆QUILT COMFORT

need it . . .

Canvas bag (model is 15" x 13" x 4")
8" square of quilt-print cotton fabric
Scraps of coordinating fabric for border
7½" square of fleece
1½ yds. of ¼"-wide matching ribbon
10 buttons in assorted sizes and colors
Matching quilting thread
Invisible thread
Straight pins

make it . . .

1. From fabric scraps, cut out twenty 3-inch-squares. Fold and press each square as shown in Diagram A. Pin five triangles together along raw edges, overlapping to make a 7½-inch border. Sew with invisible thread. Repeat three more times.

2. Place borders around quilt square with triangles pointing inside, as shown in Diagram B. Sew around edge with a ¼-inch seam. Fold border out and press.

3. Place fleece square on center front of canvas bag. Place quilt square on top of fleece and pin in place. Topstitch on seam around all four sides. With quilting thread, hand-quilt around design on quilt block.

4. Tie a bow in center of ribbon and secure to top corner of quilt block. Cascade tails around block, using buttons to tack in place.

5. Make a matching lap quilt to stuff in bag.

◆T-TOTE

need it . . .

T-shirt
Tissue paper
Curling ribbon
Safety pins

make it . . .

1. Turn the T-shirt inside out. Pin the neck and arm holes closed, leaving the arms inside the shirt. Turn shirt right side out and stuff with tissue paper and/or additional gifts. Tie top closed with curling ribbon.

change it . . .

◆ Use a team sport shirt and stuff with appropriate ball and gear.

◆ Try a swimsuit cover-up stuffed with a beach ball, bucket, sunscreen, and sunglasses.

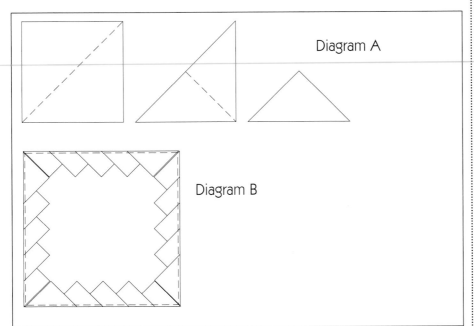

Diagram A

Diagram B

use it . . .

◆ Use this gingerbread-man bag to store Christmas cookie cutters.

◆ Cut out the front of the bag and frame it.

◆COOKIE

need it . . .

Papier-mâché sack
Small gingerbread-man cookie
    cutter
4" of 45"-wide fabric in 3 differ-
    ent coordinating Christmas
    fabrics
Golden brown, dark green, and
    dark red acrylic paint
Paintbrushes
Old toothbrush

make it . . .

1. Using cookie cutter for pattern, trace gingerbread-men randomly over sack. Paint the gingerbread-men dark red, dark green,
and golden brown. Dip toothbrush in dark green paint. Drag
thumb over toothbrush to splatter
paint lightly over sack.

2. Tear each fabric strip in half
so that there are six long strips 2-
inches wide. Using a strip of each
color, braid to desired length.
Punch holes about ¾-inch down
from top of sack and ¾-inch in on
each side. Pull braid through
holes and knot ends on inside to
secure. Repeat with other strips
for handle on other side.

3. With a scrap fabric strip, tie
cookie cutter to one handle.

◆BEE HAPPY

need it . . .

Brown paper bag with handles
    (model is 8" x 9½")
6" of 1½"-wide ivory wired ribbon
5" of 1"-wide rust wired ribbon
4½" of 1½"-wide iridescent green
    wired ribbon
3" of ⅝"-wide gold mesh wired
    ribbon
2" of 1"-wide yellow wired ribbon
2 yds. of ¼"-wide gold cording
4 black stamens
Tacky glue
Brown fabric pen

make it . . .

1. Bees–Cut two 1-inch lengths
of cording and two 1-inch lengths
of yellow ribbon. Glue a piece of
ribbon around each piece of
cording. Glue two stamens into
one end of each "bee." Pinch and
glue other end closed. Cut two
1½-inch lengths of gold mesh ribbon. Fold and glue raw edges
under slightly. Fold and glue corners back slightly. Pinch in center
and glue "wings" to center of bee.

2. Twig–Cut a 5-inch length of
cording and place in center of 5-
inch length of 1-inch-wide rust
ribbon. Wrap and glue, tucking
ends inside.

3. Leaves–Cut three 1½-inch
lengths of 1½-inch-wide iridescent green ribbon. Fold corners
of one raw edge down to make a
point. Pinch and glue other end.
Repeat for each leaf.

4. Hive–Starting about 1½-
inches down from top center of
bag, glue gold cording in a coil
shape, gradually going from 1
inch at top to 4 inches in middle
and back down again. Place
something heavy on bag until hive
is completely dry.

5. Cut a small slit in the center
of each end of 1½-inch-wide
ivory ribbon. Fold and glue inside
corners back, forming a "V". With
brown fabric pen, write "Honey"
and glue banner to center of hive.

6. Glue bees, twig, and leaves
to bag as desired.

change it . . .

◆ Use ribbon flowers to
make a bouquet.

◆ Make grapes out of
scraps of purple fabric or
ribbon and glue to bag in
a bunch.

◆ Glue ribbon yo-yos to
bag in the shape of a
Christmas tree.

use it . . .

◆ Use these cute bags to hold crayons, pencils, and markers for school.

◆BACK TO "SKOOL"

need it . . .
Bicycle Bag

Small brown paper bag with
    handles
5" gold covered wire
Scrap of foam core
Scrap of brown paper bag
Scraps of colored paper
Scrap of wrapping paper or fabric
Buttons: 2 for wheels, 1 for head,
    crescent shape for helmet
Black acrylic paint
Craft knife
Tacky glue
Paintbrush

make it . . .

1. Cut foam core into desired
shape for body. Cover with wrapping paper or fabric. Cut four ⅛-
inch-wide strips from paper bag,
each 3 inches long. Fold each
strip accordion style. Glue in position for arms and legs on body.
Cut two small rectangles for feet
from foam core and paint black.
Glue body to center of sack. Glue
on buttons for head and helmet.

2. Cut gold wire in half and
twist into "X" shape and glue to
center of body. The top wires will
be the handlebars and the bottom wires are the bike frame.
Glue buttons for wheels in proper
position. Glue feet to end of legs
close to wheels. Decorate front of
bag with narrow strips of colored
paper.

need it . . .
Teacher bag

Small brown paper bag with
    handles
Painted miniature wooden apple
Long bamboo skewer or toothpicks
Scrap of foam core
Scrap of wrapping paper or fabric
Scrap of brown paper bag
Scraps of colored paper
Button for head
Black and white acrylic paints
Craft knife
Tacky glue
Paintbrush

make it . . .

1. On top front of bag paint a
black rectangle. Let dry.

2. Glue apple to "blackboard."
Cut six ⅛-inch-wide strips from
colored paper, each 1½-inch
long, and fold accordion style.
Glue on button for hair. Glue on
button for head.

3. Cut desired body shape from
foam core and cover with fabric

or wrapping paper. Cut two small
rectangles for feet from foam core
and paint black. Cut four ⅛-inch-
wide strips from brown paper
bag, each 3 inches long. Fold each
strip accordion style. Glue in position for arms and legs on body.
Glue body and feet in place.

4. Break bamboo skewer to
form a border and glue around
blackboard. Paint a small piece of
skewer white for chalk. Paint
"1+2=3" on blackboard and glue
chalk to end of one arm. Decorate
front of bag with narrow strips of
colored paper.

change it . . .

◆ **Make button elves for
Christmas bags.**

◆ **Use large oval buttons
as Easter eggs for a
springtime gift.**

◆ **Make seven dwarfs and
Snow White and fill with
party favors for a child's
birthday party.**

use it .
◆ ◆

◆ This bag is
designed to
hold plastic
grocery bags.

◆MIXED GREENS

need it . . .

13" x 18" piece of striped canvas fabric; matching thread
1" x 5" scrap of striped canvas fabric
12" of 1"-wide green to orange ombré wired ribbon
9½" of 1½"-wide iridescent green wired ribbon
12" of ⅝"-wide iridescent green wired ribbon
3½" of 2"-wide red wired ribbon
6" of 1"-wide ivory wired ribbon
18" of green rattail cording
9" of ½"-wide cording
2" of ¼"-wide cording
Small amount of stuffing
Tacky glue

make it . . .

1. Fold 13- by 18-inch canvas fabric in half with right sides together, making a 6½- by 18-inch rectangle. Sew ½-inch seam along bottom and side. Turn and press. Fold top edge inside bag 4 inches and press. Fold top over 2 inches to make a cuff and press. Fold scrap of canvas fabric in half lengthwise with right sides together. Sew ¼-inch seam across long edge and one short edge. Turn and press. Make a loop handle and sew or glue into top left side of bag.

2. From green rattail cording, spell "bags" and glue onto cuff.

3. Carrot—Form stuffing into a 5-inch carrot shape. Starting at the top of the carrot form, wrap 1-inch-wide green to orange ombré wired ribbon, with the green edge at the top, at an angle down to the point. Tuck and glue ends under. Cut 3 inches of ⅝-inch-wide iridescent green wired ribbon. Overlap and glue raw edges, forming a tube. Pinch and glue one side of the tube, forming a cup. Glue bottom of cup to top of carrot.

4. Asparagus—Place the ½-inch cording lengthwise in center of the 1½-inch-wide iridescent green wired ribbon. Wrap and glue, tucking ends inside. Cut five 1-inch lengths of ⅝-inch-wide iridescent green wired ribbon. Fold one edge under ⅛ inch and glue. Fold corners of top edge back, forming a point, and glue. Glue "tips" onto "spear" and glue onto bag.

5. Radish—Overlap and glue raw edges of 2-inch-wide red wired ribbon, forming a tube that is a little wider at the top. Pinch and glue bottom closed, making a point. Fill with stuffing, pinch and glue closed. Make a "top" from 3 inches of ⅝-inch-wide iridescent green wired ribbon, as in carrot instructions, and glue to top of radish.

6. Mushroom—Cut a 2½-inch length from 1-inch-wide ivory wired ribbon. Place the ¼-inch cording in center, and wrap and glue like asparagus. Cut two 2-inch lengths from 2-inch-wide ivory wired ribbon. Trim so that each piece is circular. Place a small amount of stuffing between both circles. Tuck and glue edges under. Glue stem onto bag and mushroom to top of stem.

change it . . .

◆ Make candy canes out of ribbon and hang bag on the front door at Christmastime.

◆ Make ribbon flowers and use bag to store seed packets.

Enlarge FRIENDS pattern 200%. See page 105.

FALL stamp pattern full size. See page 105.

Enlarge SNOMIT pattern 200%. See page 105.

Enlarge SPECIAL DELIVERY Envelope pattern 400%. See page 113.

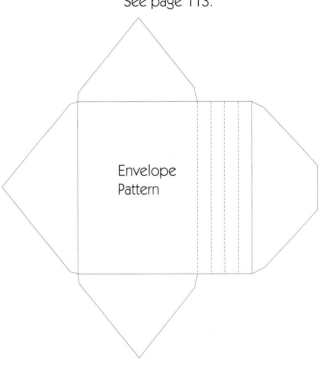

Envelope Pattern

STITCH GUIDE

#	Description	Color	Stitch
1	Flower	Light Pink	Lazy Daisy
2	Leaves	Sea-Green	Lazy Daisy
3	Flower	Mauve	Japanese Ribbon Stitch
4	Flower	Purple	Free-Form Flower
5	Flower center	Off-White	French Knot
6	Buds	Light Avocado	French Knot
7	Flower	Rose-Violet	Free-Form Flower
8	Flower center	Off-White	French Knot
9	Star	Sea-Green	Weave

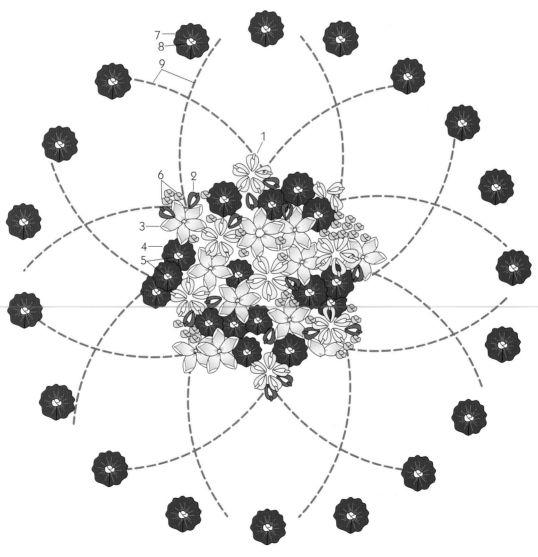

See FINERY on page 113.

INDEX

INDEX

METRIC EQUIVALENCY CHART

MM-MILLIMETRES CM-CENTIMETRES
INCHES TO MILLIMETRES AND CENTIMETRES

INCHES	MM	CM	INCHES	CM	INCHES	CM
⅛	3	0.3	9	22.9	30	76.2
¼	6	0.6	10	25.4	31	78.7
½	13	1.3	12	30.5	33	83.8
⅝	16	1.6	13	33.0	34	86.4
¾	19	1.9	14	35.6	35	88.9
⅞	22	2.2	15	38.1	36	91.4
1	25	2.5	16	40.6	37	94.0
1¼	32	3.2	17	43.2	38	96.5
1½	38	3.8	18	45.7	39	99.1
1¾	44	4.4	19	48.3	40	101.6
2	51	5.1	20	50.8	41	104.1
2½	64	6.4	21	53.3	42	106.7
3	76	7.6	22	55.9	43	109.2
3½	89	8.9	23	58.4	44	111.8
4	102	10.2	24	61.0	45	114.3
4½	114	11.4	25	63.5	46	116.8
5	127	12.7	26	66.0	47	119.4
6	152	15.2	27	68.6	48	121.9
7	178	17.8	28	71.1	49	124.5
8	203	20.3	29	73.7	50	127.0

YARDS TO METRES

YARDS	METRES	YARDS	METRES	YARDS	METRES	YARDS	METRES	YARDS	METRES
⅛	0.11	2⅛	1.94	4⅛	3.77	6⅛	5.60	8⅛	7.43
¼	0.23	2¼	2.06	4¼	3.89	6¼	5.72	8¼	7.54
⅜	0.34	2⅜	2.17	4⅜	4.00	6⅜	5.83	8⅜	7.66
½	0.46	2½	2.29	4½	4.11	6½	5.94	8½	7.77
⅝	0.57	2⅝	2.40	4⅝	4.23	6⅝	6.06	8⅝	7.89
¾	0.69	2¾	2.51	4¾	4.34	6¾	6.17	8¾	8.00
⅞	0.80	2⅞	2.63	4⅞	4.46	6⅞	6.29	8⅞	8.12
1	0.91	3	2.74	5	4.57	7	6.40	9	8.23
1⅛	1.03	3⅛	2.86	5⅛	4.69	7⅛	6.52	9⅛	8.34
1¼	1.14	3¼	2.97	5¼	4.80	7¼	6.63	9¼	8.46
1⅜	1.26	3⅜	3.09	5⅜	4.91	7⅜	6.74	9⅜	8.57
1½	1.37	3½	3.20	5½	5.03	7½	6.86	9½	8.69
1⅝	1.49	3⅝	3.31	5⅝	5.14	7⅝	6.97	9⅝	8.80
1¾	1.60	3¾	3.43	5¾	5.26	7¾	7.09	9¾	8.92
1⅞	1.71	3⅞	3.54	5⅞	5.37	7⅞	7.20	9⅞	9.03
2	1.83	4	3.66	6	5.49	8	7.32	10	9.14